LIKE THE HEROES OF OLD

KATE HALEY

I wouldn't be here without you.

CONTENTS

Visit **www.katehaleyauthor.com** for
deals and current news from the author.

CHAPTER ONE

Rain had fallen in the night. The forest was still dripping as water ran down the leaves and broke across already sparkling wet grass. Inside the thatched-roofed hut, Jak was hurriedly stacking dirty breakfast dishes in the sink. Her black curls cascaded over her shoulder and she quickly tied them back out of the way with a leather cord.

"Allie come on!" she called to her younger sister. "We can't be late today!"

"Calm down," Allie called back from the next room. "I'm just getting ready." The younger girl swept into the main room in a green dress and twirled. "What do you think?"

Jak raised an eyebrow as she watched. The two of them were three years and a million worlds apart. Same dark skin. Same black curls. Except not the same. Jak's hair was wild and she tied it back like overgrown vines to keep it out of her eyes. Allie's curls were brushed sleek and plaited down her back like a princess. She wore simple dresses, but she wore them to try and accentuate her newfound puberty and appear older. Allie was maturing way too fast. Jak dressed like a boy. In shades of brown. She wore trousers and boots, and a leather vest over her cream shirt, and she hoped no one would notice she was a girl.

"What are you doing in your good dress?" she asked. "You're going to work."

"It's my first day!" Allie exclaimed excitedly. "And Thom works at the bakery too… I want to look nice."

"Thom?" Jak criticised. "Who in the gods' names is Thom?"

"The cute boy at the bakery," Allie told her like she was stupid.

Jak stared her down. With Allie it was a new boy every week. There weren't that many of them in the village; Jak still struggled to keep up.

"How old is this one?"

"About your age," Allie shrugged.

"So fifteen?" Jak checked. She gave her sister another sharp look. "Allie, you're twelve."

"I'm of a marriageable age," Allie told her primly.

"No you're bloody not! I'm not of a marriageable age! You're definitely not!"

"You should already be married. You would be if you put in a little bit of effort to look pretty and didn't chase away every single boy who comes near you with a stick. Then, if you were married, your husband could look after us and I wouldn't have to go to work."

Jak counted to three inside her head and took a silent breath. They were not having this fight again.

"Allie, please," she tried calmly. "Put on a work dress and get ready to go. I'm doing everything I can, but I'm struggling. We need the extra cash — just for a little while."

"It's not for a little while, Jak," Allie sighed. "We

both know that. I'm thinking about my future. You should too."

"When Mum gets back—"

"When?" Allie demanded. "It's been a year, Sis. When's Mum getting back?"

Jak didn't answer. She looked to the note pinned to the wall. The paper was faded and dusty now, but she kept it there anyway. *Morning my darlings! Just popping out for a bit. Be back soon. Jak's in charge until I return. Love you xx.*

"I'm in charge 'til she gets back," Jak reaffirmed. "So go change. You're going to get it dirty."

"Then I'll wash it," Allie rolled her eyes. "I do half the washing around here anyway — and don't bother using your stupid threat on me. It doesn't work. I'm too old for that now."

Jak let out the sigh she'd been holding back all conversation. "Where's Dora?" she asked after their youngest sister.

"Probably out in the woods. No one took the bread and milk she left out on the sill last night, so she will have taken it out to Äulé in the forest."

"That stupid gnome…" Jak shook her head as she marched to the door. "Stupid girl," she added with a mutter. "Dora!" she bellowed out the front door. "Get back here!"

The rain dripped from the eaves of the thatched roof and Jak watched the still forest. It was calming. Nature always felt calming to her. It was better than being inside. Inside was where all the chaos was. It was where she was trying to raise her sisters. It was a reminder that

Mum had left and life was hard. The woods were wild and beautiful, and she didn't begrudge Dora the desire to play in them. She just needed her not to do it now.

The back door sounded and Jak turned. Tiny footsteps pounded across the floor and Dora raced in with wet grass on her shoes. The bottoms of her leggings were soaked. The little girl was beaming excitedly out of her freckled face.

"Look! Look! Look!" she yelled. Nestled in her halo of black curls was a flower crown. It was very cute. "I'm a fairy princess! A nice man just gave me a magic crown! I'm a fairy princess now!"

"It's not magic," Allie told her. "It's flowers."

"It's magic!" Dora insisted. "He said it was magic! He said that I'm a fairy princess now."

"Who was this?" Jak demanded. "Was this Äulé?"

Dora shook her head. "Nope. I didn't see Äulé this morning, but I left his bread and milk out. No, this was just a nice man in the forest. I didn't ask his name."

"Dora," Jak began patiently with the tone of someone who has had their patience tested too many times in one day. "What have I told you about talking to strangers?"

"Don't do it…" Dora muttered.

"Yeah," Jak enforced. "Don't do it."

"But I'm a fairy princess now!" Dora protested.

"Oh my gods!" Jak cursed. "I don't care if you're the bloody fairy queen! Mum put me in charge! Do as I say and don't talk to strangers or Ĝoŕgomghōul will get you! Magic powers won't save you from the god of darkness. He preys on naughty children, and he will slip out of the shadows and steal you away to turn you into soup! So just… behave! Both of you!"

Allie pulled a face behind Dora's back. It was true; that threat didn't work on her anymore. Ever since she'd turned twelve she had discovered a new level of attitude that Jak considered a problem. But Dora was still young. Tears were welling in her eyes. The threat of a scary shadow monster turning her into soup was very real. Jak sighed and knelt down to pull her little sister into a hug. If Allie was an old twelve, Dora was a very young seven.

"I'm sorry, baby," she muttered. "I don't want to scare you. I just want to keep you safe, and that's a hard thing to do. I know I'm not Mum, but that's what makes it harder. Your crown is lovely, and you make a wonderful fairy princess, but please don't go talking to and accepting gifts from strangers in the forest."

"I won't do it again…" Dora mumbled miserably into Jak's shoulder.

"Thank you. Now, come on. I've packed your bag. You're going to the bakery with Allie today — I need someone to keep her out of trouble, and it will take all your new magic powers…"

Dora giggled. Jak gave her a squeeze and let her go. Dora ran to the corner of the room and picked up her backpack. Allie gave Jak an angsty teenage eyeroll as Dora wiggled into the straps of her backpack.

"I'm ready!" the little girl announced.

"So am I," Allie challenged Jak.

Jak was prepared to concede that this was a battle she didn't need to win. If Allie wanted to wear a pretty dress and flirt with boys at work, she would soon get a taste of what working life was like. Or, perhaps, she would find her future husband and then Jak could sell her off. It didn't seem like such a bad option this morning.

With her sisters packed for the day, Jak ushered them out of the house and into town. Their little cottage was only a ten-minute walk from the centre of the village of Rutsborough where they lived. The girls were known by the locals, but it wasn't an overly friendly relationship. Jak worried that was her fault. She was not a people person. Allie was. Allie liked people, and people liked her. Jak liked… well, Jak wasn't really sure what she liked. She was sure she used to like things, but the last year… she hadn't had time to like things.

Few people acknowledged them as they wandered through the muddy streets. Given that most people's topic of choice at the moment was war, Jak was even more okay with the silent treatment than usual. Their village was in a tiny corner of the kingdom of Kosveir, but the neighbouring kingdom of Dazigh had broken out into civil war. The rumours that had reached Rutsborough were that a band of rebels had murdered the king of Dazigh and now the people were rising up. The locals here considered the behaviour barbaric. Jak considered the entire affair none of her business.

"That's him!" Dora exclaimed suddenly. Jak broke from her train of thought to see Dora pointing down the road. "That's him! That's the man who gave me the crown!"

Jak followed her sister's finger to the culprit. It was

a travelling merchant. He looked like the most ordinary man she'd ever seen. Short brown hair, weather-beaten skin, simple clothes. He was sorting his caravan and folding the back of it out into a store. Dora took off like an arrow before Jak realised.

"Shit," she muttered under her breath as she ran after her little sister. Allie chased after them.

"Hey!" Dora waved as she ran up to the merchant.

The man turned to look their way. He caught sight of Dora and beamed. His smile lit up his whole face and dimpled his cheeks. Jak felt her feet slow. He was the most ordinary man in the world until he smiled. It was a heart-warming smile that radiated from him. A smile of genuine pleasure.

"Hey Dora," he grinned at the little girl cheekily. His accent was unusual but not unpleasant. "I didn't realize you were coming to town."

"I'm going with my sisters," Dora declared proudly. "They're going to work. This is Allie, and this is Jak."

Jak reached them as she was introduced to the stranger. She didn't have time to stop Dora or halt the pleasantries. She'd been introduced now. She was going to have to people. The man's eyes washed over her and Allie. His warm brown gaze met Jak's.

"The infamous Jak," he grinned at her. "The 'I have to get home before my big sister comes looking for me' Jak." He turned his most charming smile on them. "It's a pleasure, ladies."

At a guess, Jak would have estimated the merchant was at least twice her age, and she had a horrible feeling Allie was going to swoon. She wasn't going to check though. Her eyes scanned the side of the caravan as they all stood by it.

"The Banging Wagon?" she questioned dubiously. It was painted in large purple letters across the dark wooden side.

"Absolutely," he grinned. He raised an arm and leant against it, managing to loom casually over them. "Only exploded once though."

"Twice!" another man's voice called from inside the wagon.

"The second time doesn't count," the merchant insisted without batting an eye. "It was a one-time accident and we learnt from our mistake." He held out his hand to Jak. "I'm Jim."

Jak took his hand and shook it, more to fulfil the necessities of politeness than anything else. He had a strong, warm, and reassuring grip.

"You gave Dora the flower crown, Jim?" she asked.

"I did indeed," he confirmed. "We were passing through while she was playing in the forest. Said she was looking for faeries and wanted to be a faerie princess. Well, she has the right dress for it, yeah, high-five for purple. Best colour." Jim held his hand low for Dora and she slapped it enthusiastically as he grinned at her. Jak noted that he wore a wide cloth belt in a similar colour to Dora's purple dress. They were purple buddies now. "Anyway," he continued, "I figured; you can't be a princess without a crown. So I gave her one, and here we are."

"Now I'm a fairy princess!" Dora exclaimed.

"You most certainly are," Jim agreed. "Magic crown

and everything." He gave Jak a side glance and murmured to her. "It makes the kid happy and it costs me nothing, why not?"

Jak was nowhere near close to trusting the strange man, but she felt herself settle slightly. Taking him at face value, his heart seemed to be in the right place. He was just a nice guy who had done something sweet for her sister. Unfortunately, he wasn't done yet, and the cheeky smirk on his face was directed at entertaining Dora again.

"You know, Dora…" he mused. "When you said you had a big sister looking after you and we needed to get you home before she got mad… you never mentioned how hot she was. I feel like this is important stuff. This is the kind of thing you should mention to people — that your scary sister is something of a babe."

Jak could feel her face flame with blush and it was a thousand times worse because she could hear Dora and Allie laughing. She stared daggers at her sisters but they ignored her. Dora was laughing at Jim with her big eyes turned adoringly up at the entertaining stranger. Allie was trying to hide her chuckling behind a polite hand, but she looked almost sorry for the man who had unknowingly made a huge mistake as far as she was concerned. Jak turned to usher them away. Jim softened as she moved to go.

"I jest," he apologised gently to her. "I have no intention of making you feel uncomfortable, Miss. I'm sure with a face like yours, in a town like this, you'd already be spoken for, and don't worry — I'd flirt with him too."

Jak cracked a smile. She wished she hadn't, and he didn't make her actually laugh, but it was a close call. He was a salesman. It was his job to be charming and, in a weird way, he was. In small doses it was funny. This felt like it was turning into a long dose.

"It was nice meeting you, Jim," she told him. "But I have to get to work."

"A tragedy," he lamented. "Stop by again if you're free later."

"I'm not," Jak assured. "Ever."

Jim laughed delightedly. "Ah, I like you, Jak. It has been an absolute pleasure. Have a fun day at work."

"Thank you," she inclined her head. "And say thank you for the crown, Dora."

"Thank you Jim!" Dora exclaimed.

"You are most welcome," he replied, but Jak was already walking her sisters away from the dangerously charming merchant and his Banging Wagon.

Down the road, Allie caught Jak's arm tightly. Jak didn't even have to look to know it was her sister and what it was about.

"Jak," Allie spoke insistently. "Quit your job and go back there right now."

"Not if Ĝoŕgomghōul rose up out of the shadows and ordered me to himself," Jak replied.

"He's real nice though," Dora added, completely oblivious to all of Allie's intentions. Jak nodded at her youngest sister. Jim had been nice. He was perfectly nice. He was also so far from Jak's type it wasn't funny. The only reason she didn't think he was a creepy old man was because she had a feeling that he hadn't been joking about hitting on everyone. He was one of those tactile people who made friends by flirting. She wasn't special, and he wasn't really interested, and that made him much easier to like from a safe distance.

At the end of the road Jak dropped her sisters off at the bakery. She had checked with the head baker and Dora was fine to stay out of the way there with her bag of activities where there were plenty of people to keep an eye on her. Jak certainly couldn't bring her to her own work.

"Right, have a good day you two," Jak told them. "I'll see you at home later. Allie you'll be done long before I will, so please get her home safe."

"Calm down, Jak," Allie sighed. "I've been looking after her for the last year just fine, haven't I?"

"You have," Jak conceded gratefully. She kissed the top of Allie's head. "Thank you. Be good," she told Dora.

By now she was running late. There were no two ways about that. She took off from the bakery and sprinted off up the muddy road to the other side of town. The sound of ringing steel was already pounding out of the blacksmith's forge.

"Sorry I'm late, Sam!" Jak yelled out. She was already tying on her leather apron as she rushed in.

Big Sam didn't say anything as she ran in. He just pointed at her workstation with his hammer between blows. Her boss was a giant with a shaved head and a massive grey beard. He was a man of few words, and they got on very well. Jak was on horseshoes today. She usually was. It was their biggest trade in Rutsborough.

The roads were rubbish and horseshoes were important. They were also simple and easy, so Jak was left with them because she was the new kid.

She noted Sam was forging another sword. There were nearly two dozen on his walls now. He didn't sell many, but he always said he liked making them. There was a craft to it — an enjoyable design aspect. Jak accepted this, but she felt like he'd been doing it more often recently. With all the talk of war in the town, it was starting to make her uncomfortable. Not that she was going to tell Big Sam that. Although, she might be able to mention something about swords and war over lunch, if she felt bold enough.

Jak got to work and the stress and memories of the morning melted away under the heat and rhythm of the forge. She was able to focus on her work and hammer her frustrations out into her craft. Big Sam always told her she was stronger and faster than other apprentices he had taken on, and that was why he'd kept her. Jak was pretty sure it was just how hard she worked to prove herself, but she would take the praise.

She wasn't sure of the time, but only four horseshoes had passed when she heard screaming and yelling outside the forge. Jak shared a glance with Big Sam. They were both safe to put down their work and step outside, so they did. Outside the forge, smoke was thick in the air. They wouldn't have noticed it inside. The smoke was black, but the air was still cool against the sweat running down her spine.

"What's going on?" Sam demanded.

"We're getting water from the river," one of the

villagers answered. "The bakery's on fire! There's a witch set it alight!"

Sam looked straight to Jak, so he saw the horror dawn on her face. He knew about her family troubles, and he knew about Allie's first day. Sam didn't hold to magic and fairies and witches. He knew they were out there, and he knew they had no business in his village. Jak hadn't even had the nerve to tell him about Dora leaving bread and milk out for the gnomes in the forest. Sam saw the fear in her eyes. With one meaty hand, he grabbed a sword from his display stand at the counter. It was simple but sturdy. He handed it to Jak.

"Go get them," he told her.

Jak took the sword. She was no master, but she'd had some practice and wasn't a complete amateur. She nodded her thanks at Sam and took off for the bakery. Now that she knew what was going on, it was easy enough to see. The pillar of black smoke was rising right from the corner with the bakery. She sprinted as fast as she could towards it. In her head she prayed to the ten gods of Roïgola'a'lanaū that her sisters would be okay.

Mud splashed from her boots as she rounded the corner. The crowd outside the bakery was huge. They had managed to form a bucket chain. It wasn't putting the fire out, but it was holding it at bay. Most of the bakery was alight.

"Allie! Dora!" Jak called. She stopped at the edge of the crowd and people turned to look at the dirty, sweaty blacksmith's apprentice wielding a sword. "I heard there was a witch," she offered, holding the sword threateningly in one hand.

"Oh, there is," Baker Wilma announced angrily. The tough old lady dragged Dora out of the crowd by her wrist. Dora was struggling and crying. Allie was hanging around with a scared look on her face, but she clearly hadn't been able to dissuade her new boss. "This little girl is a witch!" the baker screamed at the crowd. "She started the fire!"

"I didn't mean to!" Dora wailed.

"She didn't do it," Allie insisted. "She's not a witch! She's just a kid."

"It's my new fairy powers," Dora cried. "I didn't know."

"Oh my gods!" Allie cursed angrily. "You don't have fairy powers, you idiot! You're not a fairy princess! Shut up!"

"What is going on?" Jak demanded.

"Your witch of a sister started a fire!" Wilma screamed. "Look at my bakery!"

"She thinks she's got magic powers because of her stupid flower crown and now she's taking the blame for an accident!" Allie yelled at Jak.

"Okay," Jak mediated, even as she died inside. "Everyone calm down."

"We're not listening to you!" a boy in a baking apron yelled. "You're probably a witch too!"

"Shut up, Thom," Allie scoffed.

"You're all witches!" he yelled at Allie. "Your mum was a witch and you all are too!"

"Our Mum is a herbalist," Jak replied.

"Same thing!"

"Thom, shut up," Allie repeated scornfully. "You're

an idiot, and right now you're just advertising that. Your face is not pretty enough to excuse this level of stupidity."

Jak didn't think he was even remotely pretty, but she did admire Allie's ability to crush her crush. Although, now probably wasn't the right time.

"Everyone, Dora didn't do this," Jak insisted calmly. "She couldn't have. I promise. She's a little kid who wants to be a fairy princess, but she doesn't have any magic powers."

"But my magic crown!" Dora wailed.

"Shut up, Dora!" Jak snapped. "I'm sorry, baby, but it's not magic. Allie's right — it's just flowers. Now is not the time."

Dora began to cry again. Jak tried to count to three, but the crowd wouldn't give her the space. The villagers were advancing.

"We have ways of testing for witches," Wilma glowered. "How about we dunk the witch and see if she floats?"

"You'll kill her!" Jak roared. "Get off my sister!"

Jak tried to snatch Dora back. Wilma grabbed the little girl and twisted her arm away. Dora screamed as her arm was twisted. Jak reacted instinctively. She hadn't even realised she'd been raising the sword until the crowd drew back in alarm. She caught herself before she struck, but the blade was raised and she knew she looked as angry as she felt.

"Enough!" a voice bellowed. Everyone turned to see a stranger approaching. Jak felt her arm drop. It was Jim. The merchant had a severe look about him that didn't go with anything Jak felt she had met earlier. He was not a particularly tall or physically imposing man, but when he spoke the whole crowd froze.

"What in the name of Roïgola'a'lanaū is going on here?" he asked.

"This witch burnt down my bakery!" Wilma screamed, brandishing Dora.

"Hey Dora," Jim smiled reassuringly at her.

"Jim! Help!" Dora wailed. Jim eyed up the crowd. His eyes were still the same warm brown. He wasn't involved in this fight. His eyes were soothing as they washed over his audience. He took in their distrust at the fact that he knew the little girl, and none of them knew him.

"I met Dora this morning," he offered the information. "I gave her the crown, and you all think it's magic?" He grinned as he said it. The tone of his voice made it sound preposterous. Jak felt a wave of relief hit her as the man stared down the village.

"She's a witch!" Thom yelled again.

Jim chuckled at him and his winning smile hit the crowd like a tidal wave. "That girl ain't a witch. I've been around. I've seen witches. She is not a witch." He turned his attention to Wilma. "I'm sorry about your bakery, Ma'am, but accidents happen. Persecuting these young ladies won't change that. It will just make ugly, superstitious folk out of the rest of you. Let the girl go."

Wilma did as he bid, and Dora tore herself free and clutched at Allie. Allie grabbed her and made for Jak. Jak quickly sheathed the sword in her belt and grabbed her sisters. She looked up at Jim. He was already watching her. She felt a strange shift in her first opinion of him. He hadn't needed to get involved, but she was extremely grateful that he had.

"Thank you," she murmured.

"Get them home," he replied.

She nodded and led her sisters away with her hands around their shoulders. He didn't need to tell her twice. The way he'd told her once said enough — he didn't think this was going to stay polite. The village was ready to get nasty, and the presence of a stranger may have momentarily confused the mob, but he had no guarantee they would stay confused. As soon as they were out of sight, Jak took her sisters' hands and broke into a run. She hoped the merchant would be able to get himself away, and couldn't believe he'd thrown himself in the path of the mob to rescue them.

The girls raced home and, as soon as they were inside, Jak locked the door behind them.

"I'm sorry, Jak," Allie apologised.

"It's okay," Jak took a deep breath. "Just tell me what happened."

"I pointed at the oven and it went BOOM!" Dora cried. Jak looked to Allie who shrugged and didn't disagree.

"I was mixing dough," Allie said. "So I wasn't really looking. Dora was in the kitchen with us, just staying out of the way in the corner. She was pretending to do fairy magic, but it was harmless. A few people were giving her dirty looks. I..." Allie trailed off. She wasn't a good liar. Jak knew what she was trying not to say. It was going to be something to do with Thom. Allie was flirting and not paying attention. Jak didn't care. She nodded at Allie to continue, so her sister did. "Dora pointed at the oven and said 'magic baking fire'—"

"I didn't know!" Dora wailed. "I didn't know it would do it!"

"Hush," Jak stroked her hair. She was still looking at Allie. She didn't know if Allie was aware how traumatised she looked. Everyone had been focused on Dora, but Jak's other little sister was having quite the morning too.

"The oven just exploded," Allie shrugged, bringing her arms up to hug herself. "Huge bang and fire everywhere. That old brick oven. It's a miracle no one was hurt." She shook her head. "My ears are still ringing. But that's it. Just went bang. Bits of flaming brick went everywhere. The wall started to catch. We all started screaming and ran outside. Wilma ordered a bucket chain, but the fire grew so fast. When she saw how bad it was, she just turned on Dora and said it was her and she was a witch. It was total rubbish, Jak. It was an accident, and now people are trying to blame us."

Jak had been looking out the window as Allie spoke. She could see the faintest flicker of fire down the path through the trees. She knew that sight well. It was the sight of a torch coming up the road. This was the first time it had ever scared her. It was accompanied by another one. Jak looked to her sisters.

"Go pack," she ordered. Neither of them moved. "Come on. We're going to go camping for a little bit until this all blows over. Get your stuff. Get it fast."

Dora and Allie both looked like they wanted to say something, maybe protest, but the look Jak was giving them kept them silent. They rushed off to pack bags. They knew how serious this was. Jak wasn't sure if they knew what she knew though. The torches were getting closer, and there were significantly more of them now. They had five minutes. Jak shoved some spare clothes and food into a pack as fast as she could. In the kitchen she grabbed some of her mother's special pottery and the note by the door. She wrapped it in a spare shirt and packed it. They were treasured possessions and she couldn't leave them. She didn't know what was about to happen, but it couldn't be good.

"Girls!" she called. "We're leaving. If you haven't packed it by now, you don't need it!"

"But Binky!" Dora cried.

"I've got him," Allie soothed her. Allie ushered Dora into the main room where Jak was waiting. Just looking at them, Jak could see that Allie had helped Dora pack. She knew. Jak met her sister's eyes. Allie knew what was happening. She had sorted Dora and herself, and she had their youngest sister's stuffed toy bunny in one hand. Allie really was an old twelve. She had always been quick, and right now her scared face betrayed her understanding of their situation. Jak nodded her thanks to her. They didn't want to spook Dora more than was necessary.

"Okay everyone," Jak encouraged. "Out the back door. Let's be as quiet as we can."

Jak ushered them out. Allie took the lead and Jak brought up the rear behind Dora. They snuck out the back door and into the forest. By now, Jak could hear the angry mob approaching. They were loud and they were furious. That was a lot of torches through the trees. It looked like an ocean of fire.

"Come on, guys," Jak muttered. "Faster."

"What's going on?!" Dora cried.

"Shhhh," Jak hushed her. "Come on." Jak picked up Dora in her arms, and she and Allie raced off into the forest. They could hear yelling and breaking glass behind them. Jak could feel her heart pounding like it was going to rupture out of her chest. She wanted to cry. Crying would have to wait. They weren't out of the woods yet — literally. She didn't know if the village would pursue them once they realised they were gone, or if the destruction alone would sate them.

If the mob realised they had gone into the forest, then perhaps they were safe. Everyone knew this was a faerie forest. There were mushroom circles and rings of stones scattered and hidden in the long grasses. Children were warned never to play in the woods because they would be snatched. It had happened before. The gods could use people's lives and bodies to make magic. Faeries would snatch the lost and use them for spells. However, the girls' parents had taught them to be safe in the forest. As much as anyone could be. Be kind to the faeries, watch your footing, and they'll be kind to you.

Most of the villagers didn't hold to that. Rutsborough wasn't a faerie friendly village, but they knew better than to mess with the forest. They ignored it and it ignored them, to a point. Vandalism wasn't worth it. Messing with the faeries cost lives. The Queen of the Fae had an army of shadow assassins that Ĝoŕgomghōul had made her. The Head Hunters. Dark faeries that would come for those who had wronged the fae. They would come in the night and behead their victims to steal their power. Nearly a decade ago, a villager had decided to clear some of the woods with fire. The gnomes had doused it, but the flames had claimed a small clearing. The next day all that was left of the arsonist was blood-soaked bed sheets.

The forest was good to the girls, but it was also a dangerous place, and Jak didn't know if they would be safe here. If the mob started to burn the trees to come after the girls, would they be blamed for it? Would the Head Hunters come after them? The thought made her want to puke.

"We have to get out of here," she stated.

"Äulé," Dora offered. "Äulé will help us." She wriggled out of Jak's arms and rushed off through the long grass between the trees. Jak and Allie chased after her. They made it to the little clearing Dora always came to. In the middle sat the lumpy boulder with the Fora rune carved into it. There was a small crust of bread and a jug of milk placed by it.

"Äulé!" Dora called. She knelt in the wet grass by the stone. "Äulé, please help us!"

Jak remembered when her father used to bring her out here when she was young. He was long out of the picture now. He'd died when Dora was born. The youngest sister had never known their old man. Jak missed him. She always did, but with everything else that was happening right now it was like a knife in her chest. He had been a big believer in faeries and small folk. Always had time for them. Dora was so like him, and she didn't even know it.

Above them in the trees a little red squirrel chittered. Its beady black eyes watched them with its head cocked. The forest animals didn't touch food left for the gnomes. They knew. Well, most of the time. Legend had it that squirrels and gnomes had gone to war over a loaf of bread. With a sharp pop, the gnome appeared. He was a little man with a tanned face and giant ginger beard. His pointed red cap flopped over on his head and his mischievous eyes twinkled. He sat perched on the rock with a tiny baby gnome in his arms.

"Äulé!" Dora exclaimed delightedly.

"Mah little Dora," Äulé grinned at her. "Ah, I see yer brought treats again. 'Tis kind of yer, mah sweet girl."

"Äulé we need your help," Dora begged. "Please help us."

"Whatever's the matter?"

"The village thinks Dora's a witch," Allie told him. "They're chasing us out, and we need somewhere safe."

"And yer pray to the rune of protection," Äulé nodded approvingly, well aware of what he was sitting on. "Damn humans. Can never trust 'em. Well, yer girls have always been good to me and mine." He rocked the baby gnome in his arms. "I can trade yer some magic for the treats yer left." He raised his arm and pointed through the trees. "Go that'a way. Keep heading straight and yer will find shelter and protection worthy of Fora. Fae's oath."

"Thank you, Äulé," Jak nodded to him. "We won't

forget this."

"Debt's already paid, girl," he smiled. "Can't do no magic without payment. Go get, little girls. Yer be safe on that path."

The girls thanked the gnome and headed off exactly the way he pointed. Their parents had not been witches, but they had been knowledgeable and respectful of faerie folk, and had raised the girls carefully around such magic. Äulé's spell only kept them safe as long as they stayed on his path. If they diverged at all, the spell would break or they would lose its protection.

Above them came the chittering. The squirrel was still there. It scrambled and hopped between branches, keeping just ahead of them. It dodged and wove between trees. It was leading them. For a fleeting second Jak panicked that the squirrel might try and trick them into betraying Äulé's magic. After a breath she calmed. Not all gnomes and squirrels were enemies. Especially in this forest. They were all the children of Thænäri, after all. The goddess of the earth and forest protected her own.

Jak had no idea how long they followed the squirrel, but it kept a straight line through the trees. Eventually, Jak had to put Dora down and get her to walk again. Every now and again the squirrel would stop and look back at them. Whenever they fell too far behind it would chitter. Twice as they travelled she glimpsed a flash of red in the grass, and caught the warning sight of a ring of toadstools, but Äulé's path kept them safely out of mushroom circles. Birds sang in the canopy, and the hut and the villagers seemed far away. Jak couldn't hear them at all anymore. Light shone ahead through the trees and Jak started to feel another rising panic. It wasn't the light of fire though. It was something else.

Daylight was breaking through the trees. She looked up for the squirrel. It was gone. She had no idea where it had scampered to. Where the day shone through was a muddy dirt road. Jak felt her feet slow. She had spent her whole life playing in that forest. There wasn't a road this way for ages. Yet, somehow, here it was already. Time and distance had become jumbled. Faerie magic. Äulé had protected them from followers. It wasn't all he'd done.

As the girls stepped from the shelter of the trees onto the road, the clomping of hooves and rumbling of wheels could be heard. Jak recognised the wagon instantly. It was hard not to with the big purple letters all over the side. The man driving it gave them one of his characteristic grins.

"Well, well, well..." he smiled at them. "Fancy seeing you three all the way out here. That's a long way you got."

"Äulé helped us," Dora told him before anyone could stop her.

"Äulé?" Jim mused. "That's a faerie name... ain't he a gnome?"

"You know him?" Jak blurted. Jim just smiled at her. He leaned back against the wagon with the reins draped loosely in one hand.

"You girls need a lift?"

Jak hesitated. She was not sure about this at all. She had warned her sisters about strangers. While she was extremely grateful he had helped them get away from the villagers, she wasn't sure how far her trust extended. Something about him was still weird. Besides, they couldn't go far... they had to wait for Mum to come home...

"Yes please," Allie answered for her.

"Allie, we don't know where we're going," Jak protested.

"Away from Rutsborough," Allie answered vehemently. She stalked out of the grass and approached the caravan.

"Good answer," Jim grinned at her. "Sorry about your town, Jak, but... well, it certainly seems like a bit of a rut. We decided not to stay."

"Who's we?" Jak asked. That was the first thing she wanted to know before she fell in with a group of vagabonds. Jim grinned at her and nodded his head towards the caravan behind him.

"Come meet my friends." He climbed down from the front of the wagon and led them around to the back. He banged politely on the back and it was opened from the inside. Jak felt her jaw drop as two men climbed from the back of the caravan. At first she thought they were identical. They were tall and pale and extremely beautiful, with soft blonde hair and large pointy ears. One had a serious expression and golden eyes, and the other had soft lavender eyes and a huge friendly smile. The one with golden eyes had shorter hair, but they both wore their pale locks loose with random, interspersed braids.

"They're..." Jak started numbly.

"Fae," Jim finished with a grin. "This is Krill," he indicated the serious one. "And this is Kode." The happy one waved joyfully at them. Jim never stopped grinning at the girls. "We're the Banging Wagon," he introduced. "Want to join us?"

CHAPTER TWO

Jak couldn't have talked her sisters out of it if she'd wanted to. Jim travelled with faeries — real life faeries. Dora and Allie found this terribly exciting. Even Jak had to admit it was kind of cool. Dora was the first one to squeal.

"Fairies!"

"Faeries," Jim corrected delicately. "An important distinction."

"You're fae?" Jak asked them, still partially bewildered. "Real fae?"

"Yep!" Kode told her happily. The beautiful blonde faerie stood taller than Jim, but there was a childlike innocence and joy in his immortal expression. He had broad shoulders and a strong muscular build, yet his lavender eyes conveyed a soul that wouldn't hurt a fly. His clothes were ragged and covered him scantily. His feet were bare and the overall style looked like a choice. Comparatively, Krill was well dressed with his trousers tucked into tall boots and a shirt and tunic layered over his lithe frame. The clothes themselves were not a style Jak was familiar with, but she could pick that it was faerie.

"I've never seen fae like you before…" Jak admitted. "Not except…"

"Except?" Krill asked her. Though Jak had found them extremely similar in appearance, Krill bore none of Kode's naiveté. His golden eyes were sharp and shrewd.

"Except in pictures of the gods," Jak finished nervously.

"We are what our kind call Ha'Cās," Krill told her with a challenging stare.

Jak looked around. She had no idea what that meant. Neither did her sisters. They all shrugged at each other.

"Ha'Cās means they're half human," Jim smiled. "The Ha'Cās are half human and half D'Ihne."

"D-D'Ihne?" Jak stammered in confusion.

"Gods," Jim grinned. "Humans mispronounce it 'divine', but the proper fae word for the most powerful breed of fae is D'Ihne. However," Jim clapped his hand firmly against the side of the wagon. "I'm not here to give you an oral history on the fae. We're travelling northwest. You ladies want a ride or not?"

"We're picking little girls up off the side of the road now?" Krill asked. The more elegant of the fae folded his arms disapprovingly. He stared down at the ever-grinning Jim.

"I can't just leave them here," Jim protested. "Unless, of course, they want me to. I'm not kidnapping anyone."

"That's a change," Krill sniped. "Not what you said last week."

"He's joking," Jim raised a soothing hand at the girls. "We've never kidnapped anyone. He's just kidding." Jim stepped closer to Krill. The faerie was standing on the back step of the wagon. Jim reached up and hooked an arm around his waist. He pulled Krill in and stared straight up his torso at him. "You have an awful sense of humour."

Krill stared him down, but Jak swore she saw the faintest hint of a smile touch the faerie's lips. Krill looked up at the girls again seriously.

"If a strange man ever offers you a ride in the back of his wagon you should say no — especially if that man is Jim."

"But… why?" Kode asked. The sweet fae looked so pure in his confusion. "What's wrong with Jim? Why shouldn't we ride with him in the wagon?"

Krill pursed his lips thoughtfully for a moment. Jim cracked up laughing.

"Oh, fantastic," he praised. With a sultry look he slapped Krill on the arse and moved away. "Go on — explain that one to him."

"I loathe you," Krill told him as Jim strolled out of reach.

"I love you too, babe." He clapped. "Let's get this show on the road!"

"We can come too?" Dora asked. Her big eyes mirrored Kode's innocence.

"I hope so…" Kode nodded at her.

"No…" Jak shook her head. "I don't think we can." She was aware that her sisters were already about to climb in with the fae.

"Jak, they were kidding," Allie told her condescendingly. "It's fine."

"It's not them," Jak replied, although she did feel a

bit nervous about travelling with someone who had the nerve to sexually harass a demigod. "It's us. We can't just go. What… what about Mum?"

"Your Mom's still in town?" Jim asked curiously.

"No, she isn't," Allie snapped. "Mum went out one day and never came back. It was a year ago, Sis. She's not coming home."

"You don't know that, Allie!"

"Woah, woah, calm down, girls," Jim soothed. "You don't know where your Mom is? You ever looked for her? Where was she going?"

"We don't know," Jak admitted. "She left a note on the table to say she was popping out and would be back soon, but she never came home… We asked around. No one in town had seen her. She just vanished. I don't even know where to start looking."

"Then start with us," Jim offered. Jak looked up at him. He seemed earnest enough and he motioned to the wagon. "Come with us. We'll help you find your Mom."

"We are not getting tangled up in another bloody adventure…" Krill growled.

"Yay!" Kode clapped delightedly. "We're going on an adventure!"

"Adventure!" Dora clapped too. The little girl and the innocent faerie clapped joyfully together. Krill closed his eyes and rested his head back against the wagon. Jak recognised the motion and the three second pause. She'd done it enough times herself. With her protests undone, she watched Dora and Allie climb gleefully into the back of the caravan. Kode kindly reached down and helped them with a beaming smile on his face. Jak felt a hand touch her shoulder.

"Come ride up front," Jim invited as he brushed by her. "It's pretty crowded in there."

She didn't feel like she had much of a choice. Krill saw where she was headed and gave her a warning look. He held out his hand for her pack. Slightly reluctantly, she slung it off her shoulders and passed it to him, with the sword from her belt.

"Thanks," she murmured.

"Watch yourself," he replied with a direct look. "And if he gets too handsy, bang on the wall behind you. I'll come break his fingers."

"Is that likely?" Jak squeaked apprehensively.

"With him? Honestly? It's hard to tell sometimes. I hope not."

Feeling even worse than she had before, Jak trotted around the side of the wagon and scrambled up the side to join Jim on the seat. Krill and Kode shut up the wagon behind them once the girls were inside. Jim gave Jak one of his best reassuring smiles as he flicked the reins and got the caravan rolling again. She felt like the smile should be working, but she was far too nervous.

"What's wrong, kid?" Jim asked. He wasn't fooled or put off by anything.

"Oh, just… just something Krill said…"

"Ergh," Jim groaned and rolled his eyes. "About me, I'm sure. Don't say. I can probably guess. He thinks the absolute worst of everyone. Always." He leant his head back against the wagon and called out to it. "Babe, why are you like this?"

"Because I hate you," Krill's voice replied from behind the wall.

"That's a lie," Jim told Jak confidently. "Pretty much everything he says is a lie. He's just always grumpy. He loves me really. If he didn't, he could just leave. I think… although… maybe. He wouldn't leave Kode, so if Kode wouldn't leave me… eh."

"Are they brothers?" Jak asked, thinking of her own sisters in the back.

"No," Jim laughed. "They're not related. Well, not by blood. They're married."

"Married?" Jak echoed.

"To each other," Jim clarified like he thought Jak might need some help.

"I…" Jak paused. "I thought fae didn't do that… get married, I mean. I s'pose there's the legend of Crŷstïar and Olíriá…"

"Don't get me started on those two weirdos," Jim shook his head. "No, you're right. It's extremely rare. Generally speaking fae don't go in for marriage. It's so… limiting. Swearing yourself to someone forever is even more ridiculous when you are literally staring down *forever*."

"And… and what about you…?" Jak asked nervously. There was still something strange about him. It was the way he talked — like he knew things about the fae. It made sense given his companions, but humans and fae travelling together… that was extremely unusual. That wasn't the direction he followed her question though, and she hadn't been more specific. Jim gave her a cheeky sidelong glance.

"Why do you ask?" he replied seductively.

"No," Jak raised a hand between them. "Don't flirt with me."

"Don't flirt with you?" Jim looked around the horizon and the endless dirt road before them. "What else am I supposed to do out here?"

"We could have a conversation like real people," Jak suggested. "Without flirting."

"No," Jim shook his head. "Preposterous. I've never talked to anyone without flirting before. Never. It makes going home to see Mom and Dad really awkward…"

Jak started to laugh. It was the first time he had made her laugh, but she just couldn't help it anymore. There was something so comedic about him. He kept a straight face as he said it, but cracked a familiar dimpled grin at the sight of her laughter.

"There we go," he grinned. "See, you can smile. It's not all doom and gloom, and — by the way — utterly gorgeous." He paused as he watched her smile fade and for a brief moment became serious. "I am sorry about what happened back in the village. Truly. Violence seems to be in the air at the moment. Everyone's on edge in this country."

"It's because of the war," Jak muttered. "People are scared. They're scared the fighting is going to cross over the border and come here."

"The war?" Jim asked.

"Yeah, the war." Jak gave him a look. "You're heading northwest — away from Dazigh. You must know about the war." Jim gave no sign that he did so

Jak continued. "Some rebels in Dazigh murdered the King, and now the peasants are revolting."

"Peasants are always revolting," Jim quipped.

"That's an awful thing to say about yourself..." Jak felt like she was starting to get the rhythm of his banter. Jim gave her a bold look.

"Do I look like a peasant to you?" he demanded.

"Yeah," Jak eyeballed him. "You do."

"Ouch."

"Why?" she preened. "Do I look revolting to you?"

Jim's grin marked his dimples deep into his cheeks in sheer delight. "Ah, Jak. Have I mentioned that I like you?"

"I think you said something about it when we met..." she smiled a small smile. It was funny. The longer she stayed out here, the less she was inclined to bang on the wall for Krill. Dora had been right; Jim was nice. He was easy going, and even easier to get used to.

"They assassinated," Jim said, straightening up on the hard wooden seat.

"What?"

"They assassinated the King," he corrected her earlier statement. "You don't just murder a King — although that is literally what it is. When it's someone of import, taken out strategically, it's an assassination."

"Are you trying to sound less like a peasant?"

"Is it working?"

"... Maybe?" Jak shrugged. "How would I know?"

"Your own vocabulary isn't bad. Trust me, I've been around. As for expanding it? You can learn. I can teach you. I'm a very talented guy, babe. I can teach you lots of things."

"… I think I want to bang on the door for Krill now."

"Calm down, kid. You're the only one of us getting excited. You want him to come break my fingers? He won't. Makes him uncomfortable. He knows I get off on it when he hurts me." Jim grinned wickedly to himself as he watched Jak balk out the corner of his eye. "You want to go ride in the back for a bit?" he chuckled.

"I feel like you're trying to unsettle me…" Jak hesitated. Jim paused. He shot her a look and Jak felt for a moment she had hit the nail on the head. He sighed.

"I'm used to Krill," he admitted. "Out on the road I rely on meeting new people. The boys are great. I love them. I wouldn't be without them. Kode has… a large range of talents, but stimulating conversation isn't one of them. Not usually. Krill… well… Krill might be smarter than me, I'm not sure, but optimism isn't one of his strengths, and conversations with him can be great, but he does keep me on my toes. I'm used to banter. I'm used to having to battle with my words. It's never just a dialogue — it's a game — and," he gave Jak an apologetically honest look, "I'm extremely competitive. Sorry," he chuckled. "You probably wanted some clarity, rather than my life story."

"Actually, I wouldn't mind your life story," Jak admitted. "I've only just met you and I don't know anything about you — except that you flirt with your parents."

"Hey, that's more honesty than you'd get from most people."

"Yes," Jak agreed. "Most people would kindly keep

that level of honesty to themselves."

"Then you've already learnt the most important thing about me," Jim told her coolly. "I'm not like most people."

Jak was starting to feel well aware of that. She let the silence fall naturally between them as she contemplated the strange man at her side. He was an odd sort, to be sure, but now she was travelling with him, she would have to spend time with him. She would have to get to know him. Like all people, he would to turn out to be a great deal more complex than she had ever imagined. If they had truly parted after their first meeting, he could have safely stayed a caricature. Now the road stretched out forever in front of them, and she had a feeling she was going to have plenty of time to get to know him.

***

The day rolled on. Bunnies frolicked in the verges and nibbled the long grass by the side of the road. They didn't bounce away at the sound of the Banging Wagon trundling and bumping by, but watched it curiously. Behind them, the forest sprawled wild and endless. Travelling with Jim and the boys was fun. Jak felt like she was getting the hang of bantering with him. She had to be sharp and quick, but her mind enjoyed the exercise. She couldn't remember holding a conversation this long with someone who wasn't family. Friends were hard to come by for someone who didn't like people, but Jim made it easy. He would talk about anything, to anything. He would make flippant comments to the birds as they flew by. He would chat casually to the rabbits. Jak could contribute when she wanted to. When she was quiet, and the bunnies ignored him, he whistled an old tune.

"What is that song?" Jak asked him. The familiarity of it gripped her heart.

"Dunno," Jim shrugged. "Don't remember. A tune long forgotten, I imagine. My mom used to hum it though. Been stuck in my head all my life."

"My dad used to whistle it…" Jak commented.

"Doesn't surprise me," Jim grinned. "Around here folk learn the old songs, even if no one remembers the words anymore."

"So you're from around here too?" she prodded.

"I'm from everywhere," he grinned. "I know songs from this land and a thousand others."

"But you said your mum taught you that one…"

"She taught me all the others too," he grinned. "I can sing you some?"

"Alright…" Jak agreed hesitantly.

Jim sang. The way he sang wasn't like anything she knew. Jak had heard drunk gusto by pub doors, and holiday choirs in the street. She had heard her parents sing while they worked. Jim sang like a man alone on the road, and it wasn't good. It wasn't awful. She didn't have a desperate urge to clamp her hands over her ears, but he seemed to make up for lack of talent with enthusiasm. Luckily, the song he sang seemed to be designed for someone who couldn't sing well. It wasn't required. It had rhythm. It had style. The more she listened, the more she enjoyed it. Soon enough, she realised she was grinning as they trundled down the road.

Jim was still singing and humming tunes when they pulled off the side of the road late afternoon. The horses clomped over the grass and into the forest. The rabbits living on the edges hopped up to investigate. They had no fear of the horses or the wagon. Jak had never seen bunnies behave that way before. One little brown rabbit sat back on its haunches and sniffed the air as the creaky wheel rolled by it. Its big dark eyes blinked. She wondered if it could smell the fae. A small robin swooped overhead shrieking and chirping. Jim stopped singing and gave it a look.

"You're cramping my style," he warned the bird. It ignored him and swooped off with another sharp twitter. Jak chuckled softly. Jim navigated carefully though the trees and parked The Banging Wagon in a small grassy clearing.

"This looks like a nice spot to set up camp," he announced. "Shall we, M'Lady?" he invited Jak. She grinned at him and they climbed down to go and open the back of the caravan. Jim grabbed the doors and folded them back. Jak felt her heart stop in a panic.

There was no one in there. To be fair, this was the first time she had ever had a decent look inside The Banging Wagon, and it was so full of junk the others could be hiding. Except, it was so full of junk there wasn't much space to hide. No wonder it was called The Banging Wagon. She was surprised it didn't make more of a racket banging down the road. Jim hauled himself into the back of the wagon and started checking through the shelves of junk like he was looking for something.

"Where are they?" Jak demanded. Jim looked back at her standing panicked in the doorway.

"Oh," he caught on. "They'll be downstairs. There's more space down there." As he said it, he grabbed a trapdoor handle in the floor and yanked it open. He climbed half in and sat with his legs hanging through the hole. "Come on," he encouraged.

Jak paused where she was and bent over to look under the caravan. The bottom of it was still sealed up and there was no sign of Jim's boots or a trapdoor. She stood again. Jim was grinning at her from the trapdoor. He motioned her to come join him. Jak clambered into the back of the wagon and followed Jim down the hole. There was a ladder down into a small wooden panelled room. It was impossible, but in the last twelve hours her life seemed to have become full of the impossible.

The room at the bottom of the ladder was mostly a collection of doorways, and it was uncomfortably small. With the two of them in it there was barely enough space for them to turn around, and Jak was not okay with how close Jim was to her as she came off the ladder. It could have been worse. He had a strangely feminine floral scent about him which was quite nice. It was just the rest of him that she would have preferred at arm's length.

"Sorry Jak," he apologised. "Just 'scuse me a second." He reached around her to a door handle and opened up another room.

It wasn't much bigger than the one they were in, and

Jak didn't really have space to spill into it as she and Jim were squeezed into the doorway together. The new room had a small table in it and a few squishy beanbags around it. Krill, Kode, and Allie were lounging respectively on the beanbags and Dora was perched on Kode's knee. They were all gathered around a card game on the table.

"You kids having fun?" Jim grinned at the table as he leant past Jak through the door.

"We're learning how to gamble!" Dora exclaimed delightedly. "I'm winning!"

Jak took in the scene. Kode and Dora were playing together, sharing a hand, and taking it very seriously; Krill had the wry look of someone who was getting a kick out of going easy on everyone else to let the kids win; and Allie looked like she was spending so much of her time ogling Kode that she was completely indifferent to the fact that cards were being played. At least they were entertained. Jak was mildly glad that the fae were playing games with her sisters before Jim could get involved. Jim seemed like the strip poker type. Besides, if they were going to start gambling, then being taught by a couple of gay faeries seemed like really safe place to start.

"Excellent," Jim beamed at Dora. "I've never beaten Krill before. You'll have to tell me how you do it."

"Liar," Krill muttered behind his cards. A slight smirk played about the faerie's lips, and Jak was at just the right angle to see Krill and Jim share a wink.

"Alright team," Jim continued. "We've got a nice spot to set up camp for the night. All hands on deck, and, guys, do we know where the tent is? The big one for the girls."

"Closet," Krill answered. "Top shelf."

"Thank you," Jim smiled at him. He turned around to a door behind him and stopped. "Hm. Actually, maybe everyone out and then I can shut that door so I have room to open this one," he called.

"Okay," Kode smiled. "Who wants to come with me to get firewood?"

"Me!" Dora exclaimed, raising her hand.

"And me!" Allie copied shamelessly.

"Right, last one up the ladder is on dishes!" Kode warned.

The girls squealed and ran for the ladder. Jak stood to the side and held the door open as her sisters rushed out and clambered up. Inside the room, the fae stood calmly from the beanbags. Krill wove his fingers through the air, tracing a rune. Fäsaírm. The entwined branches. He snapped his fingers and the cards jumped back into the packet themselves. The rune of binding. He smiled at Kode.

"You don't mind playing dad?" he asked.

"I love playing dad," Kode replied happily. He stepped around the table and kissed his husband. "Last one out is on dishes," he reminded teasingly before scooting away and chasing the girls up the ladder.

Jak watched Krill watching Kode run off. The serious fae's golden eyes were so soft when he looked at his husband. She couldn't believe someone so severe could look so gentle, but once she had seen it she couldn't unsee it either. He caught her looking, but she didn't flinch. She didn't feel like she had been intruding, or that she had seen something she wasn't supposed to. The fae weren't shy about their feelings. Krill gave her a polite nod as she was still holding the door open.

"James, you're on dishes," Krill announced as he started up the ladder.

Jim laughed as he watched them all leave. He motioned to Jak and she shut the door she was holding. Jim opened his door and exposed a tightly packed closet. It looked like it was full of paperwork. He made a few thoughtful noises as he rummaged, and then pulled out an envelope.

"I think this is the right one," he mused. "And we'll need three of these…" he grabbed a few knotted rags, before turning a suggestive sideways glance at Jak. "Unless you want to stay inside and share…?"

"With you?" she checked. "I really don't."

"Suit yourself. But jokes aside, this door is mine," he indicated one of the other doors. "If you need anything don't be afraid to come knock. Or, y'know… if you change your mind."

Jak gave him a wry look. He couldn't seem to help himself.

"I won't," she assured.

He just grinned. It was the grin. It made her feel like he never really meant it anyway. It took the edge off his words and insinuations.

"Well," he shrugged, "I'd feel awkward about leaving the kids outside on their own anyway, and there's no way I'd leave them alone overnight with Kode to watch them."

"Really?" Jak asked. "He seems like the safest of all of you."

Jim sighed. "In some ways… I can see that. Kode is the simplest. Sometimes that's the best, but it does make some things… difficult. He thinks like a fae. He was raised fae. That can come into conflict with a lot of human sensibilities, and he doesn't understand enough to try and hide that. Besides, let's not be shy about this, Kode is a lot like a little kid himself. As long as Krill is watching out for them, I'm not worried at all. Krill is the safest."

"You said everything Krill said was a lie and that he's always grumpy," Jak reminded.

"Yeah," Jim nodded. "But he's also the best person I've ever met. He has a strong moral compass and he tries to do the right thing. He's a very good man." Jim shut the cupboard door. "A very good man who has lived a very difficult life."

Jak watched Jim curiously. When his flirting façade fell, he was an interesting man, and when he spoke about the fae, Jak felt compelled to hear the story. He wasn't prepared to tell it though. Not here. Not yet. He turned and his carefree smile returned as he indicated the ladder.

"Shall we? Ladies first, of course. You don't want to be stuck on dishes."

Jak smiled her thanks and climbed up the ladder with Jim following behind. Once they were out, he shut the trapdoor after them. They left the wagon. Kode and the girls were already disappearing into the woods to search for firewood. Krill was wandering around the edge of the clearing. Jak watched him as he moved around the trees marking signs with his fingers. Runes appeared over the bark as he went. Jak recognised the Fora rune.

"What's he doing?" she asked.

"Protecting the clearing," Jim answered. "It doesn't always work, but it helps to keep us safe, and warns us of any danger." Jim motioned her away from the caravan. "Okay. Let's make some space." He clicked his fingers and the horses pulling the wagon vanished. Jak jumped and yelped in surprise.

"But what—? Where—?"

"Magic horses," he explained. "They're not really real, but it freaks people out if the wagon drives itself. Come over here, but stay behind me. We'll set up the tent."

"Why do I need to stay behind you?"

She barely needed to ask. As soon as she started speaking, Jim took out the envelope from the cupboard. He took a slip of cloth from it and tossed it in front of him. The instant the fabric left his fingers, it sprang out. In seconds, it exploded into a full tent. It was large enough to fit a family in, and muddy-green in colour. The magical tent sat innocently on the grass in front of them. Jak made another small yelping sound. Jim handed her the envelope.

"You can hold onto this," he offered. "Now we just set up the beds."

"It's magic," Jak blurted.

"Isn't everything I do?" Jim smirked. He opened the front of the tent and took out the three rags. He untied each one and tossed them in. As they hit the ground, they sprung up into fully made camp beds. Jim turned his smug smile to meet Jak's stunned face. "Arrange to your liking. You girls should have plenty of space in here."

"How did you do that?!" Jak exclaimed, even though she'd watched it happen.

"I'm magic," Jim smirked, wiggling his fingers at her.

"But you… you're… wait!" Jak grabbed him by the arm as he moved to leave. "Your wagon is magic, your stuff is magic—!"

"It's what I do, Jak," Jim smiled at her. "It's what we do. We sell magic items. It's our business."

"Dora's crown?!" Jak demanded. Jim paused. He sighed.

"Is magic," he admitted slowly. "But if she caught magic powers off it, she's the first person to do so. It's made of flowers, but it will never age or brown or die — that's how it's magic. Indestructible flower crown — not one of my bestsellers."

Jak believed him, but she wasn't sure she wanted to, and she didn't let go of his arm. He moved back into the doorway of the tent with her and stood too close for comfort. The man did not have a personal space bubble at all.

"You want this to be my fault," he stated softly. Jak didn't reply. He was right, but she couldn't very well say that. He wasn't much taller than her, and he wasn't imposing, but he was so close it felt like he was looming. His proximity made her too nervous to speak. He kept talking. "You want this to be my fault because that would be easier. Then you could go home and explain the mistake and blame it all on an outsider. That's beneath you, Jak. You're better than that. The truth — whether or not you like it — is far more likely to be that Dora was playing at being a faerie princess, and an accident happened, and superstitious humans went berserk."

"I know…" Jak whispered. She let her hand drop from his arm. She hated it, but he was absolutely right. The shame of it wouldn't let her meet his eye. She stared at the floor of the tent. Jim raised a hand. Jak flinched back violently as his fingers neared her face. Jim raised his hands defensively in front of him.

"I'm not going to hurt you, kid," he promised. Everything about that promise was genuine, but he could sense her discomfort and took a step back. He indicated the interior of the tent. "You do you. Sort yourself out. Get comfortable. I'll go help the others."

Jim turned and left without another word. Jak's heart was still racing from the shock of flinching. It had been a misunderstanding. She knew that. She could be logical about it. He was a tactile person. Touching was one of the ways he reassured. She didn't like being touched. They would just have to get used to each other. She took a deep breath.

Oh man… she felt like such a dick. Yes, okay, he was an awful and inappropriate flirt. That was certainly true. But he had also given her sister a present — which wasn't something she had been able to do for a while. He had stood up to the village and saved them from the mob. He'd also offered to help them find their Mum, put a comfortable roof over their heads, and food in their bellies without asking for a single thing in return. The least she could do was say 'Sorry, that was a misunderstanding. I don't like being touched.' He'd understand that.

She ducked out of the tent, but Jim was already disappearing into the treeline. It could wait until he got back. She didn't need to chase him. Instead, she took her pack and her sisters' bags from the caravan and moved them into the tent. Then she arranged the beds around the edges to give them space to walk through and store their things. She stashed her sword under her bunk. The tent certainly was roomy. She'd never seen a tent this big. There was room to stand up in it. And it was magic. It had fitted inside the little envelope she had stored in her pocket. The envelope Jim had given her. She took it out and looked at it. It was old and worn, but thick and sturdy. She shook her head. This was stupid.

Jak pocketed the envelope again and left the tent. There was no one else around. She was alone in the campsite, but she had seen the direction Jim had headed and followed after him. He couldn't be that hard to find.

Jak had never left Rutsborough before. That village had been her whole life, and she hadn't belonged there. But the road they followed ran alongside the old forest. The forest was bigger than she had ever been able to explore. It was part of the same wild woods she had always lived in. Faerie woods. They grew thick and feral and dark. The scent of magic hung in the air of them. Jak stalked through them carefully. The ground was thick with old leaves. Here and there small rocks dotted the ground. None of them positioned in a ring. Just because she couldn't see the danger didn't mean it wasn't there. She knew to always be respectful in the forest. It could cost you your life if you weren't. No matter her new companions, she knew better than to anger or tempt faeries.

Something glimmered in the distance and she crept towards it. Rune magic. It was Krill. Jim was with him. He was standing so close to his friend that at first she hadn't realised they were both there. She headed straight for them, but something in their mannerisms made her stop and pause. She wished it had made her turn and run away too. It would have been better than eavesdropping.

"You still mad at me, Elkrillendé?" Jim asked softly. "You've been in a shitty mood all day."

Krill sighed. "Why did you pick up those girls, Jim? What in Ghōul's name were you thinking?"

"That village wanted to drown the little one!" Jim protested. "I couldn't just leave them!"

"I get that," Krill conceded. He placed an understanding hand on Jim's chest and nodded gently. "You did the right thing there. I believe that. But now they're travelling with us—"

"Just for a little while," Jim defended. He placed a gentle hand soothingly on the side of Krill's face. "Look, we'll help them find their Mom, and get them safely away from that village, and then they can go their own way. It can't be that hard. Then they'll be safe and happy, we can go back to our lives... everyone wins."

"I just feel like this was so…"

"I know. I know. I'm sorry."

Krill grinned at him. It was a wicked look on the fae's face.

"You panicked, didn't you?" he smirked, leaning so close it was hard for Jak to hear them. "You couldn't let it go."

"You don't have to tease me about it," Jim grumbled.

"Yes, I do," Krill chuckled. He leant in and kissed the human in his arms. Jim kissed him back. Jak felt her jaw drop and her heart sink as she watched the two of them embracing through the trees. She was not supposed to have seen that. That was bad. It pretty much ruined everything. She fled back to the campsite.

Unfortunately, she arrived back at the same time as Kode and her sisters. They were carrying a collection of old dry branches for firewood. He was talking and laughing with them, and they were completely enamoured with him. He was so sweet and pure. He was gormless and simple. He'd be easy to fool. Jak wanted to puke. It was horrible. The conversation in the forest… Krill had been worried about having extra people around, and now Jak knew, but no one knew she knew. This completely sucked.

"What's wrong with you?" Allie demanded of her as soon as they were close enough.

"Nothing," Jak tried to shake it off. This was not her place or her business.

But it was settling over her like a cold, damp cloak. She felt like she was carrying some horrible secret, and she had no idea what to do with it.

The girls inspected the tent while Kode dug a quick firepit and pulled some benches out from the wagon to place around it. Jak watched him work. She couldn't bring herself to say anything. She couldn't do that to this happy, dim faerie. Allie came back out of the tent to join her watching Kode. He was strong and agile and scantily glad. Jak could tell Allie appreciated it.

"Are you okay?" Allie asked her.

"Yeah…" Jak lied weakly.

"Just trying not to think about it, huh?" Allie sympathised.

Jak turned to look at her sharply. Allie didn't know… she couldn't. She was still staring at Kode as she kept talking.

"Me too," she muttered. "It's been quite a day. I'm trying not to think about home, and Rutsborough, and all that… I just… it's totally normal for us to be sad, right? I'm just trying not to think about it though. At least I have a nice distraction."

"You mean that buff, chiselled, god-body?"

"Hey, you do get it!" Allie giggled, nudging her in the side.

"Not even a little bit," Jak replied honestly. It still wasn't her thing. She could appreciate that they were beautiful in a way only gods could be, but they weren't her type. "Allie, they're magical creatures—"

"I don't want to marry one, you dork," Allie scoffed. "They're married to each other. They told us. I just like looking at them. They're soooo pretty. Especially Kode."

"Because he's mostly shirtless?"

"And beautiful. He's just got this wholesome, gorgeous glow about him."

Jak nodded. She understood that. Which made her brief excursion into the forest all the more confusing. How could Krill be cheating on someone that sweet and pretty and perfect? With Jim of all people?! Jak felt a faint sneer of distaste cross her face. Those two still weren't back yet. She didn't want to think about what they were up to. Eventually, they came back separately. She wanted to hit them both with shovels. Jim wandered back into the campsite his usual confident cheery self. He joined Kode to raid the wagon and they left Krill to make the fire.

The girls were back inside the tent. Jim and Kode were inside the wagon. Jak was alone, watching Krill arrange the wood in the firepit. Most of her brain was screaming at her to stay out of it, but it was haunting her. She edged closer to him.

"Something bothering you, Jak?" he asked quietly as she neared him. She froze, but she knew he knew the answer, and that was why he'd asked. She couldn't back out now.

"I saw you in the forest with Jim," she accused.

Krill looked up at her from under his pale eyebrows. A sardonic smirk marked his face. He snapped his fingers. The Ezian rune he had just traced in the air vanished. Jak jumped as the fire caught instantly. Krill stood and brushed the grass from his knees. He pointed and Jak followed his finger.

Jim and Kode were stacking things on the grass outside the wagon. They were laughing and fooling about. Kode grabbed a stack of plates and set them out with everything else.

"We can use the nice plates," he told Jim.

"Oh can we?"

"Yeah," Kode grinned. "You're on dishes."

Jim grinned and placed a hand to the side of Kode's neck. He pulled the teasing fae into a kiss. Kode happily obliged.

"Well then it's a good thing we've got magic for that too," Jim retorted. The two of them laughed. Jak turned back to Krill very confused and sheepish.

"It's called polyamory," Krill told her calmly. "Kode and I are in an open relationship with Jim. We have been for the last ten years."

"Oh…" Jak replied in a very small voice.

"Don't feel stupid," Krill said. "How would you know if it's not something you've ever encountered before? We didn't tell you. I'm guessing you were raised just Mum, Dad, a small village you've never left, and you will have been raised human. Fae do not have any of the hang-ups about love and sex that humans do. Your concerns are not ours. How old do you think Kode is?"

Jak didn't answer. He didn't look much more than a few years older than her, but he had that immortal glow about him…

"He's over a hundred years old," Krill continued. "I'm four hundred and sixty-two. Think about how much you have changed in the last ten years. Now try and imagine forever."

She couldn't. She had gone from five to fifteen in the

last ten years, and while part of her wanted to say that was different because she had stopped being a child, she knew it wasn't true. It wasn't different.

"I married Kode because I love him," Krill told her. "I want him forever. If anything ever happened to him, I would be inconsolable. I would raze the earth and sky and my grief would know no bounds. But that doesn't mean he will be the only person I love forever. Forever is a long time, Jak. So is ten years."

"You said you hate Jim," Jak muttered.

"Sometimes I do," Krill agreed. "You love your sisters, you don't hate them sometimes?"

Jak was quiet in response.

"Family, friends, lovers — all relationships are complicated," he told her. "That's just life."

"You're the smart one, aren't you?"

"I'm well over four hundred," he smiled. "You can't get that old and not learn something."

"I'm sorry I..."

"Don't be." He touched her shoulder gently. "You're learning. We've all had to do it."

She smiled. There was a reassurance in his touch, but it was distant. Neither of them were tactile people. He was doing it because he thought it would help, not because it came naturally. That was probably something he had learnt from Jim. It made her reconsider what she had heard in the forest too. Perhaps there was no ulterior motive to Krill's dislike of their new hitchhikers. Perhaps he was just heavily introverted and felt uncomfortable about looking after children for the foreseeable future.

"Thank you for taking us in," she murmured.

"You're welcome, but Jim is the one you should be thanking — albeit from a safe distance."

"You make him sound so dangerous," Jak grinned.

"He will shag anything that moves and a great many things that won't," Krill warned. "I do not feel special."

Jim and Kode approached the campfire carrying their bundles from the wagon as Krill said it. He stared his human lover down as he spoke. Jim was grinning at him.

"Babe, are you being hyperbolic again?" he teased.

"It feels dishonest to your character to talk about you without using hyperbole," Krill replied cuttingly. Jim brushed passed him as he and Kode set down what they were carrying.

"You are still grumpy," he commented.

"Of course," Krill replied. "Grumpy," he pointed at himself. "Happy," he indicated Kode. "And the annoying pain in my arse," he gave Jim a painfully direct look.

"Says the top," Jim laughed at him.

Jak put a hand over her eyes as she felt her cheeks flush. This was not a conversation she felt comfortable being a part of. She didn't need to know.

"What does that mean?" Dora's little voice asked.

Everyone froze as they realised the girls had left the tent again and snuck up on them.

"Nothing," Jak overruled anyone else's answer with her face buried in her hands. "It means nothing."

"Dora," Jim smiled at her. "Do you want to help Kode dish up?"

"Yes!" the little girl exclaimed. She ran around the outside of the benches to join the faerie. Jak uncovered her face to look over at what they had brought out. Jim and Kode had a stack of plates and mugs, along with a pitcher and a picnic basket. Dora was terribly excited about helping stack food from the basket onto plates.

"Where did all of that come from?" Allie asked.

"Let me guess," Jak said to Krill. "Magic jug with unending supply of water? Magic basket with unending supply of food?"

"How could you tell?" Krill smiled.

"I'm starting to see a pattern..." Jak admitted drily.

"Jim is nothing if not lazy," Krill replied. "If we can do it by magic, he insists we do."

"And you guys take your lead from him? Even though he's the human?"

"It's his wagon," Krill shrugged. "His home. He took us in. We're just grateful he was there when he was. Thank you, Dora." Krill smiled as Dora handed out plates of food. He sat back on one of the benches by the fire as the sun began to set. Evening bathed the forest in pink light. Allie took a plate and sat down beside him.

"Lazy, huh?" she asked cheekily.

"Allie!" Jak exclaimed.

Allie ignored her sister and didn't take her interrogating eyes from the fae. Krill turned his face away and covered his mouth to hide his laughter. Allie turned away smugly like she'd won something. Jak shook her head at both of them. She stalked around the fire to help Dora and join the others. Krill waited until she was safely on the other side before leaning in to

Allie.

"Perhaps he reserves his laziness for some aspects of his life over others…"

Allie giggled wickedly. "And if you can do it by magic…"

"Not always," Krill hid his answer behind his mug as he sipped at the water. "Not always."

There was an unspoken agreement between them that this conversation would not be reiterated back to Jak at any point. Allie thought she was old enough to have the conversation, and no fae was going to disagree with her. The hang-ups around the campfire were Jak's, and Jak's alone.

They ate around the warm fire as the sky darkened and the sun sank. Jak lounged on a bench with Kode and Dora. Allie had been right earlier; it had been quite a day. Jak had a feeling that at some point in the future the severity of what had happened would hit her, but for now… this was nice. She couldn't remember the last time she had been this relaxed, or this happy. She thought about it. Maybe she could remember…

But maybe that made it worse.

She looked around the boys at the campfire. The strange threesome that had taken them in so willingly. Jim lounged by one of the benches as a rabbit hopped hesitantly toward him. He grinned at it. Its long whiskers twitched as it sniffed. Its body stretched out, its back legs extended for a pause, and then they suddenly bounced forward, condensing it into a round fluffy ball again. Nothing else happened. Slowly it stretched out and hopped a little bit closer again. Its long ears twitched as it watched Jim.

"How you doing, little one?" he asked, holding out a hand to it. The bunny sniffed his fingers curiously. Then it started to lick. "No, not me," Jim protested, as though he was worried nibbling might come next. He pulled a short carrot out of the magical picnic basket and held it out. The fluffy brown rabbit fell upon the treat like a ravenous chipmunk. Tiny flecks of orange sprayed around its mouth as it devoured the carrot. Jim chuckled. He reached out and stroked the rabbit's long velvet ears.

"Bunny!" Dora whispered. She had been holding her breath watching it approach. Jim saw her big eyes shine with adoration. He motioned her over. Dora crawled from the bench and crept forward silently across the grass. The rabbit remained completely unfazed as the little girl came over and stroked its soft fur. There was still carrot to munch.

"Look at that," Jim grinned. "He likes you."

"He likes you," Dora pointed out. She was too young to know how to verbalise the distinction that the bunny tolerated her petting, while it had actively sought Jim's company, but she had recognised it.

"Eh," Jim shrugged and rubbed the top of its head. "Rabbits like me. They always have. We have lots in common."

Krill snorted. Jim winked at him. Jak watched them from across the fire. The rabbit finished its small carrot. It hopped forward, nuzzled Jim, and bounced away. Dora sat in the grass and watched the rabbit go with loving eyes. Jak watched the man that had attracted it.

She had never known wild rabbits to be curious about humans before. He was like something out of a fairy-tale. Jim looked up from where he reclined by the bench and met her eye. She wanted to know.

"So… you three have been together for ten years?" she asked.

"Yeah, must be about that," he nodded.

"Ever since we left Roïgola'a'lanaū," Kode chimed in.

"The Golden City?" Jak asked in awe. "The city of the gods in the sky? You lived there?"

"All Ha'Cās do," Krill answered. "It's where we are born and raised."

"All demigods live in the Golden City?" Allie echoed beside him. "Really?"

"Demigods are different," Krill said. His golden eyes searched the group, but no one was going to stop him, so he elaborated. "There are two kinds of Ha'Cās. Demigods are the human name, because it is usually applied to the human born. A human born Ha'Cās is mostly human — raised human, lives human, etc…"

"Like the heroes of old…" Jak supplied.

"Exactly," Krill gave her a nod. "Your heroes of old are demigods. Human-born Ha'Cās. Kode and I are fae-born. We are born fae and raised fae, but… we are not considered fae."

"What do you mean?" Jak questioned. "You're clearly fae."

"To you, maybe…" Krill smiled a small smile. There was something dark to his smile. Something that made her nervous. Both Ha'Cās were looking down. Jim was the one who finally met her eye.

"Ha'Cās are kept as slaves in Roïgola'a'lanaū," he told her softly in his lilting accent. "They are taken on by a patron god when they are young — discovered, if you will. That god teaches them to hone their craft and they live fulfilling a purpose. But they don't have rights, or lives... or loves."

An eerie tension had settled over the fire. The flames crackled and popped in the silence.

"Wait," Allie began. "You two were a forbidden love?"

"We were..." Krill agreed. "We weren't considered people, so we weren't allowed to have relationships. We kept it secret... until one day we just eloped. We fled Roïgola'a'lanaū and never looked back."

Kode got up as Krill was speaking and moved to join him. The younger fae curled up with his husband on the other bench and kissed him gently. Jak felt a strange ache in her chest as she watched them. It was beautiful, but sad.

"Wow..." Allie breathed, staring at them. "That is so very wow."

"That's awful," Jak supplied. "I'm so sorry..."

"It is what it is," Krill stated philosophically.

"It's fucking unacceptable," Jim growled. Everyone looked at him. He quickly adopted a look of mock horror and covered Dora's ears with his hands. She shoved him away with a giggle.

"No! You said a bad word!"

"I did. I say bad words all the time," he admitted. "Especially when I'm angry."

"Are you angry?" Dora asked him.

"Sometimes when I think about it… yeah," he confessed. "Gods can be bad people, little one. Power doesn't make you good. It doesn't make you right. Saving people, taking care of each other, spreading the love — those things make you good."

"You're a lover, not a fighter?" Jak grinned at him.

"You said it, sister," Jim smirked at her. "Me and the bunnies know where it's at. If more people were like me, the world would be a better place."

"That sounds awful," Krill teased him. "I can't imagine anything worse than a world full of Jims."

"That sounds amazing…" Kode said wistfully.

"I love you, baby," Jim called to him. "Krill's just a hater, and we don't need that."

"You two wouldn't last five minutes without me," Krill smirked. "Now, Jim, you can take all those feelings and use them to wield the scrubbing brush."

Jim leant back and groaned loudly in protest.

"Don't be a sore loser!" Kode told him. "You were last up the ladder! You wash the dishes!"

"Fine," Jim pouted. "You put the kids to bed then."

"That sounds fair," Kode agreed. He kissed Krill again and got up from the bench. "Come on, girls. Time to get you sorted for bed."

"I have to put a plate out!" Dora cried. She jumped up and quickly added some left-over food to her plate before running it to the edge of the clearing. The boys watched in confusion and Jak smiled softly.

"More bunnies? Or does she tame badgers?" Jim asked.

"She leaves a plate out for the faeries," Jak told him. "Every night she saves some food and leaves it for them. Back home, Äulé used to collect it."

"Lucky faeries…" Jim commented. "That is an *old* custom though."

"Our parents taught us," Jak shrugged as Dora came running back. Dora crashed onto the bench and Jak ruffled her hair under the flower crown she still wore. "They told us to pay our dues, and keep in the favour of faeries."

"Wise folk…" Jim commented without a trace of his usual flippancy. Jak nodded. He looked around and shrugged. "I s'pose you do live in Löcha-du-Bŷur though."

"What's Löcha-du-Bŷur…?" Jak asked.

"It's the name of the forest," Jim replied. Jak just stared at him. He grinned at her. "You didn't know?"

"We always just called it the forest," she shrugged, trying to hide her blush. "I didn't know it had a name."

"Everything has a name, Jak," he smiled. "Places are defined by the stories we tell about them. Everything is named for something. Löcha-du-Bŷur is a large region that was once a village of giants. Frézíān, the D'Ihne of fire, burnt the entire village during the war of creation. Back when the world was reshaped with the bodies of the enemies of the D'Ihne. This forest grew from the ashes of that ruined village. It also happens to be the forest where the D'Ihne of the earth, Thænäri, later birthed the gnomes. You get gnomes living in forests all over the world now, and a few of them are even drifters, but all gnomes can trace their heritage back to this forest. It's no wonder your parents taught you to mind them."

Jak nodded slowly. "The... the way you say their names..." she began, his pronunciation catching her attention.

"Faerie pronunciation?" he grinned at her. "You can't say it wrong, Jak. The fae have their own way of pronouncing things, but if you're talking about D'Ihne — the gods are worshipped by various names all over the world. Almost everywhere pronounces it differently. D'Ihne don't care. They know you're talking to them, about them, whatever. They way you say it only marks where you're from."

Kode shot Jim a look, warning him he could not continue procrastinating the washing up. Jim rolled his eyes. Kode turned to Dora.

"Gnomes fed?" he asked. She nodded. "Then time for bed," he finished.

There were protests, but for the first time in a long time, Jak felt like she wasn't the one who had to manage them. Kode coaxed the girls to the tent while Jim stacked the dishes and took them away. She was surprised when Krill got up and came to sit next to her. The faerie was nervously silent for a moment. His soft blonde hair hung delicately around his face in gentle strands and short braids, and his long ears protruded out the sides.

"You don't mind that I spoke the truth of the Ha'Cās in front of them?" he asked.

"Not at all," she shook her head. "You were a slave for more than four hundred years! I don't think that's something you should duck around because of some kind of propriety. That seems... wrong."

"Thank you," he nodded. "I... I don't always know what is and isn't appropriate in front of human children."

"Me neither," Jak muttered. "I don't know what to protect them from, but the truth isn't something that should be hidden. I'm just doing what I think I can, but... but I'm not Mum."

"You don't know where she is? Your mother?"

Jak shook her head.

"Do you have any clues?" Krill asked. "Any possessions?"

"Yeah, hold on." Jak went and grabbed her bag from the tent. Kode was tucking the other two in and telling them a story that seemed to involve a fluffy duckling. He was so wholesome. She came back to Krill and dug through her pack. She pulled out the shirt and unwrapped it carefully.

"What's this?" he asked.

"The note Mum left for us," Jak showed him. "And some of her pottery."

"Her pottery?" Krill took up one of the bowls and looked at it.

"Yeah," Jak told him. "Mum and Dad used to make pottery together. It was more his hobby than hers, but she kept it up once he was gone — I guess it helped her keep him close. I couldn't leave these ones behind to get destroyed..." she trailed off sadly. The hut had been so wet from the rain that it might still be standing... but it might not too. She didn't want to think about it. She didn't want to imagine her house burning down. Everything she had ever owned… all her memories…

"Anyway, this is the note," she tried to show him again.

Krill was staring at one of the bowls. It was one of Jak's favourites. Green and glazed with little white flowers.

"Your mother made these…?" he murmured again.

Jak nodded. She watched him turn each piece over in his hands. His long delicate fingers caressed the glazed clay and his golden eyes stared curiously at them. His fingertips brushed the rune marked on the bottom of each one.

"She marked them with Nari," he named the engraved rune.

"Yeah," Jak nodded. "It's the earth rune." This had all made perfect sense to her growing up. When her parents made something from clay they marked it with Nari — the symbol for earth. Krill seemed fascinated by it. He was far more intrigued by the pottery than the note.

"Keep these safe," he told her. "Keep them packed away, and keep them hidden from Jim. Don't let him see them."

"Why not?" Jak asked.

"I'm not sure yet," Krill admitted. He looked deeply thoughtful, and a small frown marked his face. "Just trust me on this. With any luck, and some of our magic, your mother shouldn't be too hard to find. Just keep her trinkets well away from Jim."

"Do you really think he's dangerous?"

"No," Krill answered as he watched Jak carefully pack away the bowls. "I know he is. But, the gods willing, you will never have to see that side of him." He stood slowly and touched her shoulder again like he had earlier. "Get some rest, Jak. With any luck tomorrow will be an easier day."

CHAPTER THREE

Jak woke to the sound of coughing. She didn't know how long she'd been asleep. Probably not long. It was still dark, and felt like the middle of the night. Dora was curled up on her bed coughing and wheezing. Jak hauled herself from her blankets, lit their lantern, and went to sit by her little sister.

"Hey, you're okay, breathe," she encouraged. She rubbed Dora on the back, but it didn't seem to be helping.

Years ago, Dora had come down with a terrible cough. Their mother had stayed at her bedside all day and night and given her medicine to keep it at bay. Dora had come right again, but Jak recognised the sound. Except now they were a long way from home, and a long way from Mum's medicine cabinet.

"You okay, Dora?" Allie asked, also coming over to check.

Dora shook her head as she coughed. She was gasping for breath between fits. Allie and Jak shared a look in the darkness of the tent.

"I'll go ask Jim," Jak volunteered. "Keep an eye on her."

Allie nodded and sat beside Dora on the bed. She patted her back soothingly. Jak ducked out of the tent and crossed over to climb inside The Banging Wagon. The sky outside was dark, and the moon was barely risen. It couldn't be late. She climbed down the trapdoor and knocked on the door Jim had indicated earlier.

"Jim!" she called out. "You there?"

She heard a slight banging behind the door and hoped she hadn't woken him, or that he wouldn't mind being woken. The door jerked open. Behind it was a sizable bedroom with the largest bed Jak had ever seen. Jim had kindly bothered to throw on a silk robe before opening the door, but that didn't protect Jak's eyes from the glimpse she got of two very naked fae sprawled on the bed. She gave a small shriek, covered her eyes, and turned away.

"Is this important, Jak?" Jim asked. "I was kinda in the middle of something."

"You mean literally—"

"Yeah. Literally. What's up?"

"Uh, actually— I don't— you know— uh nev— um—"

"You broke her!" Kode accused from inside the room.

"Jak," Krill's serious voice came sharply from the bed to bring her back to her senses. "What's wrong?"

"Dora's sick," Jak answered, still keeping her eyes covered. "She's got a cough, I was just wondering—"

"Wait here a second," Jim instructed, ducking back into the room. He came back and pulled the door slightly closed behind him to protect Jak and her delicate sensibilities. That just left them squeezed into the tiny ladder room. Jak wasn't sure what was worse.

"Give her a spoonful of this," Jim directed, passing Jak a small bottle and a spoon. "Just one spoonful. No more. Followed by a big drink of water. The pitcher is on the top shelf on the left side of the wagon. There are two of them, you want the one on the right. That's important. One on the right. If it doesn't work, or if she gets worse, come back and get us, okay?"

"Okay," Jak nodded. "Thank you."

"Of course. Feel free to come back if you want to join in too," he smirked.

"You're disgusting!"

"And you're a prude," he smiled sweetly and booped her nose with a finger. Jim disappeared back into the bedroom. Jak wiped her face with her sleeve. It was completely clean, but she didn't want to know where that finger had been earlier. The Banging Wagon indeed. She scrambled, mildly traumatised, back up the ladder and grabbed the correct pitcher and a mug before heading back to the tent. She could hear Dora coughing before she got inside.

"Here we go, baby." Jak rushed to the bed. "I've got you some medicine. Drink this."

"You look a little wild-eyed," Allie commented suspiciously. "Did that perv do something?"

"No," Jak shook her head. She poured out a spoonful from the bottle and gave it to the coughing Dora. "He was fine; well, actually, he was himself. No. I just saw something I really wish I hadn't."

"Jak," Allie sighed. "Your life would be a lot easier if you weren't so scared of penises."

"Allie!" Jak exclaimed.

"She's said that before..." Dora muttered. The little girl looked exhausted, but she took the mug of water and she was managing to drink without coughing.

"I am not scared of..." Jak started indigently, but wouldn't use the word. Behind her, Allie nodded at Dora and mouthed 'yes she is'. Dora smiled at them wearily and finished drinking from the mug.

"That's the same medicine Mummy has," Dora commented.

Jak picked up the bottle and looked at it. It was a plain clay bottle with a small cork. On the side a rune had been etched. Creachta. The rune of the goddess of medicine. The rune of healing. Jak remembered what the boys had said about the gods over dinner, and wondered how they felt about the Lady Créātā. Maybe she wasn't one of the bad ones. Maybe there were no good ones. Jak would be the first to admit she didn't know much about gods. She'd heard some legends, but they were just childhood stories. She hadn't even known her own forest was part of those legends.

"You doing okay now?" Jak asked.

Dora nodded.

"Okay baby," Jak rubbed her back again. "Try and get some sleep. I'll leave the water beside your bed, and I'll check with Jim in the morning when you can have more medicine."

Dora nodded again and snuggled down in her bed. Jak made sure her stuffed bunny Binky was tucked up with her and Dora squeezed it tightly. She gave a couple of weak coughs, but it seemed to have settled. With any luck it wasn't as bad as it had been last time. Jak blew out the lantern as she and Allie climbed back into bed themselves, and the three of them hunkered down in the dark still night.

***

Jak woke again when the night was darker and stiller. She could hear her sisters breathing. It was pitch black, and she could sense something was wrong. The sword Sam had given her lay by her bed. She hadn't known what to do with it except keep it once she had realised she had run away with it. She picked it up carefully and tiptoed out to the front of the tent. Halfway out the door, she realised she wasn't alone.

Someone else stood by the tent. A shadow upon a shadow. A dark blade gleamed in their hand, but it was held low. She couldn't work out if it was a short sword or a long dagger, but it looked dangerous. The shadow stepped backwards towards her. In front of her.

"Stay inside," Krill's voice ordered so quietly she only just caught it. She opened her mouth to ask what was going on, but he moved his hand without looking, and touched her lips with a warning finger. Jak stayed silent.

Something moved in the darkness. It was too dark to see anything. Whatever it was, it moved more silently than the wind. Unable to see or hear it, Jak could only sense it. The presence of 'other'. The sensation of nearby movement. Krill stood protectively in front of her, over the mouth of the tent. She couldn't believe someone so pale and fair could blend so perfectly with the darkness.

The trees rustled. Krill turned his head sharply. The presence left. They were alone again. Krill took his hand away from Jak and stepped forward. He gazed cautiously around the clearing. Jak crept the rest of the way from the tent. She kept the sword in her hand, just in case. The fae turned and saw her hunched by the tent with the sword clutched tightly. He shook his head.

"Put that away, child," he instructed. "They're gone."

"What happened?" Jak whispered.

"Fora worked," Krill murmured. "The protection rune held. They didn't find us."

"Who's they?"

"People you do not want to encounter." He eyed up her sword again. "And people you would do well not to draw against."

"You're armed," she pointed out.

"I know what I'm fighting," he warned. "You don't." With a sleight-of-hand twist, his blade vanished. He began walking slowly back to the caravan. Jak was fairly sure he wasn't going to elaborate so that she could learn. If she wanted to know, she'd have to ask one of the others, and that meant waiting until morning. She crept back into the tent and stashed her sword away as she climbed into bed. The girls were still sleeping soundly. She needed to try to as well.

***

Morning dawned clear and bright after the cold dark night. Cold dew had settled on the grass of the clearing, but the ground beneath the shelter of the trees was dry. The forest twisted up all around them. Birds chirped and sang in the coiled leafy branches. Several bunnies seemed to have made themselves comfortable around the base of the Banging Wagon. Jak was still fast asleep. It wouldn't last. Her sisters were up and about. She was the only one still in bed, and there was someone who didn't blame her. Staying in bed for the day seemed like quite a nice idea. Unfortunately, there were things to see and people to do.

"Morning Sunshine," Jim smiled down on her.

Jak woke at the sound of his voice, and shrieked slightly when she saw him standing over her.

"It can be shocking the first time you wake to my beautiful face," he agreed. "But you'll get used to it."

Jak groaned. She rolled over, pulled the pillow over her head, and whimpered. She did not want to get used to that. His face was fine. She didn't consider it beautiful by any stretch, but she supposed he was adequately symmetrical. Either way, she did not want to wake up to it.

"I brought you breakfast," Jim's cheeriness remained unfazed. "It's time to rise and shine like the candy-queen you are, my jellybean. We're packing up camp again."

"How's Dora?" Jak groaned from under the pillow.

"She's doing well," Jim answered. "I'll leave the medicine in the wagon for you in case she needs it again tonight, but she's doing okay this morning. Hopefully a spoonful before bed for a few nights will kick whatever she's got."

Jak nodded and resurfaced from under the pillow. Jim held out a bowl.

"Hot porridge," he offered. "It will give you the strength to get out of bed. Which you will need to do in the near future."

"Thanks," Jak sat up wearily in bed and took the bowl.

"Eat up, we're hitting the road soon," Jim encouraged. "And if I come back here and find you napping again, I'm getting in to join you. It's just a camp bed, but there's room for two if we snuggle…"

"Don't even joke…" Jak glared at him.

His laughter lingered as he strolled from the tent in amusement. Jak hunched in her bed and ate her porridge while she contemplated how much of a dick he was. Bringing someone breakfast in bed was nice, but he was just so… ugh. He clearly knew how threatening snuggles were. At least from him. That was not a thing she was ever going to want.

Jak quickly ate her porridge and dressed properly. She picked up the sword from under her bed and looked at it. The strange encounter with Krill last night seemed like it was almost a dream. Almost, but not quite. She slid the sword back into her belt the way she'd worn it yesterday. It was an unusual weight hanging there, but it wasn't unpleasant. Rather, it was somewhat comforting. Having the weapon riding on her hip, a sword of her own, made her feel tough. It was a feeling she liked. It took the edge off all the bad memories of the last twenty-four hours. It was a feeling she hoped she could get used to.

She hooked all the packs over her shoulders and scampered out of the tent as Kode came wandering by.

"Dishes!" he announced sweetly as he passed her. He was carrying a stack of dirty bowls, and he took Jak's from her hand without even slowing down as he went by. He was followed by the ever-grinning Jim.

"Up and about in record time," he grinned. "You ready to pack up?"

"As I'll ever be," Jak nodded.

"Let's get this tent down." Jim bent over and grabbed a corner of the tent. He brought it up with a flick and it shrunk to a tiny pocket instantly. Jak grabbed the envelope out of her own pocket and held it out.

"Hm..." Jim mused. He gave the tent pocket a squeeze. It was much thicker and lumpier than yesterday. "I maybe should have taken the beds down first..."

"Are you doing it wrong again?" Krill asked, appearing at his shoulder like an apparition of disapproval.

"No, it's fine. I just didn't take the beds down first so it's a bit... lumpy."

"You are so lazy," Krill scolded.

"You are so judgemental," Jim retorted. He took the envelope from Jak and carefully shoved the lumpy pocket back into it. It was a much tighter squeeze. "There!"

"I do not want that back in my pocket..." Jak muttered, thinking about the rate of expansion if something went wrong.

"It's fine," Jim assured. "Just chuck it on a shelf in the wagon."

At those words, Jak had an epiphany about how The Banging Wagon had become such a cluttered mess. At least ten years of 'just chuck it on a shelf' had become a banging, rattling lump of chaos. She could see in Krill's eyes he agreed with her. But it was Jim's wagon and that was just the kind of ship he ran. He had named it appropriately. She remembered last night with a hideous and sickening blush. All too appropriately.

The girls were with Kode at the back of the wagon, stacking away the magically clean dishes. Jak headed their way. She was still too tired to face up to a morning with Jim. Instead, she was hoping she could manage a nap on one of those beanbags in the games room. Krill followed Jim to the front of the wagon. Jak caught a glimpse of them drawing Capall in the air. The rune glowed. The horses suddenly reappeared at the front of the caravan. They stamped and snorted like they were impatient to hit the road. Looking at them now she couldn't believe they weren't real — but that was the point.

The bunnies loitering by the wagon started at the sudden apparition. Jak had wondered if they were drawn to the magic of the caravan, but they were not drawn to the magic of the horses. The Banging Wagon was ready to start rolling, and little flicks of white cotton tails marked the rabbits scampering away. The grass around the wheels looked thoroughly nibbled.

Jak climbed into the back of the wagon and dumped the packs out of the way of the trapdoor. Kode guided the girls down the hole and shut the wagon doors behind him. He motioned to Jak and indicated knocking on the back wall of the wagon. She did. The wagon bumped and lurched as Jim and Krill drove them out of the clearing and back onto the road. Kode indicated the trapdoor and Jak headed down with him.

"Kode..." she started hesitantly.

"Yes Jak?" he smiled sweetly at her.

"Last night... I woke up and Krill was outside the tent. He was armed and there was something out there... do you know what it was?"

A dark shadow passed over the faerie's kind face. His lavender eyes narrowed in concern. It was an alien expression on him, and it spooked her slightly.

"I'm not sure..." he replied. She honestly couldn't tell if he was lying. It was possible he just didn't know, but she knew she had sparked enough in him that she might be able start getting answers — if only because the younger fae might pursue them himself.

"It's okay," she smiled reassuringly. "Just asking."

He nodded, but his expression didn't change.

They made it down into the secret rooms. Even down here rocked and shook with the movement of the wagon. Kode's gentle brow was still creased in contemplation, and Jak hoped she hadn't made him think too hard. It wasn't difficult to see that he wasn't the brightest bean in the bucket. They went into the games room where the girls were already trying to play cards with each other. Their enthusiasm was enough to distract Kode, whose bright and innocent smile came back as he joined them. Jak nestled down in one of the beanbags out of the way. She wasn't up for cards. She was hoping she could squeeze in a nap before they next stopped.

***

Nap she did. Her sleep in the last twenty-four hours had been broken and disorienting. She woke with a dry taste in her mouth in the dim bumpy interior of the wagon. A small giggle sounded beside her and Jak looked down to see Dora nestled by the beanbag with a cheeky grin on her face.

"You were snoring…" Dora giggled.

"Good," Jak muttered, struggling up. "How long for?"

"Awhile," Allie grinned at her. The middle sister was sitting in her own beanbag with a book in her lap. "But you could take over if you're awake. You're better at this than me."

"Better at what?" Jak rubbed her sleepy face.

"Reading."

"Allie's been reading to us," Kode smiled. "She reads real nicely."

"Your turn now," Allie insisted, getting up and dumping the book on Jak.

"Get me some water and I'll give it a shot," Jak agreed.

Kode was the one who jumped up and scrambled up the ladder in the other room. He brought down the pitcher and several glasses. The first one he poured with practiced steadiness as they rumbled along, and handed it to Jak.

"Thanks, Kode," she smiled. "You don't want to take a turn?"

He shook his blonde head gently.

"He can't read," Allie divulged. "Sorry, do you mind that I told her?"

Kode just shrugged. There was a faint pink blush to his pale cheeks. "No one ever taught me," he admitted. "Can't read or write. Weren't skills I needed."

"Do you want to learn?" Jak asked.

He shook his head and went back to his beanbag. Dora bounced over and jumped on his lap.

"Good call," she told him, snuggling down. "Jak's a mean teacher."

"I am not!" Jak protested.

"You're so strict and you always make us do our lessons!"

"That's why you know words like strict," Jak retorted. "Mum made us do them, so I make you keep doing them. She'll be cross otherwise when she gets back."

"What's your mum like?" Allie asked Kode.

The faerie blinked in confusion. That was clearly a question no one had ever asked him before.

"I'm not sure…" he admitted slowly. "She's alright, I guess. I don't really know her that well."

"You weren't raised by her," Jak recalled. The adorable, gentle fae had been raised in slavery.

"Ha'Cās are given to the carers until they are old enough to show promise. Then they are given to their patron who rears them for their cause," Kode told them.

Jak felt a sick awkwardness settle in her stomach. She wanted to change the topic, and she looked to the book Allie had given her.

"These are faerie-tales," she announced in surprise. "Myths and legends of the gods..." So it wasn't much of a change in topic. She smiled at Kode. "Are any of them true?"

"I don't know," he shrugged. "I don't know what they say. Allie was reading to us about the original five and the creation of Roïgola'a'lanaū. That was a long, long time before I was born."

Jak quickly flicked through the index. She was surprised how many of the stories she recognised. She had always believed she knew very little about the gods, but there weren't many stories here that she had never heard of. The first generation — deities of sky, earth, water, fire, and darkness — had created the Golden City which had come to be populated by their children. That was the one Allie must have read. There were legends about the wars with the giants and the dragons. Legends about the children of the five who had become deities in their own right. Gods of sunshine and rain and poetry and music and travel and games. They lived in a heavenly city in the sky where they cursed and blessed humanity with their immortal wisdom.

"But do you think it's true?" Jak pushed. "The Golden City in the sky? The Queen of the Fae?"

"That's all true," Kode nodded. "I lived there."

"Does Ĝoŕgomghōul really make people into soup?" Dora asked desperately.

"I don't know," Kode replied. "I've never met him. He doesn't live in Roïgola'a'lanaū. He left a long time ago. Before the second generation were born. Krill knows him though."

"Krill's met Ĝoŕgomghōul?" Jak asked after the god of darkness.

"Yep," Kode nodded. "Many times."

"What about the story of Fæmör?" Allie smirked. "Is that true?"

"You'll have to be more specific," Kode laughed. "Fæmör has done lots of things."

Jak was trying to give Allie a sharp glance, but her sister wasn't looking her way. Fæmör was a second-generation deity, best known for being the god of sex. He was the deity of games and parties and pleasure. His rune was Draimor, the rune of risk. There were many legends about him. But Dora was in the room.

"Is it true he seduced his entire generation?" Allie asked. "Even his siblings?"

"Except Olíriá," Jak interrupted. She knew that story.

"Except Olíriá," Kode agreed with a nod and a smile. "He's not even related to her, but she wouldn't cave."

"Well..." Jak scoffed slightly. "They're all related, really."

"They don't see it that way," Kode replied. "It's not like humans. There are so many of you that you need to keep track. There are only eleven D'Ihne. Five in the first generation, and six in the second. The first generation are all technically siblings, and they are the parents of the second generation. Mostly the second generation care more, but only if they're siblings. That is the only way by which they consider themselves related."

"The two generations don't really mix, do they?" Allie asked. "At least, not in the stories."

"They don't," Kode agreed.

"Why doesn't Olíriá like Fæmör?" Dora asked, tugging on Kode's sleeve. She had not heard the story. At her age, she would have heard almost no stories about Fæmör. Jak tried to avoid them herself.

"Oh, she likes him fine," Kode beamed sweetly. "In fact, Olíriá and Fæmör love each other dearly. They get on very well. Fæmör is actually very kind and funny. It's just that Olíriá swore herself to Crŷstïar in a bond of eternal love, so she has made it very clear she won't have sex with Fæmör. She always turns him down." Kode chuckled to himself. "I like Olíriá. She's pretty great."

"You've met the goddess of love?" Jak asked in awe. She knew she shouldn't be surprised, but somehow the idea was still so strange.

"Oh yes," Kode smiled. "I know her well. She's lovely. Actually... I always liked the second generation D'Ihne. They were always nice. The D'Ihne... I don't think they're as bad as Jim and Krill think they are. I don't know... I know I'm not the smart one, but they weren't so bad. Not really."

"They kept you as a slave," Jak pointed out.

"It wasn't so bad..." Kode sighed. "I mean... I'm happier here. I'd rather be with Jim and Krill. But it was okay. Sometimes it was great. I liked my life."

"What did you do?" Allie asked. "Before you ran away?"

"I made people happy," Kode beamed. All around them, the caravan rumbled to a stop. "It was my job to please others. I was very good at it."

Jak felt a horrible combination of cogs click into place in her brain. Something about that phrasing, combined with Kode's sweet innocence, the gods he knew well and what he thought of them, and something Jim had said about the gorgeous fae's talents...

"Let's go see where we've stopped," Jak encouraged quickly. Kode nodded in joyous agreement and lifted Dora from his knee. Allie shot Jak a look, and Jak wondered if her sister had caught on too. They all clambered up the ladder and climbed from the wagon. Jim and Krill met them as they were coming out. Jak stopped in wonder and looked out over the view. They were on a rocky outcrop on the side of a mountain. The stone path behind them looked dusty and old. Before them stretched a forest valley with a lake, and beyond that more mountains.

"Thought this looked like a good place to stop for lunch," Jim announced. "That and I need to stretch my legs because after yesterday and this morning on the cart my ass hurts."

"You said arse," Dora giggled. She ran off to inspect the view. Allie and Kode chased after her.

"Why is that funny?" Jim stretched his back out. "Don't go near the edge!" he called after them. He turned to look at Jak. "I don't know how you do it every day. She just zooms everywhere. I suppose you're young enough to keep up…"

"And you're not?" Jak teased him.

"I'm so old…" Jim groaned, leaning back against the side of the caravan.

"Yes," Krill patted his side as he went by. "You're ancient. Perhaps we should get you to bed early tonight and actually let you sleep for a change."

"Don't be stupid," Jim scoffed, catching him around the waist and pulling him in. "My plan for lunch is to give the children food now and let them play by the edge of the cliff while you shag me senseless."

"I'm standing right here," Jak pointed out that she was very much in earshot.

"Yeah," Jim looked to her. "If he says no I'm asking you next."

Jak made a loud noise of disgust and protest. Krill laughed.

"That's unfair," he objected, grinning as he said it. "You know I can't let you harass her like that."

"I'm counting on it…" Jim replied.

Jak shielded her eyes and turned her face away. They were getting far too handsy for her liking. There was groping going on she didn't want to see, but it reminded her of the close call they may have just had downstairs with Dora.

"Dora asked Kode what he used to do in the Golden City," she said loudly enough that they could hear it.

"Oh dear…" Krill replied.

Jak turned. The two men still had their hands all over each other, but she had their attention.

"What did he say?" Jim asked.

"He said he used to make people happy. Apparently, it was his job to please others."

"Huh," Krill made a pleasantly surprised noise. "That was a very tactful response for him."

"He has no idea he responded tactfully though, does he?" Jim mused.

"I don't think so," Jak agreed. "I don't think he realises she doesn't understand, and I don't think she realises there was anything more to understand."

"Then everyone's a winner," Jim grinned.

"Maybe…" Jak didn't like how many conversations they were skirting around with Dora. She didn't want to start having to have conversations like that with her little sisters. They were all still just kids. She wasn't ready. She watched them running around with Kode. He was so sweet and pure, and yet… "So is it true?" she asked the boys. "Back in the Golden City, was he a prostitute?"

"Of course not," Jim laughed. "Don't be ridiculous. No one ever paid him."

"He was a sex slave," Krill clarified. "He was taught to exist for the pleasure of others."

"That's awful…" Jak shook her head.

"Why?" Jim asked the question, and there was a cutting edge to his voice that made Jak pause. "Did he tell you it was?"

"No…" Jak admitted. "He said it was great. He said he liked his life."

"So what's your problem?"

Jak was quiet. She wanted to ask why he left if it was so great, but the answer was standing right in front of her. He had been kept as a slave, but he had enjoyed it, and he had left because he loved Krill and their society had forbidden that. She cast her gaze back to the naïve and trusting faerie.

"He has the intellect of a child," she tried to articulate why it bothered her. "People shouldn't be using him for sex."

"Go and tell him that," Jim challenged. "Go on. I dare you."

Jak felt very small. Jim wasn't often serious, but she had stepped into Serious-Jim territory with this conversation. He was clearly of the opinion that it was Kode's body, and Kode's life, and he could do whatever he damn well pleased. Jak felt like Jim used that argument to take advantage of the innocent, gullible, and (relatively) young man. She looked to Krill.

"Doesn't it ever bother you?" she asked in a small voice.

"Our ways are not yours, child," he smiled at her. He still had an arm around Jim. "Kode is an optimist. What he does makes him happy, and he does it more than willingly. It makes others very happy. He is incredibly good at what he does — gifted. There are things he can do that no one else in either of our worlds can. Yes, he was groomed to do this, but it was partially his choice. He feels no shame, and I would request that you didn't try to make him. He's proud of what he does, and he should be."

"Oh," Jak was very red in the face.

"My only concerns," Krill admitted, "were in Roïgola'a'lanaū, where there was someone who was abusing him. Kode doesn't dwell on bad memories. Doesn't have the personality for it. It's part of why I love him so much. I protected him as much as I could, and when I couldn't stop it, I took him away from it."

"Fucking Frézían..." Jim cursed furiously.

Jak knew that name. That was one of the five. Frézían was the name of the god of fire. She didn't want to ask. Kode didn't look like Frézían still haunted him, and she did not want to be the one to start that. She gave Krill a nervous look.

"Were you..." she started. The whole conversation had made her so uncomfortable she didn't know how to finish the sentence anymore.

"I was not," Krill smiled.

"Honestly though," Jim chipped in. "Bad call that one. I think you would have been great."

"You think I'm good at that, you should see me at my calling..." Krill teased him. "No. I have never been an entertainer. I do not have any patience for pleasing others on their terms. Obedience and submission were never my strong suits. I would not have done well. I'm far too brutal."

"But fuck me, I'm so into it..." Jim pulled him in tightly again.

Jak was already turning away in a blush as the others arrived back at the wagon.

"Food!" Dora crowed as she ran back with Allie and Kode just behind her. She saw the crowd standing between her and the promised food. "Are you two making out?"

"Not yet," Jim replied honestly.

"Okay. Can I have some food?"

"Please," Jak corrected on autopilot.

"Please can I have some food," Dora adjusted.

"Help yourself," Jim invited. He untangled himself from Krill, pulled the picnic basket down from one of the shelves inside the wagon, and sat it on the back stair. Dora lifted the lid and squealed in delight.

"Sandwiches!" she clapped. "What's your favourite kind of sandwich?"

"A Jim sandwich," he answered.

"How do you make that?"

Jak could see Krill cover his eyes with a hand beside his lover. She was staring the man down with a gaze that told him she would kill him if he answered that honestly. Jim had a mildly nervous crease in his smile that suggested he just realised what he'd done. Kode grabbed him in a bear hug from behind.

"It's a snuggle sandwich!" Kode exclaimed. "And he gets to be in the middle of the snuggle!"

"Aw!" Dora laughed. "I want a snuggle sandwich!"

"You're too small for a big snuggle sandwich," Kode told her, letting go of Jim. "But you can have a little one!" He grabbed her in a bear hug too and lifted her up into the air. Dora squealed and laughed as he pinned her up.

The others watched in slightly open-mouthed awe. The squealing and laughing of the bear hug/snuggle sandwich drowned out their conversation.

"Did he just make that wholesome?" Allie asked in wonder. She folded her arms and her green dress swished around her ankles as she turned to look at Jim.

"He's like the anti-you. He just made that wholesome."

Krill smacked Jim on the shoulder. "Did you just tell a child your favourite sandwich was a Jim sandwich?!" he hissed dangerously.

"It's fine," Jim defended. "Kode saved it."

"This time," Krill agreed. "But her big sister looks like she's going to stick her sword in you, and that's not a euphemism for something fun. That's me watching while she guts you."

"I'm sorry…" Jim apologised. "I'm not good with kids. Never have been."

"Oh man…" Allie shook her head. "That was nearly a clusterfuck."

"Allie!" Jak exclaimed. "Where did you learn that word?!"

"He said it yesterday…" she pointed at Krill. Jim saw his opportunity and also pointed tellingly at Krill. The faerie sighed.

"I am also not good with children," he admitted. "Apologies."

Jak looked between them all. "Oh, fuck it," she muttered. "Give me a sandwich and stop treating me like I'm Mum."

"That's the spirit!" Jim encouraged, clapping her on the shoulder.

"Not you," Jak pointed warningly at him. "You can keep your gropey hands and slutty mouth to yourself."

She shrugged him off and joined Dora and Kode at the sandwiches. Allie gave Jim a droll look and followed her sister.

"I don't…" Jim started.

"You do," Krill put an arm around him and kissed his shoulder. "You do have gropey hands and a slutty mouth. For what it's worth, I appreciate both…"

"Really…?" Jim gave him a sultry look. "Do we leave the others to sandwiches and…"

"Hm… they are guarding the entrance to the caravan, so no."

"Unfair," Jim complained. "I'm so horny."

"Yes, we're in danger of even the child noticing…" Krill warned. "It was your idea to take them in."

"That was before I realised I was going to have to behave…" he grumbled. "Can't they just entertain themselves for an hour or so?"

"We'll see…" Krill kissed his shoulder again and gave him one last squeeze before joining the others.

By some miracle, Jim managed to behave while everyone was eating. The boys knew Jak was mad at them, but they also knew that was more to do with her own issues than anything to do with them, so they let it lie. She needed time and space, and those were easy things to give. As long as they kept Jim on a short leash. He was the only one who didn't treat her like the child she so clearly still wanted to be.

Jak wasn't watching as Kode joined his husband on the back of the wagon and muttered quietly to him. The fae turned their vibrant eyes on her curiously. Jim noticed.

"What are you two sweethearts scheming?" he inquired.

"Jak said Krill was outside the tent last night," Kode replied. "She said he was armed and something was out there."

Jim's eyes narrowed sharply. "D'rö-Hadās?"

"Fora held," Krill told them soothingly. "Nothing happened."

"You're supposed to wake me when they show," Jim growled.

"You didn't wake, and Fora held," Krill repeated. "You would have known if it hadn't." His reassurances did nothing to ease Jim's scowl. Krill had his eyes back on Jak. "How did you know?" he asked her.

"Huh?" she was still pondering the term Jim had used. It wasn't one she knew.

"How did you know something was out there?"

She thought about it. A faint blush started in her cheeks.

"I'm not sure," she admitted. "I just sort of... knew. This is going to sound dumb..." she trailed off as she thought about it, but Krill gave her an encouraging nod so she continued. "I couldn't see or hear anything, so I don't really know how I knew, but I just kinda... sensed it."

Jim and the fae shared a long look at that revelation. Jak's sisters were staring at her. She hadn't told them about last night. She hadn't wanted to worry them. Now they looked worried. A hush had fallen over their group at her admission.

"Is that bad...?" Jak asked nervously.

"It is neither good nor bad," Krill replied, standing up from the wagon. "It is merely interesting." The faerie walked away from the wagon into a clear space on the outcrop overlooking the valley. He turned and motioned to Jak. "Draw your sword," he instructed.

"My what now?"

"Sword," Krill smiled at her. "The blade you wear on your hip. The one you were so keen to swing about last night." He motioned for her to stand and approach. "Show me what you can do."

"Careful, Krill," Allie warned. "Big Sam did actually teach her how to use a sword. She's not half bad."

"Then she shouldn't have any problems demonstrating." Krill still had a slight smile at the corners of his lips. It was cunning, and matched the sharpness of his golden eyes. Jak could feel everyone watching her, and it was an uncomfortable feeling. She didn't like being the centre of attention. She got to her feet slowly. This didn't feel like an optional activity. She drew her sword and stood to face him. He wasn't even armed. He motioned for her to attack. She shot a nervous glance back to her audience.

"Don't be scared," Krill soothed. "And don't worry about them. They can have a go later if they want. The sword is yours and I want to see how well you can use it. I'm not going to hurt you."

"I'm not worried about you hurting me..." she muttered. "You don't even have a weapon."

He smirked at her. The look said quite clearly that he didn't think he needed one. He motioned her to attack. She raised her sword and centred herself. She took a deep breath. Then moved to strike. She pulled out of the attack quickly and shook her head.

"I can't," she muttered. "I can't attack you when you're not even armed."

Krill twisted his hands. Two dark blades appeared in his grasp. They looked like the one she had seen him holding last night. She had never seen steel like it before.

"Better?" he queried.

It was. She tried again. It was just a test. She wasn't in a fight. It was like training with Sam. Just the basics. She centred herself again. Wielding a blade was something that had always come naturally to her. It moved as an extension of her body and flowed with her rhythm. The sword led her as she swung into the attack. Krill flickered. As she struck towards him, he suddenly appeared off centre. His blades were gone and he whacked her blade away from him with the back of his hand.

Jak staggered and recovered. She had expected a deflection and gone in too hard. Over her shoulder, Krill looked like he hadn't even moved. He stood calmly with his hands behind his back and the same small smile. Jak went in again. She didn't swing so hard this time. If his skill was in speed, she needed to be fast, not strong. That didn't work either. She jabbed in. Again he suddenly dodged away. She didn't even see him move. One second he was there, the next he was off-centre. He batted her strike away lightly with one hand. It sent her blade off wildly. She wasn't even close to getting him.

Now it was a challenge. She wasn't worried anymore that he wasn't armed. She swung in and feinted, pulling away in the last second and stabbing in. He casually knocked the blade aside. Jak refused to relent. She kept trying. He kept deflecting. It didn't matter what she did, or how hard she tried, he was always just out of the way of her attacks. At the edge of her attention, she was vaguely aware the audience were cheering.

She didn't know when she stopped going easy on him and started really trying, but somewhere along the way her frustration got the better of her. She was supposed to be good at this. He was making a fool out of her with no weapon and one hand behind his back. The sun was hot and she could feel sweat dripping down her back. Her face and hands were slick with it. Krill was giving her a run around. Nothing was bothering him. Not least of all her.

Jak yelled as she hacked and slashed at him. Every time it was close. Every time she just missed — was just pushed off balance — had to recover and stabilise her blow. Half the time he kept his hands behind his back and simply ducked and dodged her attacks. Jak stopped swinging. She lowered her sword and held up a hand.

"I need some water," she requested, wiping her face. Dora came running out with a glass and handed it to her. "Thanks baby." Jak took the glass and downed it.

"You're not bad," Krill commented, standing off to the side with his hands behind his back.

"Don't bloody patronise me," Jak scolded. "You're going easy on me. You haven't drawn a weapon or broken a sweat and you've already handed me my arse. Right," Jak motioned Dora back off her battlefield and raised her sword again. "Again."

"We don't have to," Krill smiled.

"I'm not done yet, old man," Jak grimaced. She wiped more sweat from her face. A glint of white teeth showed in Krill's grin at her fighting words.

"Jak, if you need a bath after this I'm here for you!" Jim called out from the side-lines.

"Shut up Jim, or I will come over there and chop your bits off!" she yelled back.

Allie cackled loudly.

"She's so fiery when she's like this," Jim commented appreciatively.

Jak drowned them out and centred herself back in the zone. She was alone with the blade. The audience were a long way gone. It was just her, the sword, and Krill. She went for him again.

Nothing had changed. It didn't matter how hard she tried. He was inhumanly fast. It was magic. She knew it was. He was fae. Half-god. She couldn't even see him move. But maybe she didn't have to…

Whatever had been out there last night, she hadn't seen or heard it. She had sensed it. Perhaps this could work the same way. He wasn't trying to attack her. She didn't have to dodge anything. She just had to land a hit. Trying to strike him hadn't worked. Trying to anticipate his movement had failed.

She tried to sense him moving around her. She tried to sense his magic. She blinked as she struck. Her eyes had been distracting her previously. Darkness fell in the moment. Her blade slid where she sensed it should. It nicked something. Krill gave a slight hiss. Jak opened her eyes. She stood, breathing heavily, and held her sword low. Krill stood back from her. He touched the side of his face where a slight red line marked his cheek. Blood came away on his fingers.

"Ha! Got you!" Jak tossed her sword on the ground and collapsed down beside it.

Krill turned bewildered eyes on her, but she didn't even notice. Jak flopped back on the rocky ground. She was exhausted again, but she'd bloody got him. It was a very satisfying feeling.

"Well fuck me and call me Susan…" Jim stated. "Baby, are you bleeding?"

"I think I might be," Krill admitted in astonishment.

"You said a bad word…" Dora tugged at Jim's sleeve.

"Not now, cupcake," Jim patted her head.

Kode ran over to where Krill was standing. His pale purple eyes were huge with surprise. He kissed his own fingertips and drew Creachta over his husband's wound. The scratch healed instantly and Kode kissed it gently.

"It's just a scratch, Kody," Krill settled him.

"How did she do that?" he asked.

"I don't know… Jak? How did you do that?"

"Who cares," Jak replied smugly from the ground. She knew she couldn't do it again. She was so hot and tired. But she had managed it once, and that was what mattered. Who cared how she'd done it. Jim wandered over with a mug and the water pitcher. He held out the mug. Jak hauled herself into a sitting position to take the cup and drink. She thanked him and started chucking the water back. He stood closely and watched her.

"Not even I can do what you just did," he commented quietly. "That was super-human."

"Na," Jak shook her head as she gasped for breath. "That was luck. I'm no magician."

"You could sense the D'rö-Hadās and you just managed to land a hit on Krill. That is more than luck. I don't think you realise that."

"He was going easy on me."

"He was," Jim conceded. "Even so."

"So what?" Jak asked. She held her mug out for more water. "Say what you mean."

"If it was anyone else I would be looking for fae blood," Jim told her firmly. "But I don't sense that in you girls. None of us do. There doesn't seem to be magic in you. So, in that case, it's just... exceptional."

"I want to say thanks, but you say weird shit to me all the time," Jak told him. She took a big gulp from her refilled mug. "Does that thing really never run out?"

"The pitcher? Never."

"Just pour it straight on me," she requested.

"Uh..." Jim bore an expression that barely held back. He looked like he was torn between just doing what she asked, and kindly pointing out that she might not be comfortable with how this was about to go.

"Don't be a pervert, you pervert," Jak reproached.

"I mean..." Jim grinned and held the pitcher over her. "I can do one or the other." He poured the cold water over her head. Jak didn't even care that he was probably being a perv about it. The cold water was so cold. She bit down a yelp. In seconds it was perfect. It was such a relief after a hot run around. He poured the jug over her for half a minute and then tipped it back.

"I didn't say stop," Jak told him, pushing her wet hair from her face.

Jim snorted with laughter. Krill joined them and took the pitcher off him.

"Go get a towel and her pack," the fae instructed. Jim pulled a face at Krill ruining his fun, but didn't argue with him. He gave the fae a quick kiss and an affectionate feel before jogging back to the caravan. Krill looked down on Jak as she sat in a puddle on the ground.

"You did well," he told her. His tone was so impressed she felt a faint flickering of pride. She couldn't remember the last time she had felt like this. "Now, wipe your sword down, put it away, and leave it there. You ever think you sense something out there in the night, do not leave the tent."

"But—!"

"No," Krill shut her down. "You did better than I thought you would, but you are still very human, Jak. It's not worth the risk."

Jim came back over with a towel draped over his arm and Jak's pack slung over one shoulder. Krill took all of it off him and placed them down by the tired, sweaty girl.

"You can take the pitcher and clean and change behind the wagon," he told her.

"I like how you think..." Jim grinned.

"You are going downstairs and staying there," Krill told him firmly. "Under no circumstances will I leave you in a position to peek."

"Elkrillendé, you absolute monster," Jim protested.

"Yes, yes, James," Krill took him by the shoulders and turned him around. "You can cry to me about it inside. Kode, baby, come with us. Give Jak some privacy."

Krill took the boys inside and left Jak with her sisters. She wasn't worried about the girls. They both looked impressed with her. She was too tired to get up and wash, but the cold water was going to be nice.

"You did real good, Jak," Allie smiled at her.

"Yeah," Dora grinned. "But he still kicked your butt."

"Yeah he did," Jak sighed. "Now come help me up. I'm feeling old."

"You sound like Jim," Dora giggled.

"I do not!" Jak protested. "Don't even joke!"

She struggled up and grabbed her things. Allie and Dora went to play, but promised to stay close. Jak went around behind the caravan. She had a brief moment of concern as she undressed that there might be some kind of magical peep-hole, but she trusted Krill. She also privately suspected that he was going to keep his human lover busy, but she did not want to think about that at all.

The pitcher was like a fountain when she held it over herself. It weighed almost nothing, but water never stopped pouring from it. It didn't take her long to cool down, and once she was clean and dressed, the practice was probably the best thing she'd done since leaving home. Now all she had to do was get Krill to teach her how fight like a fae.

CHAPTER FOUR

Jak relaxed on the back of the wagon watching her sisters play. She sat unwinding with her mug and the pitcher of drinking water. The boys hadn't come back yet, and she hadn't gone to get them. Partly because she had no interest in knocking on that door ever again unless it was a dire emergency, and partly because she privately felt that the longer they stayed down there the more manageable Jim might be later.

Instead, she simply enjoyed the view from the mountainside. Birds wheeled overhead and above the trees in the valley. Other mountains rose and tumbled in the distance. The sunlight reflected off the lake in the forest like a silver mirror. It wasn't too much longer when she heard the trapdoor and turned to look. Jim clambered out the top. He grinned as soon as he caught sight of her lounging on the back stair.

"How you doing, kid?"

"Not bad," she replied. "And you?" She put sufficient emphasis on the question to let him know she was teasing.

He winked at her. It was enough of an answer and they both knew it.

"Let's get the girls inside and hit the road again," he requested. "I'm keen to cover more ground today. Not going to find anything useful up here on Shágrahiā's ass."

Jak gave him a look. He noticed and flashed his dimples.

"Shágrahiā is the name of the mountain we're on," he answered. "See out there in the distance, that's Rōshotorō and Ātŷs." He pointed to the other mountains near them. "This is old war territory."

"The mountains are named after fallen giants...?" Jak caught on.

"The mountains are fallen giants," Jim replied. "If you believe the legends. The first five D'Ihne wove the world of their own essences. A planet of stardust and the five elements. But they left holes — gaps. Magic that wasn't their own came to investigate. Giants and dragons and monsters and huge beasts, all came through to trample and claim what the D'Ihne had so painstakingly created. They couldn't see eye to eye, so came the war. The D'Ihne plugged the holes and slew their enemies. The bodies of the fallen created a new world, which the D'Ihne no longer wanted to live on once it was a battleground. So they built the city in the sky to be their home. That was Roïgola'a'lanaū, where they raised their children. New life was born from the death that littered the world, and smaller creatures that lived in harmony with the D'Ihne came to be."

"I know the creation myth," Jak nodded slowly. "I just..."

"You didn't think it was so close to home?" Jim grinned. "It's everywhere, Jellybean. The whole world. We live on the bodies of the fallen. Your village and your forest are what Thænäri grew over the bowl of fire. These mountains are the fiercest of giants who fell when Clōudiá, the Sky Queen of the Fae, led her people against them. Whole armies fell under the power of the D'Ihne. Just off the coast, that way, are the islands Kúlaghn and Hæl. Giants that still lie where Äluāknā drowned them."

"Huh…" Jak mused with more awe than she let on. "Do you know everything about the world?"

"I try," he smirked. "I know all the legends, and I know the world as much as anyone can. You want me to tell you about it?"

Jak nodded.

"Then come ride up front and I can show you," Jim requested her company for the afternoon.

"Krill or Kode aren't joining you?" she asked.

"We'll get them to look after the kids again," he replied. "They usually travel inside. I don't like it, but it's safer, and we're heading back into human territory."

Jak raised an eyebrow. Jim elaborated.

"Faeries are like penises," he told her with a straight face. "You need to make sure people actually want to see them before you get them out and show them to the village. It can end poorly."

"Do you always make sure you follow your own advice?" Jak asked, eyeballing him deliberately.

Jim turned away from her as he laughed hopelessly. Jak realised as she watched him that she was smiling herself.

"You're good company, Jak," he told her. "Please come be my friend."

"Well, since you asked so nicely…" she conceded. She called to her sisters and got them to come back inside. The girls ran back to the wagon squealing as Allie chased Dora down the ladder. Once they were inside, Jak helped Jim shut the wagon up. "Just don't make any cracks about how lonely the road gets, and keep your hands to yourself."

"I don't make cracks about that," he assured. "It's too true. Promise I'll keep myself to myself. Just want your lively conversation."

Jak gave him a nod and they climbed up onto the front of the wagon and got it moving. The illusionary horses plodded off in front of them. They had been impossibly well behaved for real horses during the lunch break. Now they kicked up real dust moving down the mountain path again. If she hadn't seen the rune magic that made them, she might not have believed it, but she had seen a lot of magic since joining the boys. Somehow they made the impossible seem mundane. It was just part of their everyday life.

Although, Jim made it sound like all magic was part of everyday life. He was driving them over the ancient remains of a giant. As she had before, Jak found herself contemplating the man at her side. The strange merchant who lived with faeries, roamed the world, and went around selling magical items. He clearly didn't need the money. He had everything he needed. This was just the lifestyle he'd chosen. Something to keep him occupied and travelling. Something to keep him excited about life. It was the strangest thought, but she realised it must be true. He seemed so jubilant all the time, but he lived this way because he needed something to get him out of bed in the morning. He needed a reason to keep going. He needed purpose.

Didn't everyone, she supposed.

The two of them watched the horizon as they travelled the mountain path. The brown and tan rocks tumbled and sloped away gently on one side, and rose sheer and foreboding on the other. Here and there they were interspersed with vegetation. Down the hill from them, a murder of magpies pecked at something in the plants.

"Five for silver…" Jim counted them. Another dark bird swooped in to join the others.

"Six for gold," Jak smiled. She used to sing the nursery rhyme with her parents. It was one she knew well.

"Well, look at that," Jim grinned. "You're a golden girl. Guess you'll be a rich lady some day."

"Unlikely," she scoffed in amusement. "What about you? Maybe you'll be rich."

"I am rich," Jim grinned. "I have everything I could ever want already, even if it's not gold."

Jak watched him as he smiled. She stared at him for so long he started to take his eyes off the road to glance at her. The path was turning steeply downhill and he couldn't look back at her for more than a few seconds at a time. There was an honest inquiry in his brown eyes, and the crows' feet creased in the corners every time he glanced up.

"What?"

"You come from money," Jak deduced. "You come

from a big family with lots of money and you left it all behind. That's why you don't care about it."

Jim lifted a discerning eyebrow at her. He didn't look impressed with her logic.

"Are these deep and probing inquiries into the soul common from you?" he asked, neither confirming nor denying her assumptions.

"No," Jak shook her head. "I'm just trying to piece you together and understand you better."

"Oh?" he leered suggestively.

"No," Jak raised a hand between them. The slope began to flatten out safely, and he could keep his eyes on her again. She kept her hand up and turned her face away.

"Uh-uh, Jellybean," he warned. "You don't get to poke me and then complain that your fingers are dirty. That was your decision. Own it."

"Alright, I'm sorry I started," she grumbled. A hot flush crawled up her neck at his analogy. Clearly he didn't want to talk about himself, and as curious as she was, she didn't feel up to braving the topic. Not if he was going to compare it to fingering. "Can we forget I said anything and move the conversation along?"

"You want to talk about something wholesome?" he grinned, clearly aware of her discomfort.

"Please."

"Like...?"

"I dunno," Jak shrugged. She looked out over the magical view. "What about that lake? You said you'd tell me the legends of the world. What's that lake?"

Jim cackled like an old witch and Jak regretted

instantly asking.

"Okay, forget I asked," she muttered. "Given that laugh I feel like the answer will just make us both uncomfortable."

"Oh honey… not both of us…"

"I don't want to know," she lied. She knew he knew she was lying. She kept her eyes on the lake and refused to look back at him. It didn't stop him. Painfully slowly, he leant over towards her until she could feel his breath by her neck.

"That lake is called Úis'tā'Mör," he told her. "According to legend, that is the spilt sweat and cum from the conception of Créātā. Apparently, Clōudiá and Äluāknā went at it hard, and when sky and water met, they created Rain — and that leftover puddle as well."

"That's disgusting," Jak told him. Her face was flaming, and her own uncomfortable sweat was beading her hot neck. But she couldn't take her eyes off the lake. If she turned away from it, she risked catching Jim's eye, and that would be worse.

"No, kid," he sighed, straightening up in the seat. "It's perfectly natural. Créātā lets the rain fall to keep the lake there. It's never dried up. Gods know where they come from." Jim looked out over the landscape. The silver lake reflected in his eyes and made them look bright. "Äluāknā has never been embarrassed that Clōudiá knocked her up to keep her from the arms of giants. D'Ihne lust is infamous."

"Isn't Clōudiá the Queen of the Fae?"

"She is," Jim grimaced. "She's a tyrant. It's her laws that enslave the Ha'Cās."

"No, I mean… how did she… how did they…?"

Jim gave her a puzzled look and then suddenly caught on. "Oh, you mean how did she impregnate her sister? Well that's easy, Jellybean. D'Ihne are energy beings. They're the life of all Fae. They choose their form, and they switch around whenever they feel like it." His smirk came back. "I imagine the ladies did a bit of experimenting to cause that lake, but whatever else went on, at the end of it, Äluāknā had Créātā. Of course, it goes both ways, because not long after that Clōudiá got herself pregnant to Frézíān and she had Ínrío almost straight after Créātā was born. Then, while those three were busy getting busy, Earth was trying to convince Darkness to stay…"

"You mean Thænäri and Ĝoŕgomghōul had Fæmör? The third eldest?" Jak realised what she was asking and quickly turned her face away. "I don't want to talk about Fæmör," she muttered.

"Good," Jim replied. "Me neither." He had the expression of someone who had started with a joke, and ended up thinking about gods for too long. The old stories were boring him. Worse than that, they were reminding him. He had not been shy at the campfire last night. Jim didn't like gods, even if he was amused by Jak's reaction to their antics. Jak didn't know how much of the world he had travelled, but she knew he had seen enough to make up his mind. Perhaps seeing Krill and Kode after they had fallen from the sky would be enough to make up anyone's mind.

While Jak tried to chase away those bleak thoughts, Jim looked like he was choosing not to dwell. His gaze roamed the mountainside and traced the patterns in the rocks rising up beside them.

"There's been an astounding lack of road markers," he observed, changing the subject completely.

"Do you need them?" Jak asked. "The path isn't diverging anywhere."

"I mean more like rune markers," he clarified. "You find them on the side of the road a lot. They're faerie portals."

"Faerie portals?" Jak echoed. So he hadn't changed the subject that much.

"You must have had one in your forest," he insisted. "Otherwise Äulé couldn't have come through."

"There was a rock with Fora carved on it. That was where we left things for him."

"Exactly," Jim nodded. "Rocks, statues, markers on the side of the road — anything like that. Different runes get carved on them and you can summon faeries to barter with."

"Is that how you get your magic items?" Jak grinned.

"Sometimes," Jim shrugged. "Not often. Mostly I just give them junk in return for directions and information. Sometimes just because I can."

"You give them junk?"

"They love it," he laughed. "One man's trash is another man's treasure. They love bits and bobs. Trinkets, coins, old rags, odd socks — they convert it into magic. It's what gives them their power. That's why you have to make them an offering before they'll give you anything. Half the time they need the junk you give them to fuel the spell."

"Huh… Wait!" Jak paused. "So… what about Kode and Krill? Their magic doesn't need junk."

"No," Jim agreed. "So, there are different power levels of fae. You've got everything from the bottom tier of fairies, sprites, gnomes, etc who convert junk to magic, all the way up to the D'Ihne. Ha'Cās are different because they are half human. They're magical, certainly, but they can't use magic the same way D'Ihne do. The thing to remember is that you can't have something from nothing. The magic has to come from somewhere. Power begets power. So weaker fae will give you weaker spells. D'Ihne take power from powerful objects and turn that into magic. It's all about conversion. Ha'Cās use rune magic. They convert the power of words into magic. Compared to humans it's unstoppable. Compared to D'Ihne it's a waste of time and energy."

"And you want to talk to a faerie around here?"

"I do indeed. You want to learn anything, Jak — ask the faeries. You want to find your Mom? Ask the faeries."

"Really?" she queried. "Äulé never told us where she went."

"Did you ever ask him?" Jim pointed out. "Directly? Faeries never give anything away for free."

"I… I never thought to," she admitted.

"Well, next time we find a marker, we ask about your Mom," Jim assured. "Honestly, I thought we would have found one already."

Jak just nodded and smiled. It made her feel better to know that was something he was thinking about.

Sometimes it felt like he'd just taken them in for reasons of his own and wasn't interested in helping them. The more she thought about that though, the less likely it seemed. For all that he had a questionable sense of humour and powerful libido, he was really a sweet guy. He seemed to enjoy helping people. Mostly he just seemed to enjoy people. She hoped the next village treated him better than her one had.

"So, tell me, Jak," Jim ruminated as they rumbled down the path. "How did you do that with Krill before?"

"I just scratched him a tiny bit," Jak scoffed. "He was going easy on me. I was bloody wrecked, and he just got a scratch. If he'd tried to hit me back, I'd be toast."

"That's true," Jim grinned. "But how did you scratch him? He was using magic to avoid you. That shouldn't have been possible."

"I just… you know how I said I sensed that thing last night? That… what was it?"

"D'rö-Hadās," Jim answered slowly.

"What is that?"

"Bad news. You were answering my question?" Jim reminded her pointedly. Jak realised she wasn't going to get more of an answer than that. Not at the moment anyway.

"Well, I tried that again," she sighed. "Instead of trying to fight him like a human, I tried to sense him. It worked, kinda."

"More than kinda," Jim commented. "I was watching. You moved damn fast for a human. Never seen anything like it, little Jellybean."

"I can't explain it, Jim. I don't know how I did what I did. What about Krill? Did he used to be a fighter?"

"Of a sort," Jim confirmed. "Elkrillendé might look like a delicate and beautiful flower, especially to human eyes, but he is one of the most dangerous men in the world. It's the only reason he got Kode out of Roïgola'a'lanaū alive."

It was funny for Jak to hear. She believed Jim when he told her Krill could be dangerous. She had sparred with him and, despite what everyone was saying, she had lost severely. If Krill ever wanted her dead, she wouldn't have time to beg, but she didn't think that would be likely. Krill had told her Jim was dangerous, and she had believed him too. Although, aside from the danger of unwanted advances, she wasn't sure what he meant. She wondered if the two men knew how cautious and respectful they were of each other.

As the hours whittled away on the road, Jak found Jim's company perfectly pleasant. She wasn't able to get any more answers out of him, but she enjoyed trying. He kept his inappropriateness mild and his banter witty. They rolled gently around the side of the mountain. The path went up again before it went down. At mid-afternoon, Jak saw a rough old statue on the side of the road.

"A marker!" she exclaimed.

Jim slowed as they went by, but he didn't stop. A sharp glance left a small frown on his face.

"What's wrong?" she asked. "Why aren't we stopping? You said we'd ask at the next marker."

"Sorry Jak," Jim shook his head. "Not that one. That

one is marked with Ondia."

"Ondia's the peace rune," Jak pointed out.

"Yeah," he conceded. "It's also the rune of the sky. It's Clōudiá's rune. Those imps you call on there will be hers. I'd rather say a prayer on Ollmahor than Ondia."

Ollmahor was the rune of darkness. The rune of chaos and wisdom. The rune of Ĝoŕgomghōul. Jak took Jim's warning very seriously.

"Sorry," he apologised again. "First marker with a different rune. Anything with Fora, Nari, Arsaid, Talámh, even Uisce — I'd stop at any of those — but nothing to do with Clōudiá. I'm not chatting to the imps of the Queen of the Slave Drivers. Too dangerous."

Jak just nodded. She didn't begrudge him that. There was clearly a lot of history between Jim and the boys and the kingdom of the fae. At least ten years of history. If Jim thought Ondia was dangerous, Jak would abide that wisdom. After all, Fora was the rune she had grown up with. The rune of shelter and protection. If he wanted to wait and call on the forest rune, she was fine with that. The next forest couldn't be too far off.

Except the sun began to set and they were still on the side of the mountain. The road was finally sloping into the valley, but they were a long way off getting there. A chorus of birds was signalling the end of daylight, and their screeching echoed up the mountainside. Golden orange light reflected off the rocks.

"I wonder if this road has a wide enough space on it to stop for the night," Jim mused. "I don't think we're making it to the treeline." They rode around the corner and a slip blocked the road. "Yeah, we're not making it to the treeline. Ugh, seriously?" he groaned. "What a pain in the— Wait here." Jim climbed down from the wagon and wandered around to knock on the back. Jak heard him stop and speak in a disgusted and sceptical tone.

"Seriously?"

"Open the doors and step away from the wagon," an unfamiliar voice ordered.

"Look, I'm only going to say this once, because neither of you are actually pretty enough to warrant my attention, but fuck off or die. I don't have time for this. Bandits are so last century."

Jak unsheathed her sword and snuck around the side of the caravan. She could see two rough-looking men holding Jim at sword point. He stood with his back to the doors and stared them down, completely unfazed. She respected that, unarmed and facing two weapons, he could still measure the importance of the encounter by how pretty (or not) his assailants were, but it didn't seem practical.

"Well, we're only going to say this once, friend," one of the men loomed — or tried to. From a distance, Jak began to wonder if it was even physically possible to loom over Jim's enormous ego. "Open the doors and step away from the wagon."

"That's the second time you've said that," Jim pointed out, at risk to his health.

"Oh, you're a smart arse, are ya?" one of them raised their sword to his throat. "Let's see how smart your tongue is when I cut it out."

Jak leapt out from behind the wagon. The bandits'

surprise was short lived. She took what she could get and rushed them, running in swinging. The sight of them threatening her friend's life sparked her ire. She yelled as she attacked. Her first blow was deflected, but she spun quickly and went for the other one.

Jak twisted and ducked and slashed between the bandits. The two of them reeled. Both managed to deflect her blows, but she was faster than them. One of them stabbed at her. She swung away from the blow. Then slashed back. The other one hit her sword down. She dragged her blade up his. It grated loudly and she knocked him back. She thrust in as she dodged an attack from the other one. Her blade sliced through his arm. She spun away and stood in front of Jim and the wagon with her sword raised.

Her breath was coming hard and fast and her adrenaline was pumping. It was two on one, but they looked worse. They looked shocked and unsure. But angry. The injured one clutched his bloody arm.

"Bitch cut me!" he declared.

"Get her!" the other one roared.

They rushed in to attack. Jak deflected both their strikes. She felt a grin forming on her face. She was in her element. The swords clanged as she danced between them, feinting and parrying. The injured one was the weaker of the two. She went for him. She pushed him further back. Each time she went for him, she gained ground. He didn't even realise she was forcing him to the cliff's edge.

"Jak!" she heard her name yelled.

Someone grabbed her around the waist and tackled

her. She hit the ground with Jim half on top of her. The sword of the other bandit cut the ground where she had been standing. She hadn't realised he'd made it behind her. Her focus had been on his friend. Jim rolled off her, but they couldn't get to their feet fast enough. Jim wasn't trying.

"Last chance!" he warned the bandits from where he sat in the dirt. "Doors are open." He pointed. Jak and the bandits looked to The Banging Wagon. The back doors were open. One of them creaked slightly in the breeze.

"We'll take what we want after we've killed you two," one of them spat.

"I warned you…" Jim shrugged.

They only looked confused for a second. Blood sprayed across the ground. Jak barely contained a shocked cry. The bodies of the bandits flew off the side of the mountain. Krill flickered into view. He was holding the heads of both men in one hand by their matted hair. The severed heads dripped blood onto the already blood-washed ground. The fae was looking down on the two humans still alive on the mountainside.

"Really?" Jim questioned in distaste. "Decapitation?"

"Old habits," Krill shrugged. He looked out to where the sun was setting. "It's getting dark."

"I know. What are you going to do with those?" Jim brought their attention back to the heads.

"Oh." Krill remembered he was holding them.

"You want to keep them?"

"I suppose not…" Krill admitted. He tossed them over the side after the bodies. "We have to get off the side of the mountain before nightfall."

"That's not going to happen," Jim told him. He got to his feet and brushed the dust off his clothes.

"Make it," Krill insisted. "We both know you can."

Jak sat on the ground and watched the lovers stare each other down. She still couldn't believe Krill had killed those two men so quickly. She hadn't even seen him attack. One second they'd been about to strike. The next second they were dead. He had separated their heads from their bodies with such force the bodies had gone flying. Both of them. In an instant.

"Krill, we'll be fine," Jim smiled at him.

"And if they show up?" the fae asked. "What then?"

Jak realised Krill was looking at her. Jim turned his brown eyes to the girl on the ground too. She realised they were talking about her without saying anything. Both of them were considering something she wasn't privy to.

"There's a block on the path in front of us," Jim told him. "How do you want to do this?"

Krill didn't answer. He wandered around to the front of the wagon. Jim followed after him. Jak scrambled to her feet. She re-sheathed her sword and hurried after them. As she came around to the front, she saw Krill draw Ezian over the rocks. The rune of fire and destruction. The slip blocking the road crumbled to dust.

"I'll meet you there. The runes will be set up when you arrive. Hurry," Krill told him. The fae stepped back into the shadow of the mountain and vanished.

"Oh goody," Jim muttered. "Come on, Jak. Let's get this over with."

He motioned her onto the wagon and quickly went around the back to shut the caravan doors. She climbed up and heard the doors bang shut. Jim was at her side in seconds. He hauled himself up.

"Hang on, sweetheart," he warned. "Shit's about to get real."

"It didn't do that when we got ambushed by bandits?"

"Eh. They picked the wrong wagon."

"You saved my life…" she murmured, remembering the way he had tackled her out from under the blow.

"You would have done the same," he grinned at her. "In fact, you did."

"Thanks, Jim."

"Keep your thanks 'til we're down the hill, Jellybean. You're not going to like this next bit." He raised his hands and drew a series of runes over the horses. As soon as he was done, he leant back against the wagon. He held on with one hand and placed the other arm protectively over Jak. She was about to protest when the runes burnt out. The horses took off. They didn't take off at a natural speed. Jak yelled out, but her cry was lost to the air.

She'd never travelled at such speed before. Probably because such speed wasn't possible. They raced down the path. The wagon bounced and wobbled. The wind raced by so fast it was hard to breathe. The noise was too loud to yell over. Everything rushed by in a blur of colour. Jak screamed and shut her streaming eyes against the assault on her senses. She could feel the wagon careening dangerously down the side of the mountain. Jim's arm felt strong and steady against her, and she appreciated it. Not that she ever planned on telling him that if they survived.

There was a sharp snap. The wagon slowed again. Jak felt the air calm around her. The noise had changed. She wondered if her ears had popped. Her face was wet from the tears that had leaked out at speed. She wiped and opened her eyes. They were surrounded by trees. The horses were stomping impatiently in front of them and pawing at the grass.

"Where are we?" Jak asked. "How did we get here?"

"Are you alright?" Jim responded.

She nodded cautiously.

"Good," he replied. "We should be okay here—"

Something smashed into the side of the wagon. Jak cried out as they were tossed from the front. She hit the ground hard. The grass was soft and damp beneath her. She crashed ribs first onto the earth. The force knocked the air from her lungs. She gasped weakly and looked up. Jim was over her in seconds. She could smell the sweet floral scent of his shirt above her. He hunched protectively, looking out through the trees. The look on his face was fearsome. There was an anger there that scared her. Except his fury was in her defence. His eyes flashed with a magical glow.

Whatever he might have been about to do, he didn't have to. Jak saw Krill flicker into view by the caravan. A shadow rushed them but the fae raised his hands. His dark blades shone in his grasp. He marked Ollmahor and Niochta, the runes of darkness and magic, in the air together. The runes shone. Then exploded in chaos and power. They blasted the shadowy figure back through the trees. Jak couldn't even see where they landed. Jim stood up and helped pull her to her feet. She drew her sword again in anticipation. Krill turned and shook his head.

"They'll stay out now," he assured. "I've already marked the area. They only got in with you. This is a good spot. The trees are strong here, and Fora will hold."

"It wouldn't have held in the mountains?" Jak asked, wondering if they could have avoided the whole ordeal somehow. Krill shook his head.

"Fora is the forest rune. It is at its strongest in the woods. The trees help spread the magic."

Jak didn't have anything to say to that. Jim clapped her on the arm.

"Come on," he encouraged. "Let's check on your sisters."

Jak tried to shake off her shock as they climbed into the back of the wagon. Her heart was still racing. She could feel it thudding in the back of her throat. The chase down the mountain and the shadow in the woods had only intensified what she had been feeling with the bandits. She'd just watched two men die. That had been her fight. Her first real fight. She'd been holding her own. But...

But could she have done it? Krill had killed those men to save her and Jim. They had died so brutally.

Their blood had sprayed with a hot, metallic, fleshy stench. She felt like she could still smell it. She couldn't shake the memory of their heads and bodies sailing separately through the air. It made her feel sick. She was glad Krill had been there. What if she had killed one of them? Would the horror of that moment have scared her out of the battle? Would she have kept fighting, driven by self-preservation? Would the bandits have beaten her and Jim?

She remembered how Jim had tackled her out of the way of a mortal blow. He hadn't engaged in that fight. She thought that he wouldn't. He wasn't a fighter. But she couldn't forget that sharp glow she had seen in his eyes when he had shielded her from the shadowy figure. Jak had assumed the magic around him came from the fae. She had assumed they were responsible for all the wonder in Jim's life. But what if...

Jim hauled the trapdoor open and called down the hole.

"How you guys doing down there?"

"Wheeee!" Dora yelled back. "Again! Again!"

"Not again," Allie requested sickly.

"Not again indeed," Jim smiled. "We're out of trouble for now. Come on out and get some fresh air. We'll set up camp."

Dora and Kode clambered up the ladder just fine. They joined Jim and Krill, and with the help of several vastly expanding small packages, they began setting up camp. Jak helped Allie from the wagon. Her little sister's face was looking a tad green around the edges, but she looked back at Jak with concern.

"Are you alright?" Allie asked.

"Yeah…" Jak nodded. "You?"

"A little caravan queasy and bumped around, but it's not so bad. You look a bit grey. What happened?"

Jak thought about lying. She didn't want to scare Allie, but then she wondered if she could scare Allie. She had to give her sister some credit — the girl never spooked, and she always seemed to know more than she said. If their positions had been reversed, Jak wouldn't have wanted Allie to lie to her.

"There were bandits…" Jak admitted. "They tried to ambush us."

Allie gave her a long look, but didn't flinch and showed no fear. Only concern. She was trying to read the situation. Allie had always been good with people.

"Did you have to kill someone?" she asked very quietly.

Jak shook her head, but she wrapped her arms around herself for comfort against the thought all the same.

"I fought them, but I didn't kill anyone. Krill did. He killed them."

"You saw it?"

Jak nodded. "He didn't even warn them. Just, bam! Like swatting a fly. Jim tried to warn them. He told them that if they didn't leave us alone they'd die. I think they thought he was an idiot. Krill… Krill cut their heads off before they even realised he was there."

"I saw him sparring with you — I'd believe that." Allie turned her gaze towards Krill and Jim, who were setting up a firepit. Her sharp dark eyes watched them.

Jak stayed with her, the two of them leant against the wagon.

"Faeries kill people, Jak," Allie said finally. "You hear about it all the time. They're tricksters and pranksters, and they can be ruthless to mortals. That's why we leave them offerings. That's why we try and buy their goodwill. At least these two don't seem like tricksters and pranksters. Krill and Kode are nice. Were those bandits you fought trying to kill you?"

Jak nodded.

"Then… is it such a bad thing Krill killed them? He was saving you and Jim. I saw him against you. If he had wanted to actually fight you, you would have been dead before you'd been able to say 'wait!' and that's not being mean. He's a scary-good fighter, and a faerie. At least he never pretends to be something he's not. Those bandits tried to kill and rob his boyfriend — they're probably lucky he just killed them."

"That's dark, Allie…"

"But I'm not wrong, Jak…" Allie touched her arm. "I know you want the world to be better than it is. You want to keep me and Dora safe, and you don't want that to be so hard. But Rutsborough tried to burn us out of town. The world isn't safe and nice. At least these guys are."

"It's not about that…" Jak sighed. "Not really. I don't think. Krill… Krill was just trying to save us. Do I wish he'd warned them off instead? Yeah… but would they have listened? Who knows. He did what he thought was right and I'm grateful, I think. I just… You're right; I do want to keep you and Dora safe… but… but am I going to have to kill someone one day to do that?"

"Not if you keep these weirdos around," Allie smiled at her. "Sis, that's not something to dwell on. It won't be good for your brain. If we find ourselves in danger, we face it then — we don't lie awake through the good times worrying about it. Mum taught me that."

Jak gave Allie a sharp look.

"It was after Dad died..." Allie admitted. "I was young... but I remember being so sad once he was gone. He was crushed by a falling tree, and I was so scared of the forest after that. Do you remember? The first year Dora was born I never wanted to go outside. I stayed inside and I'd help cook and clean and wash and take care of baby Dora, but I never wanted to do the outside chores. I always made you do them."

"I thought that was just because I was bigger and stronger..."

"I was too scared to go outside," Allie shook her head. "I was terrified a tree would fall on me — or any of us. Trees were everywhere, and one had killed Dad. Mum explained to me that trees don't just fall randomly, and that all the trees around our house were healthy, and all that stuff. She cleared it all up and made it make sense, but she also told me not to worry about freak accidents and crazy things that might happen. If I was careful and stayed away from rotting trees, I'd be fine, and other than that there was no point worrying."

"And... that worked? You felt better after that?"

"Well..." Allie smiled a small smile. "She also told me that you and her wouldn't let anything happen to me. So even once she was gone, I knew my big sister had my back…"

Jak grabbed her and pulled her into a warm embrace. Allie giggled and groaned into her shoulder.

"Ugh, don't squeeze me. I still feel sick."

"Shut up, Allie," Jak sighed, hugging her tighter. Allie giggled and hugged her back, although much gentler.

"Oooo, is this a group hug?" Jim's voice ruined the moment as it approached. "Can anyone join?"

"No, you weirdo," Allie scoffed at him. "Stop being such a perv."

"Ouch," Jim put a hand to his chest in offense as he grinned at them. "Harsh, but fair."

Jak let go of Allie and turned. There he was, all smarmy grin and way too close, as usual. She eyeballed him, but he never seemed to mind that. He liked people looking. Liked the attention. Jak sighed.

"I'll help get firewood," she offered and slipped away. She wasn't in the right mood to try and deal with him now. When she was in a good mood he could be fun, but when she wasn't he was just a pest. She didn't want to feel that way after he had just saved and defended her. Again. More than that… she didn't want to let herself be put in a position where he could ask her for something, or try to flirt with her. Not now. Not when she felt so indebted to him. The combination of that was more terrifying than the fate of the bandits.

"You make her super uncomfortable, you know," Allie told him firmly as soon as Jak was out of earshot. The girl in the green dress folded her arms sternly and adopted a no-nonsense expression. Jim smiled at her.

"Now that's a downright tragedy," he commented. "But she'll come around…"

Allie gave him a stern look. Jim barely glanced at it, and then double took. He turned a slightly startled and fearful look at her.

"Geez, kid… don't get so stern. You remind me of my Mom when you do that."

"You know Jak's gay, right?" Allie said like he was stupid. "I tease her because she won't admit it, but she is never going to be into boys. There is no 'coming around' if that's what you meant by it. If you were a woman — maybe. At least she'd be way less intimidated and way more pink in the face. She just gets really uncomfortable about turning guys away, because it can go so wrong so quickly."

"Ahhhh," he nodded. "Now that you mention it, I do get the gay vibe from her. I think I was so focused on how prudish she gets I wasn't really paying attention to anything else. I just like teasing people. So, on that note, if I was a woman, you say…?"

Allie gave him a dry look. "What?" she drawled. "You gonna go all D'Ihne on her and turn into a lady?"

"Now wouldn't that be something?" Jim flashed her a grin.

"I don't think your faerie boyfriends would approve…" she replied.

"Kode wouldn't be bothered," Jim sighed. "But Krill would definitely take issue. He's as gay as your sister."

"Yeah, I kinda get that vibe from him," Allie grinned.

"So, you feeling better?" Jim asked, placing a guiding hand on her back. "Can I interest you in dinner?"

"You can not touch me, for a start," Allie told him firmly, gliding away from his hand.

"Oh-kay," Jim drew the word out carefully. "You're the boss, Boss."

"I am," Allie agreed. "Please remember that. And, Jim, if you ever mess with my sister, I will kick you in the balls. I'm not scared of you."

"Noted," he nodded as though he took the twelve-year-old girl before him very seriously. "May I interest you in hot stew and warm bread?"

"You may," Allie nodded.

Jim held an arm out in invitation, but kept his hands very much to himself. Allie strode from the side of the wagon with him. As they came around the corner, Krill was standing with the magical picnic basket and a small smile on his elegant face.

"What?" Jim asked him.

Krill ignored him and gave Allie a slight bow. "That. Was. Magical," he smirked. "But I warn you now, Allie, he has masochistic tendencies. Careful what you threaten him with."

"Were you listening to all of that...?" Jim muttered bleakly.

"With ears like mine?" Krill smiled. "Stew?" he held the basket up.

CHAPTER FIVE

Jak slept the night through once they had sorted out the mess of the tent. The beds needed to be pulled apart and remade after being crushed together, but it was nothing the boys couldn't handle. She didn't know if the runes kept the D'rö-Hadās out, but she didn't sense anyone, and she didn't wake until morning. Perhaps yesterday's workouts had tired her enough to sleep through anything. When she slouched half-asleep from the tent everyone else was having breakfast again. She was the one who always slept the latest, it seemed.

"Morning, Jellybean," Jim grinned appreciatively at her scruffy half-dressed look. "Pull up a stool and grab some grub."

"Thanks," she completely ignored his lecherous expression and took his words at face value. It was starting to get easier. Perhaps he wasn't someone it took long to get used to. What seemed so creepy when you met him was just the way he was, and actually, it turned out to be a lot more harmless than it first seemed.

There was hot fresh toast with butter and jam this morning, and the bread was brown and tangy. They hadn't eaten this well at home in a year. Jak noticed the way Dora devoured food from the magical basket. Their mother had always been able to provide good food. She

129

could grow and cook and create in a way Jak hadn't been able to mimic. Allie was a better cook than Jak was, and she'd happily concede that, but Jak had earnt simple wages and hadn't been able to provide as much. Still, they had gotten by.

Now they needed a new way to get by. Jak looked over the remains of the warm fire as she ate. She watched Krill. The fae was not unaware of her attention.

"Krill...?"

"Yes, Jak?"

"Will you train me how to fight?"

Silence fell at the campfire. There hadn't been much noise to start with, but as soon as it stopped it was noticeable. No one was even chewing.

"I have never trained a human," he answered softly.

"But you've trained hundreds of fae," Jim cut in cautiously. "Same principle, just different talents."

"You could not learn to do what I do, child," Krill warned her.

"I know that," Jak admitted. "I know I'm not magical. But you're a fighter, aren't you? You could teach me how to be better."

"It's not a bad idea..." Jim commented.

Krill gave him a sharp look — as though this was a conversation he and Jak could manage just fine themselves without the man poking his nose in. Jim didn't relent, but he didn't say anything else. Krill contemplated silently for a moment.

"I can run you through exercises during our daily breaks," he conceded. "That may help me get a better idea of your capabilities. We can move from there. The way I taught was to push my kind to their limits. I required them to learn to be as good as I was, or else they were rejected as unfit."

Jim gave a slight snort. Everyone ignored him, but Jak got the impression Jim didn't think Krill had actually managed to train anyone to be as good as he was.

"I cannot raise you to that bar," Krill warned. "But I can see what you can do, and advise your skills. The art of the blade is the same no matter the species."

It was as close to a yes as she was going to get, and she grinned at him.

"Thank you."

"You're welcome. Besides, *he* seems to think it's a good idea." They both shot Jim a look. He looked smug.

"You always do what he says?" Jak asked.

"No," Krill smiled his delicate smile. "But I usually do what he asks."

That was the end of that conversation, and they packed up after breakfast to hit the road again. As they packed the wagon, Jak spotted the odd bunny scampering out of the way. She hadn't seen them at breakfast, but a few had been lying by the wheels of the wagon. They spooked at the sound of boots on the wood and bags banging above them. Dora watched them longingly and stroked Binky's ears. Allie laughed and ushered her into the wagon. They would just have to settle for playing with faeries instead.

Jak felt a faint fluttering of excitement in her stomach. Krill was going to teach her how to be a sword-master. Or, at least, he had agreed to try. She imagined future fights. Being able to disarm bandits and force them to run away because she was the better fighter. Being able to hold her own against faeries. Okay, maybe that was too much to hope for, but she wasn't going to know until she tried.

She rode up front with Jim that morning. He didn't even have to ask her. She just decided that was where she wanted to be. They had come a long way off the road in their frantic getaway last night, but Jim knew exactly where to drive to find it again. Jak sat beside him, trying to keep a lid on her elation. Today was going to be a good day. She could feel it. They would probably find a rune marker. Krill was going to start giving her lessons. Life was coming together in a way it never had before.

The forest around them was lush and wild and green like the forest back home, but Jak could still sense that it wasn't the same one. Not quite. It felt different. The trees grew taller here, and straighter. There was variety, but enough pine to scent the air. Dried needles littered the ground — muffling the horses' hooves and the rumbling wheels. Above them, birds sang and squirrels chittered. They weren't the only life around, and Jak could feel eyes on her.

It took a while but she finally spotted them. Every now and again, what looked like a fluffy brown or grey tail was topped with beady eyes and a pointed cap. Gnomes. Little gnomes, not much more than hats and beards, were watching them travel. Jak pointed them out to Jim. He smiled up at them.

"Yeah, you get used to it."

"Do you think we could ask them, instead of finding a road marker?" Jak asked.

"It's worth a shot," he shrugged. The invitation was encouraging, but he didn't seem overly positive. "Call up to them and ask if they want to trade."

"Uh…" Jak knew she should, but talking to people, even faeries, didn't come naturally. As always, as soon as she was put on the spot, she had no idea what to say. Jim seemed to pick up on her dilemma.

"Hey!" he called up into the trees. "This girl's looking for her mom. Anyone want to trade for information? We have old loved trinkets!" Jim flashed her a grin. "That'll get their attention."

He wasn't wrong. The air buzzed with whispers and chitters. Jak glimpsed gnomes muttering in each others' ears and turning beady eyes on the wagon. One by one they vanished from the branches. Jak waited for them to show up closer. None did. The wagon rolled along and the forest went quiet again. It felt empty.

"Huh, that's odd," Jim commented. "And after Dora left them food last night. Rude."

"Did they all just leave?" Jak asked. She couldn't sense them anymore. Wind swayed the branches above them, but the only things left up there were leaves and animals. The magic had run away.

"Seems like it," Jim agreed. "Whatever. They're all just scout gnomes anyway. You don't want to talk to them. No one in the history of the world has ever gotten a useful answer out of a scout gnome. Recluses and thieves, all of them."

Jak took his word for it, but she kept an eye out all

the same. Every now and again, she thought she might have glimpsed something, but it was too hard to tell. Instead, she began trying to spot markers. The odd flash of mushroom at the gnarled base of a tree always got her hopes up, but there were never enough to make a circle. Finally, she spotted something through the trees.

"There!" Jak pointed to a patch in the pine needles on the ground. "A marker. Is that a circle of stones?"

Jim followed her gaze. He pulled a face.

"It was..." he admitted. "Until someone moved them..." Jim rode them closer and looked down. Sure enough, there were patches of dirt and moss where old stones had been taken. There was no sign of them now, but bugs crawled in the empty space. "Very recently..." he finished.

"The gnomes...?" Jak asked, bewildered.

"Mostly likely," Jim agreed, also sounding confused. "Wow. They really don't want to talk to us. What did you do?"

"Me?! I— I didn't—!"

"I'm kidding, Jellybean. I was there. I know you didn't do anything. What did I do...?" he met her eye. "I mean recently, like, today. I don't need you listing everything."

"I don't know everything," she smiled. "You didn't aggravate any gnomes, did you?"

"You mean recently, right?" Jim reiterated.

"Jim!" she laughed.

"No, seriously, I have no idea what that's about..." he looked thoughtful for a moment. "It might not have anything to do with us. Or it might be a prank. Or it could be another instance of faeries being too busy to deal with mortals. That's been going on a bit." He sighed deeply and got the wagon rolling again. "Either way, it doesn't matter. We'll get back to the road, find a marker, and do this the old-fashioned way. Everything will go back to normal."

"How much further to the road?" Jak asked.

"As far as it is," he shrugged. "There's a path through the trees. We just follow the path to Marlámh. We'll get there."

"Marlámh?" Jak queried.

"All roads lead to Marlámh," Jim answered. "It was the first road Talámh ever laid down. A lot of people don't know that he's the youngest of the D'Ihne. His name has come to mean home, but he's the journey as well as the destination. Y'know — where you belong, as well as how you get there. Marlámh was the path he laid to get back to himself when he began travelling. All roads eventually lead back to it. You follow any road long enough, you make it back to Marlámh."

"All roads eventually lead home…" Jak mused.

"If you travel long enough…" Jim smiled.

"Is that what you're trying to do?" she asked. "Travel long enough to get home?"

Jim didn't answer. His expression clouded briefly, and Jak wondered even more about what had made him take to the road, but he wasn't going to talk about it. She was alright with that. After yesterday, she was starting to build her own theories about him, and she was prepared to try and solve that mystery herself. She also didn't want to push him away or trigger his reflexive inappropriateness if she pushed the wrong buttons. She let the silence lie. For now.

Jim was right about the path leading back. Soon enough, he rumbled the wagon through the trees and up the ditch back onto the road. They came out at the first fork Jak had seen in a long time. Behind them, the mountain from yesterday seemed obscenely far away. She wanted to claim that there was no possible way they could have travelled that far, but she knew better. One path led back towards the other side of Shágrahiā, and the forest grew lush and thick and green that way. It looked safe. It looked like home. But Jim had a dark look in his eyes and he was already turning the Banging Wagon down the other path where the forest thinned.

"Jim?" she asked.

"We're still heading inland, towards the cities," he replied. "I don't like how close that thing is."

Jak looked for what he meant. She realised he was looking at the sky. A massive cloud bank hung over the forest path. Huge and fluffy white, with gentle touches of grey. It looked like a mountain in its own right, maybe even bigger than Shágrahiā.

"What's wrong?" Jak asked him. "Is it a storm?" She didn't think it looked dark enough to be a storm. Rain wasn't falling from it. It wasn't moving quickly on a harsh wind. She was prepared to make her argument for why the clouds were harmless as weather went, but she wasn't prepared for his reply.

"It's Roïgola'a'lanaū," he answered darkly. "The Golden City of the D'Ihne. To mortal eyes it appears as mere clouds, but I'd recognise that formation anywhere. I don't like it so close."

Jak stared at it. Her lips were parted enough that she felt like her mouth was hanging open, but she knew it didn't look that way. The Golden City. She considered it. It was a truly impressive cloudbank, she would concur, but the actual city of the fae? That seemed a stretch. What if it was just a bunch of clouds? She didn't think Jim would lie or make up something like that, and she had heard the legends about the floating city, but how did you tell one mountain of clouds from another? What made this one special?

She turned to ask him, and shut her mouth instantly. The clouds may have looked like a striking natural formation, but the look on his face told her — more than any magical clouds could have — that those particular clouds really were Roïgola'a'lanaū. He didn't just believe. He knew. How could he recognise them? She didn't want to ask, but if he said those were the clouds, then those were the clouds, and they needed to be riding the other way. After the Ondia marker yesterday, and now this, she was getting the impression that Jim wanted to get as far away from this region as possible. It was reinforced by the speed he got the horses to race them away at.

They didn't talk much more that morning. The cloudbank had definitely soured his mood, but he perked up the further they got from it. Once the sky greyed and the distinctive clouds were lost from the horizon, once Shágrahiā was nothing but a memory, his usual sultry vibe began to return. Jak didn't mind his company in silence. In fact, she found she almost liked it. There was something warm and familiar about him — or perhaps the feeling of having him there, if not the man himself.

The forests faded gently into farmland. Grassy green hills divided into paddocks stretched over the horizon. Jak was daydreaming and watching the scenery when she felt the caravan slow. Jim drove off the road into the long grass of the verges and parked up. Jak looked around. Rune markers. Three of them. He had promised. She checked the runes. The biggest one was an old and worn Fora rune. A marker of the old forest boundaries before most of the trees in this valley had been cleared for farmland. The other two were newer, Daonna and Ellaigh, the runes of Man and Cattle. Markers that blessed the land for the people and their wealth. There was almost certainly a town near here.

"These ones are okay?" Jak checked.

"They're fine," Jim nodded. "Between us, Jak, I pretty much just avoid Clōudiá and Frézíān. Everyone else is fair game — or at least reasonable. The Sky Queen can be a stuck-up bitch because she's so high and mighty, and dear old Frézíān can't help being a destructive greedy monster. Other than that, the D'Ihne aren't all bad, even if I can't help giving them a hard time."

"What about Ĝoŕgomghōul?" Jak asked in a small voice. "You don't avoid him?"

Jim just laughed. There was a spark in his eye and an ironic twist to his mouth.

"He avoids me," was all the answer he gave.

Jak felt sceptical about that. "Ĝoŕgomghōul? The god

of darkness? The shadow monster who makes soup out of people's bones?"

Jim laughed. "You humans have such bizarre notions."

Jak didn't say anything. There was only one thing she could think in response to that, and she wasn't ready to bring it up. Not just yet. After all, it might just be another bizarre human notion, but she had been carrying it for a while now. He hung around with Ha'Cās, alluded to knowledge and magic, and that comment… 'you humans'… She was definitely starting to have her suspicions about strange old Jim the Merchant.

"So… what's the best way to do this?" she changed the subject instead.

"We'll have lunch first," Jim replied, heading for the back of the wagon. "It always helps to have a little extra food on hand when you're bargaining with faeries."

He opened the doors to the fresh air and called down to the others. They clambered out, glad to be able to stretch their legs. Dora flopped into the long grass by the side of the road with a giggle. Allie reached down and tickled her. Dora shot up with a delighted shriek back towards the wagon. It was good the girls were burning some energy.

Krill gave the area a sharp once over with his golden eyes.

"Why this spot?" he asked.

"We're going to ask a friend to help find their mom," Jim replied, motioning to the runes. "Like I promised."

"We're going to summon faeries?!" Dora exclaimed,

already half in the picnic basket and digging for sandwiches.

"We most certainly are," Jim grinned. "Nothing as pretty as the two we've got, but everyone has their purpose." It sounded like the usual rubbish he spouted, but his eyes were soft on his lovers as he said it. Jak had made a joke about the lonely road yesterday, but he hadn't risen to it, and she wondered now what it was like for him most of the time — driving place to place on his own all day because he needed to keep them hidden.

They all stopped for something to eat, and then Dora was allowed to take a plate of food to the runes. Kode helped her pack it and the two of them walked it over. Krill hung around Jim's shoulder nervously. His anxiety nearly dripped from him, but it wasn't catching. Jak and Allie waited near the rocks. Krill paced from one side of Jim to the other.

"Jim, she shouldn't be—"

"Calm down, babe. She's fine. It's fine. Just chill."

Dora placed the food down by the stones and knelt. She clasped her hands together.

"Dear faeries," she prayed. "Please accept this food and please come and help us and we can do a trade if that's okay and if you aren't too busy."

"Oh, she asks so nicely," Jim placed a hand on his chest. "Even I'd come out for that."

"No one ever had to stop you from coming out, Jim," Krill told him drily.

Jak watched and hoped and prayed. Even though she was anticipating it, she still jumped when someone appeared on the stones. The little gnome had a baby in his arm, and he was very familiar.

"Äulé?!" Jak exclaimed.

"Äulé!" Dora cried delightedly. "What are you doing so far from home?"

"Mah little Dora!" he replied in kind. "What are yer doing all the way out here?"

"I asked you first!" Dora protested. Jak almost flinched, but Dora had a way with faerie folk. They liked her. Most people would get a spit or a curse for talking back to fae, but the sprites always had a soft spot for the little girl.

"I ain't far from anything, wee one," the gnome smiled and bounced the baby in his arms. "Mah home is the forest. All forests. Past and present. This here's a Fora, and so here I be when humans come a-calling."

"Any forest? Anywhere in the world?" Dora asked gobsmacked. The world was a big place. Even bigger than Kosveir, which was even bigger than Rutsborough. Dora was starting to comprehend this in her travels.

"Anywhere," Äulé agreed.

"He's a Drifter," Jim commented from by the wagon. "Most gnomes have a forest, but a rare few are what we call Drifters, and they follow runes rather than trees. They can travel. I knew I knew your name when they mentioned it."

"Aye, some call meh a Drifter," Äulé agreed. "Worse things been said."

"Do the gnomes here dislike you muscling in on this rune?" Jim asked. "They seem a grumpy lot."

"Not ta meh," Äulé grinned. "Don't know how they'd find yer, James. Might think yer a lazy pansy..." Jim didn't rise to the bait. Äulé took a piece of bread from the plate and fed it to the restless babe as it started to wake. When he looked up again, he was looking at Dora. "So what yer after this time, mah wee lass?"

Dora looked back at her sisters, but Jak and Allie just nodded encouragingly at her. They had agreed over lunch to let Dora do the talking — as long as she didn't talk about her crown or try and pull rank. If she starting going on about being a faerie princess, things could go sour. Otherwise, she liked faeries, and they liked her, and it wasn't a hard question. If things got complicated, they were all right there to jump in.

"We're looking for our Mum," Dora told him. "Do you know where she is?"

Äulé went very quiet. He pursed his lips in thought and fed some more bread to his baby gnome. Then he ate some of the bread himself.

"That's an expensive question," he answered finally.

"Well," Jim pulled himself away from the wagon with the grace of a man who knows his business and a smile to match. That winning smile. He held up a fat pouch and rattled it. "I have a whole bag of loose, lost buttons."

Äulé eyed the pouch like Jim had just told him it was full of gold. He looked half set to drop the baby to snatch it, but he was a better father than that, and they all knew it.

"Oh aye...?" he tried to keep the eagerness from his voice, but he couldn't hide it in his eyes. "And all yer want for it…?"

"Where's the girls' Mom? Tell us how to find her."

Äulé stared at the pouch with desperately hungry eyes, but he looked torn. He turned his gaze between them all, and then something dawned in his expression — as though he were just seeing them all for the first time.

"Wait a minute…" he muttered. "What yer all doing together? Nice girls like yer shouldn't be travelling with a scoundrel like him!"

"Your vote of confidence is touching, Äulé," Jim drawled. "Now — buttons for info. I won't wait all day."

"Yer'll wait as long as yer like, James," Äulé grinned at him. "Yer always do. Keep yer grubby mitts away from mah little ladies."

"I'm not —! Geez! I'm taking care of them, you stupid gnome! Don't be such a villain about it. I'm looking after these girls."

Jak clasped a hand to her mouth, but Äulé didn't look like he was about to hex Jim for the insult. Instead, Äulé stared at him a moment, but there was no lie there and he realised Jim must have been telling the truth. The gnome howled with laughter. Gales of it racked his tiny body. He hooted and hollered, and slapped his hand against the rock he sat upon. He laughed so hard he snorted. Jim lost his winning smile and his patience as he folded his arms and gave the gnome a dark look. Krill stood half hidden behind him, with a weary hand over his eyes.

"Ah, James," Äulé wiped tears away. "Yer killing

meh, lad, yer killing meh."

"I'm glad you think this is hilarious."

"Yer have no idea… Yer? Looking after them? Ha! 'Tis a fine joke. Best I ever heard."

"Good. I'm a funny guy. Now," Jim rattled the pouch again. "You want these? Or should I go find someone else to trade with?"

"Yer won't find no one else," Äulé warned. "It's no wonder the others been giving yer the cold shoulder. It's expensive, Jim. They're simple folk around here." He stared at the pack of buttons. Jim watched him stare. He jingled the pouch. Äulé took a deep breath. "But I can spare a bit… Yer want the girls' Mama? Ask Roïgola'a'lanaū." He held his hand out for the buttons.

"Ask Roïgola'a'lanaū?" Jim repeated.

"That's what I said," Äulé confirmed. He gestured impatiently.

"I'm not paying you for that," Jim scoffed. "That's like telling me if I want help I have to speak to your manager, and then telling me I have to go and find them myself because you won't get them."

"Yer asked a question and I gave yer an answer — a true and truthful answer! Don't yer be trying to cheat meh now, boy!"

"You're cheating me!" Jim argued. "Just because those dickheads in the sky can tell me the truth doesn't mean you get to pass the question you can answer up to them. We're at square one, as far as I'm concerned. You give me a real answer, and I'll give you real buttons."

"I did give yer a real answer," Äulé growled. "Yer don't get to avoid paying meh just because yer don't like it."

"Äulé, please," Jak begged. She was hesitant to interrupt, but she was scared Jim was going to do something to get them all cursed. She'd never heard of someone fighting with a fae like that. Faeries often gave tricky answers, you just learnt to deal with it. But Jim was a business man. He wasn't going down without a fight. She needed to mediate it. "Please, Äulé, help us find her. Can't you give us a little more? Anything, really."

The gnome turned his eyes to Jak. They misted softly and he sighed reluctantly at her.

"Ah, Jakie," he shook his head. "Yer don't understand. Yer can't. Things are getting complicated. I want to help yer girls, I really do, but it ain't that simple anymore. Yer travelling with them. Yer in with their lot now."

"You racist little—!" Jim started for the gnome, but Krill grabbed him and held him back.

"Don't get yer panties in a twist, James," Äulé scolded him. "Yer know I ain't like that. Yer made things complicated, boy. This is on yer."

"What does that mean?" Krill asked, his face paling in fear.

"Don't pretend yer don't know what's been going on this past year, D'rö-Hadās," Äulé replied to him. "Things been in chaos, and none of yer been helping. Everyone knows. They all been talking about it."

"It's not our business or our problem," Jim sneered.

"And no one's going to tell yer otherwise if that's the stance yer take," Äulé gave him a nod. "But yer don't help us, and no one helps yer. That's how it's always worked, James. I don't make the rules."

"The rules are broken, Äulé," Jim snapped. Krill jerked him back with a sharp look. The blonde fae was scared. He hadn't wanted them to summon someone here in the first place, and he really looked like he didn't want to start a fight. Jim mellowed at the fear on his face.

"James," Äulé sighed. "I got no interest in fighting with yer, boy. I ain't stupid, and I ain't wanting to cross yer, but you ain't got a monopoly on no one either. I belong to Thænäri. Yer got problems, yer take them up with her. I ain't getting involved."

Jim sighed angrily. He tipped out a small handful of buttons and passed them to the gnome. Äulé tightened his fist around them greedily.

"Give my love to your family, Äulé."

"Thank yer kindly, lad," the gnome bowed to him.

"But, wait! Äulé!" Dora started to panic. "Help! We don't know what to do! You didn't tell us where Mum is! We—!" Dora started to cough. Her words were lost as the fit racked her body. Allie and Jak grabbed her and pulled her up as she started to choke. Kode leapt into the back of the wagon as soon as the coughing started.

"What's wrong?" Äulé demanded. "What's wrong with mah little Dora?"

"I got this, gnome," Jim waved him off. "She's just got a cough."

"Why?!" Äulé insisted, as though illness was some rare and terrifying dilemma.

Kode was already bounding back out of the wagon

with the medicine bottle. Jak couldn't remember if they'd made Dora take it last night. They might have forgotten, but she hadn't coughed in the night. Kode came over and took the little girl from her sisters. The big faerie bundled Dora into his arms and fed her a spoonful of medicine. She stopped coughing and he started getting her to drink from one of the mugs.

"She shouldn't be sick," Äulé grumbled. "What did yer do to her?"

"Nothing," Jim retorted. "She's got a bit of a cough. I'm patching it up. Don't get your panties in a twist, you hairy-butt gnome."

"I'll worry about her health if it pleases meh, yer silken tart," Äulé sniped. "Yer never had much to do with kids before, Jim. What made yer think to start?"

Jim didn't answer. Not at first. He behaved like he hadn't heard. They were all still watching Dora. She had calmed down, and she looked safe and content in Kode's strong arms. He was good at playing dad, and he rocked her gently and patted her back. They all just watched and finally Jim spoke, only to Äulé.

"They needed me," he answered. "They stumbled out of the forest and they had nothing else — not even a direction to run. They needed me."

"Oh bugger meh," the gnome cursed. "Meh safety spell sent them to yer?" he chuckled, and his eyes perused the sky as though there was something to see. "Yer ever feel like the universe is playing with us, James?"

"No," Jim replied. "I don't let it."

"Boy, yer never said no to something playing with

yer," Äulé laughed. He had a handful of buttons on one side, and a baby on the other. The gnome faded out of sight before Jim could retort again. The group of travellers were alone on the side of the road, and their help was gone. Jak looked up at Jim. The older girls were kneeling by Kode, who sat in the grass with Dora on his lap.

"What now?" she asked.

He shrugged and turned away. Jim wandered slowly around behind the back of the wagon. Krill and Jak watched him go. The two of them shared a look. There was a loud thump like fist on wood and they heard him yell.

"Fucking faeries!"

His boots clomped loudly into the wagon. Krill quickly touched Jak's shoulder. The two of them weren't touchers, and the tips of his fingers barely brushed her shirt, but he was attempting to be reassuring. He hurried after Jim. Jak listened to doors and trapdoors and more doors and ladders and people moving. Jim was angry now. Something was going on that he wasn't telling them about. Something big.

She thought about asking Kode, but she got the impression that he might not know. The whole time they had been at the runes Krill had been giving Jim looks. He knew something was up. He knew summoning one of the little faeries was trouble. He had tried to protest and warn, and Jim hadn't listened. Now he had ended up fighting with Äulé and they were all back at square one — or so it felt. There were a few things she had been able to pick up though. It wasn't all for nothing, and she might as well try and ask.

As she turned to speak, she took note. Kode was asking Dora if she was okay now. He was looking after her and she was doing better and everything was alright, but there was a sad droop to his long ears. Jak had never seen that look on either of them before.

"Kode…?" she asked softly. "What's wrong?"

He looked up her. He had such big and innocent pale-purple eyes. Those sweet eyes glanced at the wagon miserably.

"They're fighting," he mumbled. "They're always fighting. All the last year. They just fight all the time."

"What about?" Allie asked suspiciously.

Kode shrugged. "They send me out. They give me tasks or tell me to play. They don't like me listening when they fight, but they fight. They fight all the time now. I know they do."

Jak opened her mouth to ask. He had to know something. He probably knew the answer to the question she'd wanted to ask for so long now. She felt manipulative, but he was too dumb to lie. Even as her lips began to form the words, she heard footsteps on the back of the wagon. They all looked up as Krill wandered to them. The fae was usually silent on his feet. To walk so heavily was a decision. He strolled to his husband and stroked his soft blonde hair with a gentle hand.

"Kody, baby, can you go calm him down please?" he asked softly.

Kode nodded. He untangled from Dora and climbed to his feet. The fae shared a kiss and then Kode ducked silently into the wagon. Krill sighed loudly and ran his fingers through his choppy, braided hair.

"What's going on?" Jak asked him, not to be put off her questions.

"Jim's being an idiot," Krill replied flippantly. "But, then, when isn't he?"

"But something's happening, isn't it?" Jak insisted. "Something big. Something with the gods."

"D'Ihne business is not ours," Krill replied. "To involve ourselves with them now would risk our lives. They would try us and kill us before they accepted our help. We broke their laws and abandoned Roïgola'a'lanaū."

"And now you're being chased by the D'rö-Hadās?" Jak remembered the shadowy figures that had been pursuing them. Krill half-nodded, half-shrugged in something near enough to agreement. Jak bit her lip hesitantly, but pushed forward with her interrogation. "Äulé called you D'rö-Hadās... what does it mean? What are the D'rö-Hadās?"

Krill looked over all of them. His golden eyes were severe and his pale lips thin.

"They will be a few minutes inside," he changed the subject. "Do you want me to train you while we break?"

"I want you to answer my question," Jak refused to relent. She wanted to train, but not at the cost of being derailed from this. She needed some answers, even if she couldn't have all of them.

Krill sighed deeply through his nose. He looked over the girls as though he wasn't sure if he was about to make a mistake. As though he wasn't sure what was appropriate or not.

"You humans know the D'rö-Hadās by another name," he said finally. "You call them the Head Hunters."

Jak felt her blood ice over. The Head Hunters. Even mentioning their name was considered bad luck. They were an omen of Ĝorgomghōul. The army of shadow fiends that rode through the night. They claimed the bounties of the fae and dealt the final say on faerie justice. Faerie justice by way of decapitation. Jak remembered how Krill had dealt with the bandits. Her throat went dry.

"The Head Hunters...?" she whispered. "You were one of them?"

"I was," Krill gave a sharp nod.

"You collected heads for Ĝorgomghōul...?" Jak realised she had a whole new fear of the way Krill fought and killed. The efficiency with which he had beheaded the bandits was no longer surprising.

"I did," Krill responded. A slight wry smile settled on his face as he answered. "Lord Ĝorgomghōul was always a ruthless but fair master. Fair in the way the other D'Ihne so often are not. I know that humans are rightfully terrified of him. He is fearsomely powerful, and the spells he weaves with the bounties of the D'rö-Hadās are legendary even among the D'Ihne. However, it is worth noting that while he is the Patron of the D'rö-Hadās, we do not belong to him. The D'rö-Hadās are Queen Clōudiá's army, in service to Ĝorgomghōul. He trains us in magic and battle. He teaches us to shadow-walk. He makes our shadow armour and our weapons

— D'rök blades: born of mortal blood, bone, shadow, and steel — the combination of which is poison, even deadly, to fae. Ĝoŕgomghōul cares for the D'rö-Hadās like no one else does, and we are grateful to him, but we ride on the order of Clōudiá, and no other."

"Is that why you don't like Clōudiá?" Dora asked. Jak and Allie looked to her. She didn't seem shaken. For the older girls, the confirmation of a ghost story was frightening. Dora had the benefit of acceptance on her side. She had never stopped believing.

"There are many reasons I don't like Clōudiá, little one," Krill answered. "She has always been a cruel and fickle mistress. I considered her treatment of my soldiers poor, and her laws barbaric."

"Your soldiers?" Jak interrupted sharply.

A faint flicker showed in Krill's eyes as he realised what he had said. He didn't elaborate.

"Krill..." Jak stared at him. "Just who were you when you worked for the D'rö-Hadās?"

Krill sighed as he stared off into the distance. "I no longer wish to talk of this," he stated. "The memories are not good ones. I apologise that we have not found helpful answers as yet, but Jim won't give up. He never does, even when it would be better for him. We will find your mother for you. Once he calms down."

"Who is he?" Jak asked. "Why does he know so much about the fae, and why do they know him?"

"That is not my place to answer," Krill smiled. "If you want to know more about Jim, you best ask him yourself."

"But then we have to talk to him..." Allie pouted.

"And he's so… creepy isn't the right word… um…"

"Lecherous," Krill offered.

"What does that mean?"

"It means to behave like Jim," he replied.

Jak chuckled. She knew exactly what they both meant. Krill turned his golden eyes on her once more. He had made it clear that he no longer wished to talk, and his gaze repeated his question about whether she would like to train. She did. Jak pushed herself up from the grass at the side of the road and followed Krill to the other side of the wagon. The road wasn't busy, and with no one else around, it gave them plenty of room. Krill turned and faced her. Jak drew her sword and readied herself. If training was going to be anything like her workout yesterday, she would probably never be truly ready.

Krill poised himself and his D'rök blades appeared shiny and dark in his hands. A sharp smile curled his lips and his eyes narrowed with the gaze of a hunter.

"Let us begin."

CHAPTER SIX

It was all too soon for Jak when Kode and Jim appeared out of the wagon again. She'd barely worked up a sweat. Every time it felt like they were getting started, Krill would stop her and correct or adjust something. She knew this was part of the training. He showed her different ways to hold her blade, and every time she tried to use one, he would stop and correct her footwork. More than anything, he seemed to want to teach her how to defend herself.

"It is the most important part of the warrior's code, I believe," he told her. "If you do not know how to protect yourself, then you will not be fighting for very long."

"But your style is offensive, not defensive," Jak pointed out. She knew enough from Big Sam to have gleaned that much by watching Krill. She wanted to learn to do what he did — or at least the human equivalent. As far as she was concerned, there was no point learning to defend if you didn't have the offensive skills to then beat your opponent. The fae smiled at her.

"I am not a warrior," he replied patiently, touching her elbow lightly to raise her defensive posture. "I am an assassin. I was trained to kill without having to engage my targets."

"But you do fight," Jak insisted. "You fight the D'rö-Hadās."

"Sometimes," Krill admitted blandly. "I have no desire to kill my brethren. They ride on Clōudiá's order, and they are still her slaves. That I wish I could change, but for now I simply drive them away. However, I have had four hundred years to practice how to do that. You are a warrior. D'rö-Hadās are trained to kill, not fight. You do not have the soul of a killer, Jak. If you were Ha'Cās, I would send you to Ínrío to serve."

"Isn't Ínrío the god of the forge?" Jak recalled. Big Sam hadn't held much with gods and magic, but he wasn't anyone's fool, and he had kept a small shield mounted on the back wall of his forge with the Sorio rune engraved sharply into it. It had symbolised respect for Ínrío; god of the Sun and forge, and his respective blessing.

"The D'Ihne are deities of many things," Krill replied. "Everything extrapolates out from there. If Ínrío is the deity of the forge, then he would also be responsible for the weapons born of it, and similarly their use. Ínrío is the deity human warriors pray to, respect, and curse by. He is the god of human war. Although I do not believe he has ever cared for the death of anyone, he is always interested in trials by combat as tests of strength." Krill smiled warmly to himself. "Ínrío is not the brightest apple in the bunch, although he is usually well-meaning."

Footsteps sounded behind the wagon and Jim and Kode wandered over to join them. Jak felt like she'd had more of a religious lesson than a fencing one. She had to remind herself it was the first time. Things were bound to start off slow. Training with Big Sam had been the same. Krill turned to them as soon as they appeared.

"What now?" he asked.

"We keep going," Jim shrugged. "Nothing's changed, we just need sprites with less attitude." He eyed up Jak with a smirk. "How's she doing?"

"She fights like a human," Krill shrugged back.

For some reason Jak felt crushed by the comment.

Everyone began to ready themselves to travel again. Jim didn't even have to say anything. They all just knew: he was ready to hit the road. Jak herded her sisters back inside the wagon. She didn't climb in herself, but instead followed Jim to the front of the caravan. He smiled at her.

"You going to keep me company again?"

"I like being able to see where we're going," she shrugged.

"And I like having someone around, so it's a win-win," he grinned.

Jak didn't answer that, but she climbed up beside him and they set off. He let her ride in silence for a while, but she could feel her stomach begin to twist with nerves. If he'd asked what was wrong, she would have lied and said she didn't know. She was half trying to tell herself that she didn't know what was wrong. As it was, he misread her reservation.

"I'm sorry about what happened back there," he apologised.

"You don't really have to be sorry," Jak sighed. "It wasn't exactly your fault. I just wish you guys would tell us what was going on."

Jim pursed his lips slightly in thought and his eyes narrowed. For a moment he just let that hang there and then began to speak cautiously.

"A lot of it is fae business that wouldn't make any sense to humans," he began. "But for what I can tell you, there seems to be something of a divide occurring in Roïgola'a'lanaū. The D'Ihne are going all to pieces over fae politics."

Jak pulled a face at the word politics. Jim laughed.

"Yes. Unsavoury, isn't it?" he chuckled. "I know what it's like to want answers, Jak, but it's not nearly as interesting as you think it is. I promise. Most of it is tedious things that I would have to explain step by step, and at the end you'd only be left disappointed by the fickleness of gods."

Jak nodded quietly to that. Jim continued talking. He reassured her about the situation and explained that they would be able to find other kinds of markers that would give them different sprites, and that those faeries might be far more reasonable. She half listened, but while he spoke she built her courage. Finally, she interrupted him by blurting the question she had wanted to the answer to for so long.

"Who are you?" she demanded.

"Me?" he checked. A cheeky smile dimpled his face. "I'm Jim, we've actually met—"

"Don't be a dick about it," Jak retorted hotly. "I mean what are you? You travel around with Ha'Cās, you know everything about faeries and gods and the Golden City. How? How do you know all this stuff?

What are you?"

She let her question hang in the air and this time Jim didn't try and be cheeky about it.

"I'm just a man, travelling the world, and trying to make a mostly honest living," he answered as delicately as he could.

"It's amazing," Jak sighed.

"You think so?" he smiled.

"No, it's amazing how you managed to make even that sound like a lie," she muttered.

He laughed. "I'm sorry. I know that Krill and Kode make everything seem so magical — believe me — but I think this might be one of those things that isn't as interesting as you think."

She let it drop. Half of her wanted to keep fighting about it, but she knew that's all it would be. He had not done anything to convince her, but she knew she wouldn't win the fight. She couldn't force him to tell her anything. She'd just have to trick him.

He knew he hadn't persuaded her, and as they drove he would throw the occasional glance her way. It wasn't a suspicious or worried look, but more the eyes of someone measuring another's irritation. He was still waiting for her to start a fight. As soon as she realised that, she turned her face away to watch the countryside roll by. She would not give him the satisfaction.

A great deal of the area they were in now seemed to be farmland. Rolling hills of green surrounded them, and sheep grazed here and there on the grass like little puffs of cloud that had fallen from the overcast sky. They rattled on down the hard dirt road, kicking up a thin cloud of dust in their wake. The road wove like a snake through the hills and they followed its winding path. About mid-afternoon, Jak felt them start to slow. She heard Jim muse.

"That's interesting…"

She turned and followed his gaze.

"Is that a village?" she asked. Up ahead, on his side of the road, was a sizable stone building. Another road veered off beside it and ran into a valley where more buildings were visible in little clusters.

"It is indeed," he replied. "And that," he nodded his head at the building on the side of the main road, "is a church."

"Huh." Jak had never seen a church before. The people of Rutsborough were not the kind to build churches. They had the occasional personal shrine or token in their house or work, if they were superstitious enough, but for the most part their village had been wary of faeries and gods. She eyed up the building with its carvings and statues; its pillars and fancy stained-glass windows. "It's quite grand, isn't it?"

"It's no city temple," Jim shrugged. "It's like most village churches, but this one is interesting." He pulled the wagon up beside it and stopped. For a minute or so, he just sat on the seat of the caravan eyeing up the place. Then he climbed down to approach the building. Jak scrambled down and followed him. While he regarded the church with only a slight curiosity, Jak couldn't help but feel a gentle awe. It was quite certainly the most beautiful building she had ever seen. Covering the front of the church, above the main doors, were a cluster of exquisite stone statues. Pillars held the roof out over them to protect them from the elements. The statues were what Jim was looking at. Jak couldn't keep her eyes on one thing.

Behind them, the doors of the Banging Wagon opened. The familiar sound of everyone clambering out could be heard.

"Why have we stopped?" Krill asked, as they came around to see what was going on.

"Jim wanted to look at the church," Jak told him. "It's quite amazing."

"One church is much like another," Krill shrugged.

Jak began to get the feeling that her boys were a bit too well-travelled. This place was breath-taking, and they were shrugging it away as though they had seen a hundred like it. She couldn't even imagine such a thing. Her sisters clearly felt the same. Kode brought them around to join everyone and she heard Allie sigh.

"It's beautiful…"

"So pretty…" Dora agreed. Kode nodded along with them.

"It's just a simple church," Krill dismissed.

"Yes," Kode agreed. "But it's pretty. So were all the other ones."

Krill smiled at him. His husband's wonder was endless, and in a way that made it contagious. While the older fae may have disregarded human architecture and brushed aside its marvels, he was still humbled and awed by Kode's ability to see beauty in it. That, in turn, made it beautiful.

"This one is interesting though," Jim commented.

"Look at this." He motioned the statues above the door.

They all looked. Jak was struck by the beauty of all the figures, but it hardly surprised her. They were supposed to be gods, after all.

"That is interesting…" Krill agreed after a moment.

"Let's take a look inside," Jim suggested. He didn't wait for a reply, but instead opened the large, ornate, wooden door and strolled into the church. Everyone followed him. Their footsteps echoed on the stone floor inside, and the light from the windows spilled in like rainbow puddles. The building was shaped like a T with a long main room and then a slightly smaller room across the top. Both spaces seemed to be lined with alcoves, and even though there were two main rooms, the spaces seemed divided. Up the front of the main room was a large stained-glass piece set almost in the middle of the church. It depicted a woman with a crown surrounded by stars. Jim sneered at it.

"Clōudiá," he commented.

"Is that really what she looks like?" Jak asked softly.

"Most of the time," Jim nodded, confirming her suspicions. "D'Ihne change their gender and appearance at whim, but they usually have a preferred form. There's a statue and a window here for every god, and they are all done in remarkably accurate detail to the D'Ihne's most common form. The sprites around here must be particularly gossipy."

"Well, Äulé is one of them," Dora said primly. "He's a gossip."

"That he is…" Jim smiled. He looked around the main room, and his sharp eyes soaked in every detail.

There were seats and stools arranged in each nook for people to go and pray or worship the different D'Ihne, but the building was empty except for them.

"That's what's got you interested, isn't it?" Krill asked Jim. His eyes were on a dark stained-glass window in the main room. Jim nodded and wandered over slowly. Jak followed him. The light shone through the black and grey glass and made it easier to see the image. The sight made her cold all over.

"That's Ĝoŕgomghōul?" she asked.

"It is indeed," Jim replied. The red light from the window's three eyes sparkled across his face. "That's what makes this place unusual. Most churches only build to the ten gods of Roïgola'a'lanaū. This one has eleven. That is not very common. For some reason, these people still give praise to Ĝoŕgomghōul. See there," he pointed to the window where faint images of books surrounded the dark god, "most people don't know that Ĝoŕgomghōul is considered the deity of wisdom. These people, whoever they are, are quite well informed about the D'Ihne." He looked around the main room. The biggest windows were depictions of five people, including Clōudiá hanging from the ceiling and dividing the two spaces. "These are the original five," he mused. "The first generation. Born of stardust and ghosts. Born of the will of the universe." He looked at Jak. "I told you that's the thing about travelling — you hear all the legends."

His tone was inviting and Jak couldn't help but follow him around as he showed her the windows and named the gods. The three others in the main room were Thænäri, Äluāknā, and Frézían.

"From these five," Jim recounted, "was all of faerie born. The other six D'Ihne are all their children, as are sprites and demigods and Ha'Cās."

"So…" Jak turned back to Krill and Kode. "Your parents are up there?"

"Our mothers," Krill nodded. "Our fathers are humans long dead. Kode's mother is Clōudiá."

Jak started at the revelation. A hundred questions jumped into her mind, but she had the sense to stop them at her mouth. She was suddenly horrified, but she realised that was what Jim and Krill had been trying to explain this whole time. Clōudiá, Queen of Roïgola'a'lanaū the Golden City, Queen of the fae, had borne a half-human child and given him to slavery. She had done it without question or concern, probably many times. That was how the fae lived.

"Does that mean you're a faerie prince?" Dora asked Kode excitedly, tugging on his hand. The gentle fae smiled and shook his head.

"Only Clōudiá's royalty is recognised by the D'Ihne," Krill told them. "And Ha'Cās have no station at all. Their parent, although not ignored, is less important than their Patron. Who we serve and the duties we perform are significantly more important than where we came from."

"And where did you come from?" Jak asked him gently. "Who was your mother?"

Krill's golden eyes went very hard, and a brief glance to a window betrayed his answer before he spoke it. "Frézían."

Jak looked up at the demonic and pointedly masculine god of fire glowing red and orange and gold in the wall. The boys had told her several times that the D'Ihne changed their genders at will, but for her it was hard to imagine. She stared at the angry depiction of the man on the wall.

"That's your... mum?" she checked.

"Yes," Krill answered shortly.

"And they do not get on," Jim added enthusiastically, grabbing Krill by the shoulders from behind. "What is it I always say about Frézíān? Oh, yes: loves sticking it in fae and getting stuck by humans."

"Thank you, James," Krill said darkly. "Because what I really needed today was a reminder of my mother's sexual preferences."

"I'm just saying," Jim grinned. "He might wander around the halls of Roïgola'a'lanaū like he's determined to get his cock sucked, but he has hundreds of Ha'Cās children, and that says more than his posturing does. I think he's just desperately unfulfilled, so he tries to fill the gap — if you know what I mean."

"Everyone knows what you mean," Allie smirked.

"I don't!" Dora protested.

"Thank goodness," Jak pulled her into a one-armed hug. "Just ignore him, sweetie. He's being Jim again."

"Ew," Dora giggled. Jim winked at her.

"Come on," he encouraged, heading for the other room. "The other six will be through here, and checking out the second generation is always more fun." He led them into the next chamber and pointed out Créātā, the goddess of medicine, and Talámh, the god of travel and commerce. The way he looked at them was almost fond. Jak was a little surprised.

"I thought you didn't like the D'Ihne," she reminded. Jim looked slightly conflicted.

"The second generation are all nice enough," he replied. "They're not bad people, not like their parents, but they are the product of a damaged institution."

"At least most of them are partially aware of that," Krill added. "They tend to be more frugal and careful about the ways they live. They're an odd bunch."

"You mean prudish," Jim responded almost automatically.

"I mean responsible," Krill replied. "Most of them, anyway. Your opinions are your own."

Jim looked like that was a fight he didn't want to start again. Instead, he wandered off to inspect more windows. Allie looked over to Krill.

"What does he mean 'prudish'?" she asked quietly. Krill took in Allie's quiet tone and the nervous look she shot at Jak as her older sister followed Jim around the building. The faerie knew the girl was trying to keep the conversation private so that Jak wouldn't stop it. That meant she knew what she was asking.

"Jim's interested in the sexual exploits of the D'Ihne," Krill replied just as quietly. "There are only eleven D'Ihne in existence — it makes their relationships hideously incestuous by human standards. They don't consider their behaviour the same way humans do, though. The first generation are considered siblings, yet they are the parents of the second generation."

"But they're gods," Allie shrugged. "It's different."

"That's how they see it too," Krill nodded. "The only familial bond the first five see is the relationship of parent and child. That is the only line they will not cross — even so far as they recognise their Ha'Cās children."

"So… even though Kode was a sex worker for the gods, Clōudiá would never go near him?"

"Exactly," Krill whispered, pleased at how quick she was. "However, the second generation extended the taboo to their siblings — for the most part. If they shared a parent, they considered themselves related."

"Is that why the gods shag so many humans?" Allie whispered.

"Probably," Krill smiled. "The second generation were interesting in that they began to have moral hang-ups in a way the first generation never did. Save Ĝorgomghōul."

Allie gave him an inquisitive look.

"Ĝorgomghōul fathered two children," Krill explained. "Crŷstïar with Clōudiá, and Fæmör with Thænäri. That was it. He never dallied with humans. He never succumbed to the seductions of Äluāknā and Frézíān. He left Roïgola'a'lanaū, and never involved himself in the infamous passions of the D'Ihne. He found other interests instead."

"Huh," Allie mused. She let Krill lead her back to the others. They were standing in one side of the top of the T and looking at the two windows positioned in the corner.

"They have a lovers' corner," Jim was scoffing. "Look at them. The windows even match."

"Why are they running?" Dora asked, looking at the windows.

"Those two are always running from something," Jim smirked. "Crŷstïar is the god of trickery, and Olíriá is his lover. They were always getting in trouble together. Most of the big legends humans like to tell is about them."

"Because they're monogamous and humans like cute love stories?" Jak smiled at him.

"If you say so," Jim scoffed. "I think it's selfish. I mean, it's not like the D'Ihne had that many lovers to choose from regarding their own kind, so when these two decided to swear themselves only to each other it was severely limiting the pool."

"They're in love though," Jak smiled. "Olíriá is considered the goddess of love because she was the first D'Ihne to promise herself to only one person forever, and she did that because she knew Crŷstïar loved her, and she loved him back."

"Ugh," Jim gave her a disgusted look. "You're such a romantic."

"Krill and Kode's story is just as romantic," Jak insisted. "You don't mind them."

"They are forgiven everything always and forever as long as they keep banging me," Jim replied. "Romance is fine as long as I can stick my dick in it."

"You are actually the worst person ever," Jak grimaced in revulsion.

"Thank you," he smiled, placing a touched hand to his heart. He strolled off towards the last windows and Jak pulled a disgusted face as she watched him go. They followed Jim over and looked up. The man had a wry look on his face as he considered the art work.

"And there he is..." he muttered.

"That's Ínrío," Dora pointed, still holding Kode's hand. "The sunshine god. He's brother to both of you, isn't he?"

"It doesn't really count, but yes," Kode nodded. "That's not the one Jim's looking at though."

"Oh my..." Krill commented with a smirk. Jak knew the window they were all looking at now. It made her blush just to look.

"What. A. Skank," Jim judged scathingly. He had his arms folded and a fight-me expression on his face as he looked at the stained-glass image of Fæmör, god of sex.

"Are you serious?" Jak stared at him.

"He's pretty though," Allie giggled. "Is it true he seduced all the other gods in this room, even his siblings?"

"Not Olíriá," Kode reminded. "She wouldn't. But everyone else, yes. He even tricked Crŷstïar."

"He tricked the god of trickery?" Jak asked. She had heard the legend too. It was a universally scandalous story. Fæmör had appeared in a woman's form to his brother, and in the dark pretended he was Olíriá. Apparently, Crŷstïar had been homicidal when he realised.

"He did indeed," Krill was trying to hide his grin. "That's mostly why the story is so famous. Crŷstïar has considered it the low point of his life ever since."

"He enjoyed himself at the time though," Jim chuckled. "It's a shame he's so stuck up."

"He was badly duped," Krill defended. "You would be sore if someone wounded your pride that way too."

"Eh," Jim shrugged. "I don't think anyone could. Besides, D'Ihne need their pride kicked in the teeth sometimes. People already call them gods. It's not the kind of thing you want going to their heads when their society is so backwards."

Jak had been watching Jim the whole time he'd been staring at the glass, and an idea struck her sharply as he started to walk away.

"Is he your father?" she asked. Jim gave her a curious look and she elaborated. "Is Fæmör your father?"

"Why on earth would you think that?" Jim replied. "I'm not Ha'Cās."

"No," Jak agreed. "You're human. At least, you appear human. But... you also seem a bit like you're not. Also, you're rude about him in a way you're not to the others. I'm not suggesting you're Ha'Cās... I was thinking more demigod — like the heroes of old. You would have a D'Ihne father, not mother. Is Fæmör your dad?"

The room held its breath. Jak was aware of her sisters and the fae staring at her, but she kept her eyes on Jim. He met her look calmly, and with a possible hint of amusement.

"No," Jim answered coolly. "He's not. The second generation D'Ihne don't have any children. Not yet, anyway. I imagine in time they won't be able to help themselves, but for now all fae come from the first five. As for why I'm rude about him, well, look at him."

"I am," Krill cut in appreciatively. Jim stopped in his

tracks. If he'd been rattled by Jak's question, it was nothing compared to how Krill's admiration of the stained-glass surprised him.

"You… like that piece?" he asked curiously.

"You know," Krill mused, folding his arms and looking up at it softly. "I really do. I always quite liked Fæmör. Even by the standards of D'Ihne, he is stunningly beautiful. I wonder if the person who made these is around to accept a commission? I could get one and hang it over my bed."

"Our bed," Jim corrected.

"Alright then," Krill shrugged. "I could hang it in the washroom. Somewhere I could look at it while I'm bathing."

Jim actually blushed. A rosy glow crawled up his cheeks in defiance of his reluctant expression. He turned away and stalked off, muttering to himself. The girls all looked at Krill admiringly. He was still looking at the window, but he had a small smug smile playing about his lips like a victory.

"That was beautiful…" Allie praised him in a whisper.

"Thank you, child," Krill grinned. "Although, I do actually like Fæmör. We both do." He smiled at his husband.

Kode smiled back. "Fæmör was my Patron," he added. "He was always kind and fun, and he was an excellent teacher."

"So, he's actually one of the good ones?" Allie asked. She seemed quite pleased about that.

"He's one of the best," Krill smiled. "Jim knows we

like him. He knows I think Fæmör is stunning."

"So he's jealous," Jak smirked. "I did wonder why Lord Skankington was calling someone else a skank."

Krill covered his mouth with a hand, but he couldn't hide his laughter. He nearly doubled over in silent hysterics, and it was enough to make Jim stop and look back. Krill's eyes brimmed with mirth as he caught his lover's gaze across the church.

"She called you Lord Skankington," he hooted.

Jim looked over them all. He caught Jak's eye. She shrugged. If the boot fit.

"I love it," he announced grandly. "I'm keeping it. From now on, you will all address me as Lord Skankington!"

Allie glared at Jak. "What have you started?" she muttered.

"Nothing I can't finish," Jak grinned at her.

Jim was leaving, so they all followed him out. Jak shut the door quietly behind them as they left and looked for their guide. His eyes were fixed hungrily on the village nestled further in the valley.

"You want us to go down there?" she asked.

"We just poked around inside their church, it would be rude not to go and say hello," he replied. "Besides, I've been stuck with you smart-asses for days now. I could use some new conversation."

"Why is the church so far away from the village?" Dora asked.

"Because it's a farming village," Jim explained. "Lots of the people who live around here have their houses on their farms and live up in the hills. The church is just outside of town on the main road in and out, so it's easy for everyone to get to. It's a pretty common practice in villages like this."

"Is it weird that there's no one in it?" Allie asked. "Shouldn't someone be looking after it?"

"I'm sure someone does," Jim replied. "But that doesn't mean they have to be there all the time. People are usually superstitious about churches. They don't like to steal from or vandalize them. Because if they offend the wrong D'Ihne, they might find themselves growing long ears and a tail and turning into an ass — or worse." He approached the wagon where the horses were patiently munching the grass at the side of the road. "Now, which of you kind ladies and beautiful faeries wants to come spend a night in town?"

"Me! Me! Me!" Dora called, bouncing up and down. Jim chuckled.

"Alright then," he grinned. "Kode, why don't you take the girls and ride us into town? I can wait in the back with these two cretins."

"Do you think that's a good idea?" Jak asked nervously.

"I do," Jim affirmed. "That's why I suggested it. It's certainly not a bad idea." He smiled back at the church. "I have a good feeling about this place."

"Then let's go investigate," Allie encouraged, clambering up onto the seat at the front of the wagon. Kode picked up Dora and climbed up to join her.

"I have a bad feeling about this..." Krill sighed quietly to himself. Jak gave him a nervous look. "I always have a bad feeling if Jim has a good one."

"That is a downright lie, and you know it," Jim disputed.

Without changing his serious expression Krill winked at him. Jak grimaced.

"Do I really have to ride in the back with you two?"

"Yes," Krill insisted, guiding her there as they followed Jim. "You have to help me keep him from being inappropriate."

"That's impossible!"

"Thank you," Jim smirked.

"That's not a compliment, Jim," Jak grated. "You're the worst."

"That is Lord Skankington to you, missy," he corrected, and led them into the back of the wagon. He left the back door open so that they could watch the scenery roll by and the church fade into the distance. Then he knocked twice on the back wall to give the all-clear. The Banging Wagon banged and rattled down the lane.

CHAPTER SEVEN

The road was so narrow it was more of a lane. Trees lined it in thick clusters, helping to separate the lane from the fields and paddocks. The church slowly disappeared from view behind curtains of green leaves as they moved downhill. Afternoon light spilt warm and golden through the branches. The closer they got, the louder the sounds of the village grew. Music was playing and people were laughing. Delicious smells wafted up through the air.

"Is that a fair?" Jak asked.

"A festival," Jim grinned, his eyes bright.

"Did you know about this?" Krill glared at him suspiciously.

"How could I possibly?" Jim replied with feigned innocence. His expression was hungry, but not for something to eat. While his answer was fair, the whole interaction made Jak wonder. It didn't seem possible that Jim could have known there was a festival on, but the fact that Krill had asked made it suspicious. Not to mention, the look on Jim's face was akin to the expression of a cat in the cream, and they weren't even there yet.

The sounds of the festival grew louder as they approached. Footsteps sounded on the road. People were rushing towards them. Jim was standing at the back of the wagon, hanging onto the wall. All the action was at the other end and he wasn't going to miss out. From outside the wagon a voice called out.

"Are you lot faerie folk?"

Jim swung around to hang out the side of the back door on the step. "Some would call us that," he replied.

His claim was met with excited clamouring. Jim grabbed a pitcher from inside — the one that sat beside the water pitcher — and sauntered casually from the wagon. Jak peeked nervously around. It was a festival. Streamers hung from the trees and streets. Tents and stalls were set up in front of shops. It was a little cobblestone town that reminded her of the richer parts of her own village. The people were dressed in bright colours. Many of them were off dancing, but a small crowd had gathered to greet the wagon.

Jim was walking amongst them, chatting like they were old friends. He had started pouring freely from the pitcher to anyone who held up a glass. Jak noted the colour of the liquid. She could feel someone else leaning around her and knew Krill was also peering out.

"Is that wine?" she asked.

"It is," the fae replied.

"He has a pitcher of wine that never runs out?!"

"Don't worry, Jak," Krill sighed. "Luckily for us, Jim decided one vice was enough, and he went with nymphomania rather than alcoholism. Just… try and keep your distance from him this evening."

With those parting words of advice, Krill stepped lightly down from the wagon and followed Jim towards the crowd. He stopped at the front of the wagon where the girls were still waiting with Kode, fully entranced by all the attention they were receiving.

"Park the wagon up here in the trees," Krill instructed quietly. "All things considered, we should set the girls' camp up away from the party tonight, and I can enchant the forest."

Kode nodded in agreement. Jak had followed Krill out and she helped her sisters down as the two fae went to park the wagon. Dora pointed down the street to a square where people were dancing around a brightly coloured statue.

"Can we go dancing?" she asked Jak imploringly. Wary as always, Jak couldn't think of any reason to say no. Life had been hard the last year, and even more chaotic recently. The girls deserved a bit of fun. Jak gave Dora a smile and a nod, and then walked them down the street.

Word of their arrival had rushed ahead of them, and apparently it was throwing the party into a full swing. The crowd looked so pleased to see them that Jak half expected to find she knew these people. Not a single one looked familiar though. She walked Dora and Allie to the square, but as soon as they were close, the girls raced off to join the other children dancing. They were warmly welcomed, and Jak felt herself start to relax and smile as she watched them. She stood on the edge of the square and kept herself away from the dancers. It gave her a good view of the party.

It also gave her a good view of her sisters making themselves the centre of attention. Allie instantly and almost methodically drew a crowd of boys to her. Dora looked like she was enthralling the children her own age with tales of becoming a fairy princess. She was proudly showing off her beautiful flower crown, which hadn't aged a day since she'd put it on. It also gave her a good view of the dancers. The townsfolk were spinning each other in circles and passing partners to the music. It was an old celebratory jig. Jak knew it. She hadn't danced it in years. The people were laughing and smiling. She swallowed a faint wave of nostalgia.

"Come dance with me, Jellybean."

Jak looked and found Jim standing at her shoulder. He held a hand out and smiled his warm smile. Jak shook her head and waved him off.

"No, I don't— um…" she stammered her refusal. "I don't like dancing. I don't feel comfortable dancing."

"You don't feel comfortable dancing?" He stared at her in complete incomprehension as though she had just told him she'd swallowed a basket of snakes. "Everyone likes dancing."

"No, Jim, they don't," she chuckled ruefully. "I don't."

She'd never seen him look so bewildered before. His brow furrowed as he gave this due consideration.

"You used to though…" he mused. "Back a long time ago. Before boys asking you to dance made you feel awkward. Before life got hard and the village became cold. Before you cared what people thought of you. Before your inhibitions swallowed you. When you were a little girl… you used to dance then. You loved it."

Now it was her turn to be shocked. Hearing him say it like that, like he knew her, was strange. It wasn't wrong though. Her breath was caught in her throat at the memory, as though he'd conjured it by speaking it.

"I… I used to dance at the festivals…" she admitted slowly, heartbrokenly. "With my dad…"

For a moment neither of them said anything. He knew about that too. He held out his hand to her again, confidently.

"Come dance with me, Jellybean." It wasn't a command. It was just a kind invitation. Yet there was no way she could refuse it. He knew now, and he wasn't invading her life with this knowledge. He was inviting her into his. She took his hand.

The same warm, sure grip that had shook her hand in Rutsborough pulled her away to the dancing crowd. Jim spun her into the circle and the other dancers included them instantly. It was like stepping back in time. She still remembered how to do it, and the movement came naturally. Jak clasped hands with the ladies on both sides of her in the circle. She kept her feet skipping in time to the music. They stepped and turned and clapped. Jak helped spin one of the ladies beside her into the middle. The woman caught her partner in the centre. They linked arms and began to dance and spin while the group danced around them.

Jak turned and skipped one way, then the other. On one side of her was a blonde girl nearly her own age. On the other was a lady older than her mother, with grey hair and a long patchwork blue skirt. They were smiling and laughing as the group danced around the couple.

Jak realised she was too. Everyone broke off, linked arms to spin, and came back to the circle as the couple returned. Now the next two were spun in by the group. Jak was one of the next ones.

She panicked for a moment. The idea of suddenly being the centre of attention was too much, but Jim caught her and it suddenly wasn't so frightening.

"I got you, kid," he promised. "Okay. Step. Turn. Spin."

She did as she was told without pausing to think. Jim, of course, was born to be the centre of attention, and was making the dance his own. She was glad he was a strong leader, because she could follow without too much trouble. People were cheering them.

"Dip," he instructed with a grin and little warning. Jak hung on tightly as he leant her back, but he wasn't going to drop her and she was still laughing. It wasn't scary anymore. It was just fun. More than that, she knew she looked good at it. She was learning about him to. When it came to musical talent Jim hadn't been much of a singer, but boy could he dance. She had to hand him that. She just did as he told her and let him swing her around to the music. It was fun.

"Spin. Spin more. Twist. Snap. Step. Look at that! You got this! What a natural!"

"Thanks Jim," she beamed.

"I just like seeing you smile…"

"Don't make it weird!" she protested as the group cheered and broke up to link arms.

Jim let her go with a cackle as they parted to re-join the other dancers. Jak linked arms with the other ladies again as she shook her head. What a dick. Still, she was smiling, she was laughing, and she was dancing. She was dancing for the first time in years and she did love it. Maybe he wasn't all bad.

The dance continued and Jak didn't have to return to the middle again. The group was large enough that she was happy holding hands and linking arms with the other women. Every few rounds they would link up with the men and bridge and swap and turn. At some point, Jim was gone. She didn't know when it happened, but when she finally realised she was dancing only with people she had never met, it didn't bother her. These were good people. Kind people who had included her.

By the time she stopped, she was hot and breathless. With the others, she applauded the band in the street that played for them. When they struck up their next song, she politely bowed out and moved to the edge of the square. She did not need another dance. What she needed was a drink. Her sisters were still in sight and enjoying themselves. That made her smile more. It was nice to see them so happy.

"Hi," a soft voice spoke at Jak's side.

She turned and came face to face with the blonde lady from the dance. The girl was petite and her pale face was framed by her soft straight hair. She was wearing a pale rose coloured dress with a golden sash. She gave Jak a small smile and held out a steaming mug.

"You look like you could use this."

Jak stammered awkwardly. She wanted to say she couldn't afford it. Except she noticed that no one along the street of vendors seemed to be paying, and somehow the presence of the pretty girl at her side tied her tongue.

"It's free," the girl extrapolated from her stuttering with a grin. "The vendors are funded by the town on fair day. Everyone chips in." She handed Jak the mug. "I'm Alice."

"Thanks…" Jak blushed. "Um, I—I'm Jak."

"Are you one of the faerie folk?" Alice asked curiously.

"No," Jak shook her head awkwardly. "I'm not a faerie. I'm just travelling with them. My sisters and I were driven out of our town, and the fae kindly picked us up."

"You were driven out?"

"My little sister," Jak indicated. "She thinks she's a faerie, or fairy, princess, but there was an accident and the village thought she was a witch. They wanted to kill her."

"That's awful!" Alice exclaimed. She turned shocked eyes to where Dora was dancing with the other children. "What kind of town would persecute a child? And what kind of town drives out their fae?"

Jak shrugged self-consciously and took a sip from the mug. The hot drink was a mulled wine that warmed her down to her toes. She was still warm after the dance, but this was a different kind of warm. This was the same kind of warm she got from standing close to Alice. The young lady at her side was watching Dora with a frown that spoke volumes about her opinion of the girls' hometown, but she was leaning in towards Jak with an easiness that showed she didn't hold their home against them.

Drinking wasn't something Jak normally did, but she had tried a wine similar to this a few times when their mother had made it. That had only been sips from her mother's drink though. This was her own mug, and drinking it helped to avoid conversation. Conversation with pretty girls was so incredibly difficult. Her new companion wasn't put off though.

"So how long have you been travelling with the fae?" Alice asked.

"Not that long," Jak admitted. "It's strange… it probably feels longer than it has been. But I guess that's a side effect of everything in your life turning into magic."

Alice laughed. "What kind of things do they do with magic?"

"Everything," Jak declared, taking another gulp of wine. "It's bizarre and amazing. Everything is done with magic. The guy who owns the wagon is the one who looks human, and he has magic stuff for everything. He's the one who pulled me into the dance." There were cries of delight and wonder further back up the street. "That's probably him too," Jak muttered.

People were rushing back up the street to see what was going on. Jak sighed and drank more of her wine, before turning and wandering up to see what was going on. Alice followed her up the cobbled lane. They walked up through the tight crowd, under rows of flags and coloured lanterns, beneath what was fast becoming twilight. The crowd had gathered around something. The two girls edged their way towards the front.

"What's going on?" Alice asked the other townsfolk. "What happened?"

"That faerie man just unrolled this rug from the back of the wagon and laid it on the ground," someone answered excitedly. "Right there on the ground it turned into a pool of champagne! A real one! It's huge!"

Jak got to the front of the group to see a swimming pool in the ground full of rose-coloured fizzy liquid. She made a horrified strangled noise and covered her eyes with her hand as she also realised she was just in time to see Jim strip completely naked and jump in.

"No one needs to see that," she declared to an audience that wasn't listening. Alice chuckled cutely at her side. "No, seriously, why is he like this?" Jak asked plaintively.

"I think he was just born this way…" a familiar dry voice answered not far away.

Jak opened her eyes and looked for Krill. The fae stood with an alarmingly large glass of wine, watching the pool with a sardonic expression. Jak edged away from Alice and towards her faerie friend. She watched him watch the pool, then she looked back at the pool. It was nearly safe to look. Not safe enough. She averted her eyes again.

"He really swims naked in champagne? With an audience?" she said.

"You can behold your own evidence, Jak," Krill smirked at the pool. "Think about what you just said; isn't that the most Jim thing you've ever heard of?

Doesn't it just sum him up entirely?"

"Is this fun for you?"

"It is what it is," Krill shrugged. "He's having fun, and he's not hurting anyone, which is nice. I can't complain. I'm not much of a party-goer, myself. When you've been raised your entire existence just to kill people, parties don't tend to be something you attend unless it's for work."

"You two are complete opposites, aren't you?"

"Sometimes I wonder that myself…" Krill mused. He chuckled at the pool. Jak turned to look. She turned back very quickly and drained her mug. Kode was in the process of stripping down to join his boyfriend. She heard him jump in and Krill nodded his head to Jak. She turned to follow his gaze and saw Allie and Dora at the front of the crowd.

"Swimming!" Dora crowed delightedly.

Jak made a choking sound and went for them. "Oh no!" she called to Dora. "None of this! You are not getting in there!"

"Yes I am!" Dora protested, kicking off her shoes. "I want to go swimming with Kode!"

"Not in there! Not like that!" Jak insisted, reaching the little girl.

Allie saw the impending tantrum coming and snuck back the way Jak had come. Krill caught her with a look and she stopped edging away.

"What?" she challenged him.

"I didn't say anything," Krill replied, taking a long drink from his glass. Allie gave him a mischievous glance. "What?" he asked, finally acknowledging the look. He knew she'd been watching Kode strip down and swim.

"I can see why you married him..." she said cheekily.

Krill smiled deeply into his glass. He liked the middle sister, but he felt a little sorry for Jak. Sometimes Allie seemed like the smarter one, and there were certain areas where she was definitely the most mature and cunning.

"That's not why I married him," he replied softly. "It was just a bonus."

Allie grinned wickedly at him, and the two of them turned their attention to the fight that was occurring at the pool edge. Dora was shrieking and struggling out of her dress. Jak was holding her by the wrist and scolding her. They both seemed unaware that around them other people were stripping down to their underwear to go swimming with the faeries. Allie gave the whole situation a raised eyebrow.

"You'd disapprove if I pushed them both in, wouldn't you?" she asked.

"I would," Krill agreed. "You'd upset your sister, and that would make things worse."

"Fiiiine..." Allie pouted. She strode back over to her sisters. "Guys! Enough!" she yelled at them. "Jak, let her go swimming with everyone else. Dora, keep your undergarments on and you can go in. Deal?"

"No," Jak protested. "It's champagne. I'm not having her swimming in that."

"Okay, it's disgusting, sure," Allie shrugged. "But so is everything Jim does, and you seem to like him well enough. Besides, it looks pretty harmless."

"Swimming!" Dora crowed. She took her opportunity to run away from Jak and jumped in the pool, still in her singlet and pants.

Jak glowered at Allie. Allie just shrugged at her.

"She's having fun, Jak. Just let her be. Look, Jim's getting out." She pointed.

Jak turned on autopilot and then wheeled back around. "Argh! Why would you point that out?! Allie, don't look—!"

"Seriously, Jak?" Allie scoffed at her. The look she gave her older sister was almost pitying. "Are you really going to try and tell me you're not afraid of penises again?" She stared her sister down and Jak looked too shocked and angry to speak. Allie shrugged at her. "You have got to find a way past this, Sis. I'm going dancing again. I left some cute boys back there, and I'm not afraid like you are."

"Allie, don't you dare!" Jak yelled, but Allie completely ignored her and was already slipping away through the crowd. Jak wanted to yell and scream in frustration, but she didn't want to make more of a scene. Instead, she stomped away. There were side streets and back alleys in the town that didn't seem to have made the cut for the party. Jak stomped into one of them and loitered by the quieter entrance. She was still holding the empty mug, and she wanted to smash it on the ground in case it would make her feel better, but that seemed awfully rude. Instead, she just sighed to herself and let the anger seep out. She was just trying to look after her sisters, but they seemed so set on getting themselves in trouble.

"Something ails you, M'Lady?"

Jak looked up to see Jim lean against the wall beside her. He was only wearing a towel around his waist and his wet hair was slicked back. In his hands were a glass and his pitcher. The very air around him smelled fruity and he still dripped.

"Oh, not you…" Jak groaned.

"Thank goodness," Jim smirked. "I would hate to think I was the cause of any of your problems."

"You're the cause of most of my problems, Lord Skankington!"

"Do you really believe that, or are you just mad?" he asked shrewdly.

Jak's frustration wilted horribly in the face of his logic. It was terribly rude of him not to give her some kind of bait to fuel her fury when she felt like this.

"Mug out," he instructed. "Have a drink, and talk to me about what's wrong."

Jak held out her mug and Jim filled it liberally with wine. He lounged comfortably against the stone wall of the house behind them and drank from his own glass. Jak couldn't help but wonder how often he got the glass and the pitcher mixed up. She could imagine him casually drinking from both.

"So, what's up, my little Jellybean? I saw you fighting with your sisters. You didn't want Dora going swimming."

"Why is it so weird that I don't want a seven-year-old swimming in champagne?" Jak demanded.

"She's fine, Jak," Jim assured, indicating the pool.

"Look at her. She's happy. This isn't about her."

They both looked at the pool on the edge of town. People were splashing and laughing about. Dora was visible riding around on Kode's shoulders. Her dark curls were plastered to her face and neck and she was shrieking and laughing in delight.

"It's sticky!" she cried out with a giggle.

Jak met Jim's gaze at her little sister's pronouncement. The twinkle in his eye was enough to make her down her drink and hold the empty mug out. He laughed and refilled it.

"That's my girl," Jim approved warmly. "Now, while you drink that one, explain to me what scares you and why."

"What does that have to do with anything?" Jak took another sip. The pitcher wine was surprisingly good. She had not expected to like it so much. That said, it was Jim. The pool was probably delicious too. He was fairly consistent.

"The fight with Dora," Jim elaborated. "You didn't want her in the pool. Why? What scared you about that?"

"I'm not the weird one in this," Jak defended hotly. "It is not weird of me to not want my little sister swimming in a pool of champagne with naked men."

"I think you just about nailed it on the head then," Jim encouraged. "Focus in."

"No," Jak huffed, drinking more. "I know what I mean and that's fine."

"Nudity bothers you, doesn't it?" Jim wasn't really asking. He knew, but he wasn't going to try and make her say it anymore. "You're scared of nakedness. Look at her, kid. Does she look bothered to you? Do you really think anyone is going to hurt her by choosing not to wear clothes? Do you think Kode would ever hurt her?"

"It just…" Jak didn't know what to say. "It's just not decent. It's inappropriate to just… hang it all out there."

"Why?" This time he was really asking. Jak could tell he truly didn't understand at all. Jim was a very free spirit, and clothes were something he usually thought of as optional. He didn't understand indecency — of any kind, she considered wryly. Jim listed sideways and leaned in closer to her. "They're just bodies, Jak. Everyone's got one. If I took my towel off you would run away screaming, and I don't get that at all. Why does it scare you? I mean… what's the difference? You know I'm naked underneath it, right?"

"Just… leave me alone…" Jak grumbled, drinking her wine.

"You've got a high and mighty stance about this that is completely unjustified," he insisted. "You're naked under your clothes too."

"Just stop talking!" she complained loudly. For some reason it was hard to think straight, and she couldn't deal with conversation right now. She didn't like that he was so clearly articulating his argument and ignoring hers, especially when she didn't know how to effectively debate her side.

Someone appeared on the other side of Jim, and Jak recognised the soft feminine voice that spoke.

"I'm not interrupting, am I?" It was Alice, the cute

blonde girl from before. She was watching them both with an amused expression.

"Why hello," Jim smiled winningly at her. "Not at all. I'm Jim."

"Alice," she introduced herself. She eyed up Jim's casual flirtatiousness and Jak's uncomfortable embarrassment. "Are you her dad?"

Instantly they both responded with shocked cries of denial. Jak protested as firmly as she could, and Jim pulled a face at the notion.

"How old do you think I look?" he demanded.

Alice looked him very deliberately up and down. "Old enough."

Jak was fairly sure Jim had never looked so offended in his whole life. She held out her mug again. He didn't even notice. He was too busy staring down the girl, and she wasn't caving at all. Finally, he turned away. He ignored Alice long enough to refill Jak's mug again, then he stalked off with a disgusted mutter.

"Humans..." he sulked as he sauntered away. His steps took him up the road towards the party again. Jak watched him go. There was something about him. He moved through the crowd with grace and ease. People were drawn to him. He didn't bid them, but they couldn't seem to help themselves. Even as he neared the band still playing for the dancers, she heard the music slowly start to change. It became more sultry, and unnervingly she felt the urge to run out and join the others swaying to it.

"Is he really a faerie?" Alice asked at her side. The tiny blonde lady watched him critically as he stopped to flirt with the band. "He's not like any fae I've ever seen. You'd think he'd be a bit more… impressive."

"His father's a fae," Jak answered numbly. Alice looked at her, but Jak couldn't take her eyes off the strange man in the towel. "I'm so sure of it," she insisted quietly. "I can't prove it, and he won't admit it, but I think he's a demigod. Like the heroes of old."

"Like a hero of legend?" Alice questioned dubiously. "He doesn't really look like it. Are you sure you don't just… I don't know… have a biased opinion of him?"

"I don't like him that much," Jak grinned. "He's a complete dick most of the time. But… there's something about him. Something actually magical. I don't think he's truly a faerie, but I think he's half faerie. Half god. I think his dad is Fæmör."

"I think he wishes his dad was Fæmör," Alice chuckled, standing with Jak near the wall and watching him. "He's not pretty enough to have the god of seduction as a father."

"He's got to have something going for him," Jak muttered. "He managed to trick the two fae we travel with into his bed somehow. Hey—!" Jak's mug was pulled up from her grasp by long elegant fingers. She turned around to find Krill reaching over her to steal the mug. He regarded her coolly and she pulled a face. "Why are you always behind me when I'm talking about you?"

"What did I tell you, Jak?" he sighed at her.

"I dunno," she shrugged. "Give back."

"Not a chance," Krill took a long drink from the mug. "This is mine now. You've had quite enough."

"Is that true though?" Alice asked him. "Did you really end up in his sheets?"

"Jim has a lot to like about him," Krill replied.

"Like the fact that he's a demigod…" Jak muttered.

"Jak," Krill said crisply. "You're drunk. What did I tell you about staying away from Jim?"

"You're drunk," Jak accused. "You're drunk too!"

"I'm magical. I don't get drunk," Krill retorted. "I am a child of Frézíān. Nothing can stop me."

"A child of Frézíān?" Alice repeated with a touch of awe. "What kind of faerie are you?"

"I am called Elkrillendé," he introduced himself. "I was once the D'Hiris: Commander and Chief of the D'rö-Hadās, Queen Clōudiá's army of Head Hunters."

Alice stared at him for a moment. She took in the strange magical fae. He was slim and beautiful like a golden sapling. She laughed.

"No, seriously," she chuckled, "what are you? Are you like a fire sprite?"

Krill just gave her a mysterious smile and wandered away. He took Jak's mug, and if she'd been paying enough attention she would have been mad, but as it was the new revelation had hit her like a brick. Äulé had called Krill D'rö-Hadās and the blonde fae had admitted to being one of them, but now Jak understood why he really didn't want to talk about it. He hadn't just been one. He had been the head of the army. The Chief Head Hunter. Krill wasn't just good — he was the best.

"Huh…" was all Jak manged to articulate her thoughts.

"What's that about?" Alice asked, leaning in closer.

"I'm pretty sure that was the truth," Jak replied. "It makes his story even more scandalous."

"You know it?"

"Kinda…"

"Want to tell me?"

Jak looked back at the cute blonde girl grinning impishly at her. She kind of did want to tell her, as much as she thought she could anyway. Her face must have given her away, because Alice took her hand with a smile.

"Come with me," she encouraged, pulling her away from the party. The two of them snuck around the edges of the festival and Alice led her to a large empty stable. There was a small hayloft up the top, and the two of them clambered up and crashed in the hay. It was warm and peaceful up there, and Jak found she was glad to get away from it all.

"So, tell me about the faeries," Alice requested, getting comfortable in the hay and fidgeting with a piece of straw.

"So, Krill…" Jak began slightly drunkenly. "That's what we call him. We call him Krill. It sounds like he was the head of Clōudiá's army. He was the Chief Head Hunter, and he trained all the others. He's probably like the best assassin ever."

"He doesn't look it," Alice commented. "He looks pretty and delicate."

"Looks can be deceiving with faeries," Jak commented. She paused a moment. There was a brief second where she really felt she had been on the cusp of something important, but her thoughts were more slurred than her words and she lost it. "Anyway, Krill was the head of the army. Kode, the other pretty one, he's Clōudiá's son, although it sounds like she never really acknowledged him. But even so. Still scandalous."

"Because…?"

"Oh, right. They're married. They eloped. The head of her army deserted to run away with her son and they left the Golden City like ten years ago or something. Then the poor buggers ended up with Jim. I don't know how that happened, or why they stayed, or what they see in him, but there you go."

"You said he was a demigod? Maybe there's something in that?"

"There has to be," Jak agreed, flopping back into the hay. "He has literally no other appeal. To be fair, I'm pretty sure Kode could love anyone, but Jim's not Krill's usual type. Not from the looks of things. I know I'm not exactly a good judge, but I don't think he's much to look at and he's annoying and slutty. Even Allie doesn't like him, thank the gods, and she's into anything that passes for a boy."

Alice giggled and flopped back into the hay with Jak.

"Tell me more," she requested. "Do you know any other faeries?"

"Well, we know Äulé," Jak mused. "He's a gnome. A Drifter. Pretty sure he has a big family, but he pops up a lot when we summon at Fora markings. My sisters and I grew up with him about in the forest behind our house. There was a Fora rune there and our parents always taught us to leave some bread and milk out for him."

"When was the last time you saw him?"

"Oh, just this morning," Jak shrugged. "We summoned him from a road marker this morning to ask about our Mum. We're trying to find her. Jim said we should ask faeries, so we tried asking Äulé, but he just gave us a bit of a run around."

"Wait, so Jim can summon faeries? He summoned a faerie just outside of town?"

"Well, no…" Jak tried to remember. "Dora was the one who actually summoned him."

"But…" Alice looked slightly confused. She leant in closer to Jak. "Your faeries can summon other faeries, right? How else did you summon one?"

"Have you never summoned faeries? It's not that hard. You mostly just do it with food. They'll come for food. Then, if you want something, you have to have a token or something to barter with. Have you really never done that?"

"We used to…" Alice admitted sadly. "But… the faeries have stopped coming."

Jak sat up suddenly. The action nearly crashed her into the girl at her side and she apologised, but Alice didn't worry or move back.

"What do you mean?" Jak muttered drunkenly.

"The faeries stopped answering calls," Alice said. "About a year ago now. At first we were scared because we thought we had done something wrong. Then we asked around. All the villages in the region say the same thing: the faeries don't answer anymore. Most of us haven't seen a faerie in more than a year now. They used to roam the region. Pranksters mostly. They would play tricks and move fenceposts and change markers and steal socks — the usual. There's been nothing like that. No sign of them. It's like all the faeries just disappeared a year ago with no explanation. All the magic just went away. We can't even call them now. No one answers prayers. Children play in the mushroom circles without consequence. Although... unwatched bread and milk still vanish if you leave it out..." she mused thoughtfully. "That's why we don't understand what's happening. They must still be around, we're just not doing whatever they need us to. It's also why we were so excited when the wagon pulled up. Your friends are the first faeries we've seen in ages. We were scared the faeries left because we'd made them angry. That's why we we've been throwing celebrations to try and tempt them back. Surely if we have festivals in honour of the gods, they will hear us and return."

"Aren't parties Fæmör's territory?" Jak asked with dread. She blushed as she remembered the window.

"Of course," Alice agreed. "But we celebrate all the gods here." She grinned. "Everyone loves a good time. They wouldn't ignore a festival about them. Our valley builds statues and shrines to Fæmör's brother Talámh as the deity of wealth and the home, and of course to Fæmör's lover Ínrío who is the patron of the valley as well as the guardian of animals and family."

"Fæmör's what?!" Jak choked.

Alice laughed at her. "Oh, come on! Everyone knows that!"

"I suppose..." Jak muttered, nestling into the hay.

She did know it, she just hadn't been thinking about it. She was trying to forget all the information Allie had been prying for at the church about incestuous gods. Also, the word 'lover' alarmed her right now. She wasn't sure why.

"We live in Cröck'ko-rú," Alice told her like it meant something. "Our valley is supposedly the site of that story. It was made by Ínrío while he was with Ĝoŕgomghōul's sons."

"Do I want to know this story...?" Jak muttered. Alice laughed at her. She had a pretty little chuckle.

"Ínrío used Roïgola'a'lanaū to blast a crater in the earth when his little brother Crŷstïar tricked him into thinking they were under attack," she recounted. "That crater became this valley."

"Oh," Jak mused. That was actually a perfectly fine story. She wasn't looking at her new friend lying beside her, and had no idea Alice was still grinning.

"Legend has it, Ínrío and Fæmör were making love at the time," she continued. "The god of the sun was intensely and passionately distracted inside Fæmör when their little brother decided to have some fun at their expense, and shot Ínrío with a small arrow in his exposed behind. Crŷstïar burst in after firing and cried that they were under attack. Ínrío, enraged, leapt up and struck with the power of the Golden City. He'd blasted the entire crater of Cröck'ko-rú before he realised Crŷstïar was doubled over in hysterics watching him with a short-bow in hand."

Jak was scarlet and staring hard at the ceiling of the barn. The wood was a pale pine colour with an even grain that was suddenly deeply fascinating, if a little fuzzy at the edges. Still, she was smiling a bit. It was mildly funny.

"Why are all the stories about the gods like that?" she muttered, embarrassed just to hear it.

"I don't know," Alice shrugged with a grin. "Maybe they're not. Maybe those are just the ones people like to tell. They're gods after all, people probably like the stories that make them sound more human."

"The foibles of the divine..." Jak mused to the ceiling, aware of the warmth of Alice's body close to hers. "D'Ihne," she corrected herself drunkenly, trying to keep her mind on track. There was so much to consider right now, but she could only focus on one thing at a time. She didn't want that thing to be god sex. But something had been important. Before they'd gotten off topic. Something, before Alice had cast her cute looks and giggled at her. She turned back to the girl in the hay as she remembered. "You threw a party for the fae and we showed up...?"

"It can't be a coincidence, can't it?" Alice pestered. "I mean... you're not the usual sprites we would have expected, but you said they were children of the gods. You said the pretty one was the son of Clōudiá herself!"

Jak was still reeling. Some of this felt like it should be important, but she was too dizzy to make real sense of it. Alice was wearing a soft perfume that smelt of roses.

"It could be a coincidence..." she admitted weakly, trying to stay focused. "We were just travelling this way anyway..."

"Do you really believe in magical coincidences?" Alice asked. From her tone it was clear that she didn't.

"I don't know what I believe," Jak sighed. She was finding it incredibly hard to think, and had to admit to herself that she might have been slightly drunk. However, that wasn't the only thing making it hard to think. She was becoming consciously aware that she was warm and comfy here in the hay, and Alice was really very close to her. The young woman was looking at her with curious and hopeful eyes. Jak had never been looked at like that before. She realised she wanted to hold the blonde girl's hand, but her palms were awkwardly sweaty, and life suddenly seemed very strange and frightening.

"I don't believe you're here by coincidence," Alice insisted stubbornly. "Maybe you're a sign that the faeries are coming back."

"Maybe if you try summoning one now you'll find you can," Jak suggested. Her sudden realisation that she was, in fact, drunk was causing her to panic. Her head was spinning. What if she made questionable decisions? What if getting drunk was a questionable decision? She was supposed to be the responsible one. This was not responsible. Krill had warned her to stay away from Jim. Had he known what would happen? Now she was alone in a hayloft with a pretty girl. She kind of wanted to be alone in a hayloft with a pretty girl, which meant it was exactly what she shouldn't be doing, and therefore she no longer wanted to be here. Alice didn't look like she was sharing any of Jak's concerns. Which was crazy, because how could she not be thinking exactly what Jak was thinking?

"What if it doesn't work though?" Alice sighed. "How do you do it? How do you make faeries come to you?"

"I don't," Jak replied quickly. "It's been a long time since I even tried to summon a faerie — years. Dora always does it. You could ask Jim what's going on with the faeries. I bet he'd know."

"Y'know, for someone you don't like that much, you sure talk about him a lot…" Alice raised suggestively. Everything about the way she said it sounded like bait. To Jak's ears, it sounded like an invitation for admission. Alice wanted her to say she didn't like boys. Or she didn't want that and Jak was reading non-existent insinuations into the conversation in a drunken panic. Either way, she had reached breaking point.

"I have to go," she announced suddenly, getting up and heading for the ladder.

"Wait, what?" Alice exclaimed in confusion. "What's wrong?"

"Nothing. I'm just leaving," Jak panicked and made it even more awkward. She half-staggered, half-dropped from the ladder and raced out of the stables. In the furthest recesses of her mind she felt that perhaps she had been rude, but she was too scared to worry about that right now. She wasn't scared of Alice, but more of herself. She was scared of the future of drunk Jak. Scared of the decisions she might make. The easiest thing to do was take herself out of all possible awkward situations. Which was impossible, because just existing was awkward.

Outside, the party was still in full swing. If anything, it was becoming more exuberant. With a kind of sick horror, Jak realised she was looking for Jim. She felt scared and vulnerable, and she was looking for something safe and familiar. Despite the warnings, something was telling her that Jim was somewhere safe. He wasn't who she found though. Instead, she ran into Kode. The younger fae was out of the pool and dressed again. He was bouncing happily between crowds of admirers. He smiled when he saw her.

"Jak!" the pretty blonde faerie beamed at her.

"Kode," Jak caught him by the shoulders. He took in her condition with one look and his usually joyful expression became serious.

"What's wrong?" he asked. "You weren't with Jim, were you?"

"No," Jak shook her head, once again partially wondering why that would be so bad right now. "I'm just drunk."

"That you are," he smiled sympathetically. "Sit here. Wait." Kode sat her down on a garden wall at the side of the street. He disappeared into the crowd of people who wandered and danced back and forth. Jak sat on the low stone wall feeling slightly dizzy and hoping she wasn't about to fall backwards into someone's rosebush. Kode was back within a moment and he held out a glass of water in one hand.

"Drink," he instructed. Jak took the glass and gulped it down. She hadn't even realised she was thirsty. Kode held out a large hot pie in the other hand. "Eat."

It was suddenly unbelievable that anyone could

have considered Kode not to be the smart one. He was a genius, and the pie was so good. The gentle fae stood holding the empty glass and watching her eat with a delicate smile on his pretty face. Jak looked up at him as she finished eating. The pie and the water and the company had settled her down again. She was back to feeling like a person instead of an anxious mess.

"Thank you," she said.

"You're welcome," he smiled. "I think we should get you to bed though. You look pretty tired."

"I am tired," Jak agreed, suddenly realising.

"It's probably later than you think it is, if you've been drinking away the hours," he smiled. "Come on, up you get." Kode helped Jak to her feet and led her away from the party. They passed the pool on their way out of town and Jak saw people still frolicking around in it. Braziers had been erected around it to light the area properly now that darkness had fallen.

The night was cool and clear and stars sparkled in the sky. Set back in the silence of the trees was their green tent. Jak had never been so happy to see it. She stumbled on with Kode's guidance, and found everything already set up inside. The water pitcher was just inside the door, and Kode filled the glass again and held it out to her.

"Drink this and I'll go find the girls," he told her. "It's probably their bedtime as well."

Jak nodded gratefully and Kode left her to her glass of water and the peace of the forest. It felt like mere seconds later that she realised she had spent the entire evening drinking. She'd had three and a bit mugs of wine, and was finishing her second glass of water. Nature was calling. At least in the forest that had an easy solution.

Jak ducked out of the tent and crept away through the trees. She made sure she was far enough from the tent and the town that she wouldn't be disturbed, and crouched quietly behind a tree to relieve herself. As she was buckling her belt again afterwards, a sound startled her. For a moment she worried she wasn't out here alone. It sounded like people.

"I'm serious, Jim," Krill's voice came warningly through the trees. "No excuses. No apologies. You touch that girl and I'll gut you."

"I won't," Jim gasped. "You have my word. I swear. Uh, Krill—"

She crept deeper into the forest towards the sound and peered through the trees. Upon her discovery she cursed herself, her curiosity, and her exceptional eyesight.

It was the Banging Wagon. Jim and Krill were on the back step. Specifically, Jim was sprawled on the back step, on top of his discarded towel, and he was firmly pulling a half-dressed Krill over him. They were making out. From where she stood, a horrified Jak had a good angle on Krill's hand fiercely masturbating his human lover between them. Jim passionately clutched the fae tighter as they tongued each other. Krill's hand looked tight enough to be painful, but Jim was caught in the thrall of pleasure. He moved his lips to gently bite Krill's ear.

"I have you," he moaned. "I don't need anyone else."

Jak saw all of it in the fraction of a second it took her to squeeze her eyes shut and cover her face. Without thinking, and in sheer disgust, she wheeled around and fled into the forest. After about six strides she crashed into a tree. Enough of her brain woke up to explain that perhaps running through a dark forest with her eyes closed wasn't the best idea. In fact, now that she was pointing in the complete opposite direction, she could probably look where she was going while she ran away. Strangely enough, she felt suddenly sober. Sobriety did not comfort her, and it hadn't improved her cognitive processes.

She reached the tent wild-eyed and with a sense of mild insanity. She could hear the girls inside and saw Kode climbing back out the flap. Once again, his sweet smile faltered at the sight of her.

"Jak?" he rushed over to her and took her by the shoulders. "What's wrong? What happened?"

She couldn't bring herself to say. Instead, she just rested her forehead on his shoulder and tried to get her brain rebooted. Slowly and painfully, she recovered the ability to think, and promptly wished she couldn't. She straightened up with a sigh.

"I saw Jim and Krill..." she finally muttered.

"What's wrong?" Kode asked urgently. "Are they okay?"

"They were in the back of the wagon..." she couldn't make herself say it. Instead, she gestured by shaking her fist. Kode began to laugh. He looked like he was trying not to, but he clearly couldn't help himself.

"Sorry," he grinned. "Jim doesn't manage to get Krill

drunk very often, but when he does Krill can get quite frisky. That was part of the reason I thought I should get you girls to bed... before my husband and my boyfriend went down on each other in public."

"Ugh! That was likely?!"

"Well, it's happened before... I don't know if that makes it likely..." he chuckled.

"It's not funny..." Jak protested wearily. "It's gross, and I just had to see it."

"You didn't have to see it," Kode pointed out. "No one was making you look." He rubbed her shoulder soothingly. "I'm sorry it makes you so uncomfortable, Jak. But it's their bodies in their wagon — they're not doing anything wrong."

Jak wanted to protest, but she didn't know what to say. Finally, she settled petulantly for:

"Why is everyone so sex obsessed?"

Kode looked around. He regarded the tent and, in a show of concern Jak didn't expect from him, he motioned her away. They stepped into the trees a few meters and his big lavender eyes regarded her earnestly.

"Because it makes them happy," he explained. "Generally speaking, we are creatures that are biologically designed to get physical pleasure out of sex, and it makes us feel good. It's even better than eating chocolate cake that doesn't make you fat."

Despite herself, Jak giggled at his description. It certainly sounded good when he put it like that.

"That doesn't mean you have to be comfortable with it," he continued. "I'd recommend finding a way to get used to the idea, but in your own way and your own time. Don't let Allie or Jim or anyone push you around. You're very young, Jak. It's okay not to be ready to learn about things. It's okay if it takes you years to be ready. I hope it doesn't, for your sake, because the world isn't going to change, and I don't like seeing you uncomfortable in it. I'm not saying that you ever have to be comfortable walking in on other people — far from it. I'm just trying to explain that people are what they are, and they do what they do, and if you can get over the idea of it disgusting you, then you'll be happier. It's about your personal happiness within yourself and not letting others affect you so much."

Jak stared at him for what felt like a long time. "You're really very smart, aren't you?" she said finally.

"No," Kode smiled. "I'm not. I just know what I know. I'm a sex worker, Jak. People's pleasures and desires are literally my business. Making people happy and comfortable and confident is what I do. It's what I'm good at. I told you that before."

"But... making people happy and sex are different..."

"Sometimes," he chuckled. "Sometimes not. Depends on a lot of things." He gave her a reassuring half-hug. "I'm sorry life is unsettling right now. I'm sorry you're ending up in positions to see things that make you uncomfortable. But you'll get there, Jak. I know you will. In the meantime, Allie is making sure Dora gets her medicine and goes to bed. I suggest you join them."

"Why?" Jak muttered. "Are you going to go make

sure Jim and Krill's antics aren't unsupervised?"

Kode laughed. "See? You're not so startled when it's on your terms."

"I can psych myself up for banter when I've had time to get used to the idea," she muttered. "It just takes a while."

"You'll get there," he assured repeatedly, and ruffled her hair. "Now go to bed."

"Okay," Jak nodded with a smile. She left him and clambered into the tent. Inside it, Allie was climbing into her bunk after swaddling Dora in blankets. Jak joined her sisters by climbing into her own bed. They didn't speak, but they didn't let the fights from earlier hang over them either. Instead, they lay there peacefully while the muffled sounds of music and laughter serenaded them to sleep.

CHAPTER EIGHT

When Jak woke the next day she did not feel well. Her head hurt. The rest of her kinda hurt too. Her mouth tasted like sand. Dry sand. Overall it was a severely unpleasant sensation to join the day. The day in question had barely dawned. Her sisters were already up and packing.

"Why?" Jak protested weakly from the bed.

"We're hitting the road," Allie told her. "Are you hungover?"

"No..." she groaned.

Allie's answering grin told her that her little sister didn't believe her for an instant. Jak struggled painfully out of bed. Dora was still bundled up in blankets. She looked like a sleepy little mouse wearily checking her pack and cuddling her Binky bunny. The toy's long ears poked out of the nest of blankets and curls, adorned with the ever-present flower crown. The little girl gave a few weak coughs.

"How you doing, baby?" Jak asked her gently.

Dora just gave her a sleepy smile and a nod. Jak nodded back. It hurt. She haphazardly shoved everything into her pack. Her pack went on one shoulder and she tossed Dora's pack over her other shoulder. Then she picked up her little sister and carried her from the tent.

Jim and Kode were outside and they looked as bright and chirpy as dawn's first light. Jak begrudged them everything. It wasn't fair. Allie followed them out and Jim grinned at them all when he saw them.

"You ladies ready to go?" he asked.

"How are you so chipper this morning?" Jak grumbled at him.

The grin he flashed her was so smug she wanted to smack it from his face. He half shrugged as though he didn't know, and then sauntered over to the tent to bring it down. Kode smiled gently at them all. Jak turned her begrudging glare to him, except he looked rather sympathetic.

"Jim doesn't get hungover," Kode explained as he led them to the wagon. "He never has. I don't think he can."

"You're going to try and explain to me that that's not a demigod power?" Jak sulked. "What about you?"

"I don't drink," Kode smiled.

They reached the back of the wagon and stopped. It was standing wide open, and Jak recognised the still form of Krill in the back. The fae was lying on the floor between the aisles of junk. He was over the trapdoor, tangled in satin sheets, and pale even by his standards. For a moment, Jak felt worse just looking at him.

"My darling Krill, however," Kode was smiling, "can get quite seriously hungover."

"I'm dying," Krill lamented weakly without moving.

Kode grinned and climbed in over him. Jak half moved to cover Dora's eyes. She wasn't sure this was appropriate. But she kept herself back just in case. She didn't want to appear startled. Kode half-crawled, half-lay over his suffering husband and stroked his hair back from his face.

"You're not dying," he assured. "I would know. You are going to have to move though."

"Can't," Krill protested.

Jim appeared behind them all with a soft chuckle. "Elkrillendé are you still feeling sorry for yourself?"

"I hate you," Krill moaned from under his husband.

"Scooch, baby," Jim grinned. "We can't get in the wagon with you lying there."

"Why aren't we just sleeping in and staying in the village?" Jak asked. "They like us here."

"They do," Jim agreed. "But rule number one is never stick around for the morning after. The night is magic, but the next day the magic is gone. Don't ever let anyone see it. Like Krill here; stellar performance last night, can't get out of our way this morning."

"Fuck you," Krill muttered.

Dora and Allie shared a cheeky look at the cuss. Jak didn't have the energy to deal with it.

"Let him be," she grimaced. "If we have to go, Allie can travel with you two up front, and Dora and I can squeeze in with the stuff. There's space in there with Krill. The three of us are just going to keep sleeping anyway."

Everyone sober shared a glance. Jim shrugged. Kode clambered back off Krill. He looked over at Allie.

"You want to come ride with us?"

"I thought you'd never ask," she grinned. Allie

dumped her pack just inside the back door and raced around to the front of the wagon. Kode followed her gently.

Jak set Dora down on the back step. She stashed the other two packs with Allie's and then picked up her sleepy sister again.

"You sure you're going to be okay?" Jim asked.

"I'd be better if you never tried to get me drunk again," she retorted.

"Ouch," he cut in a sultry tone with a complete lack of offense. He leant in. "Way to push the blame. No one made you drink."

Jim was standing too close again, and Jak was glad she was holding Dora between them like a shield. Meeting his eye, she was hideously reminded of the last time she had seen him, and she turned her gaze away quickly with her cheeks burning in disgust. Dora was looking between them, like she knew there was something she wasn't understanding. Jak turned away quickly and clambered carefully into the wagon. She realised as she was walking that these were the same steps she had seen him on last night. Krill sprawled in the sheets on the floor was probably a remnant of where that event had gone.

"Don't move," she warned him. "We're coming by."

"Can't," Krill groaned.

Jak stepped carefully over the sprawled fae to the back of the wagon. She didn't look back at Jim, and she had no intention of doing so. He must have realised, because he began shutting the doors. Jak was setting Dora down in the back corner by a pile of junk, that included the rolled-up rug of last night's pool, when the doors closed completely and left them in the dark. There wasn't enough outside light yet to filter in through the cracks.

"It's dark…" Dora complained.

"I know, baby," Jak nodded. "You can just go back to sleep though."

There was a snap like someone clicking their fingers. Nearly a dozen tiny, dim lamps lit up over the shelves. It was plenty of light for the small enclosed space. Krill had half rolled over onto his back. He was pale and grimacing, but his body language said more about his condition than his graceful, immortal appearance would otherwise allow.

Dora nestled up against the pile of junk in the corner. She was still wrapped in her blankets and she looked cosy. Jak slid down the wall to sit on the ground as the caravan started to rumble away beneath them. Krill grimaced again as the caravan rocked and swayed. Jak shared an empathetic look with him. They both felt like trash. Within minutes, the swaying became bearable, and Dora began to snore quietly in the corner. Jak smiled at the sound. She wanted to lapse back into unconsciousness herself, but she felt too awful to relax.

"You said last night that you didn't get drunk," Jak spoke softly to Krill.

"I lied," he muttered.

Jak giggled. "Kode said Jim only manages to get you drunk once or twice a year."

"That sounds about right," he agreed reluctantly. "You'd think I would have learnt by now… but apparently not."

"For what it's worth, you look right terrible."

"Thank you," he sighed. "I feel it. You don't look so chipper yourself, child. I warned you. At least one of those hits I took for you, and it's worse at my age. Oh gods… I'm feeling all four hundred years today…"

"You were pretty drunk last night…" Jak agreed, her face flaming again.

"What would you know about it?" Krill scoffed weakly.

She thought about not answering, but it seemed dishonest. "I saw you…" she admitted with sickening embarrassment. "In the back of the wagon last night… with Jim."

"You…?" Krill's own cheeks began to dawn a soft pink. "You… saw that…?" He stirred painfully in the sheets to look at her. The blush in his face was delicate, but ashamed. "I'm sorry."

"Not as sorry as I am," Jak muttered, but she almost managed a smile. The fact that he had the decency to be embarrassed too comforted her. It made her feel that perhaps she wasn't so strange in her discomforts after all. She knew their society was different, but at least Krill seemed to think that having an audience wasn't as acceptable as Kode and Jim thought it was.

That said, she was starting to feel that perhaps Krill wasn't a normal fae. She had not forgotten his drunken slip last night — that he had been the leader of the D'rö-Hadās. Krill struggled up against the shelves and made it into a slumped sitting position. The sheets remained piled in his lap, which seemed modestly intentional on his part. Jak noted his bare torso was much leaner than Kode's but still firmly muscular. A large scar spiderwebbed across his side like white veins with a hard, knotted centre. Jak's eyes were drawn to it, and Krill noticed.

"Can I ask?" she said.

"You just did," he grimaced.

"I'm sorry." She turned her gaze down. "You don't have to answer."

"You don't need to apologise for everything," Krill replied. "You haven't done anything wrong, Jak. You ought to back yourself more often." He closed his eyes and sighed deeply. "I told you about D'rök blades — that they are poisonous to fae. I was stabbed with one. When Kode and I fled Roïgola'a'lanaū. The D'rö-Hadās caught us trying to escape. My people are fearless and resolute. I taught them nothing less. Elrïlani, the warrior who ended up taking my place, pursued us and managed to strike me while I was protecting Kode. We fell from the sky with nothing. It should have killed me. It was killing me. The wound festered and spread. Kode was capable of easing my pain, but he couldn't heal the wound or cure the poison. Not a D'rök wound. They are supposed to be fatal. We were refugees in this world. I should have died." He paused and opened his eyes. "Jim saved my life."

"Jim?" Jak echoed in surprise.

"Kode found him, or he found Kode," Krill admitted. "Either way, I don't remember it. I was delirious, unable to walk, I would not have had much time left when he found us. He took us in and he healed my wound. I was bedridden for two weeks while I recovered."

"How did Jim heal you?"

"Honestly?" Krill sighed. "I don't completely know. He's a magician, which you will have gathered by now, but I don't know the extent of his powers."

"They must be great if he can heal a fatal wound…" Jak said carefully.

"Yes…" Krill agreed with a troubled expression. "They must be."

"Is that why you think he's dangerous?"

"I've told you before, Jak; I know he's dangerous. I don't think it. Jim is one of the most dangerous people alive. I don't know the bounds of his magic, but then… I'm not sure even he knows the limits of what he can do. Sometimes I worry…" Krill trailed off with concern creasing his perfect face.

"What?" Jak asked. "You worry about what?"

"Nothing," he sighed and shook his head. "It's nothing. Can you reach the food basket? We definitely need hangover food."

"What's hangover food?"

"All kinds of things. This morning I'm thinking burgers."

"What's a bur-ger?"

"It's like a sandwich but better," Krill answered. "Usually greasy and carb-heavy."

"What does that mean?"

"It means it's delicious. Just get the basket, Jak. The food will explain itself. Also, grab the water pitcher. I don't want to feel like this all day."

***

Burgers turned out to be a life-changing event. They were followed by water and a nap, so it was a very brief life-change. However, it did mean that Jak woke at lunchtime feeling better than she thought she possibly could have when she had woken that morning. Even Krill seemed to be doing better. He had disappeared down the trapdoor at some stage and reappeared dressed and healthy. Although, he did seem to be stretching out a few kinks after sleeping on the floor.

The day was clouding over and looked like it might turn to rain. That left Allie keen to swap out after lunch. They woke Dora for food, but she was barely hungry and seemed to be running a slight fever. They gave her a little food, plenty of water, and some more medicine. Then Jak borrowed a cloak against the weather and swapped with Allie and Kode. The afternoon was grey and drizzly as she sat in the front of the wagon with Jim.

"Can you do anything for her?" she asked him as they rode on.

"Can I do anything for whom?" he replied.

"Dora," Jak clarified. "Can you use your magic to heal her? Krill told me you healed him when you met him."

"What?" Jim looked confused.

"When he ran away with Kode and got stabbed with a D'rök blade." Jak stared at him. "You were actually the one who healed him, weren't you?"

"Yes," Jim nodded at the memory once he realised

what she was talking about. "Yes, I was. It's not the same, though. Sorry, Jak. I wish I could heal Dora. Thing is… just between us, I tried. It didn't work. I don't know why. I mean… I've got several theories. But they're just theories. I haven't experimented or anything. I guess we just see how she goes for now. Sometimes with the snuffles you just have to give it a week or two and medicate the symptoms. She'll come right."

"I know," Jak sighed. "I just don't like seeing her like this. It reminds me of when she was really sick, and Mum isn't here to fix it now. Swimming last night wouldn't have helped either," she glowered.

"It won't have hindered her," Jim grinned. "Having fun is good for you when you're not well. It helps kick the bugs, and you gotta look after the soul as well as the body."

"Swimming in champagne isn't good for anyone," Jak growled. "Especially not a child."

"It's not *real* champagne. That's just what I tell people it is."

"… what is it, then?"

"It's magical fizzy rose water."

"Don't fucking lie to me, Jim."

"I'm not!" he protested. "Jellybean, please, do you really think I'm the kind of guy who would let a child swim in champagne?"

"Yes."

"Okay, well, thank you," he placed a hand over his heart. "I'm deeply touched that you believe in me, but—"

"I don't believe in you," she argued. "I think you're

a sneaky, evil, conniving monster who likes to trick people."

"And I'm touched, Jellybean, I really am—"

"And I think that you would have let my sisters and me get into trouble, and I think you would have thought it wasn't even a bad thing, and I think you cause chaos wherever you go, and… and I saw you! I saw you in the back of the wagon last night!"

"Really? Jak… if you're into watching, all you have to do is ask."

"NO!" she shrieked. "It was horrible and I ran away!"

"Then why were you looking?"

"I glimpsed it accidently!"

"You're worried about something you accidentally glimpsed? Really?"

"I hate you!"

"Now you just sound like Krill…" Jim shrugged and lounged back on the seat with the reins held loosely in his hand.

Jak turned away and took several deep breaths. It was so hard not to punch him in the face, but she knew she would be in the wrong if she did. He was so completely unfazed. He clearly knew she was just going through something. It was her first hangover, and being drunk hadn't been particularly pleasant either. It wasn't a great time in her life.

"Jak…" he said slowly, still lounging beside her and staring ahead. "Are you okay?"

"I don't know," she muttered.

"Okay," he nodded. "That's okay too."

"Please don't be understanding right now," she complained. "I really just want to hate you in peace."

He laughed at her, and even she felt better at how silly the whole situation was. She was scared for her sisters, and she was scared for herself, and she was scared for the future. Jim was an easy target. He was so irresponsible, but he was also well-intentioned. As furious as she was with him, she was also starting to build an important picture. Jim wasn't human. Not as human as he pretended to be, anyway. It wasn't just his magic and his knowledge. The more she thought about it, the surer she was. His culture was fae. He had embraced his heritage from his father's side. Now she just had to find out which of the fae had fathered him. Not that she particularly wanted to think about it, but she had to know. She had to be able to prove he was a demigod.

They drove on through the damp misty drizzle. Jak stayed huddled up in her cloak, but Jim was happy enough in the rain. The water on his skin seemed to refresh him. The rolling green hills of farmland were dotted with white sheep that frequently huddled together like poor imitations of the cloudbank of the Golden City. Small clusters of forest interspersed the farms and Jim drove right past the markers of Fora. The last thing he wanted was another run-in with Äulé, and Jak also felt she could do without watching the two of them fight. Jim had told her the dispute was born of fae politics. She wondered if his father was relevant. If, perhaps, some of Äulé's rudeness to him had come from the gnome's relationship to Jim's parents.

She also wondered about her conversation with Alice last night. The memory of the pretty blonde lady was suddenly embarrassing now. She wished she hadn't run away, but she knew, playing it out in her head, that the fantasy always ended with her running away. She just… she just couldn't. It wasn't like her.

"Jim…" she started quietly. "Can I ask you something?"

"Sure," he answered cautiously at her tone.

"I was talking with someone at the village last night, and they said that no one in the valley has seen a faerie in about a year — all the faeries left and they don't know why. That's why they were throwing the party to the gods — to try and get the faeries to come back. They don't even come when summoned."

"Do you have a question…?" Jim asked.

"Why did the faeries leave?"

"I have no idea," he replied. "I travel with two fae, but they were exiled a decade ago, and it's not our business what their people get up to."

"But you said something about fae politics yesterday…"

"I do know a bit about that," he admitted slowly. "Things have been chaotic the last year for the faeries, so perhaps it is connected. Still, you have to remember, Jellybean, fae have their own lives in their own world. This mortal world isn't everything to them. They come and go as they please. If they don't please, they don't come." He smirked.

Jak kept her eyes averted and ignored his humour. There was something else on her mind, and it was weighing it down.

"Mum's been gone for a year…" she muttered.

"Wait, you think that's connected?" Jim started.

Jak shrugged. "I don't know. The timeline matches, but you won't tell me anything about it."

Jim laughed. "Lots of things happened in the last year, babe. I got my hair done, you got a new job, doesn't mean they're connected. Was your Mom heavily involved in fae politics?"

"No," Jak mumbled.

"Good. Would have been concerned otherwise. Jak, little Jellybean, it is highly unlikely that whatever the fae are getting their panties twisted over is connected to your Mom going walkabout. We will find her, I promise you, but it almost certainly has nothing to do with faeries, so let's try and keep our noses out of their angsty magic issues to do it, yeah?"

"Yeah…" she nodded, feeling slightly reassured, but no wiser. She didn't know if he was telling the truth about what was happening with the fae. He was trying to hide that he was a demigod, so maybe he didn't get on with his dad. Maybe Krill and Kode weren't the only reason he didn't like Roïgola'a'lanaū. Maybe it was their business. She hadn't known anything about the faeries before she'd met Jim and the boys, and Äulé had never stopped showing up for them. Maybe something had happened in the valley, and she was reading too much into all of it. Still, she couldn't shake the niggling feeling that there were connections she was missing.

The sky grew dark early under the thick grey clouds. Jak watched farm after farm roll by, until she realised that the houses she was looking at had warm firelight blinking from the windows. The thought suddenly made her very homesick. She missed her own bed, and their warm hut, and being able to just sit indoors by a fire. Messing around with Jim and the boys had been an adventure, but now she just wanted to be able to go home. Remembering the way they had been driven out, the thought of their home burning, and the knowledge that they might never be able to go back, made her want to cry.

"Jak? Are you okay?" Jim asked.

"Huh?"

"I'm getting a very sad vibe from you all of a sudden. What's wrong?"

"Nothing." Jak rubbed her face as though trying to push away the feelings. "It's nothing."

Jim looked like he was about to push the topic, when something crashed into the side of the caravan. It sounded like an explosion. The force shook the ground. The caravan was thrown. It crashed on its side in the mud. Jak and Jim went flying. The horses vanished. Jak hit the soft grassy bank at the side of the road. She felt dazed and confused as she rolled onto her back. Her side hurt where she had hit the ground.

The wagon lay on its side with one wheel spinning listlessly and half the back door lying open. Jak wanted to scream for her sisters, but she didn't want to draw attention. Standing in the shadows of the overcast evening was a warrior in black. Their armour was dark and glistened like Krill's daggers. On slow and silent feet they approached the wagon. Jak felt a cold fear grip her at the sight of them. She knew what they were without having to think. D'rö-Hadās. Head Hunters.

Two more stepped out of the shadows. They advanced on the wagon. As fast as they had appeared, Krill was there. The former D'Hiris appeared on top of the fallen wagon. His blades blurred and flashed runes in the air. The runes exploded. The fight that followed moved faster than Jak's eye could follow. She caught glimpses and snatches. The air was filled with the sound of life. To human ears, the sounds of the D'rö-Hadās fighting were like the buzz of insects and the wingbeats of birds.

Jak struggled to her feet. She tried to sense the fight. For a moment, she thought she could see it. Krill danced and dodged and parried. He kept all three D'rö-Hadās at bay. But the effort of keeping the other assassins back was taking its toll. The biggest one was coming in hard and fast. Somehow, Jak knew that was Elrïlani, the new D'Hiris. There was something personal in the way the two of them fought. Elrïlani was drawing Krill's attention. The other two were trying to land a strike behind him. Jak remembered the scar on his side. A single cut with one of those blades could be fatal to a fae.

She didn't even think about it. She uncoiled from the grass and drew her sword. She watched and waited. Then she struck. She ran at the wagon. Her eyes were half closed in an attempt to sense rather than see. Her sword swung out. She aimed for the space between the magic. She was trying to protect Krill's back. Something struck her blade so hard it almost ripped it from her hands. She staggered back. Her hands clutched the sword.

"Jak!"

She heard Krill bellow her name. He moved like lightning. With a crack he was there. His blades whirled and vanished in his hands. They changed direction to meet every strike. Then Elrïlani was there too. The terrifying assassin appeared on the wagon. Jak looked up. From the gaps in the black mask, golden eyes loomed down on her. They raised their blade to strike. For a moment, Jak realised how terrifying Krill must have been once.

Jim appeared. He didn't move in from anywhere. He didn't step or leap. He simply appeared between Elrïlani and Krill. The armoured assassin froze mid-strike at the sight of him. Their golden eyes widened. Jim snapped his fingers.

Jak thought she'd gone blind. The light was so bright it scorched her vision. She squeezed her eyes shut, but still the light burnt through her lids. Everything went dark. Silence fell. She didn't realise she'd been holding her breath until she gasped silently. She was too afraid to breathe. If she made any noise, they'd find her.

"Jim..."

She heard Krill's voice whisper beside her and felt the warmth of his presence vanish. She opened her eyes. They were in a forest. The road was long gone, and she had no idea where they were. The trees were large and dark and unfamiliar. The wagon stood upright and undamaged beside them. Jim was slumped on the ground behind it. He sat on his knees with his shoulders sagged. Krill had already run to him. Jak couldn't see him well with Krill standing over him, trying to pull him up, but he looked pale and gaunt.

The door of the wagon banged open. Kode burst out with Dora in his arms and Allie right behind him. Allie had a hand to her head as though she had banged it. Dora looked startled, but unhurt.

"Jim!" Kode called as he staggered down the stairs. He set Dora down and the two fae tried to pull Jim to his feet.

"You're an idiot," Krill scolded Jim.

"You're an idiot," he retorted. "I'm fine. Set up a barrier." Jim tried to wave them off and stand on his own. His hands were shaking but he stood tall. Jak balked at the sight of him. He kept his face turned down and wouldn't meet anyone's eye, but his skin was chalky white and his cheekbones stuck out sharp enough to cut with. He looked like he'd lost nearly half his bodyweight.

"I had that fight," Krill argued.

"No, you didn't," Jim scorned. "The kid just had to step in and save your life." He staggered past the girls to the door of the wagon. Kode stayed with him and kept his hands on his body to keep him upright. "Make sure they don't come back," he grunted. They disappeared inside.

Krill's golden eyes were dark as he watched them. The girls all neared him cautiously. He was the only thing they had that was safe. He noticed them approach.

"You're injured, child," he motioned to Allie. She

stepped forward. He raised a hand and wove the Creachta rune over her head. Allie let her hand drop as though the pain had suddenly vanished. Krill had already turned from her. He raised his hands and wandered around the wagon, marking the Fora rune as he went. Every time he drew it, the rune flashed like light in the air, and then dispersed into the branches of the trees. He lowered his hands as he came back around and faced Jak.

"I told you not to involve yourself in fae battles," he growled.

"They were trying to stab you in the back!" Jak protested.

"I know." He paused, his expression still dark. "Thank you."

"You're welcome. What happened? Where are we?"

"Wherever Jim sent us," Krill answered with a sigh. "I don't know exactly. The D'rö-Hadās attacked, and he magicked us somewhere else. Somewhere safe."

"How?" Jak demanded. "How does an ordinary man get that kind of power?"

"Jim is not ordinary, Jak," Krill replied patiently. "Don't pretend you don't know that."

"Well, he says he is," Jak retorted. "He won't tell us who he really is. He won't tell us who his fae parent is, or even admit he has one. You know he's a demigod. There is no other explanation for what he does and how he does it. You're all just lying to us."

"It's his business, Jak," Krill sighed. He sat wearily on the back stair of the caravan. "I can't make him tell you, and I wouldn't try. Just like I can't make you stop asking. He doesn't like that part of his identity. He likes being human. Let him be."

Jak wanted to keep fighting, but Krill looked so tired. He looked so tired, and he looked hurt. Not physically, but somewhere deep there was pain, and fear.

"Would it change anything?" Krill whispered. He was staring down at the grass beneath them. "Would it mean anything if he gave you a name? He'd still be exactly who he is. You'd still have to put up with his lecherous, wise-cracking behaviour, just like I do."

"You don't *have* to put up with him…" Jak muttered. She knew it wasn't true as soon as she said it. Jim had saved Krill's life. The fae assassin was supposed to be an immortal. He owed Jim everything. Somehow, without knowing how or why, Jak knew it was more than that too. There was something between them. Something she didn't know about. It was whatever made Krill afraid of Jim. It was what drove all his warnings to her. He didn't want Jak to end up like him. He didn't want her to become bound to Jim. The wry and painful smile on his downcast face told her she was right, but he didn't try and argue. He knew she knew her words had been wrong.

"The basket's here if you girls would like some dinner," he changed the subject.

"I'm really not hungry…" Jak muttered.

"You're shaking."

"I'm scared," she replied. She looked up at her sisters. Allie and Dora were looking at her with big eyes. She was still holding her sword. They knew she'd been in the fight. They were scared. She was scared. They had all been through a lot.

"I'm sorry," Krill apologised. "It shouldn't— It's all just a mess. Everything got so out of hand. I don't even know how it got this bad..." He sighed and stood. "Have something to eat and stay by the wagon. I'll be back in a moment."

Krill disappeared inside and Jak listened to the sound of the trapdoor. She sheathed her sword with a sigh.

"How are you two doing?" she asked her sisters.

"We're okay now," Allie answered. "What's going on?"

"I think Jim is hiding something..." Jak glowered.

"Oh, no shit?!" Allie replied with scathing faux-surprise. "Only one thing?"

"Don't use that kind of language, Allie," Jak growled.

"Or what?" Allie retorted. "That was a dumb thing to say, Sis. You're not Mum. Your new friends haven't helped us find her. Now we're being attacked by the Head Hunters? You're getting into fights with them? How stupid are you, Jak? They will cut off your head, steal your power, and take the pieces back to Ĝorgomghōul to make soup with."

Dora began to cry. Jak glared daggers at Allie, but her younger sister didn't relent, although she did look slightly guilty.

"Don't cry, sweetie," Jak knelt down and pulled Dora into a hug. "That's not true. Allie's just making that up."

"You don't know that..." Allie muttered.

Jak shut her up with a look as she soothed Dora, but she felt bad. Allie was only saying those things because she was scared too. They all were. They had no business with Head Hunters. They'd just become entangled with people who did. Jak had a deep and real fear that she would never get the opportunity to make that argument to Elrïlani. The D'Hiris would probably kill them all at the first chance they got before Jak could say anything. Even so... she had no desire to leave her fae friends to that fate. As strong as the urge to keep her sisters safe was, she felt an obligation to help Jim and the boys. There had to be some way to get them safe and free of Clōudiá's army. She certainly couldn't just abandon them now to an endless fate of running for their lives.

"Jak...?" Dora's voice came quietly from by her shoulder.

"Yes, sweetie?"

"Can I have a sandwich?"

"Yes, baby," Jak chuckled. "Help yourself." Jak set her down in the back of the wagon and Dora pulled the magic basket closer and opened it up. While she was rummaging for food, Jak looked over at Allie. She held her arm out invitingly to her younger sister. Allie looked like she wanted to refuse and sulk, but she caved and came into the hug Jak was offering. For a moment, the two of them just held each other reassuringly.

"I'm sorry, Allie," Jak murmured. "I didn't mean to scare you."

"You didn't," Allie lied. "What... what are we doing here, Jak?"

"I don't know," Jak admitted. "What would you

rather do? Where would you rather go?" She directed the question at both girls. Allie pulled away from the hug with a sigh.

"Nowhere. I dunno," she grumbled. "I like Krill and Kode. I don't want to leave them. It's just the Head Hunters… I mean, why? Why chase them? Why not just let them be? They're so nice. It's awful to think that evil bitch's army is trying to hunt them down…" Allie glowered at nothing. Her dark eyes sharpened with suspicion. "Maybe that's why Jim won't talk about his fae heritage. Maybe he's powerful because he's a fae prince. Maybe he's one of Clōudiá's, and that's why he hates her so much."

Jak stared at her little sister like she had just struck gold, but Dora made a doubtful sound around a mouthful of sandwich.

"I don' thin' so," Dora shook her head as she chewed. "Clōudiá is Kode's mum. They would have said if they had the same mum, and they wouldn't be shagging if they were brothers."

Jak thought for a moment the D'rö-Hadās had killed her when she heard her youngest sister talking about shagging. Dora looked like it wasn't a big deal, and kept eating her sandwich.

"What do you know about that?" Jak demanded. "Where did you hear the word shagging?"

"Allie told me," Dora replied. She rattled on without drawing breath. "She said it was something grown-ups do, and that you were scared of it because you weren't a grown-up but you could be, and you're scared people will think you are, and that they might expect you to shag someone, but you don't want to. Also, you don't want to shag Jim because he's a boy, and you don't like boys. But Kode and Krill shag Jim because they do like him, and they also shag each other because they're married."

Jak turned very slowly to face a mortified Allie who was looking at Dora in the back of the wagon.

"Dora, sweetie," Allie squeaked, "you remember that we weren't going to tell Jak about that conversation — that Krill and Kode were also there for, and it wasn't just me?"

"Yeah, they were there too," Dora nodded. "But it's okay. Jak's not mad."

"Really?" Allie asked again in her high-pitched tone.

Jak was looking at Allie in agreement with Dora. She wasn't mad. She was furious. Livid. Allie was all too aware what Jak's murderous eyes were conveying.

"Look," she squeaked again. "In my defence... I am actually right, right?"

Before Jak could reply, the trapdoor opened and Krill stepped back out to join them.

"How are you girls doing?" he asked, stepping down beside Dora.

"You remember that conversation we all had that we said we weren't going to tell Jak?" Allie rushed to tell him. "Dora just told her."

Krill looked down on Dora, who looked up at him and took another big bite of sandwich. Krill smiled at her, and then turned his smile up at Jak. It was so gentle and understanding she couldn't stay mad, not even at Allie. Of course the topic of sex had come up with Kode and Krill in the room. If it hadn't been so personal, Jak would have been admirably pleased with how well Allie seemed to have managed it.

"We were talking about Jim," Jak muttered to him. "Who his parent might be, and Dora pointed out he probably wasn't related to you or Kode."

"He's not," Krill acknowledged with a nod. "I can't stop you girls talking, but I can advise that you will do your heads in thinking about this, and that at the end of the day you will almost certainly still be wrong."

"There's something about fae that's important to this that we don't know about, isn't there?"

"Why does it matter so much to you?"

"Because…" Jak trailed off. It was hard to articulate. She wanted to know because he was her companion. Her friend. She wanted to feel like he trusted her enough to tell her. She wanted to feel like they were on even ground and that he wasn't keeping shady secrets. She wanted to know because it was a mystery to solve. She wanted to know because she was nosy. That truth shamed her slightly, and it drove home that it truly was none of her business. She couldn't say that out loud though.

Krill sighed. "Come inside, girls."

Jak and Allie both followed his ushering quietly and obediently. They took Dora and the basket and went down the ladder. Krill locked the doors of the wagon behind him and followed them down. The door to the small game room was open. A lamp was lit inside and blankets had been laid out on the beanbags. Jak realised with surprise that part of her had been hoping the boys' bedroom door would be open a crack so that she could see how Jim was doing — at risk to her sensibilities. But their bedroom door was firmly shut. She followed Dora and Allie into the other room. Krill came down behind them and stood in the doorway.

"We decided it might be safer to keep you in here for the night," he said softly. "Just for tonight. We're not able to set up a proper camp, but I hope this will do."

"It will be fine, thank you," Jak nodded to him. "How's Jim?"

"Stupid as ever," Krill smiled. "He'll be fine. He just did something he shouldn't have, but he'll recover by tomorrow. He's strong like that."

Jak continued to nod slowly. She remembered the flash of white light. It had been like nothing she'd ever known. She wanted to ask what it was, but she already knew Krill wouldn't tell her. If he did, it would be some rubbish and obvious answer like 'magic'. That much she knew. The memory of the fight was so sharp and real, but here inside the wagon felt safe, even from those burning golden eyes behind the dark mask. The eyes that looked so like the ones staring at her now.

"Krill...?" she spoke softly. "The D'rö-Hadās, the big scary one, was that Elrïlani? The new D'Hiris?"

"Yes," he nodded briefly. "She was always one of the greatest trackers among us."

"She?!" Jak barely realised she'd exclaimed in surprise. Krill lifted a cool pale eyebrow at her and Jak blushed. "I just..." Jak floundered awkwardly. "I didn't realise she was a she. She... uh... I thought she looked like you. I mean, how you would have looked when you were D'Hiris."

"She does," he agreed with a shrug. "Elrïlani and I look similar. She is also a child of Frézíān."

"She's your sister?"

"I suppose, yes."

"But…" Jak looked back at her own sisters who were watching the conversation curiously. "But how can your own sister want to kill you?"

Krill smiled at them. "Goodnight, children. Sleep well. I have to go and attend to Jim again, but knock if you need anything." He shut the door on them silently, but firmly, and brought Jak's line of questioning to a close.

CHAPTER NINE

Jak slept restlessly that night. She woke multiple times sprawled uncomfortably on her beanbag. Her sisters were both still small enough that they could curl up happily and sleep through the night. Jak kept getting a crick in her neck and her side would go numb half on the floor. At one point she woke to a rattling noise, and wondered in her half-asleep daze if she should investigate. Once the rest of her mind woke up it had a new theory, and she decided it would be best left unexplored. She'd just wait for it to stop.

The memories of the fight with the D'rö-Hadās swirled during her waking hours. The knowledge that the terrifying warrior was Krill's sister somehow made it worse. She couldn't stop thinking about those murderous golden eyes. Her own sisters were everything to her. How could Krill's sister want to kill him? But then... how could their parents condemn them to a life of slavery? How could the gods think it was okay to demand a life of obedience with no thoughts or feelings? And what about Jim? Jak hated how many times her brain asked that question. How did he fit into it? Who was he?

She sighed to herself in the dark. Under the roof of the wagon the idea of gods seemed profoundly unmagical. Clōudiá had ordered her army to come after Krill and Kode and kill them. It was so wrong it made Jak grind her teeth. She wanted to scream. She wanted to march outside to the giant cloudbank of the Golden City and scream 'FUCK OFF!' at the top of her lungs. They had suffered enough. It wasn't right. She had spent so much time recently half-loathing Jim, but lying in the dark and realising how much he was doing to protect his lovers, she had to admire him a little. She respected it. She felt like her opinion of him was on a pendulum.

When morning rolled around Jak felt like she'd barely slept, yet she was still wired with adrenaline. She'd done a lot of sleeping the day before, so perhaps she just didn't need the rest. Kode got them up for breakfast and they left the wagon to a bright and damp morning. It had rained in the night, but now the sunlight sparkled down through the leaves like little droplets of gold.

Jim and Krill were sitting together on a bench on the grass. The bench was presumably another magical item from the back of the wagon, but Jak wasn't sure what it folded up into. She was busy eyeing Jim. He looked perfectly normal. The strain of yesterday was gone. He grinned his dimpled grin at her as they stepped from the wagon, and there was a wicked glint in his eye like nothing had ever happened. She refused to be fooled.

"How are you feeling?" she asked.

"Who? Me?" his grin widened. "Do you really want to know?"

Jak didn't answer. It was so easy to like him when he

wasn't around. Once he was there it was all she could do not to hate him.

"You scared us last night," Allie told him. "Good to know it wasn't serious." Allie stared him down, and Jim's smile slowly vanished. Allie had a stronger stare than he did. His joviality couldn't withstand her judgement.

"I'm sorry," he apologised. "You guys shouldn't be caught up in this."

"We wouldn't mind so much if you told us the truth," she retorted.

Jim tried to stare her out again, but once more he failed to hold under Allie's sharp, black eyes. He didn't look away. He didn't break. But he didn't resist either. When he finally replied, it was in a soft and sombre voice.

"I'm a magician," he confessed. "I learnt how fae magic works — how it really works. No one else in the world knows as much as I do about it. Except possibly Ĝoŕgomghōul himself. I learnt how to harness it and use it. That's my secret. I mastered the power of the gods."

"But... how?" Allie asked. "Not even Krill and Kode can use magic like that, and they're faeries — you must be too."

"I don't 'must be' anything, squirt," Jim smirked at her. "I learnt the secrets of the universe. That's its own power. It is not to be traded. As much as I like you girls, as much as I love my Ha'Cās boys, this isn't knowledge you share lightly."

"No one would ask you to," Krill assured, taking his

hand and interlocking their fingers. Jim smiled at him and the two of them leant their heads together tenderly for a moment. Jim broke himself from the brief seconds of gentle affection briskly, as though he couldn't maintain the softness. As though he was scared he'd catch feelings. He stood up and joined Kode who stood behind the girls with the basket. There was breakfast to sort. Jak couldn't help but feel that breakfast didn't take much sorting. She watched Krill's shrewd eyes linger on his lovers. His consistently severe expression was unreadable.

When they sat down with food, Jak took a seat with Krill and Allie. She had not forgotten the conversation last night and her sister's comments about shagging. Allie seemed to have a memory for that moment as well, and she kept shooting Jak nervous glances. Finally, Jak sighed.

"It's okay, Allie," she muttered. "I'm not mad."

Krill gave them a quizzical look. "Why would you be mad?"

"I found out what she said to Dora about shagging — and what she said about me."

"It was all true, wasn't it?" Krill asked. "I probably would have used alternate terminology, but I thought she answered Dora's questions quite well."

Jak suddenly felt less forgiving, and Allie noticed the change apprehensively. That wasn't fair though, and Jak knew it. She kept her glare on her sister, but tempered it with a small smile.

"How is it you cower from me, but you can stare Jim down better than any of us?" she smiled.

"You can be scary," Allie answered. "You're my big sister. When you start yelling, I know I'm in trouble. Jim's just a dick, and I've got absolutely zero time for his shit."

"That's how I feel but I can't stare him out like you can!" Jak laughed. "How come Jim just caves to you?"

"She reminds him of his mother," Krill answered quietly. Both girls looked at him. Krill kept his eyes on his breakfast. "Jim's mother is extremely like an older version of Allie. I think it freaks him out."

"Dear gods I hope I never have a son like that," Allie muttered. "No offense."

"You don't have to like him, child," Krill grinned. "I like him enough for all of us."

Jak felt herself smile slightly at him. There was something about the two of them this morning. Something sweet. She didn't know why, but somehow their relationship seemed gentler this morning. There was a genuine love there she felt like she'd been missing. Jim had always hidden his feelings behind banter, and Krill suffered the brunt of that. In this new and golden morning light, it was almost beautiful, and it didn't scare her. It reminded her in a way of her own parents, a long time ago.

***

They travelled through the forest that morning. The wagon bumped and banged and rattled over the uneven ground as they wound slowly through the trees. No one, except possibly Jim, knew how far they were from a road. The self-proclaimed magician drove with absolute confidence. He seemed to know exactly where they were, even if everyone else was lost. They followed a trickling stream downhill and the water bubbling and gurgling beside them was a comforting sound.

Jak had always liked being in forests. They reminded her of home. Now that the dark night was over, this forest reminded her of the wild forest that grew behind their old house. It felt safe and familiar. She knew it wasn't the same forest, although she didn't know how she knew that. Somehow she was just sure that Jim was travelling with a destination in mind, and he wasn't the kind to double back.

Wherever they had ended up, they were back in a faerie forest. Yesterday they had been in the valley of Cröck'ko-rú, and Jak had been warned that the magic had left. She hadn't felt its particular absence then, but she could feel its return now. The forest floor was covered with life. Between the trees grew patches of wildflowers and circles of mushrooms. Berry bushes crept up here and there and small birds flitted around them, pecking away and splattering the ground with juice. Small families of rabbits began to hop about the wheels and follow the wagon. Even the quality of the light filtering through the leaves above them was atmospheric. It was magical, without being magic. She half expected to see tiny fairies curled up asleep in the centre of the flowers they passed. It would not have been out of place. The morning left her with a sense of wonder as they drove.

It was only as morning was nearing its end that the

wagon bumped and rolled into a clearing. Tall twisting trees rose up around it on every side, but it was a large enough space, and a thicket of blackberries grew wild and juicy on one side. Jak knew, before Jim even slowed down, that this was their stop for lunch. The others hadn't made it out the back doors when the rabbits that had been following along began to nest in the long grass around the wagon. They flopped out with their long feet splayed to the side and their curious whiskers twitching. Jak had to tell Dora to have her food before she played with the bunnies.

As they ate, Krill offered to train her again. Jak's enthusiasm was matched by Jim's, but she refused to let him put her off. Although, she would have preferred not to have an audience, and genuinely appreciated if the audience wasn't him. She wasn't going to let anyone else stop her from becoming a master.

Krill stood and led her back from the wagon. The grass covering the clearing was long and thick and pale green. It was still wet with dew in the shade. She knew it would make footwork hard, but learning how to handle the environment was half the lesson. Krill motioned her forward with empty hands.

"You tried to involve yourself in fae combat last night, Jak," he commented. His sharp eyes gave her an extremely direct look. "I will continue to teach you on the condition that you never do that again."

"You were in danger..." Jak protested.

"I know," he nodded. "This isn't a discussion. Those are my terms. You are a human. A mortal. You could have died."

"So could you."

Krill turned away and began to walk back to the wagon.

"No, I'm sorry! I'm sorry! I won't do it again!"

"Your word?"

"I give my word: I won't," Jak flushed.

Krill seemed satisfied given the small smile he directed at her. He returned and began training while the others looked on and cheered — or in some cases jeered.

"Ignore them," Krill instructed. "Block them out."

"Don't worry," Jak grinned. "That's something I'm good at."

She barely heard the voices calling to her. Her ears were full of the sound of her blood pumping, and the voice of her sword itself. It didn't use words the way people did, but it did seem to speak to her somehow. It communicated through movement, and the sound of it, the knowledge of where it wanted to go and what it wanted to do, filled her mind.

Jak hacked and slashed and parried. She tried to force Krill to give ground. The faerie never drew a weapon. He danced and wove and batted the flat of her blade away with the back of his hand. She was reminded of the first time they had done this on the side of the mountain. Except she already felt like she was moving better. She wasn't trying to hurt him anymore. She didn't need to hit him. She just wanted to match him. She swung at him and he vanished completely.

"Much better," he complimented from behind her.

Jak turned and wiped the streaming sweat from her

face. He always looked so perfect, and a quick run around left her disgusting. It wasn't fair. Bloody faeries. She raised her sword. Krill raised a hand flat towards her. She stopped as he bid her.

"I want to try something new," he said carefully. He smoothed a loose strand of soft blonde hair back from his face. "Your technique has improved greatly over a short space of time, which pleases me. However, there is something about your talents which fascinates me. I think we should test it. I want you to attack me again, Jak, but I want you to do it with your eyes closed."

She didn't bother to question it. She knew what he was getting at, so she just nodded. He would have noticed by now the way she closed her eyes when she wanted to try and strike him — and the way she had done that last night trying to defend him. She took a deep breath and shook herself out. Once she was loose, she set herself tense again. She closed her eyes. Then she struck.

Just like the night before, she let the sword lead her. She breathed out as she swung. Without her sight to distract her, she attacked the source of the magic. Her blade struck true. It clanged like a bell as it met steel. The blow stopped short. It sent a rattling force up her arms. Jak opened her eyes. Krill's golden gaze stared back at her. Close. One of his dark blades was raised in front of his face. It had stopped her strike, but only just.

She stood down. Krill lowered his blade. It didn't vanish from his hand though. Not this time. He reached into a pocket and pulled out a long strip of cloth. It sat gently in his delicate pale fingers as he held it out to her.

He didn't need to say anything.

Jak stabbed her sword into the soft muddy ground and took the cloth strip. She bound her eyes with it carefully, and then pulled her sword from the ground and took up a defensive pose.

"No, attack," Krill instructed.

She obeyed. Jak went for him again. With her eyes closed, everything was different. Not least of all because her blade was striking another. This was practice. Her ears rang with the clash of steel. She attacked repeatedly. Her movements were different. She could feel it. She never paused to register what she could see happening in the fight. She just struck where she could feel the magic, and she defended when she could feel the magic coming for her. It came from behind. She whirled as fast as she could and brought her sword up. The sound of his blade hitting hers rang through the glade.

She had just defended an attack from a fae. She had known how. He could shadow walk. It made him impossible to catch. Yet, somehow, she had blocked his strike. It lit a fire in her. In the darkness she could forget Krill. There was only the fight. The fight against the fae. Against a D'rö-Hadās. The magic had moved away. She charged it.

With her eyes bound, she couldn't see where she was going. Her feet caught in the long grass. She tripped. With a yell, Jak hit the ground. The blade swung from her grip as she fell. It nicked her shoulder. The pain was sharp and sweet. She splatted into the mud. For a moment, she just lay there. It wasn't something she particularly wanted to get up from, but she consoled herself that she didn't have that much dignity to maintain with her present company anyway.

Jak groaned as she pulled the blindfold from her face and rolled over. Krill appeared over her and knelt down. Jak just sighed at him.

"It was fun while it lasted…" she grinned.

Krill didn't smile back. His face was very serious. His face was so often serious. With delicate hands, he reached down and signed over her shoulder. The shallow cut mended and Jak felt the pain subside. Her sleeve was still torn and bloodstained, but at least the injury was gone. He held out his hand and helped pull her to her feet.

The others were hurrying over. Kode chased after the girls and Jim sauntered behind them.

"Jak, are you alright?" Allie asked.

"Yeah," Jak grinned, wiping some mud off her clothes. "Just some wounded pride."

"You looked silly when you fell over," Dora giggled. She was holding a small rabbit in her arms and stroking its ears. It didn't seem to mind. "But you looked pretty cool before that."

"Thanks." Jak ruffled Dora's curls under the flower crown with her clean hand. She'd take what she could get.

Kode was smiling at her with her sisters, but Krill and Jim were sharing a long and unsmiling look. It really took the fun out of everything.

"What?" she asked.

"You can sense fae," Jim answered. "You can sense

magic. It's not a coincidence or as common a gift as you might imagine. You've done it too often now for it to be anything but talent."

"Jak," Krill met her eye grimly. "I have spent centuries teaching my soldiers a gift that seems to come naturally to you." He placed a hand firmly on her shoulder. "You would have made an exceptional D'rö-Hadās."

Jak had no idea what to say to that. She didn't really know if it was a compliment. Being compared to a Head Hunter wasn't really all that pleasant, but they were the greatest warriors of all time, so maybe it was a compliment? Krill didn't seem to expect a response. He squeezed her shoulder once in pride. Then he turned to his lovers. Jim was still wearing a serious and contemplative expression. Kode was ever-smiling.

"Kody…" Krill said slowly as though he'd just realised something.

"Yes?" Kode looked lovingly at his husband.

"What do you see?" Krill asked. Jim turned his head sharply to look at Kode and his eyes narrowed. The two of them were both watching the younger fae seriously in a way that made Jak nervous. He looked between them with gentle incomprehension.

"You're not surprised by this," Jim caught on. "You knew she could do it."

"No," Kode shook his head. "I didn't know. I don't know what her talents are, or who her patron would be. She's not Ha'Cās, so it's not that simple. She isn't marked like we are. She wears Domhanda on her soul."

Jim and Krill stared at him like he'd just told them

his pants were on fire. Then they shifted the exact expression to her. Jak stared back at them all in confusion. This had gone from flattering to weird, mostly because Jim and Krill looked so concerned.

"Domhanda is the world rune," she said, because she felt like she should say something and she didn't know what they meant. "The circle. The beginning and the end."

"It's the rune of destiny," Krill said. "And Kode can see it on your soul."

"That means you have one, Jellybean," Jim grinned. "Most of us just have lives, but you have a Destiny."

"What does that mean?" Jak demanded, not liking the sound of it at all.

"It means we get to sound dramatic about something we know nothing about," Jim smirked. "Honestly, having a destiny is grand, but unspecific. It could mean you're going to become Queen of the World, or it could mean that against all odds you will find your mom. Who knows. It could be a path you have set yourself on and will soon complete, or it could be something that is marked out and you won't even begin it until you're fifty. The only way to find out is to keep going."

Jak sighed. She should have known better than to expect a real answer from faeries. Krill seemed to sense her resignation, but he didn't have a better explanation. Instead, he changed the subject and turned to the wagon.

"You should clean yourself up. The stream isn't far and you can bathe properly there. We will wait for you."

"Or I can hold the pitcher up like a shower for you, if you'd prefer," Jim offered.

"You may take the pitcher to the stream if you'd like, Jak." Krill placed a hand on Jim's chest to keep him back. "We will wait for you here."

"We're going to pick berries!" Dora interjected, completely unfazed with talk of magic and destinies. Allie smiled wryly over her little sister's shoulder. Jak smiled back. She turned her smile to her teacher as Allie guided Dora to the berry patch by the wagon.

"I'll be fine, thanks," Jak told Krill. She walked with them back to the wagon and grabbed her pack before heading towards the sound of water. The stream wasn't hard to find. She could hear the water pooling and followed the sound. Sure enough, deep in the dark green forest, she found a small pool where the stream settled in a rocky dip. The rocks were mossy around the edge and the water looked cold, but it was better than sweat and mud.

Sunlight dappled the pool and the rocks. Jak took a towel from her pack and left it in a patch of sunlight to warm for her. She stripped off and rushed into the water. At its deepest, the pool only came up to her waist, and the first splashes around her ankles were so icy she bit her tongue to keep from shrieking. As soon as she was in the deepest part, she dunked herself under. It was almost cold enough to give her brain-freeze. Jak washed herself off as quickly as she could, but it didn't take long for her to get used to the cold water. Her initial panicked cleaning relaxed slightly as the water began to feel less cold. The urge to jump out became less urgent.

With a sudden strange feeling, she realised she was smiling. She pushed herself lazily backwards and forwards through the water and let the smooth cold feel of it rush over her bare skin. She remembered the thrill of the fight, and the way Krill had told her — in his own roundabout way — that she was exceptional. She had a destiny, and she could fight fae. She grinned at nothing and let herself wash at a leisurely pace.

When she was done washing herself and her clothes, she climbed from the pool and wrapped herself in the warm towel. She smiled up at the sunlight and it winked at her through the leaves. The day was suddenly too beautiful to spend on the road with Jim or cooped up in the back of the wagon. She dried herself slowly and squeezed the water from her hair. The pool was still picturesque and it continued to sparkle invitingly. As she took the scene in, she noticed something.

One of the rocks around the edge of the pool was bigger than the others. Noticeably bigger. It reminded her of something. She wrapped herself in the towel and approached it. There was something carved on it. Jak pushed away some of the moss and splashed water up onto the stone to wash it. Uisce. Water. It was a rune marker. An ancient one, but still a rune maker. Jim wasn't here. Jak internally slapped herself for even thinking it. She could go back to the others once she was dressed.

As she opened her pack to haul out clothes, she paused. She unwrapped her mother's bowls and she looked at them softly. Krill had warned her not to show these to Jim. That was why she never got them out. That was just another mystery to solve. She sighed. Maybe it was a good thing the others weren't here. Maybe this was going to work out better. Jak wrapped the bowls again carefully. She took an odd sock from her pack, kept herself firmly wrapped in the towel, and laid the sock at the foot of the marker.

Then she knelt to pray. She called on the spirits of the pool to help her, and offered to barter with them for their help. Something happened. It wasn't like all the times they had summoned Äulé. Jak stepped slowly to her feet and backed up, clutching the towel to her tightly, as the surface of the pool began to glow. Someone walked out of the water. A woman appeared. She surfaced slowly without leaving a ripple, and stepped gently from the water to sit on the rune marker.

Jak stood completely frozen. This was no gnome or sprite. She had the long, pointed ears of the fae and was taller than Jak herself. Despite walking from the pool, she was completely dry, yet her skin and hair shone and glistened like pearl. Her cool blue eyes were deeper than the sky. She looked at Jak and smiled warmly. She was the most beautiful thing Jak had ever seen in her life, and the most beautiful thing she ever would see. The girl stood there in her towel, staring. Her skin was so hot she felt sunburnt and she blushed before the woman she recognised as one of the goddesses from the church windows. The goddess of beauty: Olíriá.

"Well met, young lady," Olíriá dipped her head at Jak and spoke in a voice clearer and sweeter than song.

"Uh," was all Jak managed to reply.

Olíriá laughed like the tinkling of music. Her perfect smile when she looked at Jak with her immortal face made the girl swoon. The heat had spread from Jak's skin into her stomach and down her legs, like a warm and pleasant glow. Her knees were trembling.

"Um," Jak squeaked. "You-you're not a… a sprite…"

"No," the goddess agreed, pulling her long white hair over her shoulder. "I'm not." She looked back at the water behind her. "This is one of my mother's old pools. It hasn't been called from in quite some time."

Jak tried to recall what she knew about Olíriá. She was the daughter of Äluāknā, the goddess of water, and of Frézíān. That meant she was related to Krill, although she may not have thought so. She was the goddess of love and beauty and music, among other things.

"Um, I used it as a bath, sorry…" Jak apologised.

"I'm the deity of baths," Olíriá grinned. "Why would you apologise for bathing?"

Jak blushed even harder. Olíriá's eyes were not mocking or unkind. Quite the opposite. She had a gentle, understanding, and loving gaze. Jak felt like if she stared for too long it would swallow her. She would drown in those deep, eternally blue eyes. She wouldn't even mind. Her chest ached as she looked at the scantily-clad goddess. Somehow the lack of clothes on her wasn't indecent. It was elegant and magical. Her body was so perfect it was art. It would have been rude to cover more of it.

"You called for something, child?" Olíriá reminded.

The use of the term 'child' brought Jak sharply back

to reality. She was suddenly and mortifyingly reminded of the sock sitting at the base of the stone.

"I… I…" she stuttered. "I was h-hoping to get some faerie help…"

"Then perhaps we can trade," Olíriá smiled. "I am also after something."

"What?"

"I am searching for information. What is it you seek?"

"I…" Jak wet her lips nervously as she began to calm down. "I'm looking for my mother. If you help me find her, I'll tell you anything you want to know, as long as I can."

"That sounds very fair," the goddess's smile widened. "What is your name, young lady?"

"Jak."

"Jak," Olíriá smiled at her. "What happened to your mother, Jak? Why are you looking for her?"

"She vanished. She went out one day, about a year ago, and she never came back. No one's seen her since."

"Hm." Olíriá tilted her head sideways. "And you want a faerie to perform a location spell? I can do that."

"Can you?!" Jak blurted. That was better than she'd hoped for. She'd been hoping a faerie might have been able to give her directions or clues, but she'd never imagined they would be able to tell her exactly where to look.

"However," the goddess warned, raising a hand. "My magic is not like the magic of sprites. I need more powerful fuel for my fire, so to speak."

Jak hugged herself tightly. She knew the legends that

gods used pieces of people to perform their magic. What would she give to find her mother? How much would Olíriá ask for? The exquisite goddess was suddenly a lot more ominous. Her soft blue eyes were narrowed as they eyed up Jak.

"How about a lock of hair?" Olíriá suggested.

"Huh?"

"I will need something of significance to cast the spell. Something to help draw out and find your mother. Something to bind you together and locate her. Something with meaning. A lock of hair should do the trick."

"Oh." That wasn't nearly as sinister as Jak had thought it might be. She pulled her damp curls over her shoulder and held them in her hands. "Yeah, sure, I guess. I don't have anything on me to cut it with though..."

"Come closer," Olíriá invited.

Jak didn't think twice. She approached the goddess and felt the heat in her body radiate like a furnace as she neared her. She could smell the sweet scent of heavenly bath salts about her, and see her skin glisten and shine in the dappled sunlight. Olíriá kept motioning her forward. Jak stepped ever closer. So close. Her heart was pounding so hard she thought it would burst. A hot sweat prickled her neck and she was painfully aware of every inch of her body. Olíriá reached out with perfect pearl fingers and took the end of one of Jak's locks in her hand. She snipped it between two fingers and the curl fell away. It sat like a soft black circle in the goddess's pale palm. Jak didn't move away. She didn't know if she could. Never in her life had she felt this drawn to someone.

Olíriá didn't ask her to step back. The goddess made a fist around the curl. She brought her hand to her soft lips, closed her eyes, and blew gently over her fingers. Jak waited. Olíriá flinched. An expression of confusion, and then pain, marred her beautiful face. She gave a sharp breath and Jak felt her own throat catch in response. Olíriá took a couple of calming breaths. When she opened her eyes, tears sparkled in the corners like diamonds. Jak could see the pain and pity in those perfect eyes.

Her own grief hit her like a club, but she didn't move. Part of her had always wondered. It wasn't as much of a shock as it could have been. Part of her had been sensible. Mum had never come home. There had to have been a reason. Why not an obvious one?

"I'm so sorry…" Olíriá whispered.

Jak nodded. She couldn't move back now. She could feel the warmth of Olíriá close to her, and she needed it. She needed the feeling of someone alive beside her, because she couldn't be sure she was anymore.

"Where?" she croaked.

"Some distance from here, by human standards," Olíriá answered gently. "I only saw a grave. A small grave in a forest, marked with a single stone. It's near an old hut, outside a tiny village."

"Wait!" a surge of hope welled inside Jak's chest like a sunrise. "A tiny stone hut? Thatch roof? The gravestone is round, and there's a rosebush growing by it?"

"Yes," Olíriá looked confused. "You already know it?"

Jak squeezed herself in a hug and sighed her relief to the sky. "That's my dad's grave. Not my mum's. The spell must have got them mixed up somehow!"

"That's… unlikely," Olíriá said carefully, giving Jak a shrewd look.

"What else can it be?"

"I don't know…" Olíriá admitted. "I haven't tested anything out yet."

"But it is possible, isn't it?" Jak pressed. "I mean… if I already know it's my dad's grave then the locating spell can't have worked on my mum, right? It got the wrong parent. Mum might still be alive!"

Olíriá didn't answer. She looked like she was considering this very seriously. Jak was too relieved to care. For a brief horrible moment, she had thought that her Mum was dead and that she was going to have to tell her sisters it was over. Now she had hope again. Then a voice drifted out from the trees.

"Well, well, well…" Jim's accent smirked at them. "I thought I smelt something sexy going on. What are you two up to?"

Jak whirled around. Jim was standing not far from the pool. He was leaning against a tree with his arms folded and his usual winning grin plastered to his face. Jak wanted to snarl at him to leave, but her heart nearly faltered when she heard Olíriá's pleasantly surprised tone.

"James…?"

"Hey Olí," he grinned. "Looking good, babe."

"What are you doing here?" she smiled warmly at him.

"This is the land of mortals," he gestured at their surroundings. "I live here. What are you doing here?"

"Jak summoned at the pool," Olíriá indicated. "I answered."

"Why?" Jim sauntered over to join them.

"I was trying to find Mum," Jak muttered, hating everything that was happening now and desperately wishing she was wearing more than just a towel.

"Not you, Jellybean."

"Oh?" Olíriá gave the nickname an amused look. "Is she one of yours?"

"No!" Jak exclaimed. "I am not."

"Jak and her sisters are travelling with me," Jim added. "That's all."

"That's all?" Olíriá looked sceptical and amused. "That doesn't sound like you, Jim. You? Looking after kids? Keeping your hands to yourself? Pull the other one."

"You sound like the gnome," Jim sneered.

"It's just so hard to believe you, of all people, went soft," she laughed.

Jim's eyes narrowed. A darkness settled in his glare that chilled the blood.

"Please don't encourage him," Jak requested. "I have enough trouble with him already."

"You are his type, Jak," Olíriá shrugged.

"Everyone's his type!" Jak yelled. "Krill said Jim would fuck everything that moves and several things that wouldn't — he doesn't feel special. I will *never* be one of those things. We're just… friends. We're friends." She begrudged the word a little, but it was partly true.

Olíriá laughed openly. "Oh, poor Krill… how is he?"

"He's well, thank you," Jim smiled at her, and the troubled look in his eyes vanished. He was standing too close to Olíriá, but she didn't seem to mind. In fact, she almost seemed to move into him, and Jak found herself shrinking back from them as he continued. "They both are. They'll appreciate you asking after them."

"I'm glad they're well, and you look well too, Jim." Her smile was coy now. "I've missed you."

He grinned and eyeballed her divine form suggestively. "You should come visit more."

"Would that I could," she laid a hand tenderly on his chest, "but some of us have to work."

"That's what you're doing answering rune markers? You're stealing sprite work so you can ask questions?"

"It's been a year, Jim," Olíriá said seriously. "We're getting desperate. We'll try anything. Whoever did this… however it happened…" she trailed off wearily.

"That's what you were asking Jak for in exchange for finding her Mom?"

"Yes."

"Did it work? Did you find her?"

"Apparently not. Somehow, trying to locate her mother, I ended up with her father's grave. At least, that's what she tells me."

"Huh." Jim's eyes narrowed.

"Yeah."

"Hm."

"Yeah."

"Okay."

"Pretty much," Olíriá nodded.

"What?" Jak stared at them dumbfounded. They both looked at her, but only as much as they seemed to be regarding her. Olíriá still had her hand on Jim, and the sight sparked a flame of rage in Jak's chest.

"There's three of them, Olí," Jim told her gently. "Three girls. Sisters. Jak's the oldest. Same parents. They're unusual girls, to be sure, but not a whiff of fae blood amongst them. Not that I can tell."

"Well, you'd know," Olíriá affirmed her faith in him. "I'm not getting anything either, but it is weird."

"Very weird," he agreed. "You want to talk to her then or are you prepared to take my word?"

"You've found nothing then?" Olíriá looked at him sadly.

"If I had you'd be the first to know," he assured. "Well… second, third… you'd be in the top ten."

"You're hilarious," she said dryly.

"I know. I'm so witty," he grinned stupidly. Olíriá laughed at him and the two stood chuckling like old friends. Jak stood watching it happen feeling like she was dying inside.

"I have to go then," Olíriá sighed. "Let us know what you find, please. We need this to be over, Jim. I need this to be over. Then we can catch up again, properly."

"I look forward to it," he nodded. Olíriá leant in towards him. The two of them kissed each other's cheeks fondly. Olíriá looked back at Jak as she stepped away from Jim. She smiled at her.

"Good luck, Jak. I hope you find your mother. And… be careful around him," she cast a look back at Jim. "He may seem charming, but he has a way about him."

"Rude," Jim commented. The two of them grinned at each other again.

"You know how to find me if you need me," the goddess told her. With a final nod of farewell, Olíriá turned and walked back into the pool. She kept going until she was completely submerged, and then she was gone.

"Well, it looks like you made a good first impression, Jellybean," Jim grinned at her.

Jak glared daggers at him. One hand kept her towel tightly around her body, the other clenched and unclenched in a fist. She wanted to deck him.

"What the fuck was that?" she growled. "How do you know her?"

"Olí and I are old friends," Jim shrugged. He was eyeing up Jak wickedly. "Why? Would you like a more intimate introduction?"

Jak smacked him across the face. Her open palm echoed a resounding slap on his cheek. The strike was hard enough to turn his head. His expression didn't change.

"Oh Jellybean…" his tone was awful. It was so sultry it practically dripped from his tongue. "Looks like I know your type now. If I'm getting under your skin, it's only because I'm using the hole she made…"

Jak hit him again. This time she punched him so hard he staggered. A red mark tinged his cheekbone like the birth of a bruise. His smile never wavered. He grinned up at her. There was a sharp glint in his hungry brown eyes.

"You realise I'm into this, right?" he stood tall and held his arms out invitingly. "Keep pounding on me. I'm bound to get off on it soon enough."

Jak staggered back. Her desire to hit him vanished at his invitation. Everything about him made her skin crawl. She hated the way he looked at her. She hated the way he spoke to her. She hated the way he got off tormenting her.

"I hate you," she muttered, staggering back. "I hate you!" she bellowed. "Just fuck off! Fuck off down your own hole and die, Jim! I wish I'd never met you!"

"Do you really wish that?" he dropped his arms and his tone became serious. He didn't approach her. The further away she backed the more space he let her have. The less he tried to tease. For a moment, his gaze was as serious as Krill could be. "I can make that happen, Jak. I can erase myself from your mind. You could go back to a life with no idea who I was."

She faltered. Half of her was terrified he could do it. The other half was afraid he would. It gave her pause to consider. A flicker of his smile returned and dimpled his cheeks as he saw her hesitate. She was angry, but she didn't actually want to lose him. It was enough, for now.

"Jak..."

She didn't look at him. She huddled down on the rocks by her pack, clutching the towel to her body and staring down at the moss on the ground.

"Jak." That time his voice came firmer. She couldn't

refuse the call. She looked up and met his eyes. There was nothing teasing or hungry there anymore. His gaze was severe. Pitying. "She's the goddess of love, Jak," he spoke softly. "It would be weird if you didn't feel something."

Jak looked away again and turned her eyes to her toes scrunching the soft moss. He was right, she knew it, and it didn't do anything to ease her resentment. She just wanted him to treat her like a person instead of a plaything. If he could just be straight with her about everything… but then, perhaps, it just wasn't in Lord Skankington's nature to be straight about anything. The memory of her own ability to tease him eased the anger in her chest.

"We need to hit the road again," Jim told her. "So, unless you want to make my dreams come true running around in your towel, I need you to get dressed."

Jak looked at him warningly again. Jim raised his hands defensively.

"I'm turning around. I won't peek. I swear." He turned obediently, and she could tell from his tone he meant it. Even so, she dressed as quickly and carefully as she could. She hurriedly pulled clean clothes on under her towel. Once she was appropriately covered, she took her time adjusting her outfit and wrapping her wet clothes up in the damp towel. The entire time she kept her eyes on Jim, just in case. He didn't move a muscle. Just as he promised, he didn't look. He didn't so much as shift his weight.

For a moment, Jak just watched him stand there. He didn't even say anything to try and rush her, even though she had long since covered herself. The way he had respectfully kept his word and his distance mellowed her again. It was almost enough to make her like him the way she had before the fight. She glimpsed the carefully packed bowls again, and just for a moment, while she was trusting him anyway, she wondered about showing him.

She didn't. Just because Jim could be a decent person didn't mean he was worthy of her trust, and it made his behaviour when he wasn't decent all the more inexcusable. It almost felt like there were two Jims, but she knew there weren't. He was just complicated. She remembered the darkness in his eyes. He'd been acting out. Olíriá's comment that he'd gone soft had spooked him, and he'd taken it out on Jak. He'd wanted to prove he hadn't changed. She still wanted to smack him across the face again. If she had to choose between trusting Jim or Krill, she'd pick Krill — he was, after all, her master. She had high hopes of apprenticing herself to him. She kept the bowls a secret.

"I'm decent," she called to him.

Jim turned with a wry look. "You're always decent," he commented. "To the extent that it's disappointing. Haven't you ever thought about being the bad girl?"

"No," Jak looked down on him as she hoisted her pack.

He sighed and shook his head like she'd just told him he was in for a long cold winter.

"I adore you, Jellybean, but you are a colossal stick up my ass, and not in a fun way."

"That's funny," Jak retorted, far more comfortable

around him now that she was dressed and had worked out why he was behaving so poorly. "You're like dung on my boot I just can't wash off."

"Ouch."

"Yeah," she smirked. "This is a two-way street, you prick."

Jim gave her a long look. "I deserved that, didn't I?"

"Yes."

"Fair. Call it quits now and start over?"

Jak thought about it for a moment, but there was nothing to be gained by continuing to fight with him. She nodded.

"Alright, but next time you start on that shit again I'm calling Krill on you."

"Ooooh," Jim grinned wickedly at her. "Please. He gets so rough when he's mad…"

"Don't start," Jak grumbled. She stalked off through the trees and Jim followed after her. It didn't feel like they'd put the fight behind them. Even though they said they had, even though they'd agreed to, there wasn't any closure for Jak. She still felt that tightness in her chest and that dread in her gut. She still felt like they'd just fought.

"Why did you panic when Olíriá said you'd gone soft?" Jak asked him suddenly as they walked through the trees together. "What's so wrong with being the good guy?"

"I am the good guy," Jim grinned at her. "I just also have a certain reputation to maintain."

"Is it so important that everyone thinks you're Lord Skankington?"

"I would have appreciated you dropping that name in front of her instead of saving this conversation for now."

"Jim."

"Yeah, yeah…" he sighed. "I dunno, Jellybean. Sometimes I just…" he trailed off. "How do you want to be seen?"

"Me?"

"Yeah, you. You posture and pose and scold all the rest of us, but how do you want to be seen? How do you want the boys and I to describe you to others when we tell these tales?"

"I dunno," Jak shrugged.

"You want to be strong? Smart? Well-mannered and proper? You want to be fierce and bold and independent?"

Jak blushed. "I guess… those sound good."

"So you don't want people thinking you've gone soft under my care? You don't want people to think that I'm making you easy and delicate and sensitive?"

Jak considered this as they walked. Twigs and leaves crunched underfoot as they stepped across the uneven ground.

"Okay… I get it," she muttered. "But, I mean… you're a magician, right? What are you worried about?"

"Jak." He stopped and the tone of his voice made her pause and turn to look at him. There was a glint in his eye. A light like magic. His expression was severe, and it scared her. She almost wished for the cheeky dimpled grin to come back and make it go away. "Jellybean, I am more powerful now than I have ever been. I want people to remember that. I want them to know it when they look at me, and I don't want to have to prove it to anyone. I have no interest in reminding the Lords of Roïgola'a'lanaū not to mess with me over their own dead bodies, but if they force my hand, I will not hesitate."

Jak stared at him in shock. Fear prickled her spine like a drop of ice water running down her back. He was talking about deicide. The power to kill a god. Surely he couldn't be that strong? No one could. Nothing about him looked like he was joking.

"But... but..." Jak stammered. "But you seemed to get on with Olíriá fine. You can't dislike the D'Ihne that much."

"Olíriá is one of the best," Jim told her. The light died in his eye and he kept walking. Jak fell in beside him. "Can I tell you a secret, Jak?"

She nodded eagerly. She wished he would.

"Most people don't know this, but you've met her now. Olíriá helped Krill and Kode escape. She was the one who married them. It's possible they would have died without her. It was in direct violation of Clōudiá's orders, but no one up there knows she did it."

"Why is the fae world so complicated?" Jak asked.

"Because people live in it," Jim chuckled. "People are complicated, Jak. They complicate everything around them. It's a disorder. They can't help it." He cast her a sideways glance. "Just look at us."

Jak conceded that point with a weary look. Now she felt like they were done fighting. This time anyway.

"Why did you tell her that my sisters and I don't

have fae blood?"

"Because you don't seem to. I can't get even a whiff of fae from you."

"But why would you even think to look?" Jak pressed. "We're human. We've always been human. Why would you think otherwise?"

"Because you're weird for humans," Jim answered honestly. "Weird stuff going on with parents, spells getting mom and dad confused for instance, that's very fae. You can sense magic — extremely unusual for a human. Allie's smarter than she should be at her age — even Dora's bright, and she has a way with faeries. You girls are something, that's for sure. I just don't know what yet."

"We're human," Jak repeated stubbornly. "Our father was a man called Grey who died when a tree fell on him. He was out in the forest collecting firewood, but he was dazed and distracted because Mum had just given birth to Dora. So his mind wasn't on the task and he wasn't careful. Mum's name is Bella, and she's out there somewhere — I know it — even if the faeries can't find her."

Jim looked like he was going to say something, but whatever it was he decided against it. They reached the wagon again and the others were waiting patiently. The girls were jumping from the back of the wagon into the long grass. Dora still had berry juice staining her lips. The rabbits seemed to be treating the jumping as a game. They would hop close and nibble the grass, and then bolt away when a girl landed near them, only to creep back between leaps. Kode was supervising while

Krill lounged. The former D'rö-Hadās raised a smooth eyebrow at them as they returned.

"Here I was wondering if we were going to have to form a search party for the both of you."

"How come you let this perv come look for me?" Jak demanded.

"He said he'd be good. What did you do?" Krill glared at Jim accusatorily. Jim wandered over and laid a gentle hand on Krill's leg. He looked between the two fae who met his gaze in return.

"Olíriá sends her love," he told them. "I passed on yours as well."

"You saw Olí?" Kode's long ears perked up.

"I did," Jim smirked. "She and Jak were getting all hot and steamy in the stream…"

"We were not!" Jak yelled. "You lying little —!"

Jim dodged out of the way as Jak took another swipe at him. Krill maintained his raised eyebrow as Jim took on a feigned expression of protesting innocence.

"I think," Krill began coolly, "that given that Jak is notoriously sex-shy, and Olíriá is unwaveringly monogamous, that you might just be a lying little —, Jim." He even mimicked the brutal pause after little.

"You got to meet Olíriá?" Allie chimed in. "The goddess Olíriá?"

"No fair!" Dora protested. "I want to meet a goddess!"

"Me too!" Allie added.

"Well, next time we run into one I'll be sure to introduce you," Jim promised.

"Was she pretty?" Dora asked.

"Very," Jak nodded with a blush.

Allie snorted. Jak glared at her.

"Come on," Jim placated the younger girls, herding them towards the wagon again. "Don't give her a hard time. That's my job."

"Why?" Allie scoffed. "She's not your sister."

"Although sometimes it doesn't feel that way," Jak muttered. She shot Jim a dark look. "You're more annoying than those two combined."

"Are you going to be our new big brother?" Dora giggled at him.

"That sounds like a terrible idea," Jim replied. "Come on, stop playing around and let's get going." He tried to pick Dora up out of the grass. He scooped her under the arms and swung her up. "Oh, geez, nope. Oh, you're so heavy!"

"I'm not heavy!" Dora protested. "Kode can pick me up!"

"Yeah, but Kode has a god-body," Jim pointed out. "I have a normal body."

"You have a dad body," Jak commented.

"Hey!" Jim turned on her. "Do I insult you?"

"Frequently," she retorted.

His answering smile was brighter than the sun. He went full-dimples. With a laugh, he hauled a playfully limp Dora out of the grass and onto the back step. She was giggling and trying to be difficult on purpose. Kode took her from Jim with ease, and she threw her arms around the pretty faerie's neck. Jim approached Jak. His warm brown eyes were soft, and he stretched his back out like lifting children wasn't good for the spine at his age.

"Are we good again?" he asked gently.

She nodded in kind. "Yeah. I think we are."

"You want to ride up front?" He asked as though it really was a question. The other four were already piling themselves into the back of the wagon. Somehow, without anyone talking about it, this had just become the new norm. They expected her to drive the wagon with Jim. She didn't mind. More than that… she wanted to. She nodded at him. The way he grinned at her made it hard to imagine that dark and serious expression he had worn in the forest.

She set her pack and her laundry in the back of the wagon. The others climbed down. Jim closed the doors and led her around to the front seat. They climbed up and Jim signed the horses into being. Jak gave him a sideways glance. He met the look. They a shared rueful smile, and with a click to the illusionary horses they rolled off into the forest.

CHAPTER TEN

Jak watched the magical scenery roll by as they drove through the afternoon and contemplated the beauty of the forest. It really was extraordinary. It was nearly as beautiful as Olíriá. The thought made her blush. She wished she didn't feel that way, but it couldn't be helped. Weirdly, Jim's words had been what helped, even though he had also made everything a thousand times worse. He'd been right though. She was the goddess of love. It would have been weird if Jak hadn't felt something. Although, apparently, there were lots of things weird about Jak, so it might have been nice if not having crushes on goddesses was one of those things.

The wagon began to slow, but Jak barely realised. She was too deep in the memory. Once she was over her own discomfort, she realised she had learnt something from that encounter. Something important. Jim was still lying to her. Something was happening with the fae and he did know about it. Olíriá had mentioned that it had been a year since something. She was answering at an ancient pool instead of a sprite. Maybe that was connected to why the fae weren't answering at Cröck'ko-rú at all. Whatever it was, Jim knew, and he wasn't telling.

"Jak!" Jim hissed softly to her.

She started sharply, as though worried he could hear her thoughts. When she turned to look at him though, he wasn't looking at her. The Banging Wagon had come to a silent stop. Jim was looking through the trees. He nudged her and indicated with a nod. She followed his gaze. Something shone through the woods. Jak saw. Her heart nearly stopped.

That was magic. For the first fraction of a second she had thought it was simply two wild horses. Then she had seen the horns. The pure white coats. The gleam and shimmer off them that seemed almost to glow in the faint light of the forest. The unicorns looked their way, but didn't approach. One nuzzled the other. They nodded their heads towards the wagon, as though acknowledging their audience. Then they trotted off and vanished through the trees.

Jak was still holding her breath. She hadn't drawn breath the entire time they had been watching them. It was too incredible to breathe, but she was going to have to at some point. Silently, she sighed.

"Maybe we don't tell your sisters about that one..." Jim whispered, and then jerked the caravan into a slow roll.

"Yeah..." Jak agreed, still in awe. "They'd just be sad they missed it." She sat back and let the silence happen around them. Somehow, the bubble of wonder that had formed around her kept the sounds of the birds and the trees and the wagon muted. She had completely forgotten what she had been thinking about before. "That was so amazing..." she breathed. "And you showed me!"

"Uh, yeah!" Jim replied obviously. His tone made it very clear that he would never pass up the opportunity to show her something incredible.

"How come sometimes you're like this and sometimes you're this annoying lecherous creep?" she asked.

"How come sometimes you're like this and sometimes you're this stuck-up pain in my ass?" Jim replied. He leant sideways towards her and gave her a rueful smile. "I know you don't see it, Jellybean, but this is a two-way street."

She shoved him wryly, but she was smiling. He sat back with a grin. However much they fought, it wasn't all bad. Jak wanted to remember this moment next time she felt like stabbing him, but she knew she wouldn't forget it. Whatever else happened, she would remember Jim and the unicorns for the rest of her life. The thought made her smile as they rode on.

Within a couple of hours they had found their way onto the road again. Or rather, they had found a road. It was wide and well used. Other carts rolled by them and people nodded or called out. It wound around the edge of a sparkling blue lake, like a brown ribbon separating the blue water and the green forest. Jak stared as they rolled out from the trees. She was prepared to admit the awe of seeing real unicorns might have been affecting her judgement, but it was nice to feel so inspired by life. She had also never seen anything like it before. It was a vision of wonder. Maybe everything was. Maybe her eyes had been opened and she had a destiny and the whole world was her road now. Maybe she was seeing everything in a new light. The sunlight sparkled off the water like rippling silver. Another caravan rolled by on the other side of the road, momentarily blocking her view. The driver gave them a nod as he went by. Jak ignored him and craned her neck to see the water again.

"You doing okay, Jellybean?" Jim chuckled at her.

"It's so beautiful…" she breathed. "Is that the ocean? I've heard about it, but I never…"

"That's just a lake," Jim smiled at her. "Well… it's not just a lake. It's Othalí'taian."

Jak didn't know what that meant, but she was sure there was a story. She rolled her eyes.

"Go on then," she invited with a sigh.

"What?" he protested innocently.

"What's the legend? Who had sex to make this lake?" she grumbled.

Jim laughed at her. He grinned his beaming grin and shook his head.

"No one," he chuckled, trying to stop laughing. "It's a lake of tears. Your girlfriend cried it."

"Wait, what?"

"Othalí'taian is named because it was the lake of tears Olíriá wept when she thought Crŷstïar had been killed. This is millennia ago, before they were officially together." Jim gave the lake a contemplative look. "Although it did lead to their first kiss."

Jak stared at the lake. She couldn't even see the other side of it. A sharp pang flared through her chest at the memory of the goddess, and the thought that such a beautiful creature had wept such a giant lake.

"What happened...?" she asked.

"Olíriá heard that Crŷstïar had been killed in battle against an uprising of Soul Mages," Jim recounted. "But actually the little shit faked his death. The D'Ihne of trickery is a fucking drama queen, let me tell you. If he has a chance to pull one over on someone, he doesn't pass it up. I think he was doing it to try and get his father's attention, but I can't really remember. Ĝoŕgomghōul has never cared much about his kids, and the little snowflake wanted to teach daddy a lesson. Jokes on him, Ĝoŕgomghōul did not care an ounce. Didn't even come out of his cave. However, Crŷstïar still thinks it paid off. He'd been in love with Olíriá since they were born. When she thought he'd been killed, she hid in her room and wept until the tears poured from the Golden City and flooded the earth beneath it. As soon as Crŷstïar realised what had happened, he rushed home and declared his love for her. He told her that it had been a trick, but that even if it hadn't been, he would always return to her and not even death could stop him."

"Oh..." Jak sighed wistfully.

"No!" Jim turned on her at her tone. He raised a finger and pointed accusingly. "No!"

"That's so romantic..." Jak sighed.

"No! No no no no no! Bad! He's a lying little shit! This is not romantic!"

"It is a bit," Jak insisted.

"No, it isn't! If he'd died he would not have come back. Death is final, even for D'Ihne. It's not romantic, it's bullshit."

"I think, Jim," Jak began patiently. "That romance sometimes is a bit bullshit, but it's not about the truth, it's about the intent."

"That is dangerous thinking," Jim huffed. "Crŷstïar is a little monster. He's spent his whole life messing with people. Olí only loves him because she's a softie, and because he's always been so desperately in love with her, and because they get along really well, and they write songs together. He writes poetry to go with her music — what with him being eloquence and all. And because she thinks he's funny—"

"You realise the more you list the better it sounds, right?" Jak pointed out.

"Anyway!" Jim huffed. "That is the story of Othalí'taian. No one had sex. Or, at least, when they finally did it was only partially related and so boring and vanilla it didn't make it into the actual legend. The legend which is also so *boring* that the people who live in these parts just call this place Lake Kover."

Jak knew that name. She had heard it before. She tried to remember her geography.

"Isn't that near the capital?" she asked.

"Kinda," Jim shrugged. "Kosvo, the capital city of Kosveir, is still two days away, but we're on the road heading that direction."

"How?" Jak demanded. "How did we get so far?"

Jim just smiled at her. She blushed slightly. Of course, he'd teleported them at least twice. The first time down the side of the mountain. The second to escape the fight. Both times to run from the D'rö-Hadās.

His magic covered more space than she'd realised.

"Are we going to Kosvo?" she asked to try and cover her last question.

"Do you want to?" Jim replied.

"Um…" Jak thought about it. She wasn't sure. It hadn't been on her to-do list, but that was because she never thought she'd travel that far. Now that it was close the idea seemed very grand. She'd never seen a big city before. She'd never really seen a city before. A big city might be the kind of place to ask about her mother. If faeries hadn't been able to help, perhaps people could, although she knew it was a long shot. But then, she couldn't think of a reason not to. "Is it nice?" she asked.

"It's a big city," Jim shrugged. "The quality of life and conditions ranges horrifically. You have everything from the King, who wants for nothing and hangs the entire kingdom on his whims, to the beggars in the streets who starve because apparently the wealthy can't even spare their scraps to them."

"Oh," Jak said quietly. That sounded far less grand than she had imagined. Jim glanced her way and realised that he had been less than kind about the capital of her country. He sighed.

"Big cities… kingdoms… they're complicated, Jak," he tried to explain. "Big cities are something you get when lots of people gather together to build a society. Most of the time they are drawn together by something — resources, power, wealth — it all ties together. Humans are greedy by nature. They're self-obsessed. You always seem to end up with those that have lots, living lives that mean they still stretch their means and want more, all the while not even seeing the people they step on to get there." He turned his concerned brown eyes to her. "Humans are wilfully ignorant, they can't help themselves, it's like a defence mechanism. They need it. They tell themselves that the poor are poor because they're not working hard enough in a game that's rigged. Most of the rich in a city like Kosvo are rich because they, or their ancestors, took power by force. They subjugated others. At this point, they don't even realise that what they're saying is basically: you're poor because you don't have what it takes to murder and rob me. That's how it started, long before these people were conceived, and now they've put up rules and laws to stop others from doing the same to them."

"I didn't know that…" Jak blushed. "It sounds like politics."

"It is," Jim shrugged. "Jellybean, politics happens to everyone, whether you're paying attention or not. You living on the edge of a tiny backwater town, being driven out by a mob scared of witches — that's politics. You were in that position because of the socioeconomic conditions of your kingdom."

"I don't know what that means," Jak blushed. This conversation had gotten out of her depth. Jim seemed to realise, and he smiled at her.

"It means the system sucks, and you can do better."

"What does doing better look like?" Jak asked earnestly.

"What do you want it to look like?" Jim replied. "What do you want out of life?"

Jak didn't know the answer. She had only ever known her life in Rutsborough. Doing better there, her dream was to maybe one day take over the smithy, or perhaps even start her own. That would have been doing very well. Now she had a destiny. Now Jim was talking about kings and rich folk from a big city. Jak wouldn't even know where to start there. She had no interest in being a noble lady. What did she want out of life? She wanted to find her mother and settle down as a family again, somewhere where life could go back to normal. Maybe get another smithy apprenticeship. Maybe even get to go back to Rutsborough and Big Sam.

That didn't seem like the kind of dream she could tell Jim about though. The idea of saying it was embarrassing. He saw her life as small, and he was talking about stuff she had never heard of and didn't understand. She couldn't tell him she wanted to be one of those rich folk. But if she dreamed big… if she could be absolutely anything she wanted…

"I dunno," she shrugged nervously. "Maybe a knight? I think it would be quite cool to be a knight."

"Yeah?" Jim's response was leering and it made her blush. Of course, anything she said would have amused him, and she should have known that. It was a pretty ridiculous suggestion, but she thought that was more what he would have been expecting.

"Well… I dunno…" she muttered, trying to backtrack.

"Don't renege," Jim ordered. "You want to be a knight? Why not? You're good with a sword, nearly good enough to take on D'rö-Hadās, that's far better than most humans, and you're still just a kid. So, tell me honestly, Jellybean; do you think they'd let you? If we rocked on up to Kosvo and told them you wanted to be a knight, do you think they'd let you join?"

"No," Jak laughed. "No way. I'm not knight material."

"You should be," Jim told her without a trace of banter. "You've got what it takes. You have the skills to be one of the best. But you're right; they wouldn't take you. You've got no money, no connections. That's what matters. That's what they care about."

"So, how do you change that?"

"War," Jim answered bleakly. "Some people call it revolution, but at the end of the day it's still just a type of war."

"Is that what's happening in Dazigh?"

"Yes. That's exactly what's happening in Dazigh. The king is dead, his vaults are empty, and the people are rising up. They call it a revolution. Over here, Kosveir is judging them and calling it war. They're not wrong, but with any luck Dazigh will come out of this with a new system of government and a far more equal society. I guess we'll see."

"You're very smart," Jak told him loyally.

"You think?" Jim chuckled at her.

"You seem smart to me," she admitted. "I didn't know about any of this."

"That's not true, Jellybean," he smiled. "You knew plenty. You knew that the King of Kosveir holds all the power in the kingdom and that the people live in a monarchic system."

"Well... I suppose," she agreed, extrapolating meaning. She let the silence sit there and pondered everything Jim had told her. It was a lot to take in. Finally, she found she had questions. "Jim?"

"Yeah?"

"If people are inherently selfish and self-obsessed, then what's going to happen to Dazigh? What if new people just take over and the same thing happens again?"

"That, Jellybean, is what we call history."

"You mean... this kind of thing has happened before?"

"Not exactly the same way," Jim admitted. "But yeah, old systems are overthrown. New systems take over. Inequality grows. Breaking point is reached. The system is overthrown. You can see where this is going."

"So... what's the point?"

"Life," he answered philosophically. "We have to have something to do to fill in the time between birth and death — trying to organise ourselves is as good a thing as any. Of course, there's always the chance that we'll get it right this time. That really keeps humanity going."

"Will we get it right?"

"How should I know?" he shrugged. "There's a reason I live on the fringes of society."

"But you're hoping we will..." Jak smiled at him.

"There's always hope, Jellybean. Always hope."

Jak grinned. "It... it's funny to hear you say you hope that people will learn to be less self-obsessed."

"Why?"

"Well, y'know… you're kinda…"

"Oh am I?"

"Yeah," she giggled. "You're always doing whatever you please. Krill says you're a nymphomaniac."

"Do you know what that word means?" Jim leered.

"It means you're a sex addict."

"I'm n— I can st— Is that a bad thing?" Jim demanded, affronted.

"I mean… as long as you and Krill and Kode are happy and can manage it…" Jak shrugged, wishing she hadn't brought it up.

"That's like saying you're a food addict," Jim huffed offendedly.

"What?!" Jak laughed.

"You eat multiple times a day," Jim ranted. "You don't have to, but you like to, and it's good for you. So you do—"

"It's not the same."

"It's exactly the same!"

"Seriously?" Jak laughed. "If you don't get properly laid three times a day you get cranky?"

"Just watch me," Jim glowered.

Jak covered her mouth with her hands as she dissolved into hysterics. Other carts passing them on the road gave the sulking man and the mirthful teenager interesting looks, but neither of them cared. Jak knew Jim was struggling to maintain his glare. A smile kept teasing the edges of his mouth. He knew it was funny.

The afternoon sun was starting to sit low over the lake. The atmosphere was warm and the light was turning orange. It was a beautiful view, and the day had been so good. She barely even remembered the fight she'd had with Jim. Now that she sat here beside him, laughing at him and watching the glittering lake, she realised she was happy. Happier than she'd ever been in Rutsborough. Working in that town she had been content. This was different. She reached out and took Jim's hand. He gave her a startled look, but she ignored it. Her eyes stayed on the scenery.

"I'm just teasing you," she told him. "I know you're not really self-absorbed. You're kind and generous, and you've taken good care of us. Thank you."

"Olíriá got to you today," he quipped.

"No, she didn't," Jak smiled. "You're a nice person, Jim. That got to me." She turned to look at him, but he didn't look flattered. He looked concerned. Before she could say anything else, a voice came from above them.

"We need to pull over soon."

Jak shrieked and snatched her hand back from Jim as she gave a startled jump on the seat. She looked up. Krill was lying on the roof of the caravan above them, looking down on them.

"How long have you been there?!" Jak cried. "How did you get up there?!"

She realised Jim was grinning at her side and that Krill was surprised he had even startled her. He had that telling slight eyebrow raise.

"You're so quiet…" Jak whispered accusingly as her heart slowly stopped hammering a panicked beat into her ribs.

"You just ruined a tender moment," Jim grinned,

keeping his eyes on the road.

"You can thank me later," Krill invited. "Personally."

"Oooo, I should be pulling over then?"

"It's not that dark," Jak muttered, blushing from her own embarrassment as well as their insinuations.

"No," Krill agreed. "But I can sense them out there. They're hot on our trail, and they're just waiting for the shadows to get thick enough to walk through. We got surprised by them last night. I don't want to make the same mistake twice."

"Fair enough," Jim conceded and drove off the side of the road. The Banging Wagon bumped and rattled into the grass at the edge of the forest. They pulled back into the trees a way so that they could set up the runes. Jim didn't go far and the road was still visible. They found a clear patch to set up camp. When Jak looked up, Krill was gone, but when she clambered down from the caravan to stretch she saw him marking Fora out in the trees.

The sun set a deep blood red that evening as they set up camp. Jak slacked off to slip through the trees and watch the sun set over the lake. It was one of the most beautiful things she'd ever seen, including the goddess and the unicorns. This was what she was happy for. This was what she was grateful for. She remembered with a tinge of shame the way she had wanted to blame Jim for ruining their lives, but it hadn't been his fault, and without him she may never have seen so much of the amazing world she lived in.

As she stood staring at the magnificent scenery, she

felt a darkness at the edge of her senses. Her hand tightened on the hilt of her sword before she even realised what she was doing. She had sworn to Krill she wouldn't try and fight them again. He was her master now, and she had to keep her word. As quickly and quietly as she could, she ducked back into the safety of Fora. She felt it as soon as she passed into the protected area. The sense of the darkness vanished. It was out there, somewhere, but it wasn't seeking her anymore. She was safe. Eyes watched her from the firepit. Jak looked over to Krill, and her face flushed hot. He knew what she'd been doing, but he wasn't going to say anything. Not with words. His eyes did a lot of his talking for him.

She ducked away to help Kode and the girls with the tent. It was going to be nice to have a bed to sleep in again tonight, even if it was just a bunk. Once the camp was set, and twilight fell, they sat around the campfire for dinner. They set the benches up against the trees like hard, makeshift couches around the glowing centre of their camp. Jak lounged by the fire, warm and full and happy. It was a good life and she was grateful for it. Until, naturally, Jim told everyone what she'd said about becoming a knight.

"I said that in confidence!" Jak protested to him.

"No, you didn't," Jim chuckled. He was lounging on a bench with a tree behind him and branches spreading around one side. He was sprawled comfortably against the bark with Kode, who was lying back against him using his chest as a pillow. "Why so shy now?"

"Yeah," Allie piped up. "You being a knight actually

sounds cool."

"And then if you're a knight I can be a princess!" Dora clapped excitedly. The two girls were sharing a seat and enthusiastic expressions. Jak smiled at them. She appreciated the vote of confidence.

"It's not like I can do it anyway," she muttered, shredding a stalk of grass in her fingers.

"Have you tried?" Krill asked pointedly from beside her. She looked up at her teacher. His golden eyes regarded her in the firelight.

"I don't think I'd be allowed."

"You'll never know if you don't try."

"Would you teach me to be good enough?"

"I'd say you already are," Krill assured. "You are a formidable warrior for a human, Jak."

"Aw…" Kode smiled across the camp. "That's cute."

"I don't…" Jak muttered awkwardly. "I don't feel like I'm the best I can be."

"There is always room for improvement," Krill shrugged. "And you are young. Your skill speaks to such a future, if you pursue it."

"But you'll keep training me, right?"

"If you wish," he dipped his head.

"You can do it, Jak," Kode chuckled as he watched them across the fire. "You're naturally gifted and you're getting one-on-one training — actual training. Used to be in the D'rö-Hadās that you had to be one of the cute young men in the army to warrant one-on-one training with the D'Hiris."

Jim and Allie cackled viciously at Kode's revelation. Even Jak shot her master a nervously amused look. His eyes were on his husband. Kode was watching him lovingly, but cheekily.

"I'm not wrong," he insisted.

Krill didn't argue, but ignored their judgement and shook his pale hair regally back from his face. He bore a completely unfazed expression.

"It's true through," Jim agreed from where he lounged with an arm around Kode, who was snuggled up against him. "There were rumours about your army, Elkrillendé. You went to great pains to be discreet, but you're lucky no one wanted to bring you down. Enough people knew your weakness that if someone had wanted to take advantage of that and disgrace you, they could have."

"Like they didn't?" Krill indicated his surroundings.

"You did this to yourself, Krill," Jim replied. "No one tricked you into shagging Kode."

"Except me," Kode offered. "I started it."

"You did," Krill agreed.

"I loved you," Kode defended plaintively. "You were so beautiful and kind and brave. It was worth it — to me. Regrets?"

"Never," Krill smiled softly at him. Kode returned the look warmly. Jak watched them with a softness in her heart, but their conversation triggered a thought.

"What about Elrïlani?" she asked.

"What about her?" Krill turned to Jak.

"She took over after you. Is there any chance she set that up? Did she know about you and Kode, or help you two meet?"

"No," Krill shook his head. "I met Kode through

Frézíān. Besides, Elrïlani never wanted to be D'Hiris. She didn't even want to be D'rö-Hadās."

"Then why is she?"

"Because she was chosen. It is a great honour to kill for the Queen, and it is not a position you turn down. It's not as though Ha'Cās get to choose their lives."

Jak nodded in response. "So… you don't begrudge her then? She took your command, stabbed you, nearly killed you, and… you…?"

"She was just doing her job," Krill replied. "I do not begrudge her, Jak. If anything, I pity her. I know her well. This is not the life she would have chosen for herself, but to leave she would risk just as much as I did, and death is a frightening prospect to an immortal. I have a chance at freedom that she doesn't. I cannot be angry at someone when I have so much and they have so little. She is still trapped in slavery."

"How do we fix that?" Jak demanded.

The boys all stared at her. They stared at her like she'd told them she was going to set fire to the world. It had seemed like the obvious question, but now they were just making her feel self-conscious.

"What?" she muttered. "You must want to fix it, right?"

"One thing at a time, Jellybean," Jim warned her. "You work on becoming a knight, then you can save the world."

"Besides," Allie added nervously. "That's fae politics, and I don't think they'd like it if humans tried to get involved. The gods would smite us."

"That not fair," Jak insisted.

"Life has never been fair, child," Krill told her softly. "Perhaps the world will become fairer in time, but Jim is right: one thing at a time. It is not for you to toil on our behalf. You have your own concerns."

Jak didn't fight with him, but she didn't agree either. It was her concern. These were the people she loved, and their world was awful. There had to be a better way. There had to be something she could do. She let those thoughts chase each other around her head. Even though she didn't voice them, she could feel Jim watching her like he knew what she was thinking. He stared at her so long she couldn't meet his eye. Finally, he sighed and squeezed Kode gently beside him, before motioning him to sit so that he could stand.

"Alright," he stood up. "It's late. Let's get some rest before morning sneaks up on us like a dog."

"What about dishes?" Dora asked.

"Dishes are on me," Jim told her. "You look like you need sleep, especially if you're still not a hundred percent. You going to take your medicine tonight?"

Dora nodded. "Yes."

"Good girl."

"Can I put a plate out for the faeries?"

"Yes, you may." Jim ruffled her curls. Dora grinned and straightened her flower crown. Then she hurriedly filled a plate and took it out to the edge of the campsite to leave on the grass. The others watched her and Jim leant into Jak.

"Do you ever worry she's going to attract a bunch of feral badgers or something?"

"No," Jak grinned. "We always had too many feral

gnomes."

Jim laughed, and he ushered them to the tent once Dora was done. The packs were stashed by the door and there wasn't much room for people and bunks.

"It is kinda cramped in here, isn't it?" he commented.

"Only because you're trying to join us," Allie retorted. "Sorry to disappoint, but it sleeps three, and Jak isn't going to get changed for your benefit."

"Allie!" Jak exclaimed.

"I'm not here to perv," Jim assured Allie defensively. "Last night was a disaster and I just wanted to make sure you were alright."

"I'll believe that when I see it," Allie smirked at him as she helped Dora measure out a spoonful of medicine. Dora drank the spoonful and then took the cup of water Jak handed her and drank that as well.

"Thanks," she muttered. Jak rubbed her back soothingly. It should get them through the night. Jim watched over them protectively. He'd been well behaved since he and Jak had left the spring. Now he rolled his eyes at Allie's cheek and sighed tragically.

"You try and be nice and what do you get..." he lamented.

"To be fair," Jak commented, placing a hand on his arm. "You do deserve this, because you are so frequently a terrible person."

"Me?" Jim replied in mock horror.

"Yes," Jak grinned at him. Then she hugged him, quickly grabbing him around the waist and squeezing him. "But for all that you're a terrible person, you make a pretty good big brother." She let go quickly, before he could ruin it, and slunk away to her bunk on the other side of the tent. Jim watched her go and the girls watched him.

"I don't think my actual siblings would agree with you…" he commented.

"You have actual siblings?" Allie asked.

"A couple," he admitted. "I don't think they like me very much though."

"Wonder why…" Dora giggled cheekily. Jim winked at her. He smiled softly around the tent.

"Sleep tight, girls," he bid them, before fastening the tent behind him on the way out.

***

Jak woke to the sound of rain. She could hear it pouring through the trees and splattering over the tent. Something was wrong. She couldn't explain what, but she knew, powerfully and suddenly, something was wrong. The night was cold as she slipped from her bunk and snuck across the tent. In the darkness she tripped on the stuff by the door and cursed. She opened the tent and stumbled out into the rain.

It was dark in the forest, but the embers of the fire still steamed in the wet. Jak felt her heart stop. The Banging Wagon was gone. It wasn't a trick of the light. The caravan wasn't in the clearing. There were no tracks. No sign of where it had gone. It just wasn't there. As though by magic.

"Jak?" Allie called to her softly.

Jak turned to see her little sister peering out of the tent. Allie's expression took in Jak standing in the rain and the empty clearing. It hardened instantly.

"Jak! Get back inside!" Allie hissed.

Jak didn't move. The rain was hiding her tears. She didn't want her sisters to see her crying. She didn't want them to see she was scared and panicking.

"Jak, get in now!" Allie hissed. "You're getting soaked!"

Allie sounded so much like their own mother Jak couldn't refuse. She stumbled back into the tent, wiping the water from her hair and face. Dora was still asleep. She lay snoring quietly in her bunk with Binky's ears poking out of the blankets and her flower crown askew.

Allie was watching Jak with serious eyes. She had seen. She always saw. She always saw too much.

"They're probably just doing faerie stuff," Allie whispered. "They'll be back by morning."

Jak nodded. She wanted to believe that. She wanted to believe more than anything. They couldn't have just left them. They wouldn't do that. Jim and Krill wouldn't have left her. Kode wouldn't have left the girls. Allie watched her for a long moment. She knew Jak was struggling. She reached out a hand and squeezed Jak's shoulder reassuringly.

"They'll be back," Allie insisted. With that said, she climbed back into her bunk to wait.

Jak understood. She followed Allie's lead. She took off her wet top and climbed back into the warm sheets. They'd be back. They'd be back in the morning. She kept telling herself.

But they wouldn't. She knew they wouldn't. The same way she could sense magic she could sense its absence. They were gone. They weren't coming back, and the magic picnic basket had been left inside the tent door. That's what she had tripped on. She didn't know why, but they had up and left without saying anything. She kept trying to tell herself that they would come back for their things. But as she lay in the darkness, with her face pressed into her pillow, she silently wept.

CHAPTER ELEVEN

She was right. When the day dawned clear after the rain, the glade was still empty except for them. Jak had cried herself out in the night. Her pillow was still damp, but she turned it over to hide the tear stains. Her head hurt, and she poured herself multiple glasses of water from the pitcher to try and rehydrate. The worst part was Dora. When she woke up and realised the Banging Wagon was gone, she started screaming a tantrum. Jak didn't feel like there was anything she could do or say to calm her down. Dora's crying and shrieking was how she felt internally anyway.

"Where's Kode?" Dora cried. "Where is he?!"

"He's not here, sweetie," Jak told her wearily. "They had to go away."

"Why?!" she shrieked. "Where did they go?"

"I don't know," Jak sighed. "They didn't say anything."

"Clōudiá got them! She must have! They wouldn't leave us! They wouldn't! The faeries took them!"

Jak just sighed. Part of her had feared that too, except... she knew that wasn't what had happened. That would make it easier. If the D'rö-Hadās had caught them and taken them away, this would be easier. Then Jak and her sisters could try and rescue them. Then they could do something. But no. Jim and the boys had left. They had made sure the girls had food and water and shelter, and then they had left. She should have known when Jim came to tuck them in. She should have known something was wrong. She should have sensed it when she realised she was happy.

But they had left them with the essentials. They cared about them. Even when they weren't here, they were trying to take care of them. So why had they left?! The question filled Jak's chest like a burst pipe. It hurt. The pressure was building and building, and it had nowhere to go. She had to hold it together for the other two. Jak was hurting, Dora was despairing, and Allie... Allie was angry. Jak could tell. It was one of the things helping hold her together. Allie was quietly and resolutely angry. Seeing that kind of rage in her little sister helped calm her. It gave her something else to focus on. Something to fix.

"Dora, just stop," Jak told her patiently.

"I want Kode!"

"I want Kode too, but he's not here and screaming won't bring him back. Now, sit down. Have some breakfast."

Dora did as she was told, but she did so sullenly and with big wet tears of disappointment. Allie dished up breakfast for them and her dark eyes stayed severe and silent. It was one of the quietest meals they had ever had. With a sick dread, Jak realised this reminded her of the first weeks after their Mum had gone. Days spent around the kitchen table silently eating, not commenting that the food wasn't as good, not asking when Mum would get back. She couldn't bear it. She wasn't the only one.

"What…" Allie croaked quietly. "What do we do now?" She looked between them, but her eyes were mostly on Jak. "Do we wait for them? We have the tent, and food and water, we could just stay camped here until they come back?"

"We could," Jak nodded slowly. That was an option. But it raised the question she didn't want to think about, and couldn't bring herself to voice. What if they never came back? They had left on purpose without saying anything. If they had wanted the girls to wait, they could have told them to. Leaving in the dead of night like that… that was abandonment. "We could stay here…" Jak admitted. "But I don't think we should. I think we should keep going."

"Keep going where?" Allie muttered.

"Kosvo," Jak answered.

"You still going to be a knight?" Allie gave her a small, half-hearted grin.

"Maybe," Jak shrugged. "It's an option, anyway. Mostly I think it will be a good place to look for Mum. It's the heart of the kingdom, and if faeries haven't been able to help us, maybe humans can. Besides, at the very least we might be able to get someone official to certify that Dora isn't a witch, and once she's pardoned maybe we could even go home."

"I miss home…" Allie muttered sadly.

"I miss Kode…" Dora cried, her eyes welling up again and her lip trembling.

"I know, baby." Jak rubbed her back. "I know."

She did know. She missed them too. Jak did most of the packing up after breakfast. She turned a sock into a makeshift pouch where she stored the beds that turned into rags and the tent that folded up into the envelope. She tied it to her belt. It wasn't something she wanted in her pack in case it all decided to randomly open up. At least this way she could toss it away if it started expanding.

Once they were packed they hit the road, this time on foot. The girls had gotten used to the luxury of the wagon, and Jak was prepared for their complaining. Dora whined. Allie didn't. Jak kept sending glances her way, but Allie ignored them. They walked along the road by the lake, and Allie kept her gaze on the picturesque landscape. It softened the anger in her eyes, but Jak could still see it sitting there under the surface.

It was a quiet day. Caravans and carts rolled by on the road, but the girls tried to avoid meeting anyone's eye. Jak wasn't prepared to befriend any more strangers. Dora complained a lot in the morning. She cried that she had to walk; she cried that Kode was gone; she cried that they still hadn't found Mum and that Jak was being unfair. She said all those things repeatedly. Soon after lunch she dissolved into a coughing fit. They gave her more medicine, but the bottle was half empty now, and they didn't know how much they could give her or how long it would last. Jak and Allie shared the opinion that at least at Kosvo they might be able to find a doctor that could help.

The sickness took the wind out of Dora's sails and she was quiet for the afternoon. They had been walking all day, and even walking at Dora's speed Jak was tired. She felt like walking slowly was tiring her out faster. She wanted to run. She wanted to sprint away from her problems and break over the next hill. But she couldn't. She kept them going as long as she could. She knew that if they had been with the boys they would have stopped by now, but their new progress was so slow. It would take forever to get to Kosvo, and they had to get there before the medicine ran out. As the sun began to sink over the lake again, Jak ushered them off the path to make camp.

Allie was still watching the sunset over the lake.

"It's beautiful, isn't it?" she asked. Jak smiled at her in agreement. She was glad Allie could focus on the scenery. It seemed to ebb her rage. She didn't seem nearly as angry now as she had when they had woken, but perhaps she was just tired too.

They ducked back into the trees to make camp. Darkness was falling and Jak knew she should try and light a fire to keep Dora warm. Her youngest sister was snuggled in her cloak, clutching Binky, and looking miserable. Jak looked around the stretching shadows of the forest. She opened the basket. Dora wanted a sandwich. She always wanted a sandwich, and it wasn't a difficult request. As Jak handed her little sister the food, she felt a prickling sensation down the back of her spine. She looked up sharply.

Just shadows.

No. It wasn't just shadows. Darkness was falling, and she knew it wasn't just shadows. They were out there. Fear began to creep and tickle its way across her skin. She had assumed the D'rö-Hadās were chasing Krill and Kode. Part of her had even wondered if the boys had abandoned them to try and keep them safe from the Head Hunters — if they had thought they could lead them off and keep the girls out of danger. But now she could feel the assassins circling. They were getting closer.

"Get up," Jak ordered her sisters sharply and quietly.

"What's wrong?" Allie adopted the same hushed tone as she stumbled to her feet.

"They're out there..." Jak whispered. Her eyes darted between the trees. It was stupid to try and look for them. She could never manage to spot them. It was only with her eyes closed that she realised where they were. But looking for the threat was what came naturally. Something glinted in the forest. Something metallic.

"Run!" Jak snatched up Dora's hand and hauled her to her feet. Allie was holding the basket and they hadn't even removed their packs. Dora was too tired. She was too sick and too small. Jak was half dragging her. She scooped up her little sister as she ran. Dora hung on around her neck as Jak held her close. They raced through the trees. Jak could feel the D'rö-Hadās following them.

The Head Hunters moved by magic. Krill had called it shadow walking. She remembered the speed with which he had beheaded the bandits. There was no way they could outrun them. The Head Hunters were pursuing. She could feel it. Jak pulled up sharply. Allie nearly ran into her.

"What's going on?" Allie gasped.

"Take her," Jak ordered, passing Dora over. "Take her and keep going."

"Jak!" Allie exclaimed. She took Dora in her arms, but wasn't big or strong enough to lift her. Jak drew her sword. "Jak! You can't!"

"Keep running," Jak ordered.

"We're not going without you," Allie replied adamantly. Jak could hear tears in her sister's voice. Tears and fear.

"That way," Dora pointed into the forest. "We have to go that way."

"We're not leaving Jak," Allie insisted.

"We all go that way!" Dora pointed.

Jak looked back and met their eyes in the growing darkness. They'd run deeper into the forest and night was almost upon them now. The last vestiges of day couldn't make it here. Her sisters weren't going to move without her.

"Alright, that way," Jak agreed. She ushered the girls ahead of her and kept her sword ready. As they stumbled through the dark, she let the darkness blind her and reached out with her other sense. They staggered over leaves and tree roots. Walls of dark bark pressed in closer and closer. Jak felt it coming. She reacted with a speed and strength she didn't know she had. The attack was going for Dora. Jak shoved her sisters to the ground and leapt.

Her blade hit another sword with the sound of battle. She didn't dare open her eyes. She had no desire to. Those monsters had tried to attack her sisters. The thought was like a fire inside her. It consumed her. It drove her. The training Krill had given her burst to the forefront of her mind. Instinct took over.

She was turning even before the swords parted. She ducked. Something brushed by her cheek. Something cold. Jak spun and swung. Her blade smashed into metal. The force moved up her arms and through her entire body. She didn't falter. She swung and ducked. Every time she moved, her blade struck another. She kicked out with a yell. Her foot hit someone full in the chest. She kicked them away with a roar.

The fight was controlling her now. No matter what happened, she wouldn't let them hurt her sisters. She raised her sword instinctively. It caught a blade coming down at her. She shoved the attack back and spun away. With another roar, she thrust out. She felt her blade cut something. It grated against metal and flesh.

"Ásaïrm!" a voice bellowed.

Jak felt something jerk her off balance. She kept her feet, and her grip on her sword, but both only barely. She opened her eyes. In the last remnants of twilight she could see her sisters staring up at her from the ground. Their mouths were open in shock. To the other side of her, a familiar figure stood in dark armour. She didn't know where the other ones were, but she knew the D'Hiris was not alone.

"Who are you, human?" Elrïlani demanded. "How do you come to attack one of my warriors?"

Jak looked around. She started to be able to see the faint glimmer of armoured assassins in the shadows of the forest. One was holding their arm where Jak's blade had cut them.

"You're trying to attack us," Jak retorted.

"I ask again!" Elrïlani ignored her. "You bear mortal blood, yet fae skill: who are you?"

"My name is Jak," she answered. "You're Elrïlani... right?"

The Ha'Cās woman reached up and lifted her mask. Jak tried to hide her surprise. Krill's face stared back at her. It wasn't exactly the same, but she knew she'd have difficulty telling them apart if it weren't for their behaviour. Perhaps that was just something about fae. She had initially thought Krill and Kode looked extremely alike, and they weren't even related. It shouldn't have been a surprise that Krill's sister could have passed for his twin.

"How is it you know me?" Elrïlani asked.

"I know your brother..." Jak answered slowly. When Elrïlani looked at her with complete incomprehension she elaborated hesitantly. "The last D'Hiris..."

"Elkrillendé," Elrïlani hissed in contempt. "He trained a human in the art of the D'rö-Hadās? His treachery knows no bounds." She replaced her mask. "Kill them. Raid their bodies."

Jak knew that order wasn't for her. She raised her sword and closed her eyes. Her heart was pounding in her throat. It was hopeless. She already knew that. The boys had left them to die at the hands of the Head Hunters. They didn't have faerie protection. Jak couldn't fight them all. Not all night. She'd been lucky so far. But she would go down before she let them touch her sisters.

"Stop!" Dora yelled. Her voice was like a beacon in the night. It came louder and stronger than Jak would have though possible given her illness. Miraculously, the D'rö-Hadās froze.

"RUN!" Allie screamed. She grabbed Jak's hand.

The girls bolted. Jak snatched Dora up again. Her youngest sister yelled directions and Jak raced as fast as she could that way. One arm was scooped around her little sister, holding her close. The other still clutched her sword. She didn't know how the little girl's cry had managed to pause the Head Hunters, but she would take anything she could get. Except the D'rö-Hadās were catching up. There was no way to stop them. They came inevitably, like nightfall itself.

"Stop!" Dora yelled again. Jak couldn't tell if it did anything to their pursuers this time, but she found herself stopping. Dora tore herself free from Jak's arms. She fell to her knees in the grass. With the last tiny vestige of light, Dora scraped the moss from a rock. It bore the Fora rune. Dora began to pray. Jak could hardly believe her eyes, but she didn't have time to hope. She could feel the magic building behind her.

Jak whirled. Her sword was swinging without thought. There was only instinct. She pushed Allie down beside Dora. Her sword caught the blow. She shoved the fae back. Another blow came from the side. Jak deflected like lightning. Her sword sent a thrown dagger spinning into the woods. Two were coming at her at once. She ducked. A blade wooshed over her head. She stabbed at the stomach of a D'rö-Hadās. They spun away from her attack. Her sword grated on their armour. One of the blades nicked her arm. She felt pain, and blood. She ignored it.

Dora was still praying for help. It was their only shot. Jak just had to defend the girls long enough for Dora to save them. Then she felt it. Elrïlani was back. Jak could feel the presence of the D'Hiris stronger than the others. Stronger because she was. The cut on her arm hurt, and she was exhausted. She didn't know if she could do this, but there wasn't another option. Jak raised her sword with a challenging roar.

Elrïlani flicked into being right behind her and swung. Jak spun. She caught the blow. Just. The shock down her arms was staggering. Jak stumbled back. Elrïlani pressed forward. She took the ground. Jak stabbed at her. The D'Hiris dodged easily. She flickered away. Once again, she appeared in the shadows behind Jak. Jak didn't have the time or energy to dodge. She twisted. Jak threw her sword up. It barely caught the strike. She yelled in pain and tried to hold Elrïlani's massive sword off her. Jak raised her other arm to support the flat of her blade. She needed both arms to stave off Elrïlani's epic strength.

It left her completely exposed. There was nothing she could do. The other D'rö-Hadās could kill her while she held their leader at bay. Elrïlani wanted this victory though. Jak heard a faint pop behind her. She could hear her sisters crying. Elrïlani raised her sword again and smashed it down on Jak's blade. Jak flinched as Elrïlani broke through her sword. She cried out and fell back. The blow drove her to the ground. Her sword snapped and the blade spun into the grass. She lifted the hilt with its fragment of blade. It was useless.

Jak turned her desperate face back to her sisters. They were staring at her. They were not alone. Jak saw Äulé's stunned face beholding the scene. He was holding Dora's sandwich. The ground lurched and Jak yelled as she was thrown back. Her hand still clutched the hilt of her broken sword. She heard a crack and a smash as the world collapsed in on itself. A sharp pain exploded in her shoulder. She felt like the sky had fallen and the ground had risen. She was trapped in the middle. The universe squeezed her. The pain in her shoulder turned warm and sticky. Blood. Then darkness. Then nothing.

***

When Jak woke she felt like she was waking from death. She remembered the smell and pressure of cold, damp earth. She had been buried. It was over. Until it wasn't. She surfaced with a gasp. It felt like forever since she'd last drawn breath. The pain had gone away. Her mind had been still. There had been nothing in the darkness, and now, with a harsh sharpness, there was suddenly everything. The comfort of the earth was gone.

Jak uncoiled like a spring. She sprawled, gasping and choking, across the grass. It was still dark, but not as dark as it had been. She could see the icy touch of frost on the grass beneath her. Blood stained her clothes. It was apparent now what had happened. The hilt of her sword protruded from her shoulder, and the broken blade was buried in her flesh. She'd still been holding it when she had been tangled up, and it had stabbed her in the fall. With a whimper and a grimace, she reached up and pulled the broken blade from her shoulder. It slid out with a wet squelch and she gasped in pain.

"Jak!" Allie exclaimed. Suddenly, her sisters were there, and Jak could feel their little hands grabbing her in shock. She clutched her wound tightly to try and keep pressure on the hole. Blood was pouring between her fingers, but she could hear her sisters at her side and she knew they were okay. They had survived. By some miracle they were alright. She wanted to cry in relief and pain, and just the general overwhelming nature of the moment.

"Woah now," an unfamiliar voice spoke by them. "That's a nasty looking wound. You don't want to move that."

They all looked up. A young man was looking down at them with big blue eyes. He stood hesitantly, as though he didn't know what he had just found, but his gaze was curious. He was more than a boy, perhaps ten years older than Jak, and wore a closely-trimmed beard and wild dark curls. His breath steamed in the air. Rich furs and leathers draped him against the cold.

"Who are you?" Jak demanded. She knew she sounded rude, but she didn't care. Her trust was gone and so was her patience. The man raised a cool eyebrow at her tone.

"Forgive me, Miss, but perhaps the more pertinent question is; who are you? I'm the man who just sprung you three from a faerie trap, and, I have to say, you might be the strangest thing I've seen caught in one. I'm not used to springing live people."

"I'm sorry, my Lord," Allie scrambled to her feet and curtsied. "We beg your pardon. My name is Allie. As you can see, my sister Jak is wounded, and my other sister Dora is ill. You haven't caught us in our best state, and pain is causing her to speak in haste, but I assure you, we meant no offence."

An impish smirk tugged at the corners of his mouth beneath the beard, and he gave Allie a gracious nod. She blushed.

"Well spoken, Allie," he replied. "To answer your sister's question; I am called Chris. Tell me, how is it that three young ladies such as yourselves came to be tangled in a faerie trap?"

"What is a faerie trap?" Jak grimaced.

"It's a— oh here, let me," Chris knelt down beside Jak. "Don't move. I can stop the bleeding." He pulled her hand away and made a brief sign over her wound. Instantly, the injury scabbed and the bleeding stopped. "Don't move it," he instructed. "It's not properly healed, and if you want something more permanent we have to pay for stronger magic."

"You're a magician." Jak couldn't keep the growl from her voice.

"I can undo the magic and put you back where I found you, girl," he replied. Jak glared at him, but he had a point.

"Thank you," she muttered.

"Your thanks are unnecessary, but appreciated," he gave her a nod.

"You're too kind, my Lord," Allie told him. "We have no way to repay you."

"Just answer my questions," he shrugged. "How is it three young ladies found themselves caught in a faerie trap?"

"We asked Äulé for help," Dora coughed weakly. "We were being chased by the Head Hunters... Äulé protected us."

"It's true," Jak defended to the man's sceptical expression. "I fought them off and they broke my sword. Äulé must have put us in the trap to protect us."

"That's impossible," Chris countered dubiously. His tone was trying to be polite, but he didn't believe them at all.

"Impossible or not, it still happened," Jak told him bluntly. "The D'rö-Hadās came after us and I had to hold them off while Dora got us magical help. You don't have to believe us, rich-boy, but if you want another story, you'll have to make one up yourself."

Allie glared daggers at her sister, but Chris gave her a sardonic smile. He didn't seem to mind her tone, yet his eyes were still narrowed darkly at her language.

"What did you call them?" he asked softly.

"D'rö-Hadās," Jak answered. "It's the fae name for the Head Hunters."

"I know exactly what it is and who they are," he replied. "How do *you* know that?" he poked Jak lightly in the chest to emphasise his point.

"Why should I tell you?" she retorted.

"Because I might be able to help you — if anything you've told me is actually true."

"It is true, my Lord," Allie insisted meekly. "I know Jak's being rude, but it is true. We were travelling with faeries, and they taught us about some of their culture. That's how we know who and what the D'rö-Hadās are."

"Where are the faeries now? Tell me what happened."

"Why in the names of the D'Ihne should we trust you?" Jak demanded. "You're asking a lot of questions and not giving a lot of answers in return."

"You mean aside from the fact that I just set you free and healed your wound?" Chris answered coolly. He gave her a long, sharp look. Jak stared into his eyes. There was something about them. Something that reminded her of something else... someone else... Jak sat back with the longest and most painful groan of her life.

"You're a goddamn demigod," she cursed. "Another one."

"Another one?" Chris echoed in some surprise.

"I am so sick of your people..." Jak muttered darkly.

"Jak!" Allie exclaimed furiously. The girl placed herself between the young man and her older sister. "Enough. This nice man helped us, and we needed his help. You don't get to take your issues out on him. Just, stop."

Jak glared at Chris but stayed silent. Silence fell over all of them until Dora spoke softly.

"Are you really a demigod?"

"That's not important," Chris answered instantly.

"Oh really?" Jak sneered. "You don't have to answer,

rich-boy. We can practically smell the incestuous family on you."

"Jak!"

"No, Allie," Jak snapped. "Either we all come clean, or none of us do. I'm not getting played again."

Chris groaned and rubbed his tired face wearily. "Look, okay, fine. I'm part fae. Whatever. It's really not important. Please, I need your help. Something has gone missing from the Golden City and the D'rö-Hadās are charged with getting it back. However, so am I — to an extent — and I have to find it before they do. So, please, kind ladies, just tell me what you know. Why are the D'rö-Hadās chasing you?"

"We don't know, my Lord," Allie replied. "We thought they were chasing the faeries we were with, but then when the faeries ditched us they kept chasing us anyway..."

"Something has gone missing?" Jak questioned accusatorily. "That something wouldn't be people, would it?"

"What? No?" Chris sounded genuinely baffled. "What do you mean 'people'? Never mind." He shook his head. "Allie, isn't it? Thank you, Allie. Look, these faeries you met, did they give you anything before they left? Anything at all?"

"Heaps of stuff," she shrugged. "They gave us this basket and pitcher," she got them out and showed him. "And they gave us a tent and some beds. Jak has them."

"May I see?" Chris asked Jak tentatively.

Jak begrudgingly tipped the envelope and rags from her sock pouch. Chris opened everything up and began going through the magic items. Jak wanted to fight with him, but her shoulder still hurt, and something about him had become strangely genuine when he had talked about the missing object. It had piqued her interest, as had the way he was desperately rummaging. He really was looking for something. Whatever it was, he didn't find it. He came back out of the empty tent with an exasperated and desperate expression.

"No luck?" Jak asked.

"No sign of it," he muttered, running his hands through his wild curls. Jak raised a curious eyebrow. So it was an 'it'. Whatever 'it' was, Jak was prepared to bet everything she owned that 'it' had been missing for a year, and the faeries had dropped everything to find it again.

"You could tell us what you're looking for," she offered. "We might be able to help."

"Can't," he muttered, shaking his head. "Strict orders from on high. I dare not break them. I'm in enough trouble as it is."

"On high?" Allie asked.

"D'Ihne," he replied. "I answer to the gods."

"Like an ancient hero?" Allie nearly swooned. "You're on a quest?"

"I suppose..." he murmured. His sharp blue eyes were watching them shrewdly. "And what about you three? How did you get tangled up with faeries?"

"We ran away from home," Jak skipped a large section of the truth before Allie could spill the beans. "Our father died and our mother went missing. We're trying to find her."

Chris nodded. "I'm sorry." His sympathy sounded genuine. He looked around the items scattered about them that he needed to repack again. "This is a lot of magical gear for three humans. It's… possible… that the D'rö-Hadās could sense humans in possession of fae magic, and that's why they came after you."

"They seemed very keen to behead us first and check for guilt after," Jak growled.

Chris nodded again. "And you say a gnome helped you?"

"Äulé," Dora piped up again with another weak, rattling cough. "He's our friend."

"Is he now…" Chris mused. "You don't mind if I call him, then? If what you say is true, he can help heal your wound properly, if not… I think I'd like to know."

"Go ahead," Jak invited scathingly. "Knock yourself out."

Chris strode around the girls clustered on the ground. His black leather boots crunched the frosty grass beneath him. The first rays of dawn were starting to break through the trees. Jak realised that was why it wasn't so dark anymore. They had been in the trap all night. Chris approached the Fora rune carved in the rock. He reached into a pouch at his waist and pulled out some cheap loose change. The copper tinkled onto the rock.

Chris didn't pray. He stayed standing and spoke a single, sharp sentence. Jak was trying to make out the words, when she suddenly realised he had spoken fae. He was calling Äulé in their own language. With a small pop, the gnome appeared. He had a baby in one arm and a bottle in the other hand. The little baby gnome was suckling at the magical, multicoloured glass bottle. The coins vanished as soon as he appeared. He looked up at the group from under his brows. He was a busy dad.

"Oh, it's yer," he said unenthusiastically as soon as he saw Chris. "What do yer want, Silvertongue?" He looked around the group again in exasperation. "And what yer be doing with mah girls?!"

"Your girls?" Chris echoed. "You're the gnome who helped them escape the D'rö-Hadās?"

"What yer implying?" Äulé growled.

"Nothing," Chris replied innocently. "It's just a question. No tricks. I just want to know what happened and why the D'rö-Hadās were chasing them."

"Yer'd have to ask the D'rö-Hadās then. It's beyond meh."

"You're one of Thænäri's gnomes… that's a bold move sticking your neck out against the D'rö-Hadās. What does the D'Ihne of the earth want with these three?"

"Who says she does?" Äulé shrugged. "Could just be meh. Yer want to know what a D'Ihne wants? Ask them yerself."

"You're infuriating," Chris warned. "This is why humans cut down forests to get rid of you thieving little bastards."

Äulé grinned at him. Chris gave a long and exasperated sigh.

"Is there anything you can tell me?"

"I know yer mission, Silvertongue. If I could help

yer, I would have. These girls don't know nothing. I watched them grow up. They're good lasses. Couldn't have been involved. Wouldn't know how."

"Alright," Chris sighed. "Thank you. Here," he pulled out some more coins and handed them to the gnome. "Can you please heal the oldest one's shoulder? Just as best you can."

Äulé stared at Chris with a strange look for a long time. Then he finally sighed and swapped the coins for the baby. Chris awkwardly took the tiny gnome baby and continued to hold the bottle up with an alarmed expression on his face. Allie watched him struggle for a moment, before she shook her head fondly and took the baby from him. She held the child carefully and kept it feeding. Chris looked grateful.

Äulé approached Jak. He counted out a few coins from the collection Chris had given him and pocketed the rest. Jak was still sitting on the grass and Äulé could meet her eye as he wandered over. They shared a look, but she trusted him even though his eyes were warning. He breathed on the coins in his hand and rubbed them together in his palms. They started to glow. Gently, one by one, he slotted the coins into the wound in Jak's shoulder. She bit her tongue to keep from screaming. It was like a red-hot poker.

She squeezed her eyes shut and fought against the pain. It subsided slowly. The pain ebbed until it was back to normal, and then it kept subsiding. After a minute, it barely hurt anymore.

"Give it a wiggle," Äulé encouraged.

Jak opened her eyes to find the gnome watching her.

"It will hurt a bit for a few days," he warned. "But it will come right just fine."

"Thank you…"

"Try to stay outta trouble," he advised gently. Äulé went back to take his baby from Allie, whom he thanked. He gave Dora an affectionate pat and then vanished by the rock.

"So," Jak turned to Chris. "You know we're telling the truth."

"I know as much as the gnome was willing to share," Chris sighed, striking down the tent in a single tug. He began to pack away all the magical items carefully. "Which, with gnomes, is never very much. I'll take you at your word, though. How's the shoulder?"

"Better," Jak muttered. "Thank you."

"Again, unnecessary, but appreciated. Are you all packed and ready to go?"

"Excuse me?"

"You're excused," he pardoned. "Are you also hard of hearing?"

"What I meant was — what is it to you? You act like we're going with you."

"You are." There was a note of finality to his voice that momentarily silenced Jak. Then her indignation roared into a fresh new fire before Allie could stop her.

"We're not going anywhere with you. We're going to Kosvo."

"Good, so am I," Chris told her, packing away the last things. "I'm meeting some people there. It would be indecent of me to abandon you ladies out here and not escort you with me to the city. So, like it or not, I will drag you to civilisation."

"Thank you, my Lord," Allie blushed. "You're too kind."

"Hardly," Chris shrugged. "Any decent person would do the same." He gave a sharp whistle into the forest. There was a responsive snort and stomp. A giant dark horse strode out obediently between the trees. He had a glossy dark coat with faint touches of white dusting around his hooves like frost and speckled across his flanks like stars. His saddle was a polished black leather and he looked extremely majestic. "Your sisters can ride until they feel better and Shæúgh can carry our things. Walk with me, Lady Allie?"

Allie was definitely swooning. It occurred to Jak then, as she watched her little sister swooning over the tall, dark stranger, that Chris was probably extremely attractive for a man. Beneath his leather armour and furred cloak, he had the lithe build of a fae, or part fae, with a very regal bearing. Jak found the beard unattractive and concealing, but was suddenly sure that beneath it Chris was probably very beautiful. Allie was behaving true to form, and Jak had to suppress a deep sigh.

Yet, his disregard of anyone who thought it acceptable to abandon them had softened her slightly. She had been worried, scared even, of trusting another stranger after the last ones had run away. Still, their options weren't numerous. Now that they were lost in the forest, someone who knew the way to Kosvo, and could hopefully help them keep the Head Hunters away, was actually a much-needed asset.

"Alright…" Jak grumbled. "But not until after breakfast."

CHAPTER TWELVE

Chris had told Jak to keep her sword. After breakfast, she had been set to throw the broken hilt away, but Chris had advised her not to. There was something in his eyes. Jak knew when he looked at her that he could tell how much the sword meant. She hadn't exactly been given it, but it was a reminder of home. It was something from Big Sam, from the smithy. It mattered. But now it was broken. Chris told her to keep it because he knew someone who could fix it. He had offered that information to be kind, and now that she was healed and fed, Jak found it easier to respond to his kindness. She did actually appreciate it. He set her and Dora to ride and walked ahead with Allie. Jak didn't fight him about it.

They travelled through the forest all day. Even though it was the same forest she had trained in, the same forest she had met Olíriá and seen the unicorns in, it felt less magical now. She didn't want to think about why. The birdsong was muted in the dark trees, and the forest itself was more frightening than before. Every shadow felt like a threat, and the dim light of day barely filtered through the leaves. She glimpsed the odd rabbit hiding in the grass, but they didn't approach. They didn't follow or come to investigate. Their little white tails flicked into the distance dismissively as they turned away.

Shæúgh (and Jak wondered about the name) was a well-tempered horse who didn't seem to mind at all being loaded down with Jak and Dora and everyone's packs as they travelled. Jak was pretty sure the horse was a fae horse, and therefore magical in some way — much like his owner. Chris had Allie wrapped around his finger, but Jak couldn't blame him for that. Allie seemed happy wrapping herself up without any encouragement from him.

Jak wanted to caution her little sister, but Allie didn't give her the time or space. Jak rode Shæúgh with Dora snuggled in her lap cuddling Binky. Chris led Shæúgh by the reins and walked ahead with Allie, who practically floated at the invitation to walk with the handsome demigod. Jak had to hand it to her little sister, for all that she was swooning away, she was also talented at getting Chris to open up, and it turned out the young man was quite the storyteller once she got him going.

"So… you're a demigod…" Allie spoke in a coy and leading way. "And you can do magic?"

"Demigods can do very limited magic," Chris shrugged. "It's possible to learn rune magic, but actual fae magic… that's something else."

"How so?"

He gave her tone a sly smile. He knew she was leading. It didn't seem to bother him.

"There are five levels of magic," he explained. "How magical you are determines the kinds of magic you can do. The first level is rune magic. It's the most basic of magics. To fae it's the equivalent of a child's drawing. Impressive, if you've never seen art before."

"I've seen some amazing rune magic before," Allie said, automatically defending their old friends. Chris grinned at her.

"Only because that's almost all the magic you've ever seen. The gnome healing your sister's shoulder — that was the second level of magic: junk magic."

"Junk magic?!" Allie echoed.

"Junk magic," Chris smirked. "To be fair, I call it that. Most people call it item magic. It is where you convert the energy of a trinket into power. The strength of it ranges."

"I was healed with rune magic that was better and more powerful than what Äulé did," Jak commented. She met Chris' eye when he turned to look at her, but her expression didn't want to fight. "It hurt less too."

"That's fair," Chris nodded. "We're talking only the first two levels of magic. An experienced rune master, with a connection to you, could do an impressive job healing you — especially on minor wounds. Your gnome has affection for you, but it was my coins he was using to heal you. They had no connection to you, no affection for you, and they were just junk to me. It's not good fuel — like trying to start a fire with damp wood. You might get it to burn eventually, but it's not fun. Whereas, if your friendly gnome had used your own lucky coin, if you had one, you would probably have healed better, faster, and without pain. Like I said, the strength ranges depending on what you use."

"What are the other three levels?" Allie asked curiously.

"The third level is blood magic," Chris answered warningly. "Blood magic is the intermediary magic because it requires sacrifice, but not a permanent sacrifice. Some people mix that up and that is when magic gets nasty. You don't need to kill to use blood magic, you just need to bleed."

"That still sounds pretty bad…"

"You need a fairly powerful fae to do it," Chris nodded. "But it's not as awful as you think. For example; a practiced blood magician could have healed your sister's shoulder by using the very blood she was already bleeding. They could have turned the blood into magic to cure her wound."

"Why didn't Äulé do that then?" Jak asked.

"He's no blood magician, obviously," Chris replied. "A minor faerie like a gnome usually doesn't rise above item magic. Think about how humans practice magic with the summoning of faeries. What you offer in sacrifice at a faerie shrine determines the faerie who comes to work their magic. You three befriended this gnome through item magic, yes? Offering him food and trinkets and junk pieces — which are treasure to him because they fuel his magic."

"You could make a blood sacrifice at Äulé's shrine and get someone else?" Allie asked nervously.

"You almost certainly would," Chris confirmed. "A faerie who could use the blood would hear its call and come to answer it — probably. It's sometimes hard to know with faeries. It used to be a far more common practice than it is these days. See there," he pointed.

Jak looked through the trees. Between the scattered trunks, she glimpsed a ring of standing stones in the distance. The runes carved into them were disappearing beneath encroaching moss, but some dark reddish-brown stains were still visible on the stone.

"That's an old altar," Chris indicated. "A sacrifice circle. I imagine, way back when people still lived in the forest, they would bring animals to sacrifice and bleed there. Mostly that would be the fifth level of magic, but some people would probably have bled without killing."

"People don't do it anymore though..." Allie murmured, casting a nervous look back at Jak after spotting the ring of stones.

"Not so much," Chris shrugged. "These days people tend to lean more to full-on animal sacrifice, and they usually do it in or near the churches and temples. Blood magic requires a semi-powerful fae. By the time you get to the third level of magic or higher, you're looking at dangerous magic and dangerous users. At that point, most people just invoke fifth level magic and try for the favour of the gods."

"What about fourth level?" Allie asked.

"The fourth level of magic is spirit magic, but that's a dying art," Chris answered with a frown. "Almost no one practices it anymore because it's so volatile. You can do some incredible and powerful things with it, but using someone's soul, or even part of a soul, is a dangerous game. Of all the magics of the three worlds, it is the most likely to backfire and kill the caster. Hence why most fae have abandoned the practice."

"The three worlds?" Allie echoed.

"This world, the fae world, and the afterworld," he elaborated.

"Oh," Allie blushed. "It wasn't a term I had heard before, but when you say it like that it makes sense."

Chris gave her a gracious and understanding nod. Jak was still eavesdropping on their conversation about magic. It called to her, and her mind couldn't wander when there were interesting fae secrets to learn. The ring of stones fell behind them, but they were not done exploring its gruesome heritage. Jak needed to know.

"So, the fifth level of magic," she called to them gently to make Chris stay on topic. "Sacrificial magic? Body magic? The magic they make using people?"

"Ĝoŕgomghōul's soup magic," Dora chimed in fearfully.

Chris looked back at them and gave them a nod. "Yes. Only the D'Ihne can use flesh and bone, but they can do it, and it will produce the most powerful magic. Animal sacrifice to the gods is fairly common, but these days it doesn't really buy you that much. You get what you pay for with magic. You really want to change the world? You offer part of yourself. That's why all the legends of the heroes of old have them sacrifice something for their power."

"Like Anathea," Allie chipped in. "She was a demigod, one of Clōudiá's children, and she sacrificed her eye to her mother to be able to see the future."

"Yes, she did," Chris nodded grimly. "She was quite a woman, Anathea. She didn't get on well with the gods though. She used to travel around and warn and help people, but she always said that bargaining with the D'Ihne was a trick. Gods were a curse, she argued." His eyes narrowed thoughtfully. "No one knows what happened to her. She went crazy and disappeared, or so the legend goes. Not like Frézían's son Thaydrid, or Äluāknā's daughter Yarai, who both died in battle."

"Was Thaydrid the one who gave up an arm?" Jak asked.

"Yes," Chris nodded. "And Yarai gave up her voice. They both sacrificed to gain access to magic, which they used to help their respective kingdoms win wars. Hence why they became legends. But fifth level magic is like that. You want enough power to make history? Give up something you need."

"Have you ever done it?" Jak asked. "You're a demigod. Have you ever sacrificed something for power?"

Chris grimaced. "Not like that. I don't want the world, and for now I'm content with the abilities I have. There are easier ways to get magic."

"I met a D'Ihne once," Jak admitted, thinking about how D'Ihne magic didn't have to come at the cost of a painful sacrifice. "They used a lock of my hair to cast a spell."

"Hair works," Chris smiled. "Hair is good for basic spells. It has enough connection to you that there is functioning magic in it, but no one has to get hurt. As long as it does the trick, right?"

Jak didn't answer. She didn't want to tell him that it hadn't worked.

"I didn't know magic was so dark and scary…" Allie commented. "I mean… I'd heard about Ĝoŕgomghōul using the heads the Head Hunters bring to make magic soup… but I didn't realise all magic is like that."

"It's not," Chris shrugged. "If all you've ever seen are the whimsical tricks of the faeries, why would you think any different? Magic is an ability, Allie. A skill. However, everything comes at a price. King Ruain conquered half the world. He had the greatest empire in history, before it fell. Half of that was blind ambition and skill, but he also sacrificed his son for the power to rule the world. Like I said, you get what you pay for."

"So, when the D'rö-Hadās bring heads to Ĝoŕgomghōul, he gets the strongest magic," Jak commented bleakly. The darkness of the conversation amplified the darkness of the forest, and it kept the memories fresh. "A life has been sacrificed."

"He tends to use more than just the heads," Chris admitted. "No point in wasting the rest of the body. But Ĝoŕgomghōul is the most powerful of the gods. No one likes to talk about it because he doesn't dwell in Roïgola'a'lanaū; it's easy enough to forget him when you never see him. His magic was always the most powerful, and he found ways to weave spells no one else could. He made Clōudiá's crown when the first generation agreed to make her their Queen. That crown gave her power over faekind. She could use it to negate magic, because it was made from mortal energy — just like the D'rök blades he makes for the D'rö-Hadās. The reason those blades are so deadly to fae is because they are made with mortal bones. The blades basically poison the fae with mortality and kill them."

"That must be incredibly difficult to cure..." Jak mused, remembering Jim and Krill with a powerful curiosity instead of anger.

"It's impossible to cure," Chris shrugged. "No one can recover from a D'rök wound. That's why Ĝoŕgomghōul only grants the blades to the greatest fae warriors who have passed his training. Only a certified D'rö-Hadās can wield a D'rök blade."

Allie glanced back at Jak, and the girls shared a look. They both remembered Krill's scar. He swore he'd been healed from a D'rok wound, and that Jim had done it. Jak remembered the way Jim had threatened to kill the gods if he had to — the serious and deadly fire that had glinted in the depths of his eyes. Jim had claimed that he had learnt the secrets of magic. He had learnt magic beyond what the gods could do. Jak didn't know what she believed anymore, but part of her still believed that. She gave Allie a warning look. They didn't need to spook their new friend with stories of Jim. Allie looked like she agreed. Dora took advantage of the silence to interject.

"You know a lot about Ĝoŕgomghōul," she said.

"I do," Chris conceded.

"Are you his son? You look like his son."

"What's that supposed to mean?" Chris demanded. "You've met Ĝoŕgomghōul? You know what he looks like?"

"I saw a picture," Dora defended. "He's all dark and shadowy, like you are."

"Dora," Allie scolded her softly. "Ĝoŕgomghōul

doesn't have any demigod kids, remember?"

"Dark and shadowy…" Chris muttered sullenly.

"She means dark and mysterious," Allie assured with glowing admiration. "We know Ĝoŕgomghōul doesn't have any demigod kids."

"No," Chris muttered. "He doesn't. He barely has any children by fae standards. He doesn't like people and he doesn't like associating with them. Still knocked up two of his sisters though, didn't he?" There was a distasteful twist to the young man's mouth as he said it, as though he was sucking on sour fruit.

"But fae don't see it like that," Allie repeated what they had been taught. "The first generation were the only ones of their kind, and they don't see each other as siblings, even if humans classify them that way."

"It's true," Chris nodded solemnly in agreement. "You certainly know a lot about this."

"We travelled with faeries who told us stories," Allie replied. "And our parents used to tell us faerie tales sometimes."

"Your parents are gone now?"

"Yeah…" Allie nodded. "Yeah. They are."

"I'm sorry."

"So am I," she sighed. "But at least we still have each other." Allie turned and grinned back at her sisters. "Even if I do drive you crazy all the time."

"Oh, bite me," Jak grumbled at her.

Chris and Allie both laughed. He flashed her a cheeky grin. She knew instantly, without having to ask, that he wasn't an only child. The banter of siblings was familiar to him.

They continued on that way for the rest of the day. Jak grew increasingly complacent as they travelled. The going was slow, but she didn't have to walk. Dora wasn't well. Her cough came and went, and Jak made sure she kept taking the medicine, but that was starting to get quite low and the illness wasn't improving. They needed to get to Kosvo to find a doctor. In the meantime, Dora stayed bundled in Jak's arms on the front of the saddle, dozing in and out of wakefulness.

Jak held her close and listened to Chris and Allie talk about fae legends. Old stories about gods and monsters. Stories from days when the world was young, when the first five battled the giants and the dragons, before they built the Golden City. Apparently, Clōudiá was the first to slay a dragon. She was the youngest of the five, but she had always been the most driven and fierce. That was why the others had agreed to make her the Queen. Ĝoŕgomghōul had made her a crown of blood and stars that gave her the power to negate fae magic. It was the most powerful thing he'd ever made, more dangerous than D'rök blades.

Clōudiá had led the battle against the giants. According to Chris, they were even travelling through an old battlefield. That was why the forest felt so dark here. The mountains the trees grew on between Lake Kover and the city of Kosvo were a place where many giants had fallen. The area was called Sōr'la'Maŕ. So called because it was where Clōudiá tricked the moon and sun to chase each other. This was what had created days, and she had done it to confuse the giants.

Previously, the sun and moon had been happy to

lounge around and share the sky. However, Clōudiá began to whisper to them both, and told them lies of the nasty things each was saying about the other. Soon, the sun grew angry at the moon and sought to burn it for the horrible rumours. The moon fled in fear, and the two have chased each other ever since. Day became night, and the giants couldn't keep up. As soon as they got used to the dark, it would become light again, and vice versa. The D'Ihne were able to use this to their advantage and slay the confused giants.

For all that Chris came across as entitled and snobbish, Jak was finding that he grew on her. She liked the way he told stories. It helped to pass the time. She was grateful, even if she wasn't ready to trust him yet.

The afternoon was getting dark and cold in the forest when Jak felt the tingling in her spine. She jerked up in the saddle, startling Dora who looked up at her with wild eyes. They were here. Jak could feel it. She grabbed the hilt of her broken sword. It was useless, but holding it made her feel better. She felt a flicker around her. Jak raised the broken blade with a cry as a flash of darkness filled her vision.

When the darkness fell, she realised it had been Chris' cloak. The young man stood between Shæúgh and Elrïlani. The D'Hiris had her blade to his throat. He had a sharply glinting dirk pointed straight through a gap in the side of her armour. Both were frozen. Elrïlani's face was unreadable behind her mask, but her golden eyes were neutral. Chris' face was impassive as he stared her down. She stood down first. With fluid grace, she removed her weapon, stepped back, and bowed her head.

"I did not expect to see you here, my Lord."

"I didn't expect you either, D'Hiris," Chris replied. He sheathed his blade and it disappeared under his mountain of fur and cloak. "The children told me their story and I didn't believe it. Yet, here we are."

"We have traced the magic to them," Elrïlani stated. "They are the thieves."

Chris looked back at the girls with a raised eyebrow. Jak stared at him. She had already been staring, but she couldn't take her eyes off him, even when he looked back and met her gaze. His blue eyes were a mystery.

"I don't think so," he replied, turning back to Elrïlani. "I don't even think that's possible. You feel a strong pull of fae magic coming from mortals who shouldn't have it?"

"I feel *the* magic, my Lord. This is where it is strongest. I am trained to know it."

"It's not here, D'Hiris," Chris shrugged. "I've checked. These girls don't know anything, and they don't have it in their possession. Whatever magic there is about them is residual — or mine. I've got them in my care and I'm keeping an eye on them. You have another lead, yes?"

For a moment Elrïlani was completely silent. Then she gave the slightest of nods.

"Good," Chris nodded back. "Pursue the other lead and report back. I'm meeting my brother and my wife at Kosvo and we will work out where to go from there, and what to do with the children."

Elrïlani gave another nod. "As you say, my Lord."

She was gracious and polite, but Jak saw a hard irritation in her eyes as she stepped back and flickered out of sight. The tingling sensation that the assassins were watching lingered a moment longer, but after a second even that vanished. Chris let out a breath and it steamed in the cold air. He turned back to them casually.

"Are you alright?" he asked.

"What the fuck was that?" Jak demanded.

"Jak!" Allie exclaimed, rushing forward. "Don't be so rude! Yes, we are, Chris. Thank you so much! You just saved us!" Allie turned her adoring gaze to the young demigod. She was practically glowing with admiration. It faded slightly when Chris ignored her. He didn't take his cool blue gaze from Jak. She was glaring suspiciously at him. He turned his eyes down and adjusted his gloves.

"The D'rö-Hadās came to attack you again. I drove them off and told them not to bother you anymore."

"Why does the D'Hiris of the D'rö-Hadās call you 'my Lord'?" Jak demanded. "I thought you were just a demigod."

Chris' lips pinched into a hard line. It wasn't a question he could dodge without making it obvious he was avoiding the answer. Finally, he replied.

"Because I'm Clōudiá's son."

"So her army obeys you," Jak concluded. "You're a Prince. What are you looking for? What do they think we've taken?"

"Prince is a human term," Chris replied coolly. "Fae don't have a word for it and they don't use it. It's a meaningless title, and not one I answer to. As to what we're all hunting: that is still fae business. It is not your concern and it is not my place to tell you. We were sworn to secrecy and I will not break that oath."

"And your brother and your wife?" Jak continued. "You failed to mention that. What did you mean you'd work out what to do with us? We don't belong to you."

"No. You don't." He gave her a dry look. "Put your broken blade away, Jak. My family and I mean you and your sisters no harm. I told you I was meeting people at Kosvo. When we get there, my brother can mend your sword and my wife can cure the little one's illness. From there, we can work out if we leave you to fend for yourselves, or whether you would like to stay and continue to travel in our party. Now, do you still want to fight, or are you done making demands?"

Jak put her broken sword away very slowly and sheepishly. His eloquence shut her down hard. She was so ready to be suspicious and to jump to the defence of her sisters, but Chris had been nothing but kind to them — in his own aloof way. However, she had thought their last companions were kind too, right up until they had vanished without a word in the middle of the night. It was going to take her a while to get over that.

"I'm sorry I snapped," she muttered in embarrassment.

"I'm sorry I startled you," he gave her a nod. "You girls look like you've been through a lot. How about we call it a day here? We can stop for the night and you can get some rest." He asked like it was a question, but he acted on it without waiting for their answer.

Jak and Allie nodded meekly. Chris moved to set up a small camp in the nearest clearing. Jak dismounted carefully, and pulled Dora down from Shæúgh's back. Allie approached them, glaring at Jak.

"What was that?!" she hissed.

"He just gave orders to the commander of the fae assassins, Allie," Jak sighed. "I'd have to be an idiot not to think that was suspicious."

"He helped us! He sent them away!"

"Yeah. He did. That's a surprising amount of authority for one of the god's half-breed bastards — even if he is Clōudiá's son. You're talking about the same race that enslaved the Ha'Cās, remember?"

Allie looked like she wanted to keep fighting, but there was no point. Jak was right, even if she could have handled the situation better. Allie stormed off to join Chris. Jak looked back at Shæúgh. The horse snorted gently and gave her a reassuring bunt on the shoulder. Then it wandered to go and join its master. Jak felt a tugging on her sleeve. She looked down at Dora's big, earnest, brown eyes.

"Thanks for looking after us, Sis," Dora whispered in her now croaky voice.

"That's alright, baby," Jak kissed her curls. "Come here." Jak scooped Dora up and hoisted her onto her hip as the little girl held on around Jak's neck. She could feel Binky's ears rubbing against her cheek, and holding her little sister close nearly made her smile. She carried Dora over to join the others.

Once the tent was set up, Jak put Dora to bed. The little girl was almost asleep again anyway. Chris seemed to be having some problems lighting a fire, so Allie took over. He stayed to supervise, for all the use it was, but Allie enjoyed having him around to pester.

"You never told us you were married," she commented slyly.

"You never asked," he replied.

"Does she know you're a demigod?"

"She knows everything about me. We have no secrets."

"How did you two meet?" she pestered. "Was it romantic?"

"We've always known each other," Chris smiled. "As long as I can remember. Our families were… close, so we grew up together."

Allie rolled her eyes with a sigh. "So when did you know you loved her then? The details, Chris. I want to hear the romantic story. What's she like?"

Jak opened her mouth to say that Chris didn't have to tell her if he didn't want to, but he was grinning openly at Allie's cheek, so she stayed quiet.

"She's the most amazing person in the world," he answered softly. "She is kind, beautiful, and clever. I was hopelessly in love with her as a boy. I was always terrified I would lose her to one of my older siblings. I have three older siblings — my sister was aloof and uninterested, thank goodness. But I had two older brothers… they were both handsome and charming and… loud. They are both loud, still. They draw attention to themselves like they're each a one-man talent show." Chris shook his head. "I was a very quiet and shy child. With my siblings, attention was always hard to get, and even if I got it, I didn't know what to do with it. My brothers used to charm her, and she would banter with them, and I would feel useless…"

Allie's eyes were misty as she looked up at him. No one seemed to have the faintest care that she had managed to light a crackling fire for them. She was captivated by his story. Chris was looking into the flames with old memories in his eyes.

"I used to hide from the others," he reminisced. "It wasn't that they were cruel or unkind, but they were boisterous and… deafening. I used to sneak away and hide on my own for the peace and quiet. I started writing her poems… and she… she would turn my words into songs. She would follow me and join me when I snuck off. I don't even remember when it went from her following me to the two of us just sneaking off together…" Chris grinned into the fire. He set another log on it now that it was cheerfully burning. "It didn't stop me from being jealous of the others for years though. I used to play pranks on them to show off for her. I was always good at magic. One time, when my oldest brother was playing around at the pool, I froze the top of the water just as he tried to jump in." Chris laughed to himself. "He went splat on the ice, and he was wet, so he froze to it. It was pretty hilarious. It was less hilarious when he unfroze himself and chased me through the halls with a sword… but it was still worth it."

"You sound like you had a fun childhood," Jak commented.

"I did, for the most part," Chris agreed. He turned

his sharp blue eyes to her and gave her a long look. "I had a very privileged upbringing. There was a great deal of freedom and space for us to grow and learn. We got to play most of the time. Self-education was encouraged. Our parents wanted us to learn things for ourselves."

"And how did that turn out?"

Chris smiled, but didn't answer. Instead, he held his arms out as though inviting her to inspect him and make her own judgement. She wasn't interested. He was what he was, and she was what she was. Her opinion of him didn't matter. She turned away and went to grab the magic picnic basket for dinner.

That evening she spent sitting around the fire with Chris and Allie. Allie asked every question she could think of and Chris told her more stories about growing up rich. Jak sat quietly and listened while she ate. Allie ate her food daintily and did her best to appear ladylike while she fished for stories. She was a hopeless romantic, and swooned for tales about Chris and his wife. It turned out she had proposed to him — in a song. Jak had to grin at her sister's reaction. Allie wasn't even mad that Chris was taken. She was just in it for the tales, and the account of Chris' wife — or at that point girlfriend — turning a public show she was performing into a personal love letter made the little girl swoon. Allie seemed to approve of Chris' choice of woman. She was clearly looking forward to meeting his family.

"And what about your magic?" she asked.

"What about it?"

"You said you were good at it. You said you froze

the top of a swimming pool. How? What kind of magics can you do?"

Chris smiled mysteriously. With quick dancing fingers, he traced the Stiar rune in the air and blew through it towards the girl at his side. A cold wind blasted over her. Allie gasped. She cast her face down and pulled her cloak tight. When she looked up again, there was frost on the grass around her and in the folds of her dress.

"That was unnecessary!" she exclaimed.

Chris chuckled. "Sorry. Edge closer to the fire, you'll defrost."

Allie stood in a huff and held her hands out to the blaze. In a minute she was toasty warm again, but she still gave his cheeky expression a miffed look. The night was bringing enough of its own cold, and he could tell by watching her that her eyes were heavy and she was tired after the last days spent walking.

"You should get some rest, Allie," he advised gently. "It's at least another full day of travel to Kosvo."

She looked like she was going to object for a moment, but decided against it. With a gentle smile and a gracious nod, she took herself off to the tent where Dora slept. Jak watched her go silently. Allie was being so well behaved — almost certainly because she wanted to make a good impression. Jak tossed another log on the fire and watched it crackle and burn. She didn't see or hear Chris move until he was beside her. The strange man in the dark cloak gave her a look, and when she didn't object, took a seat beside her.

"You don't talk as much as your sister," he

commented.

Jak shrugged. It was true enough. She didn't know what she wanted to say to him anyway, if she even did want to say anything at all. He didn't seem to mind, but he also put in the effort to carry the conversation.

"You don't trust much either," he observed.

"I have to be the one to look after them," Jak replied wearily. "Mum and Dad are gone. I have to look after my sisters and make sure nothing happens to them. Sometimes you just can't afford to trust."

"Sometimes," Chris agreed. "And sometimes you can't afford not to. Your problem is your past. I can see it in your eyes. You've been hurt. Betrayed."

Jak gave him a sharp look, but Chris stayed watching the fire as he lounged at her side.

"I recognise the look," he shrugged. "You really think you're the only one?"

"It doesn't matter," Jak shook her head. "It wouldn't matter if this was perfectly normal and everyone in the world had been through what I have. I'd still feel the way I feel, and other people having felt the same thing wouldn't do anything to change that. Other people's pain doesn't change mine. It doesn't matter."

"It matters a great deal," Chris disagreed. "You're right that it doesn't change your pain, but the fact that you are not alone is important, and one day you will see that."

Jak watched him quietly. He let her look for a minute before turning to face her. His clear eyes were still sharply blue in the firelight. His expression was a severe one, and there was an anger and a haunting behind it.

For a moment, Jak wondered if that was what her own expression looked like.

"You are not the only one," Chris told her solemnly. "You are not alone."

"Thank you," Jak replied simply. She kept watching him. There was something about him… it was the same thing that had betrayed his heritage earlier. She couldn't stop seeing it, but she had no idea what it was or what it meant. "You were hurt too?"

"I was betrayed by someone I trusted," Chris answered. "I trusted them and they made a fool out of me with that trust. They think their behaviour so harmless… I wish I could show them what it was they really did…" A darkness settled over his eyes as he spoke. A darkness so black it brought out the demigod in him. Jak went cold just looking at it. She didn't want to ask, and was grateful that he didn't seem to want to share details.

"I… I should probably get some rest too…" she changed topic carefully, glancing to the tent.

"Of course," Chris conceded, letting the darkness fall away. "Sleep well, Jak. I'll see you girls in the morning."

"Thank you. Goodnight." Jak didn't wait for him to say anything else, but climbed to her feet and moved to the tent. She kept her pace slow, so as not to seem like she was running away, but she didn't look back either. She dipped through the flap and saw Allie smiling at her as she entered. She returned the smile as she closed the tent up and climbed into bed.

"Jak?" Allie's voice whispered out of the darkness. "Yes?"

"He's nice, isn't he?"

"Yes, Allie," Jak smiled. "He is." Chris seemed to be a lot of things, and Jak had a feeling there was more going on than she had figured out. There was a piece missing. She could feel it. She had almost worked it out. There was just one little bit… like a word on the tip of her tongue. Something important she just hadn't remembered. But whatever else he was, whatever else was going on, Jak could concede that Chris was nice. Enough.

LIKE THE HEROES OF OLD

CHAPTER THIRTEEN

Morning broke crisp and frosty. Jak had slept with her cloak spread out over her bunk like an extra blanket against the cold. She knew the seasons were turning, but she missed the warmer climate of home. She pulled on her boots, wrapped up back in her cloak, and stepped outside. The fire was still going, and Chris was still there. Jak had steeled herself for finding him gone and having to explain it to Allie, but as she stepped out into the icy morning, he looked over to her from where he was checking Shæúgh's saddle.

"Good morning," he smiled.

"Morning," Jak nodded to him. "You're still here."

"I said I would be," he replied. He stood, rubbing one black-gloved hand on Shæúgh's midnight neck. The man and horse were very similar, and Shæúgh butted Chris' shoulder affectionately. They stood like the silhouette of dark shadows beneath the trees. Chris continued. "I don't know what kind of people you used to keep company with, Jak, but I'm a man of my word. I'm the kind of guy who sticks around."

"Just ask your wife?"

"If you want to," he shrugged. "We're making adequate time. I'm hoping to have reached the city by nightfall."

"And then?"

"We can work out the 'and then' when we get there."

She couldn't fault his answer. It wasn't like she had a better one. Allie would almost certainly want to stay with them, if they'd have her, and Jak… well, Jak wasn't sure what she wanted anymore.

Once Chris was happy with Shæúgh's condition, they struck camp. Breakfast was quick and Allie didn't even complain about being woken. Dora did. Their youngest sister wasn't doing well. She was pale and weak and her cough rattled deep in her chest. Jak shared a worried look with Allie and Chris as they waited for Dora to eat breakfast by the fire.

"The best thing we can do for her is travel," Chris told them in a hushed tone. "My wife is a healer and she will be able to help her. One of you ride with her and keep her in the saddle."

"Jak can ride," Allie offered instantly. "I'll walk with you."

"We might need to move faster than we did yesterday," Chris warned.

"I can do that," Allie assured. "Jak, you look after Dora."

Jak just nodded. She had no problem with the plan as long as they got Dora medical care soon. They didn't have much money to pay a doctor, so the fact that Chris' wife was a healer was remarkably convenient; Jak wasn't going to look a gift horse in the mouth. She was going to get on the horse and ride as fast as Chris and Allie could walk.

Once they were ready, and Jak had Dora bundled up

on Shæúgh, Chris cast a frost spell over the fire and they set off.

The sun rose over the forest as they travelled and thawed the air beneath the canopy of sheltering branches. They hadn't been travelling long before an unexpected sound began to drift through the woods. The sound of singing. Jak cocked her ear to listen. It was a man's voice, and they weren't particularly good or bad, but they were enthusiastic. He sang with gusto. It reminded Jak of Jim. He had that same sound of someone who thinks themselves alone, or doesn't care if they aren't. The memory became a sharp pain in her chest, like she'd been stabbed all over again. She quickly blinked back tears. Chris, however, began to glare.

"What in the world…" he glowered.

"It's alright," Allie consoled him, smiling at the sound. "They sound harmless. It could just be a hermit."

"That's no hermit," Chris growled. "What in the name of all that is holy is he doing all the way out here? Come on." Chris turned towards the sound and began to lead them to the singer. His mood hung over him like a thundercloud. Allie hung back closer to Shæúgh and shared a curious look with Jak. They followed the voice to a clearing, and Chris burst in with the grace of a storm.

"What, by the golden walls themselves, are you doing out here, you idiot?" he demanded.

Jak and her sisters stopped with Shæúgh at the edge of the clearing and looked in. They stared. Allie made a small sound. There was a man resting by a campfire. A knight. He was tall and impossibly handsome with golden skin and honey-blonde curls. He wore a full suit of silver armour, detailed in gold, with the sun of Kosvo on the front, and a golden cape. He looked up at Chris with a smile so pure and beautiful it probably knocked Allie's socks off.

"Brother!" he exclaimed, rising to his feet and embracing Chris with enough force to wind him. The girls just stared. If Chris was a demigod, this man put him to shame. Jak could feel Allie swooning beside her. Chris did not look pleased to be crushed in his brother's loving, steel-encased arms. He shoved him away.

"What are you wearing?"

"I'm a knight," he explained happily, as though Chris was stupid and couldn't tell. "Why wouldn't I wear this?"

"You look like you're wearing everything but the kitchen cupboard, and you sound like a pot that's been kicked down the stairs," Chris replied scathingly. "What are you doing all the way out here?"

"You hadn't shown up," his brother shrugged, oblivious to any insults. "We were wondering why you were taking so long, so I came this way looking for you."

They could see Chris struggling with this. He clearly wanted to keep chastising his brother, but there wasn't a fault in that argument — save the point that wandering into a forest to look for someone wasn't sensible because the odds were that you would miss them. Except that he hadn't. Chris had been late to meet up with them, and his brother had come and found him. The younger brother sighed.

"Well, it's a good thing you brought two horses," he indicated to the other side of the clearing. Two horses Jak had not noticed before were tied up to a tree. "I found company. We haven't been travelling so fast since two of us are walking." Chris motioned to the girls and both men looked over to them. His brother took stock of their company and bowed fluidly.

"My ladies," he addressed them courteously. "Had I but known that my brother was waylaid in your service, I would have hurried back faster to aid you."

"Don't faint," Jak muttered down to Allie.

"As if," she hissed back fiercely, wearing her most winsome smile.

Chris was eyeing his brother in a similar fashion to the banter between the girls.

"Not bad," he complimented softly. His brother winked at him.

"We are most grateful, Sir Knight," Allie replied to him, taking the lead and approaching. "If we had but known that such help was awaiting us, we would have hurried faster."

"Isaac," he held out his hand to her.

"Allie," she responded, offering her own hand. "My sisters are Jak and Dora." He took her hand and kissed it. Jak rolled her eyes. Chris gave her cynicism an empathetic eyebrow twitch.

"The youngest one is sick," Chris interrupted their moment. "Is Olivia still meeting us at the city?"

"She is," Isaac nodded.

"Good. We'll need her skills. Let's ride." He cast his frost spell at Isaac's fire to quench it and strode for the horses.

"Ride with me, Lady Allie?" Isaac asked. Allie looked like she could fly. She joined the men by the horses and Isaac lifted her into the saddle behind him. Chris swung himself up onto the other horse. He gave Jak a nod and she returned the look with confidence. He took point and led them off into the forest.

As they travelled on, Jak felt Dora tug at the edge of her cloak. The little girl's face was pale and dark bags hung under her eyes, even though she was sleeping most of the time.

"What's up, baby girl?" Jak asked softly. "Do you need to stop? We're trying to get you to a healer."

Dora shook her head. "I don't think they're lords," she rasped quietly. She leant in closer to Jak and whispered conspiratorially. "There weren't two horses with Isaac when we got there. They appeared when Chris pointed them out." She covered her mouth with her hand carefully and looked at the men they were following suspiciously, even though it seemed impossible that they could hear her. "I think they're con men."

"They're certainly something..." Jak agreed carefully, keeping Dora bundled close. She had her own growing suspicions about Chris and Isaac. Jak didn't want to get Dora worked up when she was so unwell, so she just gave her a cautious nod of affirmation and warning. Dora took the hint. She knew Jak would protect them. When the time was right, she would act. Jak just had to wonder what the right time would be, and the right action — especially if her own theories were also right. She kept her silence and they rode on.

As they travelled, Isaac asked his brother about the curious entourage he had attracted, and Chris recounted the tale, complete with their run in with the D'rö-Hadās. The brothers shared a joint fascination in the knowledge that the girls had been saved from the Head Hunters by one of Thænäri's gnomes. In Jak's head it made sense — you needed a faerie to stop faeries, and Äulé had always been their friend. Their new friends did not seem to agree. The idea of a gnome doing something to thwart the D'rö-Hadās was controversial.

Chris also explained that he found them because they were where one of the leads he'd been tracking led him, which was why the D'rö-Hadās were involved anyway. Jak listened as intently as she could to the conversation for any clue as to what they were after. Isaac, obviously, had had no luck either. Whatever they were looking for, no one had seen any trace of it, but for some reason one of the leads kept circling around to Jak and her sisters.

She was so absorbed in their account that she didn't even sense the danger until it was upon them. Dora was asleep in her lap. The trees were pressed in thick, tangled and wild. Suddenly, a bear charged towards their group. It came at them from the side. The horses shrieked and reared.

"Shit!" Chris cursed, trying to rein his horse in.

Allie screamed and clung to Isaac. Shæúgh pranced nervously away but kept his cool. Jak appreciated the courage of the fae horse. She kept one arm protectively around Dora, holding the reins. The other drew her broken sword. The bear was looking to them. It had picked them as the weakest of the group, instead of going after the demigods. She didn't know if she could keep it back with half a weapon, but she was prepared to try.

The bear was twice the size of a horse. It had thick shaggy brown fur. The colour almost blended into the forest. But saliva dripped from its white teeth and red jaw. Jak brandished the broken sword with a growl. The bear growled back. It was a deep, hungry, and terrifying sound. A small reactive terror quivered in Jak's chest at the noise. Her fight or flight response was telling her to ride hard in the opposite direction.

"Halt!" Isaac commanded. Everyone froze, including the bear. With a tight grip on his reins and a regal bearing, Isaac rode forward to place himself between the girls and the bear. Allie clung on in terror behind him, but he kept himself pointed towards the threat. His poor horse rolled its eyes madly, but he stroked its neck reassuringly as he forced it forward.

"Calm down, Peanut," he soothed. Then he looked to the bear. His mannerisms changed completely. He raised one hand. It wasn't quite signing, at least, not in the way Jak recognised it. He gestured at the beast and nodded to it. At every motion it became less aggressive, until, after less than a minute, it whined and rubbed its face on a shaggy brown paw. "Go on," he encouraged, motioning it away. The bear gave a tired groan, and then lumbered away. They watched it shamble off with great purpose. It didn't look back once as it set off with a certain direction.

"Show off," Chris muttered now that he had control of his horse again.

"Don't be sour, brother," Isaac told him calmly. "You have your uses as well."

"I have my uses? Seriously? You want to be like that?"

"You do, Silvertongue. Don't let anyone tell you otherwise," he smirked.

"You waved your hands and pulled faces at a bear, don't make more of it than it is."

"You screamed a bit and cursed aimlessly. I'm sure you could have been helpful if you wanted to. If I'd given you more time, perhaps, you could have driven the bear away with some poetry."

"Oh, piss off. No one asked you to help," Chris sulked.

"They didn't have to," Isaac shrugged. "It's just what I do."

"Oh, sure," Chris drawled. "You're incredibly helpful. You help yourself into the beds of admiring ladies from here to the far sea. I'm sure everyone you meet feels oh so *helped*."

Isaac raised an eyebrow at him. "Are you done?"

"Are you?" Chris countered.

Isaac rolled his eyes and looked to the girls. He noted Jak's blade and they way she still sat defensively, ready to strike if necessary.

"My Lady, your sword," he motioned.

"It was broken in a fight with the D'rö-Hadās," Jak answered. "You can talk to bears?"

"It's not that difficult," Isaac shrugged. "He was just hungry. I conveyed a nearby location with significantly easier food. I can mend the blade if you'd like."

"Once we get to Kosvo," Chris ordered. "The little one needs a healer and we need to find out if Olivia found anything. The sword can wait. Besides, you can just wiggle your fingers at any threats on the way."

"Next one is all yours, brother," Isaac invited. "Anything else tries to come after us, you can talk it to death."

"I'm sure your passenger would appreciate it," Chris replied scathingly as he turned his horse to lead on. "Young girls don't tend to appreciate being placed in the area of attack."

Isaac looked back at Allie still holding on behind him.

"Lady Allie?" he inquired as though he'd only just remembered her. "Apologies, my fair maiden, I didn't mean to frighten you. We were never in any danger, I assure you."

"It might have been nice to know that before you rode up to the bear," she muttered softly.

"I won't do it again without warning you," he promised.

Allie laughed weakly. She had the expression of someone who would prefer that he not do it again at all, but she couldn't fault his honesty. Jak watched her carefully as she sheathed her broken sword. Dora was still cuddled into her, and Allie seemed to be settling again under the great knight's watch. Everything was fine once more — for now.

***

They rode without incident for the rest of the day. Dusk was falling when they crested the hill at the edge of the forest overlooking Kosvo. The trees stopped abruptly along the skyline, as though they knew not to get too close to human territory. Jak struggled to keep her jaw from dropping as they rode out of the trees and looked down.

Kosvo was massive. It stretched as far as the eye could see. Clusters of stone houses and paved streets blanketed the horizon. Large buildings and temples rose up from the crowded suburbs. In the centre of all of it rose the castle of the King. Jak had never seen or imagined something as big as the capital city of Kosvo. It was incredible. The sun was setting over it in dusky pinks and blues. Lights were beginning to twinkle in the windows like a sea of stars.

Jak nudged Dora awake to look down. The little girl was too sick and sleepy to pay much attention, but she gave her older sister a nod. Chris looked back and noted her awe.

"You've never been here before?"

"No," Jak shook her head. "We come from a small town a long way from here. This is our first city."

The brothers shared a look and a smile, possibly at the innocence of their companions. Jak didn't care. She remembered the way Jim and Krill had been the same. She had considered them so worldly, and they had considered her so stupid — in hindsight. They had thought of her as a burden and left her behind. She had imagined she would be looking at this city one day with them. Now here she was, and they were long gone. The thought brought a lump to her throat, but she blinked the emotions away fiercely.

Out of the shadows of the trees, a lone rider came towards them. Jak instinctively reached for her sword. The failing light made her tense and watch for fae. She still expected the D'rö-Hadās to return. The stranger was not D'rö-Hadās. In fact, they were not even a stranger. Jak felt her theories about their new friends fall into place as she watched Chris ride forward to meet his wife. The lady on the white horse was cloaked, but she pushed her hood down and leant over to kiss her husband as he pulled up beside her. She was breathtakingly beautiful. Her pale platinum hair was coiled in braids and her eyes were a pale blue. The two conversed briefly and then Chris rode back to the others.

"Olivia has a camp set up just inside the woods," he told them. "We'll rest there for the night and she can heal your sister."

"Thank you," Jak nodded, accepting him at his word for now.

The woman on the horse rode back into the trees and Chris followed with their guests. They didn't have to go far. A minute back into the wild tangle uncovered a clearing with a roaring campfire and a tent already set up. They dismounted and Isaac saw to the horses. Jak carried Dora, and Allie set up their own tent with a sharp flick of the cloth. The girls organised their bunks and Jak put Dora to bed.

When she came out again, she motioned Allie to join her. Her younger sister could tell from the look Jak was giving her that something was up, but Jak wasn't going to spoil it by telling her. She also wasn't going to leave her in the dark about this. Although, she wasn't sure how Allie would take the news that her new friends weren't what they seemed. As if it wasn't obvious enough that they were too beautiful and magical. Allie seemed to have expensive taste in men.

When they came back out of the tent, Isaac had finished what had been an incredibly quick tend to the horses — if they were even real; Jak had to wonder. He had joined his brother and sister — Jak knew that's what they were now — and the three of them stood close by the fire conversing intensely in hushed voices. The orange light danced across their faces and Jak was struck by their uncanny fae beauty. She couldn't believe it had taken her so long, but it was the beauty she had come to associate with half-fae after her time with Krill and Kode. She was prepared to believe in demigods. But her demigod had not been this pretty. This was something else.

"Jak?" Allie inquired softly by her elbow. The little girl grinned. "She's pretty hot."

"She's more than just 'pretty hot', Allie," Jak replied. She was surprised to find that the memory was painful. It wasn't a pain she wanted to acknowledge. She didn't miss them. She didn't miss him. He was a jerk, and he always had been. She strode forward. Her heart was hammering like it wanted to break through her ribs. She was about to out them, and she didn't know if she could do it. What would happen if she pissed off the gods?

"Girls," Chris turned to them as he saw them approaching. "This is my wife, Olivia—"

"You mean Olíriá," Jak corrected. "We've met. I recognise her. You don't fool me anymore."

"Jak," Olivia smiled at her. "What a pleasant surprise." She maintained her human appearance, but Jak recognised her completely. She recognised that smile. It was the same way she had smiled charmingly at Jim. Somehow it wasn't so pretty anymore.

"You know these girls?" Chris asked.

"I met Jak a few days ago," Olivia shrugged.

"Wait," Allie interrupted everyone. "What?! You're— You mean—!"

"She's the goddess Olíriá," Jak insisted. "Which means you must be the gods Crŷstïar and Ínrío." Jak gave Chris a sharp look. "I could almost have bought the idea of you as a demigod, *Slivertongue,* but these two? Nope. Not a chance."

Olíriá and Ínrío shared a look, but Chris stood between them, holding Jak's eyes with his own. As she held his gaze, he morphed into his fae body. It was subtle. Nearly a shrug. Suddenly, he was godly. Olíriá and Ínrío followed suit. Allie gasped audibly as they were suddenly faced with gods at the campfire.

"You're very sharp, girl," Crŷstïar complimented. "And deeply suspicious. How is it that one such as yourself can pick out gods and battle the Queen's assassins? We're looking for a fae thief, and you aren't doing yourself any favours stacking your hand against ours."

"Calm down, Crŷs," Olíriá urged. She pronounced his name Cr-ice and placed a gentle hand on his arm. "She doesn't know anything. We'd know if she did."

"How can you be so sure?" Crŷs replied. "My main lead brought me to these girls and something about them doesn't sit right. It never has."

Olíriá turned her attention to Jak. Allie was still staring at them all in shock, but Jak had known this would happen. She lifted her chin defiantly as the gods turned their attention to her. She refused to show weakness. Not here. Not now. Even if she could feel her nerves tremble. She wouldn't give the D'Ihne the satisfaction.

"How did you come to be here, Jak?" Olíriá asked. "What happened to your last companions?"

"They left," Jak answered. Her voice quivered when she said it and she bit her tongue. Not now. Not here. Keep it together. "They just left one night. When we woke up, they were gone."

Olíriá stared her down. She knew. Jak felt tears building in her eyes as the goddess looked at her. She bit her tongue harder to keep them back. Don't cry. Don't cry. Don't fucking cry. Olíriá was staring at her with such sympathetic eyes.

"It's not the first time he's done that," she said gently.

"It's not the first time who's done what?" Ínrío asked boldly.

"When I met Jak, she and her sisters were travelling with Jim and the boys," Olíriá answered, without taking her eyes from the suffering girl.

"She what?!" Crŷs exploded. He rounded on her. "You fucking what? You never said you were with him!"

"You never asked!" Jak yelled back. "And I wasn't with him. You gods are all the same. You don't even give a shit. You just make assumptions."

"We give more of a shit than he does," Crŷs snapped. "What were you doing with him?"

Jak stared at him. Her throat was trembling inside her and she didn't think she could answer through the lump building inside it. She took a deep breath through her nose. As the air steadied her lungs, a single tear finally escaped and dripped tragically down her cheek. Well, shit. So much for that.

"Fuck. Off. Chris." Jak whispered each word like a bite. It was all she could manage. Her grief for the life she could have had under Krill's tutelage, and the days of fun Jim had insisted on them living, was trying to break out of her like a storm. The gods didn't see that, but they did see something. Crŷs was watching her like she was about to detonate.

"What did he do to you?" he asked.

It was the final straw. Hot tears splashed down her face. Jak cursed and threw her hands up to hide her distress. She turned away as she began to break down. A tiny hand on her back told her Allie was there, trying to comfort her. She shouldn't have to. It shouldn't be her little sister's job to look after her, but she couldn't stop crying enough to breathe properly, let alone force words out. Jak hunched down, hiding her face, and wept as quietly as she could.

"Jak, what did he do to you?" Crŷs repeated. The gods were all gathered around them now. He asked the question so intensely it sounded almost threatening.

"Back up, god-boy," Allie warned him. She'd lost her infatuation. Family always came first for her, and she didn't like feeling stupid. Being tricked by gods would not have endeared them to her. "I don't know what you're trying to imply, but Jak's gay, so there's none of that going on."

"That's never stopped him before," Crŷs warned coldly. Allie paled slightly and shut up quickly.

"Let her answer," Olíriá encouraged. Her calming touch rested on Jak's shoulder and rubbed it soothingly. "Jak? What did he do?"

"He left," Jak sobbed through her hands. "He l-l-l-left. They a-b-b-band-doned us with n-n-no-w-where to g-go and no id-dea what to d-d-do." She hated the way she sounded, and wished she wasn't so upset, but the more she wished she would stop crying, the harder the sobs came.

"Wait…" Crŷs paused. "You're upset because he left you alone? Why? Ow!"

Olíriá smacked him on the shoulder. She shot a daggered look at him.

"What?" he protested.

"Oh, brother," Ínrío sighed at him. The god of the sun rubbed Jak's back reassuringly. "It's alright, child. I understand what it's like, even if my smartarse brother can't see past his own personal grudges."

"How can anybody want that prick around?" Crŷs

protested.

"He was fun," Jak muttered, wiping her face miserably. They all stopped fighting to look at her. She took a deep shuddering breath and wiped away more tears. It had been a hard thing to admit out loud, but the pressure in her chest lessened as she said it. She was finally shedding the weight of the truth. "He was rude and gross sometimes, yeah, but he was fun to have around. It was like… it was like having a big brother. I know this sounds stupid, ye gods it sounds so stupid, but… but he kinda reminded me of Dad."

Jak looked up. The others were all looking down on her. Even Allie. Allie's eyes were misty at her confession. Jak sighed. She'd almost stopped crying again.

"When Dad was around…" Jak reminisced softly, "we used to have fun. I was just little, but we used to play all the time. Life was… better. After he died… we didn't play anymore. We didn't even cry. We just buried him. Mum became sombre. We had a new baby to look after, and no Dad to help out. We just had to work all the time. And… and I miss him." Fresh tears fell like rain. Jak tipped her head back as she finally cried for the loss of her father. "I miss him every day. I miss him so much. And then Mum went too. I have no idea where she is, or if she's still alive, or how to find her, or how to look after my sisters…"

Allie threw her arms around Jak's neck. She fell into her big sister's lap and squeezed. Jak squeezed her back and kissed the top of her head.

"I was so mad at Jim," she breathed softly through

her tears. "I was so mad at him for so long, but when he came into our lives we got to play again. He brought back the kind of fun I hadn't had since I was a little kid, and it reminded me of Dad. Then he left us. In the middle of the night without a word. He just ran off and abandoned us. Now... now I don't know what to do anymore."

"Then start by resting up," Olíriá suggested. "Get warm by the fire and, for tonight, don't go anywhere. I'll go and see what I can do for your sister."

"Thank you," Jak sighed, sagging into the empty space left by all the emotions that had just escaped her. Allie stayed in her lap, hanging on around her neck in a reassuring embrace. Jak hugged her sister. She hadn't wanted to put any of that on her, but she felt so light now that she'd said it. All the weight that had been piling up since their dad had died, and all the weight that had been crushing her since their mum left, was suddenly gone. She knew it would come back, but even if she was only free for tonight, it was something.

Olíriá was back in an instant.

"Uh..." the goddess' hesitation sounded behind them. Everyone turned to face her. "Did you leave the little one in your tent?"

"Yes, why?"

"She's... not there..." Olíriá answered slowly. Jak met her eyes. Olíriá wasn't lying. Dora was gone.

CHAPTER FOURTEEN

Jak was on her feet instantly. She raced to the tent, calling for her youngest sister. There was no one in there. She checked the other tent. That one was completely empty. Clearly Olí's tent was just for show.

"Dora!" Jak called into the forest. Allie was already yelling into the trees. Suddenly, Ínrío was beside them, swinging into the saddle of his horse.

"I'll find her," he declared. "She can't have gone far." For a second he closed his eyes, and then they snapped open and he whirled Peanut as he charged off. Jak was so dazed that, for a moment, she couldn't work out how he had untied his horse and ridden off so surely and quickly, until she remembered he was a god. Her nerves weren't up to this. It was too soon. She wanted to cry again.

"It's alright," Olíriá soothed her again. The goddess' hands were warm on her shoulders as she guided her back to the fire. "He'll find her. There's no way a little girl can escape the greatest hunter alive."

Crŷs placed an arm around Allie's shoulders, enfolding her in his cloak, and led her back to the fire as well. The two sisters were in shock, and they sat down together by the flames under the watchful eyes of the gods. It was too much. Everything that had happened since they had left home… Jak had been there for all of it, and she still didn't understand how this had become her life. Sitting here and doing nothing was unbearable, and yet she felt too dizzy to act usefully. Their future was now in the hands of the gods — very literally. They were very 'hands on' gods.

"I… I have to get her medicine…" Jak muttered, scrambling unsteadily to her feet and weaving back to the tent. No one tried to stop her. No one pointed out that when Dora got back Olíriá was going to heal her and the medicine wasn't necessary. She knew part of her was hoping that she would open the tent flap and Dora would be there piled under the blankets wondering what all the fuss was about. She wasn't.

Jak stared around the empty bunks in the tent. Dora was so sick… how had she gone somewhere on her own? Did something take her? How? The gods would have seen it. Except… they were faeries. The most powerful and dominant of all creatures, yes, but still faeries — and faeries were child snatchers. Especially if the children had done something wrong. Did they think Jak and her sisters had done something wrong? Did they think Dora had done something wrong? They kept saying the lead everyone was chasing drew them to the girls… did the gods think the girls had stolen something?

Jak could feel a rising panic, until she remembered the way Olíriá had defended her against Crŷs. She didn't believe they were thieves. That wasn't a trick. She just had to trust them. Ínrío would bring Dora back safe and sound. Any second now. If he didn't… then they could start wondering what the gods were up to. Jak opened her pack and dug around for the medicine. The clink of pottery sounded and her heart skipped a beat.

With gentle yet trembling hands, she pulled out the shirt with her mother's bowls inside it. She could already feel the broken pieces through the fabric. With a horrifying lurch in her stomach, she remembered the shattering sound she had heard as they had been swallowed by the faerie trap. She sat the shirt in her lap and carefully unfolded it. The bowls were broken. Every single one was in pieces. She began to weep again.

There was nothing else to do. She was too tired to function, and this was too much. She sat on the floor of the tent, on her own in the half-dark, and she let the tears roll free and fresh down her face. After a moment, the tent flap opened. Jak looked up expecting to see Allie and have to show her the damage. She was surprised to see Olíriá enter and kneel down beside her.

"Jak? What's wrong?" the goddess asked.

"They broke," Jak answered pitifully. "I brought them with me to keep them safe, and they broke."

"That's an easy fix," Olíriá smiled. "If you want me to."

"I... I c-can't pay you..." Jak snuffled.

"Oh Jak..." Olíriá smiled sweetly. The goddess raised her hand over the broken pottery and made some quick signs. The runes seemed to glow in the air and then rained like glitter over the bowls.

Jak stared in amazement as the pieces quickly stitched themselves back together. In seconds, the bowls were sitting complete and unharmed in her lap, without so much as a crack. She picked one up and began to inspect it in awe. It was as perfect as the day it was made.

"It's just rune magic, Jak," Olíriá smiled. "It doesn't cost anything. Well, no more than the words you use. Now, if you want me to make them unbreakable, give them a core of steel, or turn them into gold — that will cost you."

Jak set the bowl down gently to wipe her face with both hands. New tears of gratitude were trying to overwhelm her.

"Thank you," she breathed.

"You're welcome." Olíriá reached over and picked up a bowl. She inspected it carefully, turning it over in her long pearlescent fingers.

Jak was starting to breathe properly again, but now that she was calming down she was suddenly aware of how close she was to the beautiful goddess. Olíriá's scantily clad form was sprawled casually next to her, and the goddess' hands kept reaching between Jak's thighs to switch between the bowls. A hot blush raced up the girl's chest. Olíriá was totally absorbed in her inspection of the pottery.

"Where did you get these?" she asked.

"They're Mum's," Jak answered nervously. "She made them. Mum and Dad used to make all our dishes. These are some of her special ones. I... I didn't want to leave them behind when... when our house..."

"Your mum made these?" Olíriá echoed, focusing on that part of the tale and letting Jak escape having to finish her sentence.

"Yeah," Jak answered, growing suspicious at her tone. "Why?"

"Did Jim ever see them?"

Alarm bells went off in Jak's head. "Why do you ask?"

Olíriá gave her a look. She knew she'd triggered something. "It's a yes or no question, Jak."

Jak couldn't out-stare the goddess. The whole conversation felt half-familiar, and the pale woman reminded her of Krill. It shouldn't have been a surprise, the two of them were related, she recalled. Krill's mother was Olíriá's father — if that made any sense.

"No," Jak told her. "I never showed them to Jim. I showed them to Krill and he ordered me not to show Jim. What's so special about them?"

"Ah Krill..." Olíriá smiled, ignoring Jak's question. "He is clever, that one. And he's right; make sure Jim never sees these. There's no telling what he'd do."

"Why?!" Jak demanded. "What's so wrong with Jim?"

"I mean, if I had to whittle it down to the basics, I would say his questionable morals and inability to apologise," Olíriá mused.

"It's a reluctance, not an inability," Jak disagreed. Olíriá stared at her. Jak shrugged. "He's apologised to me before."

"Really?"

"Yeah..."

"A proper apology, Jak — not just wiggling around until everyone forgets about it."

"Yes, a proper apology. Well, he's said sorry to me before."

"Sorry? He actually said 'sorry'? With his mouth?"

Jak laughed. She wiped her damp eyes and shook her head at herself. She should be worried. She should be scared. Dora was missing. But she was hiding in a tent, alone with the goddess of love, and laughing about her old friend.

"Yes. He said sorry with his mouth. He has admitted to being in the wrong."

Olíriá stared at her like she had just said the world was going to end tomorrow. Slowly, she turned her dazed blue eyes away and stared blankly across the tent. A small smile hovered at the corners of her lips.

"Good," she whispered so softly Jak barely heard her.

"Who's he related to?" Jak asked. She gently packed away the mended pottery. "I know he's a demigod, but who's his father? How do you all know him?"

Olíriá opened her mouth to answer, when the thudding of hooves cut her off. The women shared a sharp look. Dora. They both bolted from the tent. Crŷs and Allie were on their feet by the fire. Ínrío reined Peanut in sharply and the mighty horse pranced and snorted. Jak recognised the bundle of blankets in the god's arms.

"Dora!" she cried.

Ínrío slid from the saddle with the little girl cradled in his massive golden arms.

"She has a fever," he told them. "I found her wandering through mushroom circles calling for her mother. It's a miracle she wasn't snatched. This is one of Thænäri's forests. It's still wild, and a dangerous place for humans to tread."

"She was in mushroom circles and the faeries didn't take her?" Olíriá echoed, taking the girl from her brother.

"At least we know they're working hard," Ínrío shrugged. "If they were too distracted to notice a child walking through their circles, it's a testament to their devotion to our cause."

"Or something…" Crŷs muttered suspiciously.

"Let me see what I can do for the child and then we can get back to the mission," Olíriá told the boys. She turned and swept back into the tent with a whimpering Dora in her arms. Jak watched her go nervously and hugged herself. Ínrío and Crŷs shared a look, and the god of snow followed his older brother away from the firelight. The two gods conversed briefly in hushed voices. Allie wandered over to Jak.

"She'll be alright," Allie assured. "They found her and they'll heal her."

"Yeah," Jak agreed. She pulled Allie into a one-armed hug. "Yeah, they will. Thanks."

"It's okay. I didn't realise you were so upset about Jim…"

"I didn't want to be," Jak muttered. "I mean, he is a dick. I just… they were fun to have around, and it was an easy way of life. I had all these dreams about how Krill was going to teach me to fight like a fae, and we would go on adventures with them, and learn fae secrets and then… suddenly they were gone. So were the dreams. They didn't even say goodbye. It hurt."

"If I see him again I'm going to kick him in the nuts."

"Allie!" Jak laughed.

"I am," she grumbled. "He's a jerk and he deserves it. No one makes my big sister cry but me."

"Yeah, you're a little rat when you want to be," Jak poked her in the side. Allie poked her back. The two of them laughed. Everything felt strangely normal. As though they could get their lives back. Despite the gods and the magic and the illness and the trouble, everything was alright again.

"I'm kinda hungry," Allie commented.

"Yeah, let's get some food," Jak agreed. They hadn't packed away the picnic basket and a warm dinner by the fire sounded like a good idea.

While they were eating, Ínrío came to join them. The god sunk down wearily by the fire and Jak offered him some food.

"Thank you," he replied graciously. "You ladies are kind and generous."

"Well, it's not even really ours," Allie admitted. "It was Jim's, but he left it in our tent when he ran away."

"I recognise his magic," Ínrío laughed. "It's not always easy to place, but sometimes you find things that couldn't have come from anyone else. Speaking of magic," he looked directly at Jak. "I spoke to my brother of your sword. He told you I would fix it."

"And he told me how D'Ihne magic works," Jak shivered. "I'm not sure it's worth it."

"What were you expecting to pay?"

"I don't know," Jak shrugged. "I don't have much

money. I'd be prepared to work off my debt to a swordsmith, but I'm not giving you a finger or an ear or something."

Ínrío laughed again. "What about a dance?"

"A dance?"

"A dance," he repeated with a nod. "My sister is the finest musician in the three realms. Would you take a turn with me about the fire to one of her songs, in exchange for the repair of your weapon?"

"She would," Allie answered.

"Allie!"

"Jak, you have to."

"I don't have to do anything!"

"No, you don't," Ínrío chuckled at them. "You don't have to answer immediately either. Think on it."

"This isn't some kind of euphemism is it?" Jak asked nervously. "How do you get magic from a dance? What level is that?"

"It is not a euphemism," Ínrío laughed. "It is old magic. A twist on item magic. A favour for a favour. They can still be bartered, if the fae in question knows how to turn a favour."

Jak didn't need to ask if the god of the sun knew how to turn magic from a favour. As she thought about it nervously, Crŷs came to join them at the fire. The younger brother sank down by the flames like a shadow. He watched the conversation with curious eyes. Ínrío met his brother's look and answered the unspoken question.

"She thinks I'm trying to trick her."

"You're not smart enough to trick her," Crŷs grinned

impishly.

"I'm not as stupid as you like to think I am, brother."

"No," Crŷs agreed. "But she picked you as D'Ihne a mile off. She's too quick for you."

"She picked you as D'Ihne too. Don't get so smug."

"I'm better at it though," Crŷs gave Jak a sharp look across the fire. His eyes were mischievous and cunning. She gave a reluctant nod in return.

"Crŷs was more convincing," she admitted. "It's strange, after all the legends about gods walking among men, I thought you would be better at passing for human — like I thought you'd be able to pass as actual humans, not just demigods or barely demigods."

"Ouch," Ínrío grinned at her.

"You know what I mean…" Jak muttered.

"Those disguises do pass us as human to most other humans," Crŷs replied. "You have exceptional skill at picking fae from a crowd. I will concede, as a being made of magic it is difficult to pass as a creature without it. Trickery aside, Thænäri was always the best at passing for human. The forest D'Ihne was the most curious about humanity, and the closest to them. She could pass as human, and she taught her children to do the same."

"She's your auntie?" Allie asked.

"Yes, I suppose," he shrugged. Crŷs looked like he was going to say something else, until he saw Olíriá standing by the opening to the girls' tent. She motioned to the men, but her face was otherwise unreadable. The two gods quickly excused themselves and went to meet her without waiting for a reply. Jak stared after them, half-risen to her knees. She wanted to follow, but knew she hadn't been invited.

The three gods spoke in hushed voices and Jak felt her heart racing at the look on Olíriá's face now. She saw Crŷs curse and run his hands through his hair in frustration. Ínrío and Olíriá were both shooting looks back at her, but trying to be subtle about it. It was hard to be subtle when the person you were glancing at was staring at you like you were the centre of the universe. Ínrío jerked his head at the girls, and Olíriá nodded. The two of them approached the fire while Crŷs loitered by the tent, irritably biting a knuckle.

"What's wrong?" Jak demanded as soon as they were close. "What happened?"

"I brought her fever down and she's sleeping peacefully," Olíriá answered soothingly. "But I haven't been able to cure her."

"How is that possible?" Jak demanded. "You're a god! What do you need? Someone's blood?"

"It's not about resources, Jak," Olíriá mediated calmly. "It's—" she stopped sharply and shared a look with Ínrío. The god of the sun raised his hands submissively and shook his head. He wasn't getting him involved. The look she returned him was dry. She turned back to Jak with a sigh. "Dora's been sick before, hasn't she?"

"I never told you about that…"

"No, you didn't. You didn't have to. I… I think that Dora has been healed by D'Ihne magic before…"

"How?"

Olíriá shared another look with Ínrío. He still wasn't

getting involved. She shrugged.

"There are ways," she answered vaguely. "It's possible your mother prayed for Dora to be healed. However it happened, I believe that the spell that was cast over her to heal her when she was a small child is still in place, and it's blocking any of my spells from taking effect."

"So, what do we do?"

"We wait," she replied. "I will reassess her condition in the morning. If she doesn't seem to be improving naturally with the help I can give her, then I may need to go to Roïgola'a'lanaū and find out what was done to her, by whom, so that I can help her."

"If she's already got a healing spell on her, why isn't it still working?" Allie asked.

"I don't know," Olíriá admitted. "I'm sorry. I've never encountered a problem like this before. Previously my magic has always worked."

"Except with us…" Jak interrupted softly. Olíriá met her look. They both remembered what had happened at the pool. The goddess grimaced.

"That was slightly different, but yes. There is something about you three, so now we need to find a way around it. If Dora is doing better in the morning, then that means my magic is working, albeit slowly. If she isn't, then something is blocking me and we need to find out what."

Jak and Allie shared a nervous look. Olíriá touched Jak's shoulder.

"Get some rest, girls. We can't do anything more tonight."

Jak wanted to protest. She wanted to do something, but Olíriá was right, and it was easier to take Allie and head to bed than start a fight with gods. She'd already broken down in front of them once tonight. She didn't need to throw a tantrum about this as well. Allie didn't fight either. She looked disheartened, as though the D'Ihne weren't really living up to their reputation as gods.

They went to bed, but neither of them slept. Dora was snoring quietly in her blankets, and she did look better. It eased Jak's worry. But while they lay awake in their bunks, the gods spoke outside. Jak caught snippets of their conversation.

"I think you're right about those girls, Olí," Crŷs muttered.

"I'm pretty sure I'm right too, but that means we need to be gentle."

"We don't have to stay. They're a dead end. A red herring. A false lead."

"We absolutely have to stay, Crŷs," she insisted. "You really want to pull a Jim?"

"Don't call it that," he protested disgustedly. "I'm nothing like him."

"You're talking about doing exactly what he did."

"We don't know he knows."

"We don't *know* anything," Ínrío leant on the word as he joined the conversation. "But Olí is right; we have to stay. We have an obligation to the family."

"You two are soft. We have an obligation to report back. We're overdue as it is."

"They can wait," Olíriá told her lover.

"We've been gone weeks! It's been missing a year!" Crŷs hissed. "I have to get back on the trail."

"Brother, what is time to an immortal? We will pursue this, but we cannot neglect all other duties as well. This is important. It doesn't have to be you that finds it."

"But they think I did it," Crŷs growled.

"No one really thinks that, my love."

"They blamed me."

"That's because you usually do it," Ínrío replied heartlessly. "Something goes missing or a prank is pulled — it's usually you. They know you didn't do it this time. You would have fixed it if you had. No one is working harder on the recovery than you. Our mother can see that."

"Everyone thinks I stole it," Crŷs muttered. "They think I pulled a prank and then fucked something up and now it's gone."

"We don't," Olíriá reminded him pointedly. Silence fell outside the tent, but Jak was lying tensed under her blankets. She wanted to jump up and run outside screaming for answers, but it wouldn't do her any good to admit she'd been eavesdropping. With a horde of nervous questions chasing each other around her mind, she lay there for hours before sleep finally took her.

***

When she woke in the morning, Dora was coughing. Jak rolled from her bunk as Dora's rattling, racking cough nearly shook the tent. Allie was already at Dora's side, spooning out the last of the medicine.

"Get Olí!" she ordered.

Jak raced out of the tent only half dressed. Olíriá was already up and moving from her tent to theirs. She passed Jak with a nod and ducked inside. Jak was left standing outside in just her shirt. It was too cold a morning for that, but she wasn't sure there was space to sneak back in and get dressed. Dora was the priority. Instead, she tiptoed across the frosty dirt to the fire, which was still blazing brightly. Her feet forgave her as soon as she was standing on the warm earth nearby, and her legs soon followed suit while she held her hands out to the blaze.

"Lady Jak," Ínrío addressed her from behind. Jak turned and watched the god approach with a fresh armload of firewood.

"Lord Ínrío," she bowed her head to him. She quickly tugged at her shirt to make sure it was long enough to be decent, but she needn't have worried. She turned back to the blaze as he dropped the logs nearby. He approached her.

"The little one isn't better?" he asked.

"I don't know," Jak muttered nervously. "She doesn't seem to be."

"Perhaps this will brighten your day." From behind his back, yet also seemingly nowhere, Ínrío materialised a sword and held it out to her. Jak stared, but he was watching her and holding the sword in both hands like an offering. She reached out gently and took it.

It was lighter than her old sword. Faster. She unsheathed it. The blade was double edged with the

Neart rune on it for strength and the Trodai rune of the warrior, while the handle bore Ínrío's own rune Sorio. The balance was better than her old blade. This had been forged by gods, not men.

"It's beautiful," she commented.

"I'm glad you like it," he smiled. "It's yours."

"I can't accept this, Ínrío. We never agreed to a price."

"Call it a kindness," he replied carefully.

"I've never heard of faeries giving away gifts like this as a kindness…"

"I'm no ordinary faerie," he grinned. "I'm D'Ihne. We do as we like. Besides, I was talking to my brother, and he said you and your sisters are no strangers to fae kindness. Jim and the Ha'Cās took you in and gave you faerie supplies, and apparently you lot are all friends with one of Thænäri's gnomes."

"Äulé," Jak nodded. "Crŷs seemed weirdly hung up on that. Why are you all so concerned about it? What do you think is going on?"

"We're not sure," Ínrío answered. "Gnomes are not usually friendly creatures, so the fact that one likes you enough to stand up to the D'rö-Hadās is unprecedented. Add that on to everything else that is going on with you three and, well… you girls can safely be termed unusual."

"But what do you *think* is happening?" Jak pressed him.

"I think it's too cold to be standing around outside without trousers," he gave her a pointed look. "Or a bra."

Jak flushed and hugged one arm across her chest. She glared at him reproachfully in embarrassment.

"What?" he asked.

"You don't think that's an inappropriate comment?" she pointed out.

"How is that inappropriate?"

"It's unseemly for a man to comment like that about a girl's body."

Ínrío raised a quizzical eyebrow at her, and pointedly shifted into a female form. She shook her blonde curls back and eyed Jak archly. "Better?"

Jak stared at her with her mouth hanging open. She knew her jaw was agape, but she was too stunned to close it. She also had a horrible feeling that her type was goddess. Her pink blush of embarrassment was not cooling in the presence of the stunning goddess of the sun.

"Now who's being rude?" Crŷs' voice teased as he approached. "There's no need to stare, Jak."

"I'm sorry," Jak dropped her gaze bashfully. "I just... I..." she stammered. "I've heard about the abilities of the D'Ihne, I've just never seen it before. It's strange to think you just... do that."

"Humans are so weird," Ínrío grinned at Crŷs.

"So weird," Crŷs agreed emphatically. "That said, you make a very pretty lady, sis."

"I do," she agreed smugly.

"But then..." Jak tried to insinuate herself back into the conversation shyly. "Why do you always go around as a man?"

"I don't," Ínrío pointed out. "I prefer my male body

because it feels stronger and heavier, and I like feeling that way. Olíriá prefers her female body because she says it feels lighter."

"I prefer this because it feels slimmer and sneakier," Crŷs offered with a shrug.

"So, who's the most fluid of all of you?" Jak asked.

"Fæmör," the answer was unanimous and instantaneous. Crŷs said it with a sneer and Ínrío with a smile. She grinned at her brother. "You do a great imitation of her. Show Jak."

Crŷs looked reluctant.

"Oh, come on," Ínrío pouted.

Crŷs rolled his eyes, and then slowly shifted into his female form. She swept her black curls over one side. Then adopted a sultry expression and an accent.

"It's not a compulsion… it's just fun," Crŷs purred, biting her bottom lip on the word 'fun'. Jak felt hot around the collar just watching. She was surrounded by beautiful goddesses, and one of them was playing coy. Her eyes were wide and she couldn't help but wonder what she had wandered into. Crŷs shifted back into his male form and gave Ínrío a scathing look. "Can you look less aroused when I do that?"

"Probably not," Ínrío grinned, also fading out of his female body. "You do it very well and she's very sexy."

"She's a creep and a rapist," Crŷs snarled.

"Oh, calm down," Ínrío retorted. "Just because she tricked you—"

"It is not about my pride, brother!" Crŷs exploded. "I don't know why I can't make you understand — this is not about my pride. My sister pretended to be my wife to sneak into my bed." Crŷs looked like he was going to puke into the fire. "It was rape. I know that word scares you, but I'm going to keep using it until I get it through your thick skull. She is not cute. She's a monster."

"It's been decades, Crŷs!" Ínrío exclaimed. "You're still taking this far too personally. It was a prank — just like all the ones you've pulled on people. She finally got one over on you, and you've never been able to live with it."

"That is not what happened," Crŷs shook his head in disgust.

Jak looked around for anything she could use to escape the situation. She wanted to sneak away to get dressed, but she didn't even need to make excuses for that. Olíriá and Allie were approaching from the tent. At the sight of them, Jak genuinely forgot about the conversation she was trying to escape.

"What happened?" she asked urgently. "How is she?"

"Still sick," Olíriá answered solemnly. "I don't know what else I can do for her. We'll have to go to Roïgola'a'lanaū and ask the others. In the meantime, you may want to find a human doctor — you're nearly out of medicine and she needs something."

Jak ran a hand through her hair in fear and exasperation.

"We've made it to Kosvo, Jak," Allie reminded. "The best doctors in the kingdom will be here."

"How do we find them and how do we afford them?" Jak asked the hard questions.

"Go to the King," Ínrío shrugged. "Kings always have the best healers."

"The King wouldn't see or talk to me, let alone help me," Jak pointed out.

"You're one of his citizens."

"So? That doesn't mean anything. I'm just one of hundreds, possibly thousands, of poor people clamouring for help. I wouldn't even be granted an audience."

"You would be if you were a knight..." Allie suggested in a small voice.

"Give it up, Allie," Jak shook her head. "I need real solutions right now, not crazy dreams."

"What's this?" Ínrío asked.

"I..." Jak sighed and stared off through the trees. "When we were travelling with Jim, he asked what I wanted to be if I could be anything. I said I wanted to be a knight — but I can't be. I'm just a blacksmith, at best. Human society doesn't work like that."

"Human society is flawed," Ínrío replied.

Jak had a strong urge to comment on D'Ihne society and the host of their problems she had heard about, but knew it wasn't the best time and held her tongue. Fighting them on Ha'Cās slavery was a battle for another day. Today's fight was about helping Dora. Crŷs sighed through his nose and gave her a serious look. He was still in a bad mood, and Jak didn't blame him.

"If you can get to the King, I can help you," he offered. Everyone turned to him. His eyes stayed stormy. "We can't find you a doctor, but if you can get to the King, I can make it so that he is drawn to your words. Whatever you ask for, he will be compelled to give you. You want a healer? He'll give you the best in the Kingdom. You want to be a knight? He'll swear you in on the spot."

"And what will that cost me?"

"Call it a gift."

"I can get you to the King," Ínrío added. "I spent two weeks in the city searching for clues. I didn't find anything to help us, but I know the King is hosting a ball tonight, and I have an invite to it. We're heading back to the Golden City, so you should attend for me."

"I can't attend a ball..." Jak muttered.

"You have to," Allie told her. "For Dora. I can't go. I'm too young to be unattended, but you could pass. You're the only one of us who could."

"You're gods," Jak protested to them. "Can't you just go down there and announce yourselves and get them to give us a healer?"

"No," Olíriá shook her head. "Not a chance. We are not permitted to interfere so directly, and we would be forced to answer to our Queen. However, we can help you help yourself. Take the invite and the spell and we will make sure you are ready for the ball before we leave."

"There's no other way?" Jak asked desperately. "I've never even seen a real Lord before! I can't talk or walk or dress like them. I can't even dance like a noble!"

"Then we have our work cut out for us," Olíriá smiled. "Take the offer, Jak."

"You're being awfully free with gifts..."

"Perhaps you'll find a way to pay us back one day," Crŷs shrugged. Olíriá elbowed him sharply. She smiled at Jak.

"Just think of us as your faerie godparents," she grinned.

"What does that mean?" Jak asked nervously.

"It means I'm probably going to collect on that dance…" Ínrío chuckled.

CHAPTER FIFTEEN

Gods were wily, Jak had to give them that. Somehow she felt like she'd been tricked, she just wasn't sure how. Allie spent the day half tending to Dora, and half laughing at the gods' attempts to make Jak a lady. Jak felt like an idiot. Crŷs was teaching her how to talk. The spell he cast over her that would sway the King involved him whispering onto her lips. She thought she could handle that, until Allie caught her eye and winked. Jak nearly choked. Crŷs, at least, seemed to understand how she felt. He never pushed her, and he never laughed. She wondered if he was still angry from before. It wasn't something she knew how to ask about.

Ínrío was going to get his dance, and Jak couldn't help but wonder if he had somehow known that when he had produced the sword. Learning to dance was what Jak was most worried about. She could take a turn at a small town festival. She had, and it had been fun, but learning to dance for a royal ball was an altogether different skill. And she would be alone this time. It scared her. She had never been a lady. She had never aspired towards being a lady. She had no idea how to blend in at a party at the King's Castle, and she wasn't sure she wanted to learn, except that she had to in order to save her little sister.

"Dancing is like fighting, Jak," Ínrío told her grandly. "Crŷs tells me you fought off the D'rö-Hadās, which means you can use the blade I gave you. If you can wield a sword, you can dance a waltz."

"I don't think that's true at all…" Jak replied.

"Let me show you." He motioned her towards him and set their hands. His grip was warm and dry, which only made her more aware that she was nervous to the point of mildly sweaty — which made her more nervous. "Dancing is all about fluidity of movement. If you can hold your own against the D'Hiris, you already have more skill than any other human. Think of your partner as your opponent — you need to anticipate how they move, and move with them. It's an art, like any other."

"Does this make any sense to you?" Jak asked the others as they watched. Olíriá smiled as she played her pipes. It was the clearest, sweetest sound Jak had ever heard, and she wanted to fall in love to it. Unfortunately, she was stuck with these undesirable clowns, so love was well off the cards.

"It actually does," Crŷs smirked. "My brother is known to have a spot of wisdom… from time to time."

"Step back and turn," Ínrío instructed. Jak did as she was told, trying to keep to the rhythm of Olíriá's tune. She wanted to argue that dancing and fencing were completely different skills, but even though she was sure she was right, it helped to think of Krill. In fact, she couldn't get him out of her mind. He had the same golden eyes as Ínrío, although the god's were gentler and less serious. She remembered those sharp eyes, and his sharper tongue, as he had corrected her footwork. It was almost like hearing his voice as she stepped and twirled in Ínrío's guiding hands.

"I feel like a right fool," she commented grudgingly.

"You look like a natural," Crŷs replied from where he lounged like a black cat. "It's been a very long time since I saw anyone pick anything up this quickly."

"Krill said I was a fast learner…" Jak admitted before she could stop herself. A noticeable chill settled over the crowd at the campfire. The blaze still crackled and popped, and the pan flute didn't falter, but Olíriá glanced sharply at Crŷs. He watched Jak with curious and shrewd eyes from under dark brows.

"And how is the old D'Hiris?" he asked smoothly. "He is the one they call Krill, yes?"

"Elkrillendé," Olíriá nodded, lowering her pipes.

"How do you know that?" Crŷs asked curiously. "I can never remember all their names."

"I knew him," Olíriá answered. There was a confidence to her voice that answered Crŷs' challenge. If he had been trying to trick her into saying something, she had just stated very clearly that he wasn't about to get one over on her. She tossed her pale hair back and looked to Jak. "So, we know that you can talk the talk and walk the walk."

"I wouldn't say that," Jak disagreed.

"You're passable, Jak," Olíriá insisted. "I was never particularly worried about you in those regards. My biggest concern has always been how will you look?"

"With my eyes…?" Jak's answer was nervously earnest.

Crŷs snorted with laughter. "We definitely need more time with your conversational skills."

"Leave her alone, Crŷs," Olíriá sighed. "Jak, appearances are everything to these people. We are going to need to dress you up like a princess."

"That's impossible," Jak chuckled. "I don't even own a dress, and I can't afford the kind that we'd need. With that kind of money I could afford a doctor and save us all the hassle."

"Do you have an old shirt?"

"Uh… yes…"

"Good. Go change into it. We'll wait."

Jak was running out of will to argue. She stalked off towards the tent.

"Jak!" Olíriá called after her. "Just the shirt! Leave the boots and trousers behind!"

"Oh come on!" Jak protested. Trying to make her a lady just wasn't worth it. Except that when she entered the tent she saw Dora lying pale and weak on her bunk, and it was completely worth it. Her little sister was barely conscious, and when she was awake enough to talk it was all mumbles about finding Mum. But Mum was nowhere to be found, which meant that it was all up to Jak. She had to help her little sister.

With her resolve restored, she changed into one of her old, torn, and bloodstained shirts and scampered from the tent back to the fireplace where it was warm. She held her shirt down awkwardly around her butt, feeling horribly exposed. Olíriá stood to join her by the flames.

"So you're going to magic me into a dress?" Jak

asked, assuming the fae would solve this problem like all the others.

"Yes," the goddess replied. "Hold still." Olíriá raised a hand lightly and whistled into the trees. A bird responded to her call and swooped down to alight on her finger. Olíriá whistled to it again and the bird whistled back delightedly. It shook its little blue-grey body happily. Olíriá reached up and closed her other fist around the small bird tightly. It didn't even have time to realise what was happening to it. Olíriá squeezed, and before it could scream the bird squished in her hand. It glowed brightly as she crushed it into light and glitter. With a gentle wave, she let it go and blew the sparkles over Jak.

Jak was still biting down a scream from watching the bird explode. The poor little thing had been turned to dust as its life was exchanged for magic — D'Ihne magic. She flinched as the magical glitter rushed towards her and rained down on her. Her eyes squeezed shut. But she could feel the changes over her skin. Jak hadn't worn a dress since she was a little girl, and it was a strange sensation.

When she finally opened her eyes, she couldn't suppress a start at the sight of herself. The gown was made from layered silk and it was more beautiful than she had imagined. She didn't have the knowledge or the imagination to picture something like this without seeing it. It was fancier than anything she had seen the ladies who occasionally strayed by Rutsborough in. It wasn't her at all. Ínrío gave a sharp whistle.

"Very nice," he complimented.

"Purple?" Crŷs raised an eyebrow.

"I didn't pick the colour," Olíriá shrugged. "She did."

"I didn't pick the colour!" Jak protested. "I didn't pick anything! I look ridiculous!"

"You look lovely," Ínrío told her.

"It is very flattering," Crŷs agreed. "We just do something with your hair and you'll pass for a lady of high station. What were you thinking about to get the colour?"

"I don't know!"

"It's the same colour as Dora's dress," Allie said quietly. Everyone looked at her and she gave them a small smile. "You look very pretty, Sis. I know you don't want to, but thank you for doing this for her."

"I feel like it should be you," Jak muttered. Allie's revelation had calmed her somewhat. Every time something happened to remake her for high society she panicked, so it was good to have the constant reminder why.

"That's alright," Allie gave her a cute smile. "Once you're a knight I'll get to be a lady every day and have lots of nice dresses. Perhaps we can sneak me into a ball next year. I'll definitely be of a marriageable age then."

"Not even close," Jak shook her head. "Not for at least another ten years."

"You're such a prude!" Allie laughed. "But at least you look good. Never thought that would happen. It must be magic."

Jak stuck her tongue out. Allie replied in kind.

"Okay, none of that," Olíriá ordered them. "Real

ladies don't poke their tongues out."

"I don't know how to pass for a real lady!" Jak protested. "This is a nightmare! I don't even have anywhere to put my sword!"

"Well then, if this is such an inconvenience shall we just call it a day and you can give up?" the goddess asked sharply. Jak shut up quickly and blushed in shame. She wanted to complain, but they were doing her a huge favour and spending magic they didn't have to.

"I can sort out the sword..." Ínrío mused.

"Ladies don't carry swords," Crŷs pointed out. "In fact, no one at a King's ball should carry a weapon except the guards. They'll take it off you before you're allowed in his presence."

"Really?" Jak asked curiously.

"Of course," Crŷs replied. "You can't draw weapons in the presence of royalty — well, you can, but they might execute you for it. It's to stop assassination attempts." He paused and gave her a look. "We might need to teach you some of the rules of noble etiquette before we send you out tonight."

"You teach her the rules and I'll fix the sword so she can take it," Ínrío touched his brother's shoulder.

"She can't use the sword — just don't give her one!"

"It will make her feel better, and you never know when the girl might need a sword."

"At this point I feel like you're just trying to show off your sword," Crŷs accused.

"Would I do that?" Ínrío grinned. Crŷs glared at him. Jak watched their banter. This was going to be the longest twenty-four hours of her life.

***

The afternoon was turning to dusk when Jak was finally ready. She was desperately trying to keep all the rules and lessons in her head. It was too much. She was just going to have to try and make the best of it. Crŷs was clearly itching to be on the move. He was ready to leave the mortal world behind and get back to whatever their desperate recovery mission was. Ínrío was less edgy, and offered to be the one to take Jak to the ball.

"Someone has to take her," Ínrío insisted. "It's the way things are done. She can't very well walk there across the city on foot."

"Knock yourself out," Crŷs shrugged. "But I'm not waiting for you. As soon as Olí is done tending to the little one again, we're off."

"Then I'll meet you at home once I have seen our lady safely to her ball."

"Don't try anything, Ínrío."

"I don't know what you mean," he defended.

"Dark curls, purple dress," Crŷs glared at him. "We all know who she reminds you of. Don't get fresh."

"I'm a gentleman. I would never," Ínrío defended calmly. He grinned and kissed Crŷs' forehead as he passed him. "You're getting terribly angsty in your old age, little brother."

"I just felt it needed to be said," Crŷs grumbled.

Ínrío patted his cheek affectionately and nodded to Jak. She was loitering by the tent entrance with Allie, while Olíriá had one last attempt at healing Dora.

"You got this," Allie told Jak, taking her hand and squeezing it. Jak squeezed Allie's hand back and patted herself down. Olíriá had braided Jak's hair and put her in a dress and slippers. Ínrío's sword had been shrunk down into a hairpin and now pinned her braids in place. He had assured her that once she drew the weapon it would return to normal size, should she need it. She felt like some kind of stupid doll, but she was as ready as she'd ever be. Ínrío had affixed a carriage to Peanut and transformed himself back into his ostentatiously grand human form. They were ready to go.

After the briefest of farewells, Jak bundled herself into the carriage and Ínrío drove them off. Jak had never been in a carriage before. It reminded her of the wagon, only nicer. There was no clutter. Windows on either side gave her a view. But the bump and the rattle were the same. A painful homesickness welled in her chest, and it hurt to realise she still wasn't over it. She wished she could ride up front with Ínrío so that she had someone to talk to, but that was more of the same, and she wanted to laugh at her own nostalgia.

Instead, she kept herself distracted by looking out the window as the city rolled by. The gates to Kosvo were the largest she'd ever seen, and they sat in a mountainous stone wall thirty feet high and ten feet deep. She tried to not to stare as they drove through. It was incredible. Every single street was paved. The wheels rattled and Peanut's hooves clopped along the cobbled ground. She remembered Jim telling her that Kosvo had everything from beggars to kings, but from where Jak was looking everyone seemed quite fine. They were certainly all better dressed than Rutsborough, and there was a consistency to it. Although, she had to concede that the further they went the fancier people appeared.

It took them forever to reach the castle. The sky had turned a dark indigo by the time they arrived. Jak kept looking around to see if they we trying to drive to the next city, but it was just that Kosvo was seemingly infinite. They passed through another set of heavy gates and finally Ínrío parked up. It was the grandest building Jak had ever seen. Grander than the church with the windows of the gods. She had seen the castle sitting on the hill from a distance, but seeing it up close was something altogether different.

The turrets rose to the sky, and the building looked like it was the size of a small village. Jak was pretty sure she could have fitted her hometown inside. Carriages of fancy dressed nobles were pulling up outside the doors and rows of servants were greeting them. Ínrío held the carriage door open while Jak climbed out as gracefully as she could. She stared at the marvellous building and glittering attendees. She wished Allie was here.

"Are you sure you can't come with me?" she asked Ínrío nervously as he helped her out.

"Alas," he sighed tragically. "I would love to accompany you, my Lady, but Crŷs will be spitting and I really should get back. You'll be fine though; just remember, stay on your toes and treat your partner like your opponent."

"I suppose your mission is more important..." Jak

muttered. She gave Ínrío a sidelong glance. For all that he played sly, he wasn't as clever as his siblings. There was a slight vacant purity to his eyes that reminded her of Kode. They were related, after all. It was worth a shot. "But why is Crŷs so worked up about it?"

"Our mission is a farce." Ínrío pulled a face and leant in. "Between you and me, someone is playing silly buggers with the D'Ihne. We're not supposed to tell anyone, but mother's crown has been stolen. That crown is the centre of D'Ihne power over the fae. Everyone assumed Crŷs did it because it's exactly the sort of stunt he would have pulled as a prank, but he swears he didn't and now he's trying to clear his name — except no one can find it to prove it wasn't him. The whole thing is a mess."

Jak was frozen. The crown of the Queen of the Fae was missing?!

"Anyway, good luck," Ínrío touched her shoulder reassuringly. "Hopefully we will see each other again soon."

Before she had time to collect her thoughts and respond, he had climbed up onto the front of the carriage and ridden away. She thought about calling out to him, but he was nearly back out the gate. It had been a year... that's what they all kept saying. Queen Clōudiá's crown had been missing for a year and everyone had dropped everything to look for it. Jak had a niggling suspicion at the back of her mind, but first things first — she had to survive the ball and talk to the King.

With trembling hands, she clutched her skirts and

the paper invitation Ínrío had given her earlier and headed for the door. The light and noise on the other side were almost enough to knock her back. One of the servants at the door took her invite and motioned her in. They referred to her as Your Ladyship. The entrance hall was grandly decorated and lit. Ornate lamps lined the walls and rich tapestries hung between them. People were talking and laughing as they moved through the entrance hall into the main ballroom. Jak joined the crowd, but she froze as she stepped through the doorway.

She had never seen anything so grand in her life. The ballroom was gigantic. A massive chandelier hung from the ceiling, illuminating the room. Crowds of people gathered in the wings, talking and drinking. The centre of the room was full of people dancing and they twirled between each other like jewelled humming birds. A band played near a balcony door and filled the air with gentle song. Jak just stared. She knew she shouldn't. She knew it made her stand out as someone who didn't belong. She just couldn't help it.

A sharp peal of laughter broke her from her reverie. People had clearly separated into factions, and small groups were clustered around the edges of the dance floor. The laughter had come from what was by far the largest group, situated on the far side of the hall. It was ten times bigger than any of the others, and everyone in it seemed to be having an exceptionally good time. Other groups were shooting them dark looks. Jak had a strong urge to avoid the crowd, which meant it was probably exactly where she needed to go.

"My Lady," someone addressed her at her shoulder. Jak turned and came face to face with a tall young man about her own age.

"My Lord," she responded, desperately trying to keep the stammer from her voice as she curtsied to the best of her ability.

"I haven't seen you around here before, wherever do you hail from?" he inquired.

She couldn't tell the truth, but she wasn't a very good liar either.

"Far from here, Sir," she murmured nervously. "Near Dazigh."

"Oh heavens, you're not a refugee from there, are you? I heard the peasants are killing everyone in Dazigh. It sounds awful."

Another wave of raucous laughter drew their attention to the large group on the other side of the room.

"Is that the King over there?" Jak changed the subject. "I really need to speak with him."

"No, that isn't the King," the young man replied. "That is someone as out of place as you. At best, they're the entertainment for tonight; and at worst, they're a charlatan; but these people won't mind being cheated as long as there's a juicy scandal in it for them."

Jak turned back to the young man in surprise. He had a sardonic expression on his face as he watched the crowds. He noted her surprise at his tone with a smile.

"I'm Tomas Brakmare," he introduced himself, noting Jak's lack of reaction with an even wider smile. "And the fact that you don't know what that means tells me more than anything that you're not really supposed to be here."

Jak's heart was pounding in her throat. She'd barely made it through the door and she'd been busted. Social etiquette was not her strength, and she didn't know what to do. Her mind had emptied in a blind panic. All her training was suddenly forgotten.

"Well, what were you planning on doing about it?" she demanded quietly.

"I was planning on asking you for a dance so that you didn't risk outing yourself to anyone else by talking to them," he replied smoothly, and offered her his hand. Jak didn't know what to say. Half of her just wanted to bolt for it, but half of her was intrigued by the dry rich boy asking her for a dance. She took his hand. He led her out to the floor.

"And what might I call you, my Lady?"

"Jak," she answered. He looked like he expected more so she elaborated. "Just Jak."

He chuckled. "If you were planning to infiltrate the King's ball, you maybe should have come up with a better cover name."

Jak stepped lightly to keep up with him as he twirled her around the hall. It was harder than it had been with Ínrío. She couldn't sense Tomas the same way — probably because he was human. Still, he kept a firm hand on her waist and guided her gently. She just had to be aware of the subtle ways he led so that she could follow. Anticipate your opponent.

"So, Jak, what is your business with His Majesty?" Tomas asked as they danced.

"I just have to speak to him about something," she blew off the question. "If I can get to him, he'll hear me out."

"What you have to say is that important?"

"It is," she nodded. They both turned towards the sound of more laughter. The large crowd seemed to be home to a source of great entertainment. Tomas had looked briefly serious at her claim.

"The King should be here within the hour," he told her. "He enjoys being fashionably late to his own parties. There should be a fanfare, but I can point him out to you if you need."

"You know the King?" Jak knew she shouldn't sound as incredulous as she did, but she couldn't help it.

"Of course," he smiled. "I'm a Brakmare."

Jak gave him a dry look in response. He knew she didn't know what that meant. He laughed gently in reply and leant in.

"The man in the green tunic," he whispered in her ear, and then twirled her out towards where he had been looking. Jak spun and her skirt flared in a circle. She caught a glimpse of a tall man with grey hair dressed in green. He stood in one of the smaller groups, glaring daggers at the larger crowd. Jak spun back in and caught Tomas' hand. He leant in again to speak quietly in her ear.

"That's my father, the Lord Brakmare. He's the King's cousin. Everyone in Kosvo knows our family. Tonight, he's terribly put out that half his audience is off cavorting with a man with a bad stage name."

"You sound rather pleased…" Jak commented.

"My father is a vain and petty man," Tomas smirked. "It's nice to have him put back in his place sometimes."

"By a man with a bad stage name?" Jak smiled.

Tomas laughed quietly. "He's calling himself 'Appetite', and apparently he's insatiable. The ladies are losing their minds, and I'm losing control of my gag reflex just watching the nightmare unfold. These people are all so horrifically trite, and it's made so much worse by the fact that they think they're special."

To her surprise, Jak found that she was starting to like her dance partner. He had a kind of dry charm she found endearing. His tempered dislike of the nobility mirrored her own, and the fact that he hadn't outed her when he had realised instantly that she wasn't one of them was a kindness she appreciated. His grip on her tightened warningly and he leant in again.

"He's coming over here," Tomas whispered. "Watch yourself."

"You're worried I'm going to go bananas for a charlatan?" Jak smiled.

The band finished their song and the dancers stopped to applaud. Jak stood side-by-side with her new friend and clapped politely. She felt someone approach behind them as the band struck up a new song. A voice with a familiar lilting accent purred behind her.

"Jellybean, you dressed to match me…"

Jak felt her stomach drop a mile and the colour drain from her face. She turned with Tomas to come face-to-face with an old friend in a purple suit. The large crowd had dispersed once their entertainment had walked off. 'Appetite' was leering over her now.

"You!" she hissed venomously.

"Me indeed." Jim grinned at them. He went full dimples and his smile was brighter than the chandelier. "You look ravishing, Jellybean."

"You know him?" Tomas asked her curiously. Jak's eyes flashed dangerously as she stared Jim down like an angry tiger. Tomas read the look. "Ah." He summed the situation up carefully.

"Don't worry," Jim winked at him, "she never stays angry for long. If I may steal this dance? I'll have her back to you in a moment."

He didn't wait for a reply. He gave the young man a sultry look, took Jak's hand, and twirled her away. She was too angry to talk. Her hands kept wanting to ball into fists. Instead, she settled for digging her fingers into his arm hard enough to bruise. He didn't seem to care. He caught her around the waist and held her close. Across the room, a man on the piano crooned a soft tune to the accompaniment of violins.

"Isn't this romantic?" Jim whispered.

"I hate you," Jak growled.

"Uh-huh," he didn't sound convinced. His eyes were still on Tomas as they stepped slowly. "He's very cute — I didn't think you went in for that type."

"What are you doing here?"

"Look around, Jellybean. I belong here. What are you doing here? Aside from getting familiar with the younger Lord Brakmare... he has a sister, if you're interested."

"I'm not looking for love, Jim. I'm looking for help!"

"And here I am," he smiled winningly at her.

"You're not help," she told him disgustedly. He met her eye and his smile faltered. That made it worse. It was easier to be angry when he was being a cheap flirt. His serious eyes made her chest hurt. Jak wasn't going to break down here. She'd done her crying yesterday, but her voice caught a little as she laid her accusation in a sharp whisper. "You. Left. Us."

Jim leant her into a dip. She clutched at him tightly as he bent her backwards, but he held her close and wasn't going to let her fall.

"Yet here you are…" he whispered in return. They straightened up and Jak realised how intensely she was clinging to him.

"Give me one good reason not to strangle you here right in front of everyone," she hissed. He didn't reply. They turned around the dancefloor listening to the music. "Jim?"

"I can't," he said. "Sorry, I was thinking, and I can't think of a single good reason for you not to. It sounds hugely arousing. I'd be very into that."

Jak couldn't hide her disgust. Her nose wrinkled as she pulled a face. That. That was the best reason ever not to take her anger out on him violently.

"You're a pig."

"Na," he grinned. "But if you say the right things in your prayers I'll turn into one."

She rolled her eyes and surrendered. It wasn't worth trying to insult him. She could never win. Words rolled off him like water off a duck's back, and insults were turned into innuendos. He twirled her back to Tomas, who had moved carefully to the side of the dancefloor.

"There we are, my gorgeous young Lord, returned as promised. Be careful of this one — you give her a moment to move on to someone else and she will," Jim warned him suggestively.

"Shut up, James," Jak did her best Krill impression. She was quite proud of it. Apparently, so was Jim. He kissed her cheek.

"You two are so cute. I'm very into it. Don't go anywhere. I'll be back in a couple of minutes."

"Where are you going?" Tomas asked him.

"Unfortunately, you two aren't the reason I attended tonight, and I have business that needs dealing to. However," he eyeballed them both up and down very deliberately. "I can see you being the reason I stick around afterwards. So, take good care of each other until I get back. I will be as fast as possible. Save me a dance — both of you." With one last winning smile and seductive wink, Jim and his dimples vanished off into the crowd.

"I want to tie him up in a sack and throw him in a lake..." Jak sighed.

"I'm sorry I didn't come to your rescue," Tomas apologised. "You didn't look like you were having fun out there."

"I want to drown him."

"Is he really that bad? He's not... I mean... he's a little... colourful, sure... but that's not really a bad thing. He's sort of... charming, in his own way."

"No..." Jak groaned. "Not you too!"

"What do you mean?"

"He got you too! Everyone likes him! I used to like him. It's not fair. He's a monster."

"He's just a bit of a flirt," Tomas smiled.

"No, my Lord, I think you're just a bit of a flirt, he's… *insatiable*," Jak leant on the word darkly. She was also giving Tomas a serious look. There was in his smile the smitten twinkle of someone for whom it was already tragically too late.

"Oh dear…" he replied consolably, although his smile didn't waver. "I take it he's the kind whom, if you give them an inch, will take a mile?"

"No, if you give him an inch he will show up stark naked in your bedroom tonight with a rose between his teeth — if he doesn't get the best of you behind the stables first."

Tomas laughed. Jak gave him a long look.

"I'm not joking," she told him. He stopped laughing. Jak watched the crowd. She had tried to follow his path with her eyes, but he had disappeared over the other side of the room.

"What is he doing here and what is he up to?" she muttered to herself.

"You don't trust him, do you?" Tomas commented.

"No sane person would," Jak replied. "He's trouble. I think he might even be more trouble than I first realised. One of his boyfriends used to warn me away from him… He gets handsy when he shouldn't and he can't stop doing things he's not supposed to."

"You want to follow him, don't you?"

"I think I should. He can't be up to anything good."

"I can't let you go alone," Tomas insisted. "But I have no idea where he went."

"Don't worry," Jak assured. "I can find him." She was sure she was right too. She took Tomas' hand and led him around the edges of the ballroom. Jim was nowhere to be seen, but Jak had an ace up her sleeve. It had occurred to her that dancing with Jim had been easier than Tomas, and not just because she'd done it before. She had been speculating on theories about her shady friend almost since she'd met him. Now, she was about to put them to the test. She closed her eyes and sought him.

"That way," her eyes flashed open and she indicated down a side passage flanked by two guards. "He went that way." She grinned a grin worthy of her opponent. Now she had him, and now she knew: fae blood.

"He can't have," Tomas shook his head. "The passage is guarded. No one is allowed down there."

"Well, Jim just got down there, so we have to too."

"How can you possibly know that?"

"I can sense him," she answered honestly. "I can practically smell he went that way. Probably the same way he snuck down there. He's not all human."

"What?!" Tomas hissed.

"Jim is half faerie," Jak told him. "That's probably why he's so much trouble."

"Let's get past those guards," Tomas declared and led her over to them. The guards both nodded at Tomas as he approached. He nodded back at them. "Gentlemen, this lady has an important message for the King. It cannot wait."

"I'm sorry, Master Brakmare," one of the guards apologised. "No one is allowed through."

"Sergeant, this is a matter of life and death. This woman is from Dazigh and she has information the King needs to know."

The guards shared a worried look. "If there is something the Captain should be told..."

"This is for the King's ears only," Jak insisted resolutely.

"You have to believe us, men. I'll put in a good word for you once this is over," Tomas promised.

They shared one last worried look and then waved them through. Jak still held Tomas' hand as he led her through dim torchlit stone corridors. She waited until they were out of earshot to harass him.

"You could have done that the whole time?" she hissed.

"I had to be sure about you though," he shrugged in reply. "I think I've finally worked out why you're here."

"I'm here because I need to save my sister," Jak confessed.

"Not because you need to warn the King about a plot against his life?" Tomas queried.

"What?" Jak started in bewilderment.

"A-ha!" he exclaimed, misreading her confusion. "I knew it. You said you needed to see the King and you've been nervous all night."

"That is not what this is about —"

"You don't have to worry, Jak," he consoled her. "I'm on your side. I can help you. He's family — I don't want anything to happen to him either. This is all because of what's happening in Dazigh, isn't it?"

Jak groaned. "Just take me to the King, Tomas."

"I thought we were chasing your friend James?"

"I can get Jim later. If you can get me straight to the King, my business with him is more important."

Tomas nodded and led her through the corridors. He had the excited gleam in his eye of someone who believed they had just uncovered a great conspiracy. He was going to be so disappointed when Jak just asked for a doctor. Once Dora was healed, she would have time to tell him the whole story and maybe he'd forgive her. Right now, it was too outrageous to tell and hope that he'd believe it. He led her to a large wooden door flanked by two more guards.

"Master Brakmare," they both bowed to him.

"Gentlemen," Tomas nodded in return. "This good lady needs to see the King at once. She has the most urgent news for him and he must hear it immediately."

"He is alone, my Lord, but he asked not to be disturbed," one of the guards replied.

"It can't wait," Tomas insisted.

The guard reluctantly turned to knock on the door.

"Your Majesty?" he called out as he knocked. There was no reply. He reached for the handle. The door was yanked open before they could get there. The guard lurched slightly and straightened, nearly colliding with the man in the doorway. Jim grinned at all of them.

"Oh, there's quite a crowd," he commented, and gave Jak and Tomas a sly look. "You little stalkers... Here, hold this." He passed the item he was holding to Jak, slipped between them all, and took off up the hallway. The whole thing was over in seconds, and everyone was too surprised to move. Until they took stock of the scene.

Jak was holding a bloody sword. Inside the room, the body of a man in regal attire lay in a pool of blood on the floor. A head that looked like it belonged to the same man lay a good two meters from the body. Jak shrieked and tossed the sword back inside like it was a live snake. Everyone took in the horror.

"STOP THAT MAN!" one of the guards yelled and raced off, drawing his sword. Jim was already turning a corner.

Tomas began to scream for more guards. The other guard pulled the door shut.

"Master Tomas," the other guard began. "We have to secure this room and get you and your lady somewhere safe."

"Oh fuck that," Jak cursed. She stepped away from them and drew the pin from her hair. Her curls fell around her shoulders and the pin grew back into the shining blade given to her by the sun god. "He's mine. JIM!" she roared and gave chase.

Tomas and the guard watched her go with stunned expressions.

"I don't think you're going to have to worry about this…" Tomas muttered. "I think she's going to kill that man."

"It looked a bit like it," the guard agreed, pale and shaking. "Master Tomas, you sound like you're in shock."

"Oh, I rightly am," the young man agreed,

swallowing nervously. The faint sound of pounding footsteps still echoed away from them.

Jak raced down the halls. She had her skirts bunched in one hand with her scabbard so she wouldn't trip on them, and her sword in the other. She had no idea where in the castle she was going, but she knew who she was chasing and she could sense him up ahead of her. A flicker of purple turned the corner down the hall.

"Jim!" she bellowed after him. She raced up the stairs in pursuit. Her feet protested the delicate slippers. But her long legs took the stairs two at a time. The staircase wound in a circle up one of the towers.

"You there!" a group of guards called from the bottom. "Stop!"

Jak ignored them. She didn't have time to explain what had happened to people who hadn't been there. Jim just kept going up. Jak kept after him. She was pretty sure her legs were going to hate her tomorrow, but she had to catch him. She broke out to the top room. It looked like a library or a study. She stared around. A door on the far side of the room banged gently in the cold night breeze. It led out onto the top of the wall. Jak looked out the door. She could see the man in purple racing between the parapets to the next tower.

The pounding of armoured feet sounded behind her. She took off across the wall. It was high enough that she didn't want to look down. She didn't realise people built things this high. It rivalled the treetops back in the wild forests of home. But she kept her eyes on the prize. She saw him yank open the door to the next tower and disappear inside. It didn't matter. She didn't need line of sight on him.

She was more than halfway across when something thrown from behind tangled her feet. Jak cried out and staggered. She tripped, but caught herself on the parapet.

"Get her!" a guard yelled as the group of them chased after her.

"Not me, you idiots!" she roared at them. They weren't listening. A group of half a dozen guards were rushing her, swords drawn. Jak cut the bolas from her ankles and raised her blade. The moonlight shone off it dangerously. They didn't stop. She didn't hesitate. The first one reached her. She swung her sword up and caught the blow. She struck back so hard it ripped the guard's sword from their hands. The blade sailed over the edge of the wall. She knocked another blow from the guard behind that one. With a grimace, she kicked the first guard full in the stomach. The slipper was not designed for kicking steel and she knew it. It hurt like a bitch. Still, it was better than getting stabbed. She got them with the flat of her foot and set them crashing back into the others. They sounded like the contents of a kitchen cupboard being thrown down the stairs.

"He's getting away!" she yelled at them, now that there was a chance they might be listening. Then she took off for the tower. He was still in there. She could feel it. She rushed inside and stopped. Her sword was held low at the ready. There he was. Jim was standing by the open window with a rope in his hands. The room here was an expensive bedroom with a large fourposter bed. Jak wasn't going to let the furniture get in her way.

She leapt across the bed, dropping her skirts and scabbard so that she could hold the blade to his neck with both hands.

"I've got you now," she hissed. "You're not going anywhere. You're stuck in here with me until those guards arrive."

Jim leant in towards her. Jak balked as she watched the blade press hard against his neck. He clicked his fingers. The door she had just run through slammed shut. A bolt fell into place across it, barricading it. The sound of men in steel hitting the door hard came through the wood. There was pounding and yelling as they tried to break through.

"Actually, Jellybean," Jim purred. "You're stuck in here with me..."

CHAPTER SIXTEEN

Jak stood with her sword to Jim's neck. He didn't look threatened. In fact, he was leaning into it, while Jak was starting to feel more like running away than cutting off heads. Except he'd blocked the doors.

"You don't want to do this, Jak," he told her. "Put down the sword and come with me."

The pounding against the door grew louder as the guards tried to break it down.

"You just killed the King!" Jak protested. "I have to stop you! You're a monster! You ruined my life!"

"For the better," Jim smiled at her.

"You can't ruin someone's life for the better!"

"I just did," he shrugged, causing her blade to shift against his skin. She couldn't take her eyes from it. Any second he was going to cut himself. He looked down at the blade too, and his smile deepened. "Is this Ínrío's handiwork? My goodness, Jak. What have you been up to? I only left you alone for a few days."

"We needed help," Jak said it like an accusation. "The D'rö-Hadās tried to kill us! I had to fight them!"

"The D'rö-Hadās?" His smile fell. "They shouldn't have. They were supposed to follow us."

"Well, they didn't," Jak snapped. "They came after us. We had to get Äulé and the gods to save us."

"And they did?" he sounded surprised. The guards were still trying to bang down the door. Jim grimaced at the sword. He stepped closer and Jak flinched, drawing the blade back so that she wouldn't cut him. She still kept it raised against his chest, for all that he seemed to notice. "Elrïlani must be better than I thought. Tell me everything."

"We don't have that kind of time."

"Then we'll just have to make it." He held out the hand not holding the rope. "Come with me."

Jak shook her head and pressed the sword against him. He finally seemed to realise it was still there.

"Jak," he began patiently. "You can't stay here. They will assume you're with me. They've already assumed that. They will throw you in prison. They will execute you. I can't let that happen. Stay your sword, and come with me."

"You killed their king…" She shook her head.

"Yes, I did. It was the right thing to do, and I'd do it again. He was not a good man."

"You killed the king in Dazigh too, didn't you?"

"Of course. The system is broken, Jak. It has to change. I'm forcing it to. That's what I do. I'm part of a small group of people who have seen the full extent of the inequality in the worlds of the living. I have seen the damage and the needless death it causes. I will show the world how to change, and I will bring that change by my own hand where I must."

Behind her, Jak could hear the door start to splinter as the guards hacked through it. Jim was still watching her seriously.

"Come with me, Jak. I can't just leave you."

"You did it before," she accused.

"Yeah, where it was safe — or so I thought," he defended. "Look at where we are. I knew I was coming here. I knew how dangerous it would be. I'm part of a rebellion. I didn't want you girls to end up in danger because of it. Jak, little Jellybean, I never would have just left you. You know me, I wouldn't do that. I couldn't lead three little girls into this kind of danger, and I couldn't tell you about the plot to murder someone — even if they were a bad man. You have to believe me. I thought I was taking care of you. I'm sorry, I never imagined that leaving you behind would have put you in just as much danger."

Jak could feel a slight tickle against one cheek, and she had a horrible feeling it was a traitorous single tear. The guards had half broken through the door. They were yelling at them. Jim emphasised the hand he was holding out to her.

"Come on, Jellybean. I can't leave you to this fate."

Jak took a deep breath. She looked behind her. The furious guards were halfway through the door. She looked back. Jim's warm brown eyes were almost earnest. As earnest as she believed he could be. They seemed to reflect the purple of her dress. He'd just said everything she'd wanted him to say, but... but maybe it really was true too. Maybe he did care. Either way, he was the best hope for her and Dora now that the spell to persuade the King was as good as gone. She sighed.

"Gods forgive me," she muttered and sheathed her sword again. Jim grinned. With the blade safely stowed, she threw her arms around his neck. He scooped his arm around her waist. His other hand still held the rope as they stood on the window ledge. The drop from the tower was a terrifyingly long way down.

"You're insane and we're going to die," she accused, staring down to the ground.

"Maybe," he agreed like that was half the fun.

He jumped and took her with him. The door smashed open. Jak buried her face in his shoulder and resisted the urge to scream. They swung through the air. It felt like falling. Above them, the guards burst into the room and rushed to the window. It occurred to Jak that the guards could cut the rope and kill them both. As the panic of that realisation gripped her, there was a bright flash through her eyelids. She remembered that flash. Her feet hit the ground and she crumpled.

She knew that the ground beneath the tower had been much further away, and quite rocky. So, when she fell safely and comfortably on a combination of Jim and grass, she knew magic had been involved. Again. She opened her eyes and looked up with a gasp. After the events of the evening she needed the oxygen.

They were outside the city, near the road in one of the valleys leading to Kosvo. She could see the wall. The castle still glittered like stars on the hill in the distance. She was lying half on top of Jim where they had fallen in a soft ditch. He grinned up at her.

"Hey."

"No," she replied, climbing off him and staggering to her feet.

"Jak?" a surprised and familiar voice sounded

behind her. She turned and found the Banging Wagon sitting by the side of the road. Krill was hanging from the back door with one foot still on the stair and a quizzical eyebrow raised.

"Krill!" Jak exclaimed quietly. She rushed over and threw her arms around his waist. It hadn't occurred to her she would be this glad to see him again. He was certainly taken aback by the sudden display of affection.

"Ah," he said softly, and put a gentle hand on her shoulder. He wasn't the hugging type, but he understood. He kept his golden eyes on Jim, who stood and brushed himself off. "Do I want to ask?"

"Raging success," Jim replied. "We should probably make tracks."

"I mean why Jak is with you in a matching dress and seemingly overwhelmed," Krill clarified. "Are you alright, child?"

Kode appeared beside his husband from the depths of the wagon. "Jak? Where are the girls?"

"That way." Jak let go of Krill and pointed into the darkness. "We're camped outside of town at the edge of the forest. Dora's sick — she's really sick. I was at the castle trying to get a healer —"

"Take us there," Kode insisted.

Jak nodded gratefully. Jim signalled the other two into the back of the wagon. Whatever his own plans for the rest of the night had been, the two Ha'Cās made it very clear with their expressions that they were going to the girls' camp. Jim wasn't going to fight them on it. Jak followed him to the front of the wagon and they set off. It didn't feel like old times though. For a start, she was painfully aware that they were dressed ridiculously — in the outfits the city guard would be searching for if anyone came their way.

There was also a sombre intensity hanging over them now. Dora's illness, coupled with the fact that Jak had just seen Jim murder a man, was like a dark cloud over them. She didn't know what to say. He had told her that he had left her to keep her safe, and he had refused to abandon her again in the castle. Relief and gratitude tempered her anger, but it didn't erase it. Half of her wanted to break down and cry again with the joy of having them back, but half of her wanted to grab him by the throat and pin him to the side of the wagon until she squeezed every last secret out of him. The mixed feelings left her quiet, unless she was giving directions, and Jim didn't offer to fill the silence.

They crested the hill and moved into the forest. The light of the campfire drew them to the girls. Allie was still sitting by the flames, tending them. She looked tired and worn and dirty, but Jak was so glad to see her. However, the feeling didn't seem to be mutual. The caravan rolled into the clearing. When Allie looked up to see them trundle into the firelight, her expression was blacker than the night.

"What the fuck is this?" she demanded.

"Don't use that kind of language," Jak told her as she climbed down from the seat.

Kode was already bounding out of the back of the wagon. The pretty faerie didn't say anything to anyone, but headed straight for the tent and entered without a word.

"I will use whatever language I fucking want," Allie retorted. "You were supposed to get a healer. What's this arsehole doing back?"

"Jak said Dora was sick," Krill answered, before following his husband into the tent.

"Allie, I know you're angry," Jak sighed. "But things got out of hand. The King is dead, and I ran into Jim at the party. He can help—"

"What kind of bullshit did you spin my sister so that she would buy your sob-story, you piece of crap?" Allie demanded of Jim. She strode up to him and stared him down as he climbed from the wagon. Jim stood straight and turned to face the little girl. Jak stared at them. He looked pale in the firelight, and he seemed taller than she remembered, but maybe that was just because he was standing by Allie. He stared back down at her.

This time Allie faltered. Jak didn't know what her sister saw, but Jim stared down at her with no trace of his usual light humour. His expression was severe and Allie cowered from it. He didn't step around her, but waited for her to back down and move away. Then he strode straight to the tent. Jak watched it all happen like it was a dream. There was something there that scared her little sister. Allie snuck back to her, all of her anger and bluster forgotten, and huddled beside her. Jak watched Jim. She couldn't take her eyes off him. A deep and powerful dread was settling in her stomach.

Jim reached the tent but didn't go inside. He looked at it, as though seeing it for the first time. The shabby olive-green fabric. The small cramped space. He pursed his lips for a second, as though it simply wouldn't do.

Then he clicked his fingers. The tent snapped up into a pavilion instantly. The trees bent back and the fire jumped five feet to accommodate the new structure. The front doors were tied open by the flames to let the heat in. Jim stepped casually inside. The Ha'Cās were by Dora's bed. Kode was kneeling beside her with his hand on her forehead. Dora smiled up at him and murmured his name in a happy daze.

"How did he do that?" Allie whispered fearfully by Jak's shoulder. "He didn't burn anything to use magic. How?"

"He…" Jak wet her lips to murmur in reply, but the dread in her stomach was turning into an all-consuming lump. She could hardly breathe. "He said once that he was more powerful than the gods… that he could destroy them if he had to."

"That's not possible," Allie hissed. "Is it?"

Jak didn't answer. Everything was finally falling into place. The dread was a sick weight now. It wasn't going anywhere. She pressed her lips together as she fought back tears. They wouldn't fall. She could hold it together this time, but she couldn't stay quiet. Watching him there in his fancy suit had sparked a thought. Everything about it made sense. She finally understood. She walked silently through the front door of the pavilion with Allie right behind her. Jak took a deep breath as they entered.

"How's she doing?" Jim was asking.

"Not good," Krill replied. "Kode can ease her and make her feel better, but that's not the same as curing her. She needs your help."

"Olíriá herself couldn't heal her," Allie told them nervously from where she stood with Jak. "And she's a goddess."

"Olíriá's sweet, but she isn't the D'Ihne of medicine," Jim replied, kneeling down by Dora and rolling up his sleeves.

"Neither are you," Jak retorted. "Fæmör."

The entire room froze. For a second, no one moved or spoke. Jak took another steadying breath.

"I'm right, aren't I?" she called to him. Beside her, she could feel Allie staring at her like she was mad. Jim turned back to her. Jak stared at him. He stared back. It was the same severe stare he had directed at Allie before, but Jak didn't flinch from it. She wasn't scared of him, even if she should be. She stared him out.

"You're nuts," Allie told her.

"Maybe." Jak didn't take her eyes off Jim. "But I'm right too. I know I am. I thought Crŷs was a demigod when we first met him because he reminded me of Jim. It's the same vibe. That was the first clue when I saw you again. The second was that he hates you. Crŷs always got worked up when anyone mentioned you or Fæmör — the same kind of worked up, because you're the same person. He said Thænäri was the best at passing for human, and that she taught her kids. Fæmör's mother, *your* mother, taught you how to pass for human. That's why you're so much better at it. You claimed to have learnt Ĝoŕgomghōul's secrets for magic. Of course. Because he's your father. That's how you learnt from him. You are the god Fæmör, and that," Jak pointed to the flower crown Dora was wearing.

"That is Clōudiá's crown. The item all of faerie is searching for. That's why the D'rö-Hadās chased us. You're the thief. You stole it and dumped it on us. Why? Why can't the other fae see it? How did you do it?"

The whole room was holding their breath in the wake of Jak's accusation. Silence reigned. Krill was the first to move. He shifted slightly towards her and spoke in his softest voice.

"Jak—"

Jim cut him off with a tiny gesture. He stared at Jak. His expression was still severe, but there was the faintest trace of his humour returning. An impressed smile hovered on the corners of his lips, barely noticeable. He stood. As he stood, the illusion of his human appearance melted away to reveal the god underneath. Allie made a noise halfway between a gasp and a whimper and sank to the floor. Jak felt her breath catch and her throat tighten.

Fæmör had thick black curls and radiantly violet eyes. His skin had the same pearlescent quality as Olíriá's. He was tall and slender and incredibly beautiful. There was a similarity to his younger brother in his mischievous face. A floor-length robe of the softest, most delicate, purple silk was draped over his shoulders. It was slit completely up the sides and hung open at the front. He was extremely naked under it.

Jak felt her blush start in the pit of her stomach and burn up to her hairline. She wanted to cover her eyes and flee again, yet at the same time, she couldn't look away. Even by her standards, the god of all things fun was breath-taking. He held his arms out slightly from his sides as though inviting an opinion.

"Well, Jellybean?" he purred.

Jak couldn't talk. She had the truth now. A lot more of it visible than she'd like. Her mouth was dry and her throat felt too tight to speak. Allie answered.

"Well, that explains a lot..." she muttered. Her cheeks were just as pink as Jak's. The usual contempt she bore for Jim had melted with his human appearance. Now she looked flustered, as though she wanted to wrap up in her cloak and hide. Despite her awkwardness, she tried to keep her cool. She didn't flinch from looking at him, even if her embarrassment was stained across her face. The little girl looked to Krill. "I always wondered what you saw in him. He didn't seem your type. Now I get it completely."

Krill didn't respond, but cast his eyes down demurely.

"That's rude," Jim chuckled at her. "I love my human body."

"Love whatever you like," Allie shrugged. "It's still not Krill's type. He seems to like pretty and sleek."

"Doesn't he just," Jim winked at her. Allie blushed, if possible, even more.

"I don't understand..." Jak muttered, shaking her head. "Why?"

"Why what?" Jim replied. "You're going to have to be more specific."

"Why everything?! Why did you steal the crown? Why did you give it to Dora? Why are you killing kings?! You're a god! Humans worship you. They pray to you. You could have just gone down to the city and told them what you wanted. They would have done it. You're... you're Fæmör!"

"Jim," he corrected. The girls stared at him blankly, so he elaborated. "My name is Jim. I changed it years ago. I mean... what kind of stoner hippie calls their child Fæmör?" he scoffed. "My mom went through some phases... it shows. I needed something fun and original. Something a bit different."

"And you went with Jim?" Allie exclaimed in disbelief. Jak shook her head at her little sister. From the perspective of a fae James probably was an interesting name. He was grinning at them like he understood.

"Why did you do it, Jim?" Jak repeated her question seriously.

"Because someone had to," he answered honestly. "Maybe a dozen or so years ago now, I began to see the flaws in my society. After thousands of years in Roïgola'a'lanaū, I began to finally see the slavery I was complicit in. I left the golden city and came down to the world of mortals to contemplate this and try and get an outside perspective on it all. This world, I discovered, wasn't much better. Except that the power shifted across the years."

Jim reached out a hand and gently stroked Kode's cheek. The young fae was still kneeling by Dora's bed. He shared a fond look with the D'Ihne who had been his patron.

"Then these two fell from the sky," Jim continued. "I knew who they were, what they'd been up to, and what had finally happened. It was everything I was afraid of for them. I took them in and healed them up. For years, the three of us lived together down here, exiled from Roïgola'a'lanaū. We were happy. It was fine. But I could never shake the knowledge that there were those left behind. Krill and I used to discuss it a lot. The ones who didn't make it, who couldn't risk it, who were trapped."

Jim looked back over his shoulder where Krill stood just behind him. The blonde fae gave a slight nod.

"Clōudiá's power over all other fae comes from the crown," Jim told them. "Ĝoŕgomghōul made it for her using a similar magic to the D'rök blades. The crown negates magic. Clōudiá could literally steal the magic of other fae. She could bind them into submission. That's why no one crosses her."

"Except you," Jak commented.

"Except me," Jim grinned. "I studied the way my father uses magic. He doesn't have to burn things. The D'rö-Hadās bring him corpses and all those bodies turn into magic for dear aunty Clōudiá. His own magic is his — more powerful and potent than anything his siblings use, and he doesn't spend flesh or blood or souls to get it. I worked out how to do the same. Then I used that magic to steal the crown right off her smug, conceited head. I had hoped that the Ha'Cās would rise up when they realised that they were free," Jim pulled a face. "But unfortunately they are all still jumping at her orders and trying to find the stupid crown for her. Killing the mortal kings and getting their people to turn against them... that was much easier. I've been hoping now that the Ha'Cās will see the behaviour of the humans and learn from it. Alas, we're still not quite there yet. However, another country is about to follow suit, when they realise the King is dead and his vaults are empty, the country will collapse. The people will be able to rebuild."

"You're insane," Jak told him.

"No, Jellybean," Jim sighed. "You just don't understand. You want things to be black and white. You want it to be simple and easy. It's not. It's politics. I can't lead the Ha'Cās against Clōudiá. I can't start a war between immortals. I have to show them how to do it for themselves. I'm making the worlds better — all of them — I just have to break a few eggs to do it."

"Why involve us?" Jak demanded. "Why involve Dora? Why give her the crown? Were you trying to make her a target? Were you trying to get the D'rö-Hadās to chase us instead when you abandoned us? Is the crown making her sick?!"

"I don't know," Jim answered honestly. "I had no idea what would happen if I put it on a human. I hoped that because it renders fae mortal it would do nothing on a human — it would become impossible to find again. I didn't think it would do anything, but I could be wrong."

"You didn't know what it would do so you gave it to a little girl?" Jak couldn't have sounded angrier if she'd tried. Jim glared at her tone.

"I wanted to be rid of it. In the hands of humans it shouldn't have any power, and I didn't want to give it to someone who might pass for a thief. I figured if the fae traced it to a little girl, they would assume something had gone wrong with their magic — especially if they couldn't see it. I placed a spell over the crown to disguise it from fae eyes, so that even if they were staring straight at it they wouldn't see it." Jim smirked and lifted his chin proudly. He stared down the girls watching him. "You met other D'Ihne. Tell me, is my magic stronger than theirs? Did they suspect anything?"

Allie shook her head. Jak just glowered.

"The crown negates magic," Jak grated. "It's what stopped Olíriá from healing Dora. She thought our mother had prayed to the D'Ihne to heal Dora before, and that the spell still lingered and blocked other magic. If that was true, would the crown be undoing the healing spell over her and making her sick again?"

"Those are all possibilities," Jim conceded. Jak strode up to him. She felt like she was having a heart attack, and she didn't want to be this close to the immoral naked god, but she had to stand up to him. She glared him full in the face. He just smirked at her closeness.

"Take it off her and fix her," Jak growled. "Or so help me, James, I'll show you first-hand what deicide looks like."

"I love feisty you," he purred. Jim reached out a hand to touch her face, but Jak smacked it away.

"Heal Dora!" she barked at him. "You did this to her. You did this to us. I was right; you ruined my life. All of this, everything that happened to us, is your fault. I used to think you were some kind of hero — some friendly demigod who had taken us in and looked after us — but you're a monster. A villain. You're responsible for everything we've been through."

"Yes, I am," he retorted. Jim stepped closer and

loomed over her. His purple eyes flashed bright and she cowered from him. "I made you, Jellybean. Without me, you'd still be slaving away in that shithole of a town, struggling to feed your sisters, friendless and alone — wishing you could be allowed to make a sword, let alone swing one. I gave you everything you could ever need. Because of me, you have travelled further than you could imagine. You've met gods. You've danced at a King's ball. You've fought mythical assassins. You've become stronger than you even knew how to measure." Jim reached out and grabbed her by the back of the neck. Jak gasped and writhed. She snatched her sword, but he casually knocked the blade from her hands. It banged and rattled on the floor. He leant over her until his face was almost touching hers. "You're welcome," he purred, and dropped her.

Jak crashed onto her butt on the floor. She sat shivering on the ground and grabbed at her neck where he had been holding her. It hadn't hurt, but it had been uncomfortable. She rubbed the feeling of his fingers from her sensitive skin. A glint caught her eye.

Krill was still standing behind Jim. His serious eyes were narrowed, and his D'rök blade was just visible, half drawn, up his sleeve. He was watching his divine lover with warning eyes. Jak met his look. He realised that she had seen. His expression eased, and the blade vanished. Jim was still looking down on her, with no idea what she had just seen.

He turned away from her. Krill stood back respectfully, all hostility gone. Jim moved to Dora's bed. He stood at Kode's side and reached down. His long pale fingers plucked the flower crown from her head. She stirred and murmured in her feverish daze. In one hand, Jim kept the crown. The other he held open, palm down, two feet above the sick girl. A glow started in his open hand. A deep purple light that matched his eyes. Dora's breathing became heavier. She rolled onto her back and her chest heaved. Jak could almost see the energy passing from her chest to his hand.

Jim closed his fist. He snatched it into his body and turned away from the bed, hunching over as a thick chesty cough rattled his lungs. He coughed twice, caught his breath, and straightened up. He took a deep steadying breath. Then he held his hand out indicating Dora on the bed as though she was a display piece. Most of the colour had returned to her face, and she was breathing easily. She looked peaceful as she slept.

Jak stayed sitting on the floor. She didn't say anything. Allie didn't comment either. Jim took their silence as gratitude. He gave them a nod and motioned to Kode. The sweet young fae climbed off the floor and joined the other two faeries as Jim signalled them all out.

"It's been a long night," the god commented as he passed by. "We'll leave you girls to get some rest in your tent." As they exited the pavilion, Jim snapped his fingers again. The structure shrunk back down into a tent. Jak felt the world lurch as everything moved back to where it had been before. She found herself suddenly sitting on her bunk instead of the floor. It made her feel motion sick. Allie leapt to the door of the tent and looked out. The firepit had moved back too. She turned back to Jak.

"They just went back into the wagon..." she reported.

Jak nodded. Good. She didn't know what else to do or say. Dora was fixed. Probably. She looked better. Jak didn't want to wake her. She was too tired to think or feel beyond that. Now that the goal had been accomplished, the drive that had been keeping her going was gone. With trembling hands, she changed from her dress into a fresh shirt and leggings, and then collapsed into her bunk. She felt Allie place an extra blanket over her and heard her little sister climb into her own bed. She didn't hear much more after that.

***

When Jak woke, sunlight was streaming in through the front of the tent. The flap was pulled open to morning, and Allie was shaking her shoulder. Her dark eyes were large with apprehension and her expression was nervous.

"What's wrong?" Jak muttered, rolling over to face her.

"They're gone again," Allie muttered. "There's no sign of the wagon..."

"Okay," Jak sighed and nodded. "That's alright." She didn't want to say it was good, because she didn't know if it was, but she wasn't angry this time. She wasn't hurt. Jim and the boys were gone. That was fine. It was easier than facing him again this morning. She didn't know what she'd say to him. It was hard to be grateful now. He had cured Dora, but she was certain he had also made her ill. He had rescued her from several things, but always because he had caused the situation that she needed to be rescued from. He had murdered and stolen and raped. She couldn't shake the memory of Krill drawing his dagger last night when Jim had grabbed her.

Across the tent, Dora gave a loud yawn and stretched out of her blankets. Her curls were a mess and Binky the bunny was looking well-squished in her arms. Jak climbed from her bunk and she and Allie both descended on their little sister.

"Hey baby girl," Jak murmured to her, stroking back her curls. "How are you feeling?"

"Hungry," Dora answered honestly. "I had the weirdest dream. I dreamt that Kode came back, and that Chris was here but that he was really really super pretty and dressed in purple." She looked Jak full in the face. "He was so pretty even you would have liked him."

"That is nuts," Jak smiled at her. She didn't laugh. She also noticed that Allie didn't laugh either. They were probably both still spooked by the memory of what had actually happened.

"If you're hungry what do you want for breakfast?" Allie asked, grabbing the basket from the corner of the tent.

"Sandwiches!" Dora declared. She sat up and clapped her hands joyfully. It was hard to imagine she'd been half-dead with a fever last night. Jim's magic had worked. Jak smiled as she watched her youngest sister root around in the picnic basket for sandwiches. She was grateful to the dangerous god, but not so grateful that it would stop her from making her next move. The plan began to form in her mind as they ate breakfast.

"Do you think you'd be up to a little walk after breakfast, Dora?" Jak asked curiously.

"Where are we going now?" Dora pulled a face.

"Not far," Jak smiled. "We can stay camped here. But you've been quite sick and a bit of a walk and fresh air might do you some good."

"Oh," Dora shoved more sandwich in her mouth. "'eah, o-k. 'Hat so'nds 'ood."

"Don't talk with you mouth full," Allie laughed at her. "Dora, that's disgusting."

Dora opened her mouth wide to show Allie all the chewed-up food.

"Ew!" Allie laughed. "You're so gross."

"You know... when you were sick..." Jak commented slowly. "You ran off when we first got to the campsite. Ínrío had to go and get you..."

Dora thought about it. "I don't remember that..." she muttered. "I... I remember looking for Mum, but I might have been dreaming."

"He said he found you in some mushroom circles."

"Did the faeries kidnap me?"

"No," Jak smiled and shook her head. She did not tell Dora that the faeries probably tried to, but that the anti-magic flower crown she had been wearing prevented it. The faeries had undoubtedly been deeply confused too. "Dora... you know how I can sense faeries when I fight? ...You can sense fae magic too, can't you?"

The three girls went very silent. Dora kept her eyes on her food and ate quietly. Allie gave Jak a sharp look. Jak gave her a soothing nod and turned back to the youngest.

"You're not going to be in trouble, baby," she assured. "I just want to know. You can sense rune markers and faerie circles? When we were running from the Head Hunters you were directing us. You knew where to go to find Äulé. You weren't running around by accident. You know how to find them."

Dora nodded slowly and nervously.

"Could you do it again?" Jak asked. "Could you find Äulé for me?"

"You want to see Äulé?" Dora asked. "Yeah. Yeah I could do that."

"Cool beans," Jak grinned at her. "So after breakfast we can go for a walk to find him?"

Dora nodded enthusiastically and grabbed some extra sandwiches from the basket. Allie gave Jak a curious look, but Jak just returned a reassuring expression. She didn't want to say what she was up to. Her sisters were just going to have to trust her.

After she had eaten her fill, Dora packed up the extra sandwiches in a handkerchief and they set out. Allie volunteered to watch the camp. Jak argued that they should all go, but her sister said that as long as they were going to come back someone should stay and watch their things and tend the fire. Jak could hear the exhaustion in her voice still, and realised Allie wasn't up for another adventure yet. She had to respect that.

Dora led Jak deeper into the woods. For the first

time, Jak really began to look at where they were. She had always been so focused on Dora's illness, or the D'rö-Hadās, or their suspicious companions that she had barely noticed the forest. This wild fae forest that Olíriá had hidden in because humans didn't enter it. They kept to their safe roads, and the faeries didn't snatch them.

Here the trees grew twisted and wild. The underbrush was thick, and the deeper they went the more wildflowers grew. Shimmering butterflies danced through the air and dipped down to kiss the flowers growing up to their knees. Light filtered in through the leaves and Jak could see the rays shining down around them like golden rain. The beautiful sight filled her with an overwhelming sense of calm. She felt like she'd just come home after a lifetime away, and she couldn't believe it had taken her so long. Any second now, she would step into the clearing near the edge of the woods and see her little house with its thatched roof.

"We're here," Dora whispered.

Jak stopped and looked around. Just in front of them, so close she was lucky she hadn't stepped in it, was a mushroom circle. It was perfect. The kind that their parents had told them stories about. Each little toadstool was red with white spots, and they almost blended in to all the colourful flowers around them.

"It's not a Fora rune," Jak commented softly. "Will it still work?"

"It should do," Dora shrugged. She knelt down in the grass by the circle and carefully placed the sandwiches in the circle. "Dearest Äulé," she prayed.

"Sorry I've been so slack leaving you food. I've been sick, but I'm better now! If you're not too busy, we need your help again please."

"Do yer just?" the gnome chuckled, appearing in the circle. He had one baby gnome cradled in his arms and another fast asleep and dribbling in a sling on his back. He gave the girls a dry look. "Yer not being chased by anything and I see yer got rid of Silvertongue. He didn't run off with the other lass?"

"No," Jak smiled. "She's back at camp getting some rest. Äulé, if possible, I need you to do me a favour."

"Oh aye?"

"I need you to get a message to Olíriá."

"An what would yer have meh say to her radiance?"

Jak took a deep breath and looked him square in the eye. "Tell her I know where Clōudiá's crown is, and I know who took it."

CHAPTER SEVENTEEN

It was mid-morning when Jak dumped another load of wood down by their fire. Allie and Dora were resting in the tent, and she was taking care of the camp for the day. There wasn't much to do but wait. Äulé had disappeared in a puff of smoke as soon as Jak had told him her message. He'd even left half the sandwiches behind. She knew he'd pass it on. She didn't know how long it would take, but she knew he would make sure the knowledge got to the right people. In the end it didn't take long. She was adding another log to the fire and stoking it when three shadows fell across the flames.

"That was quick," she commented.

"How's Dora?" Ínrío asked.

Jak looked up to see Ínrío, Olíriá, and Crŷs standing on the other side of the fire.

"She's fine now," Jak answered. "We found someone who could heal her."

"Who?" Olíriá asked.

"Jim," Jak answered simply. She looked up at Crŷs. "You never told me he was Fæmör."

"You didn't know?" Crŷs raised an eyebrow.

"Didn't have a clue," Jak replied. "Until I met him for the second time. After meeting you lot, I worked it out."

"And he could heal Dora?" Olíriá queried.

"Once he took Clōudiá's crown off her so that the magic could actually get through, yes," Jak replied. "It turns out that was what was making her sick."

"What do you mean she had Clōudiá's crown?" Crŷs asked. "She didn't. We would have seen it."

"It had been enchanted so that you wouldn't," Jak sighed. "That's why the power of it drew you and the D'rö-Hadās to us, but then once you had us you could never actually find it. There was a spell over it making it invisible to fae eyes."

"That's impossible," Ínrío stated.

"Could Ĝoŕgomghōul do it?" Jak asked.

The three gods shared a long look. They kept glancing between each other. Mostly Olíriá and Ínrío looked to Crŷs. Eventually, the trickster god shrugged.

"Possibly," he conceded. "He is capable of things the rest of us aren't, and he did make it. But that would be unbelievably out of character for him. He doesn't get involved in fae politics, and if he wanted something, he would talk to us. He's not a thief."

"But his son is," Jak said.

"Wha—! I'm not!"

"Not you, Crŷs! Fuck," Jak shook her head. "Your brother. Jim. He stole the crown. He gave it to Dora to try and keep it hidden on a human, but that was a complete disaster, and now he's taken it back. Jim has the crown. He's the thief you're looking for."

"That's impossible, Jak," Ínrío refuted gently. "The crown disappeared from mother's head while Jim was here in the mortal world. She's been living in that rickety caravan with those Ha'Cās the whole time."

"She?" Jak looked confused.

"He means Jim," Olíriá explained. The three gods shared a wry look of contempt for limited human understanding. Jak tried to get her head around the idea of Jim as a woman.

"Look," Jak refocused herself. "Jim said he learnt his father's way of doing magic. He doesn't have to burn anything to use it."

"Impossible," Crŷs shook his head.

"I've seen it!" Jak protested. "I've seen him do it multiple times! He transports us places! He healed Dora! He does all kinds of stuff, and I have never once seen him use anything but a gesture to do it!"

"That's not possible, Jak," Crŷs insisted wearily. "Magic cannot come from nothing. That's like clicking your fingers and having a loaf of bread appear. You can't do it."

"Well, he's found a way," Jak argued. "He found a way to magic the anti-magic crown from Clōudiá's head in the fae realm to his hands in our world. He used his power to keep the D'rö-Hadās off him and his boyfriends for a year now, and made sure no one could find him or work out what he'd done. Now, he's going around killing human kings to start uprisings in the hope that it will inspire the Ha'Cās to fight back against Clōudiá now that she doesn't have the crown."

Silence reigned.

"That's impossible," Ínrío disputed gently. "She wouldn't do that. Not Jim. She's not the type. She wouldn't betray us like that."

"Will you two stop saying it's impossible," Olíriá snapped. Everyone looked to her. The goddess folded her arms seriously. Her perfect brow was creased in thought.

"You think he did it..." Crŷs murmured.

"Jak has no reason to lie to us," Olíriá replied. "Whatever has actually happened, she believes she is telling the truth. So, my question to you is this: what if she is?"

"Jim wouldn't do that," Ínrío repeated stubbornly. His siblings both ignored him.

"I absolutely believe he would," Crŷs nodded to his beloved. "It's only a question of if he could."

"Who else could possibly have kept the D'rö-Hadās from their target for so long?" Olíriá shrugged. "They have never spent more than a week on a target — now this has been going for a year and they are no closer. They could never identify who the thief was. Jim has the previous D'Hiris on his side. Between the two of them, with the crown, they would be impossible for the D'rö-Hadās to catch. It explains a lot."

"And he stuck the blame on me..." Crŷs growled. "That shitty little snake..."

"That's a little narcissistic, brother," Ínrío commented. "I'm sure it wasn't the intent. Just a coincidental and valuable lesson about messing with people."

"So now what?" Olíriá asked. "We're entertaining the theory that Jak is right. We have to tell the others, presumably. But then what? How do we stop him? A rogue D'Ihne? With the crown of the fae? Not even the D'rö-Hadās can catch him, and they were the contingency Clōudiá created to stop fae kind from stepping out of line."

The three of them stood there with deep concern etched on their faces as they thought. Jak watched them contemplate the problem.

"I'll do it," she told them. "I'll catch him for you."

"That's kind of you, Jak," Ínrío chuckled appreciatively, and laid a hand on her shoulder. "But we are talking about the most dangerous being in creation. A D'Ihne wielding the crown of all Faerie. You're just a human, and no match for a D'Ihne."

"I would be a match for him if I had a D'rök blade..." Jak argued softly. Now she had their attention. She met their eyes and continued. "D'rök blades are made the same way as the crown. They're anti-magic. I could fight a fae with one of those, and I'm human, so he couldn't destroy me by using the crown to negate my magic."

"As much as I appreciate your enthusiasm," Crŷs smiled at her. "You're talking about suicide. Besides, D'rök blades are made for an assassin when they officially join the D'rö-Hadās. It's not like we have some lying around we can lend you."

"But she could have one made..." Olíriá commented. "Her own D'rök blade..."

They all looked at the goddess. She still stood with her arms crossed seriously, but she had a leading expression on her face.

"No," Crŷs shook his head. "We're not getting him

involved. No way."

"It's a good idea, Crŷs," Olíriá insisted. "This is how we beat Jim. We can't take him by force alone, and he's smart enough to rival any of us. The only way to get him is to play to his arrogance. Make him underestimate us. He will never see her as a threat, and he will underestimate her every step of the way. That's our secret weapon."

"It's insane," he argued. She held his gaze. "*Insane*," he repeated as though no one had heard him the first time.

"Well, Jak?" Olíriá turned to her. "You offered us your service. Did you mean it? Will you travel with me to Fäsaírm and forge your own D'rök blade to help us stop Jim?"

"I thought Fäsaírm was a rune...?" she replied.

"It is," Crŷs nodded. "But the rune and the symbolism come from the place. It is where my father resides, in the binding between the realms."

Jak looked between them all. Crŷs' expression was telling her she didn't have to say yes, and Olíriá's was neutral, leaving the decision entirely in her hands. Ínrío didn't look like he knew what to think. The revelation about Jim was still hitting him hard.

"I will," Jak answered the goddess. "But what about my sisters?"

"Crŷs and Ínrío will look after them," Olíriá volunteered. She turned to her lover. "It's better if you don't come along, and someone needs to watch the girls and report home. I'll get word to you once we're ready and you can join us then."

"I hate this plan," he told her gently, resting a curled finger beneath her chin.

"I know, my love," she replied. "But we don't have a better one." The two of them kissed and Jak averted her gaze. She turned away towards the tent. If this was happening, she'd better pack to hit the road. She had no idea how far the bridge between realms was. Jak entered the tent and began to pack her things quietly. It wasn't like there was all that much to pack.

"What are you doing?" Allie asked behind her. Jak turned. Allie was lying awake in her bunk, looking at her big sister.

"The gods are here," Jak told her quietly. "I'm going on a quick trip with Olíriá to get a magic sword to stop Jim. Crŷs and Ínrío are going to watch you two until I get back."

Allie threw off her blankets and sat up. "You can't go."

"I have to, Sis," Jak insisted. She moved over and gave her a half hug by the bed. "I won't be gone long. This is important. They need my help."

"Do they?" Allie asked seriously. "Or do you just need to give it?"

"Someone has to stop him." Jak dodged the question. "At the rate he's going, he will plunge the entire world into war. I can't let him do that. I couldn't live with myself if I didn't even try and help."

"At what cost?"

"So far? Not much. Once we have the sword, we'll come back. I won't do anything crazy without you, and Olíriá won't go after Jim without Crŷs. I promise."

Allie sighed. "What am I going to do when Dora wakes up and I have to tell her you're gone too?"

"Be honest," Jak shrugged. "I'm coming back. You can distract her with the gods too. She was jealous when I first met Olíriá, and she's been semi-conscious for all our other divine interactions. It might be nice for her to meet them properly."

Allie sighed again, but this time it sounded like she was giving in. "Stay safe," she requested.

"You too," Jak kissed the top of her head. "I'll be back as soon as I can. I don't know what travelling with a god is like."

"Don't you?" Allie arched an eyebrow. Jak just rolled her eyes. The nap had been good for Allie. She was back to being as sharp as ever, and Jak couldn't keep up with it. She gave her little sister's shoulder one last squeeze, and then hauled her pack from the tent.

The gods were still waiting where she had left them. Jak hoisted her pack onto her shoulders as she approached them.

"No time like the present?" Olíriá smiled.

Jak nodded. She looked at the other two. "You'll take good care of them, right?"

"Of course," Crŷs promised. "Ínrío will look after them like they were his own sisters. I won't, because no one wants that. I will make sure no harm befalls them."

"Thank you," Jak nodded.

"I'll get word to you soon," Olíriá promised her beloved. "It shouldn't take us too long to reach Fäsaírm. Let me know what the others say. I don't envy you the job of telling your mother."

"I can manage the D'Ihne," he assured. "As long as you can manage my father."

She nodded. They shared one last kiss goodbye. Olíriá hugged her brother farewell, and then turned to Jak. The two women shared a nod of agreement that they were ready to go, and then Olíriá led Jak back into the depths of the woods.

The trees grew in a tangle of branches above them like a net of green. It seemed the way they were headed was even thicker than many of the other pathways Jak had taken. In these parts, nature ruled. Squirrels and birds nested above them, and bunnies hopped away from them. She remembered the way rabbits used to chase the wagon. That was just another mystery solved. They walked in silence for the first few minutes, but Jak had too many questions to maintain that for long. Eventually she had to ask.

"So… where is Fäsaírm?"

"There are entrances scattered across the world," Olíriá replied. "The closest one is at the bottom of the country."

"The bottom of the country!" Jak exclaimed. "And we're walking?! It will take all year!"

Olíriá gave her a dry look. "We're going to cheat, Jak."

"We are?"

The goddess laughed and looked around the wild forest. "We are, and we might as well start here. Take my hand."

Jak did as she was told, and slipped her hand nervously into the goddess' grasp. Olíriá's hand was warm and soft. She held on tightly. The goddess reached out her other hand and placed it carefully against a tree. Jak felt the whole world lurch.

She gasped, and when everything steadied again, she was staring through the last rows of trees to the road by Othalí'taian, or Lake Kover. She recognised it instantly. They had just covered days of travel in a second. However, Jak felt a tad unwell. Specifically, like she was going to hurl. She put a gentle hand on her stomach and caught her breath.

"You feeling alright?" Olíriá asked.

"Mm," Jak responded half-heartedly.

"Good. Come on." The goddess still held her hand, and she dragged Jak with her across the road. They stepped lightly across the packed dirt road into the grassy verge leading down to the water's edge. The grass was slippery and the sand beyond it was wet but soft. Olíriá pulled Jak along. Lagging behind, she didn't have the stomach to ask what was about to happen next. Olíriá reached the water, still holding Jak's hand. One pale foot dipped beneath the surface. The world lurched again. This time it took longer. It was like lying inside a wheel and being pushed.

Jak hit the ground on her hands and knees, tearing away from Olíriá's grasp. The goddess looked down on her and placed a hand on her back.

"Are you alright?" she asked again.

Jak puked on the grass beneath her. She couldn't make her head stop spinning. Or anything else, for that matter. All her organs were churning, and the world was having its own problems staying still.

"Ah," Olíriá patted her back. "Yes. Okay. We'll walk for a bit."

Jak crawled away from the vomit. She curled up in the grass with her eyes closed and her head in her hands. She needed a minute, and Olíriá looked happy enough to give it to her. She stepped back into the water and stood peacefully, as though rooted to her realm.

When Jak finally opened her eyes again, and the world stopped spinning, she took it in. All sign of the lake was gone. They were on the bank of a river. Upstream, mountains rose blue and hazy in the distance, and around them a completely different forest grew. Jak had no idea how far they had travelled, but she wouldn't have been surprised if they had covered most of the distance of their journey already. The air down here was warm and mild. Despite the pleasant temperature, Jak was still shivering queasily as she sat back up.

"Where are we?" she asked.

"Only about a day's walk from where we need to be," Olíriá turned back to her. "Fae methods of transport are far quicker than human."

"I feel like I've been liquified…" Jak groaned.

"In a way you were," the goddess shrugged. "I'm sorry. I didn't know what kind of effect spirit travel would have on a human."

"Egh. You sound like Jim."

Olíriá smiled at her. "The difference is I knew you'd be alright."

"How could you possibly know?"

"Because I know something about you that he

doesn't..." Olíriá smiled. She stepped from the water and started up the bank. Jak watched her walk by and waited for the elaboration. It didn't come. Olíriá kept walking towards the trees without a word, smiling her mysterious smile.

"Wait!" Jak called after her weakly. "What does that mean? Hey! Wait up!" she struggled to her feet and staggered after the goddess. It was tough going and Olíriá didn't slow or wait. By the time Jak managed to catch up with her, she had forgotten they were even talking. The trees grew straight and even around here. The forest was cultivated, not wild. It didn't feel magical. Jak only realised there was a difference when she felt the lack. She still felt sick, and her legs were trembling as she chased after the goddess.

"Wait!" she gasped. "Seriously, do you even care? I can barely walk."

Olíriá turned back to her. "I'm sorry, Jak. I'm not used to travelling with mortals."

Jak looked at the distant gaze Olíriá directed her way. She stopped. There was something vague in the goddess' eyes, like she was only half there.

"What's going on?" Jak asked. "What's wrong?"

"You mean aside from the fact that one of the D'Ihne has gone rogue, is trying to collapse our empire, overthrow our aunt, and that you and I are venturing into the heart of all worlds to find a blade that can kill him? Aside from that?"

"Well... yeah..." Jak wheezed. Olíriá smiled, but it wasn't a real smile. It was strained. She looked back towards the water again, but the view of the river was fading as they headed inland.

"I just... I can't help but wonder if this is partly my fault..."

"Wait, what?" Jak caught up with her. "How? Olíriá, this can't be on you. Jim stole the crown. He killed those people. You didn't have anything to do with it." She paused. "Did you...?"

"Not as directly as you're implying," she sighed. "I had no idea it was him. I never suspected him, until the moment you told us. As soon as you said it was him, all the pieces fell into place. It was the only thing that made sense... but to believe he'd actually do it..."

"You like him, don't you?" Jak pestered. "When I first met you at the pool, you two were so close — like old friends. You actually like him."

Olíriá shrugged in agreement.

"*Why*?!" Jak exclaimed.

"Because it's complicated, Jak," the goddess sighed. "Because everything is complicated, even when we don't want it to be." Olíriá turned and began to walk through the trees, but she moved slower so that Jak could keep up. The girl had caught her breath, and it was easier now.

"Didn't he... rape Crŷs?" she asked uncomfortably.

"That's one of the things that makes it complicated," Olíriá answered darkly. A shadow came over her eyes at the mention of it, and Jak regretted bringing it up. But she needed to know. She needed to understand. Olíriá sighed beside her, as though she could sense that need.

"Jim has done terrible things," Olíriá began. "Does that make him a bad man?"

Jak felt like it was a trick question. She listened to the leaves and twigs crack under her feet as they walked through the forest.

"Yes…?" she answered hesitantly.

"He's also done wonderful things," Olíriá continued. "Does that make him a good man?"

"Um…"

"Jak," Olíriá sighed. "He's not even a man. Jim is D'Ihne — a powerful breed of fae, and while I refer to him, others of our kind refer to her in equal measure. Jim has spent forever switching between genders and species and elements, and that confuses mortals. You don't seem to be able to grasp it. Is he a good or bad man? He's neither. That's only the beginning of why this is complicated."

"Well, what's the good stuff he's done?" Jak demanded. "Does it balance the bad? Weigh it up."

"How do you measure it?" Olíriá asked.

Jak was left to ponder some more. Olíriá stopped for a moment and sighed again. She closed her eyes, and when she opened them she changed direction slightly. Jak continued to trail after her.

"He's… he's killed a lot of people…" Jak started. "How would you even balance that?"

"What about Krill?" Olíriá countered. "He had been killing for four hundred years. Is he a bad person?"

"He was a slave," Jak defended. "He was doing what he was ordered to. He had no choice."

"Didn't he? What about when he ran away with Kode? Was that not a choice?"

"It's not the same," Jak insisted stubbornly. "Krill is

a good person who has had a hard life. He's had horrible decisions to make. Jim is just a spoilt brat."

"Really?"

"He's a god. An all-powerful being who can do whatever he wants, and he does. He just travels around shagging everything he comes across and killing people he doesn't like."

"Is that why he's doing it?" Olíriá gave her a pointed look. "Is that the reason he gave for his recent behaviour? Jim is thousands of years old. He's killed hundreds of people. Do you think he was just doing it because it was fun? Do you think he enjoys killing?"

"Well…" Jak muttered. "He said he was trying to end slavery… but he's going about it all wrong!"

"I agree," Olíriá nodded. "That is why we are going to try and stop him. However, I don't want to drag you into this if you don't understand what it is we are doing. Jim started his wars as revenge for eons of Ha'Cās slavery. His methods are atrocious, and there must be a better way, but the things he did were done for love. How can I, of all people, judge him poorly for that?"

Jak was silent for a moment. "You really think that?" she asked finally.

"I know it," Olíriá sighed. She clutched a fist to her chest. "He's trying to hide it, but I can feel it even from here. He loves those two. He has since we first started watching out for them, just the two of us. Their persecution and exile hurt him. He wasn't even in the city. He'd already left by then. We knew when they fell in love. No one else in the city knew. We kept it secret, even Krill and Kode didn't know that we knew. He was getting too close to it, so he went to travel the mortal realm for a bit. I could feel how intense his emotions were becoming. That's why, when they were discovered, I married them and sent them to him. I knew he'd keep them safe."

"Why are you telling me this?" Jak muttered.

"Because I need you to understand."

"Understand what? I'm just confused now."

"Good. Confusion means you're thinking. It means you are beginning to understand the situation. You asked for a D'rök blade because you know what it does — what it is capable of. If I'm going to help you get a weapon that can kill my kind, I need to know that you understand the responsibility you will have, and the consequences that will bring. You believe that what Jim did was so wrong, but he believed he was doing the right thing by killing those kings. You want a sword that can kill him, but if you use it, where will that put you?"

"Why are you defending him?"

"Because it's complicated." Olíriá finished, bringing home the point she had been trying to make from the start. Jak was really starting to loathe this conversation anyway. She let it drop. It was certainly a lot to think about, and… kill? She wasn't sure she wanted to kill Jim. She wanted to scare him; to put him in his place; to make sure he could be tried for his crimes… but actually kill someone? Kill him? She didn't know if she could. Then why was she asking for a D'rök blade? Krill had said those blades were poison to fae. A simple wound with one could end a faerie's life. Jim had saved him from that fate, but it was the only instance in history where that had been done. Could Jim cure himself if he was the one wounded?

Olíriá stopped with another sigh. Jak felt like the goddess wasn't done explaining, but that she also wasn't sure how to finish her argument. Instead, she just signed in the air. The glowing runes turned into two white horses, and Olíriá transformed herself to appear human.

"We might as well ride," she told Jak. "We'll cover more ground faster that way, and there's something I want to show you."

Jak didn't argue. She had a lot to think about. They mounted up and rode off through the trees.

By early afternoon they hit a road cutting through the forest. Olíriá still dictated their direction, and Jak followed contemplatively behind her. It didn't take long for the road to lead them to a small but sprawling village. The houses ranged on the small side, but the fenced properties were large. Down here, they seemed to build from wood rather than stone, and Jak marvelled at the panelled walls. She didn't marvel for long. Something else caught her eye. One of the houses had a giant wooden statue of a rooster in the front yard. The bird stood proud and its head rose higher than the roof next to it. Jak gave it a bewildered look, and she could hear Olíriá struggling to keep back a chuckle at the sight of it.

"What is that?" Jak asked.

"A statue," Olíriá chuckled. "I tell you what, let's stop by the inn and get you fed, and then we can go ask about it."

The inn was close. They tied up the horses outside and entered. Olíriá paid for a meal for Jak, while the girl sat down at a scrubbed wooden table and stared out the window at the strange carving. She watched the world outside as she ate, contemplating the people wandering by, while unable to ignore the pompous bird with the stupid expression. It was easier than meeting Olíriá's eyes. She didn't want the goddess to ask her about killing again.

Jak ate quietly. After puking on the riverbank and settling down again as they travelled, she was now ravenous. Olíriá insisted she would need her strength for what they were about to do. Jak knew she was right, but she was confused enough without engaging in more difficult conversations. The whole time she kept glancing to the statue. For reasons she couldn't explain, it annoyed her. Olíriá watched her. When she was finished, they left and didn't spare any extra time at the inn.

Olíriá led her back into the afternoon sun with a smile.

"Now, let's go ask about that rooster."

"Why?" Jak asked. "You already know what it is, don't you? Is it a god thing? Do they worship animals here?"

"We're here, Jak, so that you can learn about it. So let's go do that."

Jak gave the goddess a suspicious look, but Olíriá ignored it and walked her through the gate of the property with the rooster. The rooster sat on the lawn, although it had been sitting there long enough that it now seemed to be more in than on. She didn't know how far the base plinth had sunk into the ground. The front yard was mostly a neat lawn, with a packed dirt path leading from the gate to the front door of the wooden house. It was a little house, after seeing the size of the buildings in Kosvo, but it was bigger than the hut she had grown up in.

They walked straight up to the front door and Olíriá knocked. Jak could hear children laughing inside. The sound became louder as the front door was hauled open. A young woman with an open, smiling face stood in the doorway. She had a baby on her hip and two young children racing around her legs. She laughed as she ushered the kids back inside and looked up at them.

"Can I help you?" she asked.

"I'm looking for a relative," Olíriá told her. "I have reason to believe you may have seen them." For the briefest second her illusion faltered and the woman at the door saw her fae form. An expression of reverence crossed the woman's face and she bowed her head.

"My lady goddess, thank you for all you have done for me."

"You're most welcome, Charlotte." No one asked how Olíriá knew the woman's name.

"You're looking for Fæmör?"

"We are."

Charlotte looked back inside at her children. Jak looked too. The two still chasing each other looked to be twins, perhaps four years old. Jak felt herself cringe inwardly as the lady answered.

"I'm afraid Fæmör hasn't been seen around here in five years."

"Oh, you didn't…" Jak muttered, half to herself.

The women heard her. They both shot her looks.

"The children aren't faerie, Jak," Olíriá smiled. "They're her husband's."

Jak couldn't quite shift the disbelief from her expression. Charlotte smiled sympathetically at her. Olíriá nodded her head at the woman, as though instructing her to tell her story to the girl on the doorstep.

"My husband and I were struggling to conceive after we were married," Charlotte admitted discreetly. "I prayed for help. I prayed to Thænäri and Fæmör for assistance. A month or so after I started, a rickety old wagon rolled up outside the gate."

"The Banging Wagon," Jak grimaced. "He's had it for a decade or more now."

"You know Fæmör too?"

"We're acquainted," Jak muttered. "He's a dick."

"Fæmör was kind to us," Charlotte countered, bouncing her baby on her hip. "My husband was unsettled at first, having a divine one in the house, but the goddess quickly eased his worry. Fæmör stayed one night under our roof and did what they could for us. The next day they left. There was no sign of the wagon or the company, except for the statue." She smiled at the looming wooden bird as though it was an old joke. "Soon after, we discovered we were pregnant. I absolutely believe Fæmör was responsible for fixing whatever was wrong. I have three beautiful children now, thanks to divine help, but I haven't seen Fæmör since that night."

"Thank you for your time, Charlotte," Olíriá nodded to her.

"Anything for you, my goddess. Thank you for all the love you have brought to my life."

The goddess and the lady nodded to each other and Olíriá led Jak away again as Charlotte closed her door.

"What was all that?" Jak asked as they walked away.

"That was a story of something good that Jim did, and it's not the only one of its kind."

"And he left her a giant rooster?"

"Fæmör left a giant, hard cock on her lawn, yes."

"Ye gods…" Jak groaned, covering her face as she finally got the joke. "Why is he always like that?"

"You used to laugh at some of his jokes, Jak."

"That was before I knew about all the awful stuff he's done! He's a monster."

"You don't know all the awful things he's done, Jak," Olíriá sighed. "You only know some of them, and you know even less about all the good things he's done. He has given far more life than he has taken, which is more than I can say for some of our kind. He helps people. He helped you and your sisters."

"But he's a creepy pervert!" Jak protested, as they collected the horses and began to ride out of town. The white steeds clopped gently down the street, and Jak barely noticed the village disappear behind them. "I don't get why you're defending him, Olíriá. He raped your husband."

Olíriá's expression was bleak. "She did, yes," the

goddess agreed. Her pale eyes looked out at the landscape solemnly as they rode by. "Immortals aren't good people, Jak," she finally sighed. "Think about how many turns a human can make in their meagre life. We have forever. Sometimes we are good and just and kind. Sometimes we are vengeful and vindictive and cruel. Always we are powerful. I want to tell you a story. A true story."

Jak waited patiently and expectantly. Her eyes conveyed that she was happy to listen.

"A long time ago now," Olíriá began. "There was a village so far away that you would never have heard of them. They were a tribe of people that worshipped Fæmör. They were good people. I'm not sure if you would have liked them — they had their own way of life that was very different to yours — but they were happy, and they were generous and loving. One night, the church they had to Fæmör burnt down. Crŷs found out about it and took a look around. He came back to Roïgola'a'lanaū and told Fæmör that the people had turned against him. They had burnt down the church as an act of defiance and taken up gruesome and unsavoury practices — which he described graphically. Fæmör was devastated, not just for his own vanity, but for the sake of his people who had become so abhorrently sadistic. He sailed Roïgola'a'lanaū over the village and unleashed a divine storm to cleanse the earth of such horror, and to exact vengeance and justice in the D'Ihne way."

"I've heard legends about the storm of the Golden City taking vengeance on people for dishonouring the gods," Jak nodded. "I didn't know he did it."

"Most of us have done it at some point or another," Olíriá shrugged. "We are vain and ruthless creatures who do not handle defiance well." Her expression was extremely bleak. "Crŷs lied, Jak. The church had burnt down in an accident one night, and the village had intended to rebuild it. They had not changed. Crŷs was just playing one of his pranks, and when he found out what Fæmör had done... Crŷs thought it was hilarious and told Fæmör the truth."

Jak felt her blood run cold. She had assumed Olíriá was telling her a story about smiting out cannibalism and incest or something horrible. Instead...

"That's..." she couldn't even get the words out.

"That was the prank that went too far for Fæmör," Olíriá admitted. "Those two had been causing havoc with each other for centuries, but Fæmör was devastated when she realised she had wiped out a village just because she had trusted her little brother. That was why she tricked him into her bed. Vengeance. Fæmör was so distraught by the nasty trick Crŷs had played that she was determined to hurt him just as equally."

"And you still love Crŷs after all that...?"

"Jak," Olíriá sighed. "There is no possible way for me to make you understand what it is like to be D'Ihne, but I am trying. We are all a mix of good and bad, with eternity to make our decisions, and the power to level cities or build them up. Even then, our lives are not simple or easy, and there are only eleven of us in all of existence. Fæmör has not lead an untroubled life. His mother was always flighty, and his father was completely absent. He was one of the oldest of our generation, and they practically raised themselves before helping to raise us. There are hundreds of stories I could tell you — good and bad and in between."

Jak shook her head. "I'm sorry that happened to him, but it doesn't excuse what he's done."

"No, but it does explain it," Olíriá countered. "What about you, Jak? One of your parents died and the other abandoned you. The man who filled the void they left betrayed you and abandoned you again. His betrayal almost cost your sister her life. Will I be telling this story one day, not to excuse your behaviour, but to explain it?"

"No," Jak responded instantly, and then realised she was only hoping it was true. She didn't know, but she was starting to get it. She took a deep breath. "At least... I hope you won't... I guess... I guess things are complicated."

"Yes, they are," Olíriá smiled. "You are so adamant that you dislike Jim, but you barely know them. You have spent time with one human form of an immortal D'Ihne. You haven't even met the goddess."

"If she's anything like the rest of him, I can do without," Jak muttered.

Olíriá gave her a long look as they rode on between rolling hills. Jak tried to ignore it, but the goddess' gaze was boring into the side of her face.

"Jak, you are so sure you can withstand his charm. You see him as... what was it? A creepy old pervert? You see only Jim, and even as Jim you did come to trust him — to love him — if only for a short while."

"Well, now I know him better," Jak stated with more conviction than she felt.

"Jak, I want you to do me a favour…"

"Oh?"

Olíriá looked at her very directly. "If you ever meet the goddess Fæmör… I want you to run as fast as you can in the opposite direction."

"You think I'd be in danger from her?"

"I think you'd be in danger from yourself around her," Olíriá commented coolly. There was something in the look Olíriá shot her. The goddess knew what her own form did to Jak, and her tone regarding her lover's sister was warning. Jak blushed hot in the pit of her stomach. She couldn't imagine Fæmör taking a form that would make her forget Jim, and she couldn't imagine ever being attracted to Jim. A small thought began to niggle in her mind at Olíriá's warning though. A thought about the way Olíriá had been trying to warn her since they left; about the way Charlotte had acted like all love was a blessing from the goddess; about how Olíriá had confessed that she felt partially responsible for the mess they were in.

"You've had sex with Jim," Jak accused.

Olíriá turned to look at her with a startled expression, but Jak had a hunch now and she wasn't backing down.

"You have, haven't you? All the legends say you're the only one that didn't, but you have. You love him. You love a lot of people, even if you love Crŷs the most. You're responsible for Jim falling in love with Krill and

Kode — that's why you feel guilty. You made him fall for them…" Jak relaxed back in her saddle as she finally worked it out. "You did it as revenge for what he did to Crŷs, which was revenge for that village, and so on and so forth back to the beginning of time."

Olíriá stared at her for a long time. The longer she stared, the surer Jak felt.

"How in the name of my mother did you work that out?" Olíriá muttered.

"Because it's what you've been trying to tell me this whole time," Jak replied. "All the stories, all the lessons, they all come back to this. Does Crŷs know?"

"Yes," Olíriá admitted softly. "He was there. I told him what I was going to do, and while he hated the idea, he decided he would rather live with the memory than the nightmare. Jim likes group activities, so he didn't mind, and he was too busy thinking of it as a win to notice I was trying to trick him."

"How did you trick him?"

"We can affect each other," Olíriá sighed. "Fae. We can mix our magics — the magic that is just part of what we are made of."

"So, if you let him have sex with you, you can make him fall in love?"

"That's a gruesomely basic way to sum it up, but yes," Olíriá agreed. "I just… I just wanted him to feel what it was like to be in love, and how much it can hurt. What he did to Crŷs hurt me, even if I know why he did it. I was hurt and I wanted him to hurt. I thought… a little bit of love magic, what harm could it do?"

"And now he's trying to destroy your society…"

Olíriá shared a look with the girl riding beside her, and then the goddess began to laugh helplessly.

"Fae are a mess, Jak," she chuckled sadly. "We're all a mess. We love each other, but we can't stop bickering, and when gods fight, the world trembles. I... I thought, with Fæmör... I thought she might fall for Ínrío. The two of them kept company all the time anyway. I thought it might be good for her — that I'd be able to accuse her of being like me after all the time she spent laughing at the way I was with Crŷs."

"You didn't count on Krill and Kode?"

"I did not," Olíriá shook her head. "No one saw that coming. I did not account for the possibility that Fæmör could have fallen in love with Ha'Cās. It was unheard of. Now I have to fix what I started... and I don't know how."

"Can't you just take the love spell off him?"

"Whatever magic I wove over him ended years ago," Olíriá sighed. "Now his feelings are all his. Whatever he loves or doesn't — that's on him. He's just far more prone to it than he ever used to be."

"Well..." Jak sighed as they rode on. "This is fucking complicated."

"Yes, it is," Olíriá smiled. "Glad to see you're finally getting it."

"I don't know how to put it right," Jak admitted. "But I think getting a D'rök blade will help."

"Then let's get you one," Olíriá nodded. She thumped her heels into her horse and it took off down the road. Jak followed suit. She wasn't a good rider, but the horse was faerie, and it knew to follow the goddess.

They galloped along twisting roads between emerald green hills. Jak felt like the world was flying by. The warm air felt cold as it whipped by her face. At this speed it was too difficult to talk. She just had to hold on and keep up. The air became colder as night began to fall. The sky began to darken and the clouds became thick.

Jak had never been much of a rider before in her life, but it occurred to her as they galloped that fae horses might move a lot faster than regular horses. She certainly felt like she was moving at an alarming rate, and the jerking speed was starting to make her feel sick. Eventually, they veered off the road and began to slow as they headed uphill.

The landscape jutted and rolled in vivid green clumps nearby, and beyond that, forests and mountains had begun to encircle them, like birds of prey under charcoal clouds. Wherever they were, it was a boundary. Somewhere where nature and its magic were looking to reclaim where humanity encroached.

Off the road, their path soon became cluttered with large boulders. Some looked to have been carved with faerie runes. Jak let her horse step carefully after Olíriá's, but she could see the rocks clustering up ahead. There was a slim chance that she could clamber over the boulders, but the horse wasn't going to make it unless it could fly. Still, Olíriá led on. Jak could see the path they meandered through the rocks becoming a clear dead end. She wondered if Olíriá was just going to blast a path through, but the goddess didn't seem the blasting type. More than that, they were now getting close enough to the blockage that the debris might hit them if it exploded. Instead, she rode straight into the dead end and turned around. Jak rode up beside her.

"What are we doing?" she asked.

"Taking the road to Fäsaírm," Olíriá indicated.

Jak looked behind her. Olíriá was facing back the way they had come, looking through the jagged cluster of rocks. For a moment, Jak just stared at the path they had walked. Then she began to see something. She shifted slightly in her saddle and turned her mount to get a better view of what Olíriá was looking at.

The carvings on the boulders lined up. As Jak tipped her head further, she saw it. From this very specific angle, a small cluster of the rocks formed a doorway back towards the crawling forest. Olíriá gave her a smile, and then started towards the doorway. Jak followed. She found her curiosity piqued. It was an illusion, but not one born of magic. It wasn't like anything she had ever seen, and it had a powerful aura about it. She hadn't felt it until she had seen the door, but now it was like electricity in the air.

The hairs on the back of her neck prickled as she passed through the doorway. It felt like there was a thunderstorm about to crack. The rock was thick and heavy around them. Jak could feel the weight of the stones pressing down around her. For a moment, she felt like she could understand things beyond her. The rocks had looked so natural, but it was clear that someone had placed them. Perhaps, then, all of nature had been placed by someone, somewhere. Hands that humans couldn't fathom had created the world.

Immortal hands.

Just like that, the moment passed, and Jak found herself riding through a tangled forest. A magical forest. It felt like home. This place was different, but Jak recognised the vibe of a faerie forest. She had grown up on the boundary of one her whole life. It seemed suddenly strange that the wild twisting branches groping out for her could feel safe, or that the shadows and creaking of trees could be homey. The canopy was thick and dark green above them. It began just over their heads, close enough to touch, and reached up further than Jak could imagine.

"Is this Fäsaírm?" she asked in wonder.

"No," Olíriá shook her head. "This is one of the oldest forests in the world. It's called Vætor-ō-Ĝōul. This is where Ĝoŕgomghōul slew the last dragon. This was the place the war ended and balance was restored, just before they crowned Clōudiá. Fäsaírm rests in the centre of Vætor-ō-Ĝōul, and the area is still considered Ĝoŕgomghōul's territory." The goddess smiled to herself. "However, Thænäri's creatures will venture here. Those two were always close. Thænäri was closer to Wisdom than anyone else ever was. Which I guess is how we got Jim in the first place..."

Jak didn't want to think about it, but she would concede that it was curious to think that Nature and Wisdom had resulted in Jim. This forest was what that looked like. The further they travelled, the stranger the forest became. Tiny lights like fireflies danced through the air, but their colours changed and faded as they moved. Beneath the undergrowth, the earth shimmered. The rocks here shone and sparkled dimly in the half light under the canopy.

They rode by a cluster of toadstools that came up to Jak's shoulder. The red and white fungi became larger and larger as they rode through. By the time they were over Jak's head, she barely recognised them. From underneath, they looked like a circle of crinkled, closed fans. Half of her wanted to reach out and touch them, but half of her was still riding nervously to avoid them. She knew what legends told of people who trespassed in faerie circles.

Still, it was hard to feel afraid in the magical forest. Part of her knew she should. She was a mortal in a world that wasn't her own, but she was with Olíriá. More than that, this felt like somewhere she belonged.

The trees began to thin out, and yet Jak felt the essence of the forest stronger than ever. The ground sloped up and Olíriá led them through long grass, up a small hillock surrounded by higher peaks. At the top of the hill was a twisted tree. It stood alone, and it stood so mighty that no other trees dared near it. As they rode closer, Jak realised it was two trees. A yew and a birch. The two trees had grown in a twisted spiral together until they had become one tree. From the bottom of the hill it had seemed a mere tree. The closer they got, the more massive it became, until it seemed to dwarf the mountains around it. The rest of the forest hung back from it, if only so that the smaller trees could still feel the sunshine. Only grass grew in its shadow.

Jak felt her jaw drop as they neared it. She didn't know how reality was warping around the tree, but it had to be. There was some kind of magic about it. Nothing could be that big. The roots crawled out and tangled over the top of the hill, standing higher than a castle. At the base, where the two trees met, there was a gap between them. A small crack like the entrance to a cave. Inside was only darkness. The tree stood so tall Jak could never hope to reach the branches, and the canopy itself became the sky. She couldn't imagine it ever shedding leaves.

"What is it?" she asked in awe.

"This is Fäsaírm," Olíriá answered, dismounting and laying a gentle hand on the bark of a tree root. "This is the entrance to the binding between worlds. This is where Ĝoŕgomghōul lives."

Jak also dismounted, slowly, staring into the darkness of the gap. A darkness so pure she had never seen its like. A cold wind blew out of the entrance. A thousand times colder than the evening breeze. The chill it sent through her body rattled her bones. This was the realm of the god of darkness. This was where the Head Hunters were born.

"Do you still want to do this, Jak?" Olíriá asked.

"I have to," Jak insisted. She knew it as she said it too. She had promised the D'Ihne that she would help. Their petty vengeances had been costing human lives since time began. She needed to do what she could to stop them from making it worse.

Even if staring down the darkness now made her wish she didn't have to.

With a deep breath, she squared her shoulders and set off between the trees into Fäsaírm.

CHAPTER EIGHTEEN

It was a dry cold. It sent shivers down her body and Jak pulled her cloak tight against it. The darkness pressed in on all sides. It was thick and cloying. The first scents had been of dirt and decay. It was impossible to see, but it felt like stepping into an underground tunnel. It felt like it travelled deep under the earth, into the heart of the world. Yet, at the same time, as she walked forward, Jak felt like she was travelling to another realm entirely. The sounds that came back at her were echoes, as though from two separate spaces, and neither were the world she had just left.

The ground was hard under her feet and the soles of her boots clipped on it. The noise bounced back. From one side it came muffled and whispery. From the other it was clear and clean. Where the sounds met in the middle was like the sigh of a bell, and Jak paused as she listened. It was a pulsing clang, but it was soft like the beating wings of a moth.

"What is that?" Jak whispered, hoping Olíriá was still near her. Her voice was snatched away by the darkness around her and distorted both ways. She twisted around to see where her whispers went, but there was no sense of space anymore. The idea of walls was long gone. A voice spoke behind her, but it was not

Olíriá who answered.

"That is the heartbeat of your world. Where immortality meets death. The sound of life. The balance of existence."

Jak turned. A giant cauldron, almost as tall as her, sat on a stone floor. It looked like it had been carved from black marble, with engraved runes and patterns, and heavy clawed feet that dug into the stone beneath it. The fire under its belly had burnt down to little more than embers that glowed in the darkness. Most of the light came from inside the cauldron. Whatever was bubbling in its depths emitted a soft glow that illuminated the area it occupied in the middle of the darkness, and the man standing behind it. His body was completely shrouded in black robes. The face that gazed out was as pale as a skull, but his wild hair and beard were blacker than night. He looked like a colourless spectre rising out of the darkness behind the cauldron, except for his eyes. All three of them were marked with burning red irises that appeared so stark against his otherwise black and white complexion. His third eye sat in the centre of his forehead, and blinked at her with the others.

"Ĝorgomghōul," Jak addressed the god of darkness and wisdom respectfully.

"Jak of the mortal realm," he nodded to her, "and Olíriá of Roïgola'a'lanaū. What brings you both to my domain?"

Jak was aware of Olíriá standing at her shoulder, but the goddess didn't appear to be in any hurry to speak. Jak knew she had to be the one to ask, but, suddenly faced with the bogeyman from her childhood, she felt a lot less sure of herself. From here, she could just glimpse the contents of the cauldron as it simmered. It was the colour of blood.

"I seek a D'rök blade," Jak answered. Her voice quivered timidly, but she had summoned the courage to answer.

"And what would a mortal want with a D'rök blade?" Ĝoŕgomghōul asked calmly.

"I need a blade that I can use to stop Jim — uh, Fæmör — a rogue D'Ihne."

"You come seeking a blade with which to slay my first-born, and you think I will grant you this?" The faerie's tone didn't change, but Jak heard the warning in his words.

"I'm not going to slay anyone," Jak shook her head. As she said it, she knew it was true. She wasn't a killer, but that didn't mean she wasn't a fighter. "I don't need a sword to kill Jim, I just need a sword that can stop him. I need a blade that can end wars, right wrongs, and repair injustices. I'm not a murderer, and I don't have to be. If I really must, I can pretend, but mostly I just have to convince him to shut up long enough to listen to a reason other than his own."

Ĝoŕgomghōul smirked knowingly. He looked pleased with her answer. Jak felt confident in what she had said, but the dark faerie still made her uncomfortable. She turned back to look at Olíriá. The pale fae woman was vivid in the darkness, and she looked impressed with her companion.

"Your request intrigues me," the god nodded, gazing into his cauldron. "However, a blade that could stop a D'Ihne is no small thing. You cannot have something from nothing, and a sacrifice must be made to cast such an item from magic. The D'rö-Hadās bring me the heads of their victims in return for their D'rök blades. What would you offer, Jak of the Mortals?"

Jak thought about it. Jim had told her once that Ĝoŕgomghōul had mastered the art of magic without sacrifice, but she felt like that wasn't wholly true. It couldn't be. The god was right; you couldn't get something from nothing. They had found a way to burn something else — some new type of magic, but Jak wasn't privy to it. She couldn't ask. She could only go with the five stages of magic Crŷs had taught her about, and she knew which one was required to create a D'rök blade...

"I can't offer you the life of another," she answered timidly. "I'm not prepared to take it. There's no point offering mine, because I can't use a sword if I'm dead."

"Then don't offer me a life," Ĝoŕgomghōul replied.

Jak swallowed nervously. There were legends she knew of the heroes of old. Stories of demigods that had bartered with the D'Ihne, giving up eyes and ears and limbs in return for wisdom and power. She was on the precipice of such a deal, but what to offer? She needed to be able to fight. It was what she was good at. There was no point offering something that rendered her unable to wield the blade. If Jim saw her crippled, it didn't matter how intimidating the sword was, he wouldn't be afraid. So it had to be something that cost without crippling. She didn't feel like there was all that much of her that wasn't essential. Maybe a kidney?

She'd heard you could survive with only one of those, but what kind of sacrifice was that? What kind of sword would she get from an organ? She needed a sword that could defend the innocent and protect the weak. She needed…

"I can offer you a piece of myself," she mumbled. "A rib? Would that make a D'rök blade?"

She heard Olíriá hiss sharply behind her.

"If I take it from you myself, yes, it would," Ĝoŕgomghōul answered. "Is that what you are offering?"

Jak looked back at the goddess behind her. Olíriá's blue eyes were clear, but unreadable. She knew this would work, but her expression gave away no indication as to whether or not she thought Jak should make the deal. It was her decision alone. Jak turned back to the faerie by the cauldron.

"I am."

"Then we have an accord. Remove your coverings and approach the cauldron, child." A white skeletal hand appeared from the swathes of robes and motioned her forward. Ĝoŕgomghōul had already turned all three eyes away to search the darkness. Jak discarded her cloak and shrugged out of her vest.

"You don't have to do this, Jak," Olíriá whispered nervously at her shoulder.

"Do not fear your guilt, Olíriá," Ĝoŕgomghōul bade her, without looking back at them. "I know well that Crŷstïar told you not to come here. I have seen things the likes of which you have not yet dreamed of. I know the sequence of events that led to this moment. I know who this girl is, how she is connected to my first born, and the plans destiny has laid out for them. You do not control as much as you think. From what I have seen, perhaps, you are simply playing a part as much as any of us. Your guilt brought her here, would you have it make her decision too? Are you that afraid of it?"

Jak looked between the two faeries. Ĝoŕgomghōul wasn't watching them, and Olíriá looked torn.

"It's no one's decision but mine," Jak stated. "And I've decided." She pulled her shirt off over her head and dropped it at her feet with her vest and cloak. Her arms wrapped around her torso self-consciously as soon as her hands were free, and the action staved off the cold of the darkness. She approached the cauldron slowly. For all her bravado in making the decision, she couldn't ignore the sharp fear gnawing at her gut. At the edge of the cauldron she stopped and looked in. It definitely looked like blood.

A hand rested on her shoulder. Jak looked back to see Olíriá standing with her. Ĝoŕgomghōul looked back to them with a nod. That was not new information to him. He stared back into the cauldron. Jak followed his gaze to the bubbling red liquid.

"A sword to strike fear into the hearts of men and gods and faeries," Ĝoŕgomghōul mused. "A sword to end wars and save the fae. You are ready to trade?"

"I am," Jak nodded.

Ĝoŕgomghōul looked up. His three red eyes blinked gently at her, then his gaze lifted to Olíriá.

"Hold her," he ordered.

Jak felt Olíriá pull her arms behind her back. The fae

woman's pale hands were strong and determined, and Jak could feel herself trembling in return. Ĝoŕgomghōul stepped around the cauldron and drew a wicked-looking, curved blade from under his robes. The light from the cauldron glinted off the weapon. Jak realised what was about to happen. She opened her mouth to protest — to recant, but he struck before she could beg him to wait.

The knife bit into her flesh. She screamed as he sliced into her side. The dark fae's skeletal face remained passive and his red eyes didn't blink. Jak writhed and screamed at him to stop. She knew she was changing her mind, but it was too late now. He cut into her with the skill and patience of a surgeon. She could feel him sawing through her rib. Slowly hacking it from her spine.

Olíriá had an arm around Jak's shoulders, over her chest. She pinned the girl back against her own body. Jak was sobbing. She could feel hot blood gush from her side. Olíriá's hands seemed to be all over her at once. She struggled, but she couldn't gain an inch. The goddess had her trapped at every angle. The pain was unimaginable, unlike anything she had known before. Whatever she had thought she was getting herself into, she had not been prepared for this. Jak screamed and begged them to stop. To let her go.

With a sharp and painful snap, Ĝoŕgomghōul broke the bone free. Jak collapsed. Her legs gave way from the pain and blood loss. The only thing holding her up was Olíriá, and the goddess had her tightly. Jak's head rested back against Olíriá's shoulder. She could feel her own tears wet between her face and the goddess' skin. It felt like her brain had stopped. She couldn't think. There was nothing but the haze of pain and panic.

One of Olíriá's hands was against her side. Jak could feel the gentle touch against her searing wound. She was vaguely aware that the wound felt wet, but that nothing else did. There wasn't enough of her mind working to interpret what that meant. She felt half dead. It hurt to breathe.

Ĝoŕgomghōul turned away. His long, elegant hands were drenched red and he held her glistening bone between them. With loving care, he placed the severed rib into the bubbling liquid of the cauldron. It sank beneath the surface.

Jak felt everything go dark. Her whole body was shaking, spasming… she felt like she was dying. Olíriá still held her tightly as the goddess sank them both gently to the floor. Jak lay shivering on Olíriá's lap with her eyes closed. She could feel the faerie trembling beneath her as well. Olíriá's grip was no longer strong. She'd been spending magic.

"When the blade is forged you alone must take it and walk it from Fäsaírm," Ĝoŕgomghōul told the slumped girl. "It will seal the blade as yours. If you cannot own it in the moment of its creation, it will never truly belong to you."

Jak was too weak to respond, but she had heard him. Now she could do little more than lie on the floor and breathe weakly, but she spared a prayer that the sword would take a while to create. She needed the recovery time. Reality was slowly starting to come back into focus, and she was vaguely aware that she wasn't bleeding. Olíriá had been healing her. She was still in agony and she was too weak to talk, let alone move, but she wasn't actually dying. She didn't know how the goddess had done it, but it had cost her too.

The cauldron was bubbling fiercely. Jak couldn't see inside it from where she and Olíriá were sprawled, but she could hear it. The light from inside it was flickering and darkening. Something was happening. As she lay there, she could feel her body trembling uncontrollably from the trauma. The shaking didn't stop, but she slowly began to regain control of her breathing. Strength returned to her legs with a tingling sensation. She couldn't stand yet, but she could feel them. She could tense her toes in her boots. Jak took a deep breath. Her side pulled with a searing pain that nearly sent her crashing again. But she could breathe. She wasn't gasping. Tentatively, she forced another breath. She could do this.

"Olíriá?" she rasped weakly.

"Yes, Jak?" Her reply was soft.

"How long does it take to make a D'rök blade?"

"I don't know," she answered. "I've never been here before."

Jak tried to comprehend that, and then she realised what the goddess meant. She had been to Fäsaírm before, but she'd never entered Ĝorgomghōul's lair before. It was probably taboo with the fae. Or it was just well established that the god of darkness didn't like company. Jim had described Ĝorgomghōul's magic as more powerful than the rest of the gods. If that was true, then the dark fae was probably feared by his own kind. It made sense that they kept their distance.

Jak took another breath as she prepared to ask her next question, but the words never made it to her lips. Inside the cauldron, Ĝoŕgomghōul's magic was boiling. Jak's missing rib seared as the power cracked through it. Even though it had been cut from her body, she felt it. The scream choked her and barely stuttered out. Her eyes rolled up in her head. Everything went dark.

When she blinked again she was back home. It was dark. Night had fallen and no one had lit the fire. Not even candles were burning. Still, from the faint starlight spilling through the windows, Jak recognised the old hut. She could smell home. Everything was just how they had left it. She stood in the main room with the kitchen bench to her back and the scrubbed wooden table before her. The pain in her chest was marked by a desperate yearning for the life she had lost. In this house she was still a child. Her parents would be through in their room. She was home, with her family, and she didn't have to grow up.

She stepped forward. The floorboards creaked under her feet. The sound sent a great tearing shriek through the hut. Jak froze. She watched in horror as the centre of the floor began to buckle and bulge. It thumped like a heartbeat. Like something was trying to break through. With a crash, the floor burst up. Jak collapsed back with a cry. The table and chairs went flying. The floorboards splintered and snapped. Beneath them, the bubbling liquid of the cauldron seethed. It had turned dark in colour, and a faint green steam wafted up from the hole.

It drifted lazily into the room like a green mist. It didn't come alone.

Something else began to climb from the hole. Something made of shadow. Something so dark the night shied away from it. Something so dark the sun wouldn't risk rising in its presence. It rose head and shoulders from the bubbling ooze. Where it sprouted, nothing could be seen beneath it, and soon the liquid was no more than a memory. The figure shifted. What had momentarily appeared humanoid was suddenly sharp. Everywhere. Spikes protruded from the darkness. It was nothing but teeth and claws. Still it grew. It went higher. Larger.

Jak lurched back. The pain in her side nearly crippled her, but the spikes where shooting towards her. The darkness grew. It wouldn't stop growing. It hit the roof. It tore straight through it. Jak cried and threw herself down as the roof exploded over her head. Splinters rained around her. Spikes shot into the wall over her head. They shredded through the cupboards behind her. Spikes shot out of the spikes, and still the body of the darkness rose further. Jak curled up tighter in her desperate attempt to avoid being impaled. She couldn't run. She was too badly injured to try and escape. She lay sprawled on the floor and looked up through the nest of spikes blocking out the sky. A shadow in the night.

She blinked. From this angle she could see the darkness rising. The spikes reaching into the sky. Branches. A tree. A single tree, that on its own was nearly as big as Fäsaírm, and was still growing. Jak reached out a hand and took hold of one of the spikes. With an effort that made her cry out in pain, she hauled herself onto the branch. It pulled her off the floor as it kept growing. She held on tightly. The tighter she held, the less fear she felt.

This was home. This was the forest. Every forest. All life. She had known this feeling since before she was born. It was a part of her. The wildness of the forest. The untameable fierceness of nature. It was part of her soul. She could feel the magic of the fae in every living thing. The energy that comprised their true forms was the force that drove existence. It was in everything. That was what made them immortal. They couldn't die. They had to be unmade. She understood. She grabbed a small branch that had begun to grow out of the one she clung to. She snapped it off.

Jak woke with a jerk, still shivering in Olíriá's lap on the cold floor. The first thing she saw was the blade. It was a longsword with a simple hilt. The entire piece glinted in dark steel. Runes Jak didn't recognise ran up the centre of the blade. They burned fiercely. Ĝorgomghōul held the blade up by the hilt, pointing it at the ceiling. His three red eyes were all on Jak. It was the moment of truth.

With all the strength she could summon, Jak hauled herself off the floor. Ĝorgomghōul held out the blade.

"Behold, Shrïgkyvsh," he intoned in his godly voice. "Named Godslayer in Old Fae — the language we spoke before the age of our children. Take him in your grasp, name him, and walk him from Fäsaírm alone. Once complete, he can never be used against you."

Jak reached out her hand. One arm was pressed tightly to the side of her body where she could feel the missing rib. She couldn't make it come away. All of her instincts were overriding to make her keep pressure on the wound. She was going to have to do this one handed. She curled her fingers around the warm hilt.

"Shrïgkyvsh," she repeated as clearly as she could, and lifted the blade from Ĝoŕgomghōul's grasp. Her hand shook and wavered like a leaf on the breeze, but all her strength gripped the hilt as tightly as she could and she didn't let the blade fall. Ĝoŕgomghōul smiled at her and gave her a slight nod. "Thank you," she said, her voice trembling as she spoke her gratitude, not just for the sword, but for the wisdom he had also been gracious enough to impart.

"You are welcome," he smiled, clearly pleased that she knew what she had been given. "But it is not over yet, and you are still in Fäsaírm. Until next time, Jak of the Mortal Realm." He bowed his head and closed his eyes.

Jak took the hint. She turned slowly and began to stagger back the way they had come. Olíriá was watching her with giant terrified eyes. The goddess gave the girl and her weapon a wide birth. Jak pushed on. Her steps dragged. Her hand shook. She keeled sideways. The arm holding the sword crashed into the wall, but she kept herself propped upright. Her other hand was wet. The wound was bleeding again. Jak gritted her teeth. She pushed forward.

Shrïgkyvsh was a part of her. It was made from her. Born of her bone and blood and pain. Born of her sacrifice. She couldn't fail. She had to carry it from the realm of the gateway. She had to bring it into the mortal world. Her world. She could feel blood running down her leg. Just a little further. There was light up ahead. She could hear Olíriá calling out from behind her. She couldn't make out any words. Her blood was pounding in her ears. Just a little bit more.

The doorway was visible now. Blood was running into her boot. She dragged her soles across the ground. Her footsteps shuffled. She staggered. A groan escaped her lips. It hurt. Everything hurt. So much. She pushed herself off the wall with the arm holding Shrïgkyvsh aloft. A little more. She was panting now. Her other hand was tight on her wound. Both hands gripped with all the force she could muster. One on the sword, and the other trying to stop her bleeding out.

With the last of her strength, Jak forced herself through the doorway of the two entwined trees. Night had fallen and everything beneath the canopy was truly dark. Jak remembered the tree of darkness that had destroyed her home. The heart of nature. There was soft grass beneath her. The rustle of branches above her. She was back where she belonged. She was home. She raised the sword above her head. Her arm was shaking so hard the trembling ran into a quake through her entire body. She could feel the strain in her toes.

"Shrïgkyvsh," she announced to the world. Her voice didn't tremble. With a cry, she drove the sword down. The perfect blade pierced the soft dirt and slid into the earth. Jak kept her hand on the hilt, now positioned perfectly at her waist. Her grip slackened.

She didn't have to hold on anymore. Her eyes rolled up. She fainted.

***

Jak woke to a crackle and pop. Fire flickered at the edge of her vision. She was warm and safe. Her body was too heavy to move, but she had no reason to. She felt like she could lie there forever. Unfortunately, the world had other plans, and now that she was awake, the pain was beginning to return. It blossomed like a spring flower in her side, growing and opening. Roots of pain stretched through her abdomen and into her spine. She groaned weakly.

"I see you're awake again…" Olíriá commented nearby.

Jak turned her head and blinked weakly. The goddess was kneeling by the fire, carefully tending it. It was still night. They had moved back near the treeline of the forest, but the edges of Fäsaírm's canopy still sheltered them from the world and blocked the sky. Jak was lying on the grass near the fire. She was wrapped snug in her cloak, with her shirt and vest tucked as a pillow beneath her head. Olíriá wasn't looking at her. The firelight made the faerie look more golden than silvery. Her pale hair and bare skin still shimmered in a way that gave Jak butterflies, but she looked weary. Jak groaned again and tried to shift.

"Careful," Olíriá warned. "The wound is still fresh. Try not to move it."

Jak moved her hand up under the cloak. She could

feel thick bandages around her torso.

"How did I get like this?" she muttered.

"How do you think?" Olíriá responded drily.

Jak struggled and grunted weakly on the ground for a moment, but couldn't lift herself up. The faerie sighed.

"You can't sit up, Jak. You're too weak to support yourself. You lost a lot of blood and right now you just need to rest."

"Can you help heal me magically?" Jak asked.

"What do you think I've been doing?" Olíriá replied. "The way he cut you was fatal, Jak. Without my magic, you would have died, and he knew that when he did it. What you asked for was unlike anything I have known him to make. He had to take a steep price to create it. He took your life — your pain as you died from a wound he inflicted and the bone that was promised. I spent your blood making sure that wound didn't kill you like it should have."

"Thank you..." Jak whispered. "I... I didn't..."

"I know," Olíriá sighed. "I know, Jak. What you did was incredibly brave and stupid. I just hope it pays off."

"It will," Jak insisted. Her hand tightened on the bandages firmly. "You saw Shrïgkyvsh. This will pay off. Where is he?"

"At your side," Olíriá answered darkly.

Jak looked down and saw the dark hilt glinting beside her. The blade was encased in a tough brown scabbard.

"You made that?" Jak asked.

"I borrowed one of Ínrío's," Olíriá admitted. "He doesn't know I borrowed it. That thing needs to stay covered, Jak. You can't just go waving it around. It is a powerful and dangerous weapon. Arguably, it should never have been made."

"Making Shrïgkyvsh was the whole point of coming here!" Jak protested weakly from the ground. "Why are you so angry that it worked? I thought you supported this plan."

"I supported you getting a D'rök blade to wave in Jim's face and convince him to back down," Olíriá glared. "I don't support this. Jak, I don't think you realise what he gave you. That blade is an abomination. It is a threat to the existence of my people. Forget using it, if you so much as draw that blade in the presence of D'Ihne, you will have the attention of the world." Olíriá glared over the flames and stoked the fire gently. "It is easy to forget that the hermit is the biggest show-off of us all..." she growled.

"That's where Jim gets it from?"

"Some could argue," Olíriá agreed with a shrug. She stiffened suddenly and cocked her head. Her long fae ears twitched. "Do you hear that?"

"Hear what?"

Olíriá stood slowly and stared intently out into the trees. "We just had to speak of him, didn't we..." she growled.

Jak could hear it now. That familiar bumping rattle. Her heart skipped a beat at the sound. Half of her felt elation at the familiar and safe sound of the caravan, but half of her realised what that meant and panic aggravated her pain. She couldn't move. She couldn't even sit up. Just trying sent crippling waves of pain through her side. She was worried she was going to tear the wound open again. She finally had the sword, but Jim was here — the showdown was here — and she couldn't wield it.

The sound of the Banging Wagon was too loud to ignore now. Its creaking wheels clattered through the forest path towards their campfire. Jak felt her grip tighten on her bandage when she heard the familiar chuckle. The banging stopped, and signalled the arrival of their company. He was as droll as ever when he spoke, and Jak realised with a flicker of surprise that his accent came from his father. She hadn't noticed in the cavern, but Ĝoŕgomghōul had the same lilt in his voice she had always associated with Jim.

"Fancy seeing you two here," the god of pleasure drawled as he parked up.

"If it's all the same, Jim, we could really do without your company at the moment," Olíriá replied. She had stood between the god and the girl.

"And if it's all the same with you, Olí, I want to have a word with you ladies before you do something stupid." His boots clopped casually on the stairs as he clambered down from the wagon. He brushed by Olíriá with a smirk, and she made no move to stop him. Jak saw him stroll into view in his human form. It was the only skin she'd ever really known him in. Short dark hair, warm brown eyes, and those dimples. He flashed them at her as he approached. "But it looks like I'm a little late for that… huh, Jellybean?"

Jak didn't say anything. She just glared up at him. Jim squatted down beside her and looked her up and down.

"If I didn't know any better, I'd say someone's been visiting daddy." He met her eye without changing expression once. "You got that look."

"I have a sword—" Jak began to threaten.

"Oh, I bet you do, and I'm only going to say this once — because these are unholy words that probably shouldn't be spoken at all — but, maybe don't pull it out and wave it around just now." Jim flicked his gaze up to Olíriá. "How bad is it?"

Olíriá looked down on them with her arms folded. She held herself defensively, and there seemed to be a reason for abiding Jim.

"It's not good," she admitted finally. "She won't die, but it's not good."

Jim finally stopped smiling. Jak watched as the darkness flickered in his eyes. She'd only seen it a few times before, but somehow it was even more frightening now that she knew where it came from. He stuck his fingers in his mouth and gave a sharp whistle. Without taking his eyes off the girl on the ground, Jim reached out a hand to gently pull the cloak back.

"Keep your hands off me!" Jak snarled.

"Oh shhh shh shh," Jim waved her off dismissively as he pulled back the cloak. Jak blushed as he exposed her bra and skin to the eyes of the world, but not even he seemed to be looking that way. His eyes were on the bandages around her ribs. Her hand pressed tighter to her side. She realised the wrappings beneath her hand were red, and her body dipped in more than it used to. Jim grimaced as he took the sight in.

The back door of the wagon banged open and Jak heard footsteps clambering down. She only heard one set, but she could sense both faeries.

"Jak!" Kode's familiar voice cried out, and his footsteps sped up. He raced to her side. Krill was not far behind.

"Hey guys," Jak grimaced at them as they gathered around her. Jim was prying her fingers away to get at the bandages. Jak didn't even know if she should be trying to resist. She had done this to stop him, but now that he was here, he looked like he wanted to help. His lovers even more so. Kode crashed down at her side. The sweet fae looked down on her tenderly, and concern creased his lavender eyes. He took Jak's hand in his own to keep it out of the way. As he laced his fingers through hers, she felt an intense calm wash over her and the pain seemed to almost disappear. Jim pulled the bandages away and hissed at the sticky mess beneath.

"Fuck me sideways," Krill cursed, crouching down at Jim's side.

"Maybe later," Jim interjected, both of them staring at the bloody mess. Krill ignored his boyfriend and peered closer. His elegant face was twisted in a grimace.

"He butchered her," Krill growled.

"You sound surprised, my love," Jim smiled. "I mean… Dad was always renowned for his mercy and kindness…" He sat back thoughtfully. "No, wait… that was you, wasn't it?" He pointed at Olíriá. "You're the only one of all of us who was ever reputed to be merciful and kind — which I'm guessing is why we can be grateful our girl here is still breathing?"

"Olíriá saved my life," Jak answered dreamily. She felt so soft and sleepy and peaceful holding Kode's hand. His grip was warm and strong. The warmth it sent down her arm was pleasantly tingling, like sinking into a hot bath, and her whole body felt completely relaxed.

"As grateful as I am," Jim continued, looking up at Olíriá. "It looks like you panicked." He smirked. "Performance issues in front of the father-in-law?"

Olíriá didn't smile. "I was the one who had to hold her while he did that. I had to keep her from struggling so that it wasn't any worse, and I had to keep the injuries from killing her while he did it. So yeah," she glared. "I panicked a bit."

"Why didn't you just say no, Olí?" he sighed. "Why didn't you just stop it?"

"Because it was her decision," the goddess replied, sinking back down by the fire. "She wanted this. She wanted the D'rök blade. She wanted to trade a rib for it. She wanted to prove herself. I'm not her mother, Jim. I wasn't going to undermine her by negating her deal. She chose this. I just held her hand."

They both looked down on the dozy Jak. Krill was carefully inspecting the wound in her side. He looked up at them and his golden eyes glinted in the firelight.

"I can fix some of this," he told them.

"Do what you can," Jim nodded at him. The god looked up at Olíriá as Krill got to work. He stood and crossed over to her. Olíriá didn't shy away as Jim sat down next to her. Instead, she rested her head against his shoulder as he put a comforting arm around her. It was a good thing Jak was half asleep. Jim sighed and kissed Olíriá's forehead.

"You're too gentle to have been the one left to do this," he told her.

"And yet I managed," she replied. "I always do. The rest of you are always so quick to dismiss me —"

"We don't dismiss you, Olí. We admire you."

"Then be more like me," she retorted. "Crŷs is the one who always saw it. He knows. You all marvel at how kind I am. You think it makes me soft. Kindness, Jim, makes you hard enough to always do what has to be done. The rest of you could learn a lot about it." They were silent together for a moment until she sighed. "And yet here you are..."

"Here I am," he agreed. "And I want her to be okay too."

"When I wanted to teach you how to love, it never occurred to me that you would come to love so many..." she smiled.

Jim chuckled. "What can I say? When I get a new talent I take it and run with it."

"You are a show-off," she agreed. "If things had been different... if all our positions had been reversed, and you had been the one with her, what would you have done?"

"I wouldn't have let her do it," Jim answered instantly. "I would have talked her out of it."

"You're not her mother either, James," Olíriá sighed. "It is not your position to make her decisions for her."

"I might not be her parent..." Jim admitted. "But...

she told me once that I make a pretty good big brother."

Olíriá stared at him. The second she realised he wasn't joking, she erupted into peals of laughter. Jim pulled a wry face. Olíriá curled up over her knees as she laughed. Kode was grinning at them openly, and Krill was biting his bottom lip to keep focused. He still glanced up and met her eye. They both knew. She could see it. She laughed harder.

"Okay, sure," Jim grumbled. "I can see why this is funny… but it's not *that* funny."

"Oh Jim," Olíriá laughed. "If you only knew… I take it she said that before she learnt who you were?"

"I took good care of those girls, Olí," Jim insisted.

"I know," she agreed. Her gentle blue eyes regarded Jak's peaceful face. "I know you did, because I remember watching her cry when she talked about you leaving. You broke her heart, Jim." Olíriá took a deep breath and sighed. "You do that to a lot of people."

"I suppose I must…" he agreed wryly. "Given that I don't even know specifically who you're talking about. But I don't mean to. I didn't want to hurt her, Olí. I was trying to protect them."

"I know," she kissed his cheek. "But look where your protection has gotten her. She nearly died trying to find a way to stop you. Don't make her fight you, Jim."

He turned his dark eyes on her sharply. She met his look. Their gazes stayed locked. His was defensive. Hers was imploring. Both were unrelenting.

"Give it up, Jim," Olíriá requested. "Give back the crown. Tell them it was a joke. Prove to everyone you're a better prankster than your little brother and that you showed him up. Again. Let him wear this shame, just don't start this war."

"You think I want this?" Jim turned on her. "You think Crŷs has even crossed my mind or that I give a single solitary fuck about his reputation? Roïgola'a'lanaū is my home. I love it. There is nowhere in any realm of existence more beautiful than the Golden City, and my heart would shatter into a thousand pieces if it burned. But it was built and run on the backs of slavery and I cannot be complicit in that. It has to stop. I cannot believe you of all people would ask me to stand aside and let them keep doing this."

"Well, I am," she snapped. "I'm scared, Jim. I saw what your father made for Jak, and it frightens me. He created that monstrosity, and he gave it to a mortal. I am scared for my people. I am scared for my city. I am scared for all our kind and what you might be about to unleash on them by starting something you can't finish."

"Look at them," Jim ordered. The god and goddess didn't break eye contact. He repeated his command with a roar so fierce his voice changed timbre. "Look at them! You know exactly who I mean, Olíriá. Look at them!"

Slowly, she turned her eyes to the two Ha'Cās sitting by the fire. Both were sombre in the wake of Jim's outburst. Krill kept his eyes on his work as he hunched over the wounded girl. Slowly and painstakingly, he spent runes to mend and stitch her torn flesh. Kode sat at her side, with her hand clasped in both of his, but he met Olíriá's eyes. He blinked gently at her. Olíriá was reminded of a deer, or a rabbit. Something sweet, innocent, and pure. Something naïve. Like a child. The D'Ihne considered her kind. She had nothing on this simple creature who had given his whole life over to making other people happy.

She also knew, as though Jim's gaze was stabbing it into the side of her brain, just how much Kode had suffered in Roïgola'a'lanaū. The young faerie always saw the good, and most of his memories of his time in the Golden City were pleasant. But not all of them were. It was her own father who had been the worst culprit. That was how Krill had found him. Olíriá and the former D'Hiris shared a parent. A parent they both knew had a penchant for great cruelty.

"You're scared because right now it's not you suffering," Jim warned. "But you can't tell me they don't, Olíriá. I know they do. You know that mine are always the most mistreated, because people get nasty when it comes to sex. You think I haven't taken Frézían to task hundreds of times for the way he treats mine? He doesn't care, because they are slaves and they have nowhere else to go. It's also not like he's alone. Olí, this is wrong. You know it's wrong. It has to stop, and I won't stop until it does. The Ha'Cās deserve to choose. They are owed that freedom."

Olíriá dropped her gaze and turned back to him. He could see the tears in her eyes, but she wouldn't cry.

"Think about what you're asking, Olí," Jim insisted. "If our positions were reversed, if you could have your precious, safe, little world back and all you had to do was lock Crŷs up and throw away the key, do you think

I'd even ask?"

Olíriá pressed her lips together tightly. She knew the answer to that question, and it made her feel ashamed. With a trembling breath, she replied.

"Then I won't ask again, but I will ask for space." She stood, and didn't wait for a reply. His accepting silence was the only one he gave, and he let her go without protest. She stepped lightly across the grass and vanished into the trees. Jim turned his gaze back to the others. Krill met his eyes around the fire.

"Even for you, that was impressive," the faerie murmured.

"You think so?" Jim smiled.

"Sometimes," Krill began softly, "I am astounded by how beautiful you can be in a human body." The Ha'Cās watched the god tenderly, but his smile was strained, and sweat beaded his forehead from the effort of magic he spent. Rune magic could heal minor cuts and abrasions. A wound like this was the equivalent of thousands of small cuts, and each rune could only heal one. He was burning magic rapidly.

Kode took one hand from Jak to reach out. He used the edge of his shirt to dab his husband's forehead. Once it was dry, he kissed it gently. Krill smiled and continued working. Jim watched them both with the eyes of someone completely devoted, yet touched at the edges by anger. He stood and retreated to the wagon. The soles of his boots thudded softly on the wooden interior, but he was only gone a moment. He returned with fresh, clean bandages and approached the group.

"Here," he knelt down at Krill's side. "Let me have a

go."

Krill sat back wearily and wiped his face. He had only made it roughly a quarter of the way around her side, at best a third. Jim raised a hand over Jak's wound. It was the same gesture he had used healing Dora. He marked no runes. He spoke no words. He made no discernible trade of blood or soul or flesh. A faint purple light burned in the centre of his palm. The same violet light shone in his eyes and erased the warm brown. His skin paled and his face thinned as his illusion faltered. Beneath his hand, Jak's wound began to stitch itself back together like a zip fastening in her skin. It pulled slowly, but noticeably faster than Krill's work had been. Jim didn't break a sweat, but the longer he worked the brighter his eyes became.

"You know she's out there contacting the others, don't you?" Krill asked Jim.

"Olí has to do what's right for her," Jim replied evenly as his magic slowly burned.

"And us? She will be telling them everything. What we've done. Where to find us. What do we do?"

"We stay here and heal Jak," Jim answered like it was the most obvious thing in the world. Krill watched him a moment, before kissing his brow and standing slowly. The faerie looked unsteady on his feet, but he took a deep breath and seemed to stabilise himself. He reached down a hand and stroked Kode's hair.

"Are you alright?" he asked his husband. Kode nodded, but he too looked tired. Ĝoŕgomghōul had required a powerful sacrifice to be made to create Jak's new sword, and it had taken a lot out of all of them to try to heal her. She would never be the same. Jim saw the toll it had taken on them. He slowly squeezed his hand into a fist and the last of the savage cut knitted together. It still left a large and angry red wound across her side. A good deal more healing would be required.

"That's enough for now," Jim gasped, letting his hand drop. He sat on the grass, half in and half out of his human form. It was strangely alien. Enough to pass for human over D'Ihne, but not enough to convince anyone he wasn't at least part faerie. Through it all, his violet eyes burned bright. "You can let her go, Kody. She'll be okay."

Kode nodded and slowly let Jak's hand drop. He looked at his lovers trustingly, and then, as one, they turned their eyes to Jak. She groaned weakly. Jim and Krill looked on empathetically. They knew better than anyone what Kode's touch could be like, and how harsh everything could feel when it was gone. Krill could remember his own weeks of lying in bed while the wound in his side healed.

"Ow..." Jak murmured weakly.

"How you feeling, Jellybean?"

"Everything hurts..."

"Yeah..." Jim chuckled. "That's the feeling of consequences."

"You'll be alright," Krill added softly, as Kode squeezed her shoulder. "But you need to rest and recover. Your injury is no small thing. It will take time to heal."

"I don't have time," Jak muttered.

"Why?" Jim asked. "What's so urgent?"

"I have a homicidal maniac to stop."

"Well," Jim smiled and brushed her cheek with the back of his fingers. "How about I hold off until you get better? A fight isn't fun if it isn't fair, and Krill is right, you need to rest. In fact, we could all do with a rest."

"Someone should keep an eye on Jak," Krill suggested. "I don't want to leave her like this with no one around."

"I'll stay," Jim offered. Krill paused. Jim gave him a sardonic look. "Really? She's lying on the ground bleeding and I just helped patch the hole. What don't you trust?"

The pause lasted another second, and then Krill sighed.

"Nothing," he answered apologetically. "Nothing. I'm sorry. Of course I trust you." Krill leant down and kissed the top of Jim's head. He helped pull Kode up from the ground and the two started towards the caravan. Krill paused again. "I'm going to go and check on Olíriá. See you inside?"

Kode nodded. The two of them kissed. Krill vanished into the forest and Kode disappeared into the caravan. Jim stayed sitting in the grass by Jak. She lay there stiffly and the fire crackled and spat beside them. The orange light was warm in the thick dark of the night. Jak sighed deeply.

"So big a sigh for one so young..." Jim murmured.

"I just sacrificed a rib for a sword that can kill you," she replied.

"Is it a big sword?" he asked in his ever cheeky and insinuating tone.

Jak clutched her side desperately and grimaced. "Don't make me laugh!" she begged. "Please, Jim. It hurts." Jak squeezed her eyes shut and tried to sit up. Whatever they had done to heal her had restored some of her energy. She was alert enough to know how much pain she was in, but she didn't just want to lie there anymore. Jim only watched her struggle for a moment.

"Here, let me," he offered, and scooped an arm around her to help sit her up. He levered her gently upright, but it became apparent very quickly that she couldn't hold herself there, even though she was trying. He rolled his eyes. "Alright, come on." Jim scooped her up, cloak and all, and carried her to the Banging Wagon. He sat her down on the back step so that she had something to lean against. "Better?"

"Thank you," Jak sighed. She held the cloak over her otherwise exposed torso.

"Don't sweat it. You might have me at the top of your hit list, but I bear you no ill will, little Jellybean."

"You don't look like you at the moment," she commented, eyeing up the way he was still struggling to maintain the illusion.

"Yet, I don't look like anyone else either..." he mused. His gaze didn't stay on her, but looked back the way they had come. His eyes saw through the darkness, beyond the fire, to Fäsaírm. Jak watched him look. She wondered how they had come to this. She had felt close to him once. She had felt kinship for him. Right now, in the wake of his help and kindness, she could feel it again. But they were only here because she had asked for a sword with the power to put the fear of death in him. Olíriá was right; it was complicated.

"I had a dream…" Jak murmured, looking out at the gateway with him. "When I was dying in Olíriá's arms on the floor of Fäsaírm."

"That sounds kinky," Jim commented, sitting down beside her. "Details?"

"I was back home," Jak smiled, ignoring his insinuations. "And this great tree grew up. The biggest tree ever. Bigger than Fäsaírm. It was the tree everything grew from, and I took a piece of it for my sword, the same way Ĝorgomghōul took a piece from me to make it."

"I know the tree," Jim smiled.

"You know it?"

"Of course," he grinned. "Half of me is that tree."

She gave him a quizzical look. He smirked.

"I hope you get to meet the other half of my family one day," he pondered. "I think you'd like them. My mom and my brother. Not Frosty McFuckface, my other brother, Talámh. On Mom's side. Dad and Crŷs you've met. The dark blood. But my mom… my mom is the goddess of the forest. She is all that is alive and good. Talámh takes after her more than I do, but, like her, we're both deities of the people. He's the D'Ihne of travel, so he gets around too — just in a different way."

"You love these people, Jim," Jak sighed. "Why are you fighting them?"

"Because what they're doing is wrong, and I shouldn't still have to explain that — least of all to you and Olí. If anyone was going to understand, I was sure it would be you two. You know Krill and Kode. You know their story. How can you stand against me?"

"Because you're killing people. I want to help the Ha'Cās, I really do, but starting wars that will kill thousands of people is absolutely the wrong way to go."

"But you want to kill me to stop that?" He turned to look at her. His eyes were still purple, and she couldn't meet them like that. They weren't Jim, even if they were his real eyes. They were god-like.

"I don't want to kill you..." she whispered, betraying her hand. "I don't want to do that, Jim. I want there to be another way. I want to free the Ha'Cās without anyone dying."

"Then you're living the naïve fairy-tale of the young," he scoffed.

"Maybe you're just living the jaded pessimism of the old," she retorted, turning on him. As soon as she tried to stare him down, she wished she hadn't. His illusion was failing, and it was hard to stare down a god. Her time with Olíriá hadn't made it easier. Not with him. Jim was dangerous in a way Olíriá never would be. Jak had been warned about him so many times, by so many people, and he was so close right now. She could feel the warmth of his body right next to hers. She turned her face away quickly and stared at her knees.

"Are you scared of me, Jak?" he asked gently.

She didn't answer. She just bit her lip awkwardly and kept her eyes down. It wasn't a question she knew how to answer. The truth felt too hard to explain, and she was still sore.

"You shouldn't be," he encouraged, slipping from the step beside her. He stood in front of her, and his pale fingers tucked themselves under her chin to lift her face. He didn't force the action when she tried to keep her eyes down. Jim sighed and let his hand drop back. In the other, he still had the fresh bandages. "At least let me patch you up while you're sitting there."

The request sounded so sensible, but as soon as he reached for the cloak Jak tightened it around herself. She could feel his scepticism rise from there, and she shook her head.

"I am the way I am, Jim," she defended.

"You are," he agreed. "Let's see if I can help with that." He dropped the illusion completely. Jak felt her jaw drop with it. Her throat closed up and her heart started racing. Pale, delicate hands raised the clean bandages.

"Now can I help?" the goddess requested. Jak was too stunned to reply. She was too stunned to protest. The goddess Fæmör gently pulled Jak's cloak away and sat it on the seat behind the girl. With soft hands, she placed a wad of bandages over the wound around Jak's ribs. Jak just stared. She felt like she was going to have a heart attack.

Fæmör had pearlescent skin like Olíriá, but the split purple silk robe she wore was covering more of her body than it had last time Jak had seen it. She had thick black curls that tumbled around her shoulders and long dark lashes around her purple eyes. Her lips were the colour of plum and they smirked cheekily in her perfect face. She was so beautiful Jak felt like she was getting stabbed all over again.

The goddess didn't say anything as she carefully

began to wrap the bandages on and tie them around Jak's chest. Her touch was light, but firm. She moved her arms gracefully as she wound the bandages. The silk robe wasn't fastened, and as she moved it slipped. Jak glimpsed a perfect bare breast through the gap, and then realised she'd been looking for it. She couldn't breathe. She felt like a fire had been lit underneath her. Colour rushed into her face with burning ferocity. It was so hot. Everything was so hot.

"Jak? What's wrong?" Fæmör asked as she knotted the bandage. "Your heart's racing. Are you okay?"

"I just… I just need a minute," Jak gasped. She could feel sweat on the back of her neck. Fæmör didn't step back. She stayed close, pressed in, with her fingers resting gently against Jak's chest.

"You don't have to be scared of me," Fæmör whispered. "You know that, right? I would never intentionally hurt you." She raised her hand to Jak's face and let her fingers caress the girl's cheek. "I would never force you to do anything. Ever. But if you're curious…"

She leant in and pressed her lips to Jak's. Jak had never been kissed before. The goddess' lips were so soft. So sure. Before she realised what she was doing, Jak kissed her back. She raised her hands to the goddess' face. Her skin was so smooth. Jak tangled her fingers in Fæmör's curls. The faerie slipped her tongue inside Jak's mouth. It was hot and wet. Jak realised she was gasping even as they kissed. Her chest rose and fell, pressed against Fæmör's body. The wound pulled painfully and she winced sharply, but Fæmör held her gently and guided her back onto the stair.

Jak lay back, relaxed yet tense, a tornado of conflicting sensations. Her head was whirling. She felt dizzy. There was no way she could form a whole thought. Fæmör lay against her, kissing her passionately. Jak pulled the goddess to her tightly. She felt Fæmör's lips smile against hers.

"You can touch if you want…" the faerie whispered against her skin. Fæmör took Jak's hand in her own and guided it under her robe. Her skin was as soft as the silk she wore. Jak groped at her bare breasts. They were heavy and smooth in her hands. She squeezed. Her thumb brushed against one of the goddess' nipples. She could feel it harden under her touch. Jak squeezed her harder as their tongues locked again.

Fæmör's own hand traced up the inside of Jak's thigh, guiding her legs apart. Jak felt like she was going to catch fire. The warmth was spreading from her groin up her body. She didn't even notice the pain anymore. Fæmör's hand pressed firmly between her legs, and the faerie began to rub her through the fabric of her trousers. Jak moaned as the goddess' lips left hers and began to kiss down her neck. Fæmör pressed harder. Jak was panting now. She knew she was. She'd never felt anything like this. The goddess was on top of her, kissing her hot skin, moving against her. Fæmör's lips kissed down her neck, along her chest towards her bra line.

"Oh shit…" Jak moaned longingly. She tried to pull Fæmör's lips back to her, but she heard the faerie chuckling. Fæmör kissed her again, but it wasn't like it had been. Jak felt the goddess' hands leave her as she pulled away. "Wait, what…?" she gasped.

Fæmör still leant over her. The faerie pressed in and kissed Jak again, firmly and passionately. Then she pulled away and rolled to her feet. Jak tried to raise herself up. It hurt. She couldn't think. Her brain felt foggy and confused. She looked up at the goddess standing beside the wagon. Fæmör was half draped in purple silk, but the way she stood Jak could see the bare skin and flowing curves of her naked body. She was stunning. Just looking at her brought a hot lust between Jak's legs and up through her still quietly panting body.

Fæmör smirked at her. With a sickening twist, Jak recognised the smirk. Even in the most beautiful face in the world, it was still a familiar expression. The goddess approached her again. With gentle fingers, she brushed Jak's cheek and kissed the side of her face. Jak didn't try and kiss her back.

"I can't be your first, Jellybean," she purred. "I'd be your best, and I can't condemn you to a lifetime of disappointment like that."

Her fingers traced Jak's skin teasingly as she pulled away, and the goddess strode carefully over her, up the stairs, and disappeared inside the wagon. Jak lay half-collapsed on the back of the stairs, gasping for breath. Her mind was still trying to work out what had just happened.

Once she worked it out, she threw herself off the back of the caravan. Jak hit the grass on her hands and knees with a small cry of pain. She hunched there, shivering and retching. Nothing came up, but she wasn't sure if it would. She felt sick. The wound in her side burned, and she wasn't sure it was the worst pain she was feeling.

Her stomach heaved and the pain made her want to scream as it pulled her side. She didn't vomit, but she began to cry. It had been him. It had still been him. No matter how he looked. She sat on her knees in the grass, in the dark, holding her bandaged side, and she cried. He said he wouldn't hurt her. He wouldn't force her. But he tricked her. Her body shuddered and hiccupped as tears streamed down her face. She felt so dirty. So foolish.

Something moved in the trees nearby. A voice called her name sharply, fervently.

"Jak!" Krill was at her side in an instant. His hands reached for her, but she flinched from him violently.

"Don't touch me!" she cried. Her fear of physical contact was strong enough to override her natural aversion to pain. The wound pulled near tearing as she jerked away from the fae's touch. The pain was so intense she felt her vision go dark for a moment. She thought she might faint. The tears came harder. She felt so dizzy. So weak. So sick. She sat back in the grass, curling against the wheel of the Banging Wagon for support. Her hands wiped desperately at her tears.

Krill stood back and watched. He had frozen at her order, and he had abided it. He made no move to touch her or help her again. He just looked on. Jak didn't look up at him. She couldn't. There was no way she could meet his eye. Not ever again. Not after what had just happened. He was angry. She could tell. He was staring at her, those golden eyes unblinking, and the rage was emanating from him in waves.

"What did he do?" Krill asked quietly.

Jak just shook her head and wiped more tears. They wouldn't stop falling. It was like her eyes had become the reservoirs behind burst dams, and the water would never stop flowing. Her chest fluttered unevenly as she gasped for breath between sobs, and every gasp hurt. The pain made her cry harder. She held her breath, trying to stop it hurting. It didn't work. It stabbed her fresh and the wince made her draw breath. Breathing hurt more. Krill knelt down in front of her.

"You are not alone, Jak," he told her softly. "You are not the first. You are not defined by this. I'm here for you. Just tell me what the fuck he did this time."

Jak shook her head and snuffled pitifully. She was beyond words. Her throat was so tight she couldn't get them out if she wanted to. He didn't understand. He couldn't understand. He loved Jim. He didn't know what this was like. She wanted to tell him that, but she couldn't. She just glared and sobbed and shook her head. Somehow, he seemed to get the message anyway. He sat down in the grass with a sigh. The fire was behind him, and it cast him deep in shadow, but he was so pale that even the faint light was almost enough to make him glow. His golden eyes were hard. Harder than Jak had ever seen them, but he was no longer looking at her. His gaze was lost in the back of the wagon. He seemed to be seeing through it, beyond it, to another time or place.

"You're not alone, Jak," Krill sighed again. "I know

what it's like. I know what he does, and how, sometimes, it's not the things he does, but the things he makes you do."

Jak almost managed to steady her breathing. She watched her old master sitting severely in the grass, staring into the distance. Now it was he who wouldn't meet her eyes.

"What do you mean...?" she breathed through her tears. Krill was silent a long time. Jak thought he wasn't going to answer, but she had no interest in talking herself. She did nothing to fill the silence, and eventually he did.

"The first time..." Krill whispered. "The first time... what I did... I... I never would have... not in a million years. I never would have done that. I didn't even know what I was doing. I was still sick. I'd been in bed for weeks. I didn't know who he was, or where I was, or what I was doing. I was still healing from the D'rök wound. I was dazed and confused and hurt..." Krill touched his side tenderly where his scar marked his ribs. "I never would have. I wouldn't. But he wanted me to. He was in my head. I didn't know it at the time. He enjoyed it. He loved it. I didn't know that at the time either. He was making me... he was in my head..." Krill placed his fingers to his temple. His hand tensed and contorted. He grimaced, like he could still feel it.

Jak stared at him. She didn't know when she had stopped crying, but she had.

"But... but I thought you loved him..."

"Sometimes, I still think I do," Krill admitted. "Before, by the fire. Sometimes, when he's kind, or passionate, or distracted… I think I'm madly in love with him. But he always goes back to being himself. That will never change. And I can feel him… all the time… I can still feel him in my head… messing with my thoughts…" Krill clenched his hand by his temple like he was in pain. Like he could sense something damaging that he couldn't pull out. He finally turned back to her, and she could see the pain in his eyes. It was real. "You think I don't understand, Jak, but I do. I know better than anyone. I have been exactly where you are — hurt and confused, and vulnerable to him. Now… I belong to him."

"Why don't you leave?" Jak asked, aghast. "He can't control you…"

"It's not control. It's influence." Krill looked pained. "I tried to leave once. I packed my bags and I headed for the door. He begged me to stay. He got on his knees and clutched at my legs and begged me to stay. Kode was watching. He…" Krill grimaced with such agony. "I can't explain to him how Jim is a bad person. He doesn't understand. He loves his patron. If I left… if I left… what if he didn't choose me? What if Kode chose to stay, and I lost him? I couldn't do that, Jak. I love him. More than anything. I can't leave Jim if it means losing Kode, and…" he stopped sharply, as though the words hurt too much to say.

"And some days you love Jim too…" Jak felt sick again, but not for herself. All of a sudden, her pain wasn't so frightening. She could have it worse. Krill looked like he wanted to throw himself on his sword. He stared down at the grass and shook his head. His pale hair swayed around his pointed face.

"Jim doesn't understand the difference between consent and coercion. He thinks persuasion is half the game — especially in his human body. That's why he likes it so much. People worship his D'Ihne form, everybody wants it, but his human body is just that: human. It's a game, and he thinks he's winning. He doesn't understand the effect he has on people — the power he has to make them think and do and feel. He charms people, and then, when the illusion wears off, he doesn't understand why the husbands and wives and serving maids and stable boys and strippers and brothel owners run him out of town."

"How can he not understand this?" Jak demanded.

Krill shrugged and spread his hands helplessly.

"Ĝoŕgomghōul always said that wisdom came with age, and he couldn't work out why his sons were still such idiots."

Jak almost smiled, but they didn't have enough to smile about yet.

"You have to get out of this," she told him.

"I can't," Krill swallowed. "I can't, Jak. He's too deep in my head. I don't know if any of my thoughts or feelings are my own anymore. I can't escape that. I can't help myself, but I can help you. I told you to stay away from him, and while this shouldn't be on you, you are easier to convince than he is. I won't let him hurt you again."

"He doesn't get that he's a rapist," Jak murmured. "He doesn't think what he's doing is wrong, because when people spurn him, he comes back and shifts into their fantasies to win them over. They like it. He thinks he's won, and if they're happy, then he can't be the bad guy..."

"That is an acute summary," Krill nodded sadly. Jak stared at him. The whole situation was more horrifying than she had ever first imagined. She didn't know what to say or do. As she opened her mouth to speak, hoping that anything would do, Krill turned. His ears pricked up. He quickly unfolded into a standing position like a leaf unfurling towards the sun. His delicate head dipped respectfully.

"Olíriá," he greeted the goddess as she returned to the campfire.

"Elkrillendé," she nodded in return.

"We were waiting for you. Jak is still healing. Will you watch over her for the night?"

"Of course," Olíriá smiled.

Krill nodded to her again. Without meeting anyone's eye, he turned and hurried into the caravan, shutting the door behind him. Jak hated watching him go, but she appreciated what he had done for her. Olíriá was watching her. The goddess' gaze took in everything. The girl, the tears, the bandages, the cloak. Olíriá sighed.

"I see you met her then..."

"I don't want to talk about it," Jak replied shamefully, rubbing her nose.

"You're not alone, Jak," Olíriá sighed. "We've all been there."

Jak shook her head despairingly as she thought about the last ten minutes. "Do you know what's going on with Krill and Jim?"

"Better than they do," the faerie hugged herself as though cold. "But that's their issue, and I can't help them with it. It's more complicated than you think."

"That's your answer to everything, isn't it?"

"It's a common truth," Olíriá sighed. "Come, let's get you back to bed. You need to be resting."

Jak struggled up from the ground. She kept her hand pressed to her side as she gathered her cloak, and went back to the spot by the fire Olíriá had set up as her bed. The hilt of Shrïgkyvsh still glinted in the firelight. Suddenly, the blade seemed far more threatening than it had before. Maybe she was just scared of what she might actually do with it now. Jak curled up stiffly and tried not to aggravate her wound.

"Jak," Olíriá called softly. "Sleep with Shrïgkyvsh at hand tonight. You might need him in the morning."

Jak didn't give any indication she had heard, but she reached out a hand from under her cloak and clutched the scabbard. It was warm and comforting. She didn't need Olíriá to tell her she might need the blade tomorrow.

CHAPTER NINETEEN

Jak woke lying on her good side. Her hand still clutched Shrïgkyvsh to her breast. Despite feeling as though she had been lying like this for some time, her hand wasn't cramping. The scabbard felt warm and comfortable in her grip. The rest of her felt like it had been lying wounded on the hard ground all night. Her body was stiff and sore and she felt tired. She had vague memories of Olíriá's voice in the night, but couldn't remember what the goddess had been saying — or who she had been speaking to.

Day had broken, and sunlight filtered through the giant branches of the tree above them. Jak could feel the warm light twinkling through the leaves and over her cloak. Slowly and gently, she tried to sit up. It was painful, to put it mildly. She groaned and whimpered as she pushed herself tenderly off the ground. The severed muscles along her side protested vigorously as she used them to hold her torso upright. Her eyes watered from the pain, and she squeezed them shut to keep back the tears. Once she was sitting, she stayed for a moment, bent over her legs, and just breathed as deeply and as slowly as she could. Next, she pushed herself to her knees.

From there, she was able to pick up the bundle that

has been her pillow. She unwound the clothes and pulled them back on. It was scruffy at best, and she didn't even think about bothering to try and tuck her shirt in, but it felt good to be properly dressed again. She remembered the night before with a nauseating blush and a strong desire to bathe. As soon as she thought about it, she could feel Fæmör on her skin and she felt sick and dirty all over again. There was nothing she could do though. Not yet.

As she sat there struggling for breath and working out her next move, she heard footsteps racing towards her, and someone screamed her name. They were small footsteps, and the sound brought a hopeful leap to her heart.

"Jak!"

"Dora?" Jak turned to face the sound. "Allie!" Her sisters were pelting towards her from the edge of the trees. "Girls, be gentle!" she cried desperately as they moved to collide with her. Fortunately, they heard her warning just in time, but Jak still grunted in pain as the girls collapsed on her. She gritted her teeth through the embrace. She was pleased to see them, more pleased than she could say, but she could have done without the hugs.

Crŷs and Ínrío were standing at the treeline where the girls had come from, and Jak could guess they had been her sisters' transportation. Olíriá was already gliding over to greet them. Jak watched her kiss Crŷs before the faeries moved back towards the camp. The Banging Wagon was still sitting innocently on the grass nearby, and Jak noticed Crŷs look at it with the same apprehension she felt.

"Jak, what happened?" Allie exclaimed, looking her up and down.

"I made a deal with Ĝoŕgomghōul," Jak admitted quietly. "He took a piece of me to make a sword."

"So, he gave you a D'rök blade then?" Crŷs checked as they approached.

"He did," Jak nodded sombrely.

"Can we see it?" Dora asked excitedly.

Jak held up the sword, still safely sheathed in its scabbard. The dark handle glinted in the morning light. All the faeries watched it with cautious and narrowed eyes.

"Is that my scabbard?" Ínrío asked.

"I took it," Olíriá defended quickly. "We needed something to keep the blade contained."

"You need but ask, sister," Ínrío shrugged at her. "However, Jak, I can make you one much nicer, if you desire it."

Crŷs was still watching the situation with the intelligent eyes of someone who had calculated the circumstances instantly. Everything in his stance was wary. He was watching the sword with even more trepidation than he had shown the wagon.

"What is his name?" he asked softly, taking in Olíriá's desperate warning about the blade, as well as the visible craftsmanship of it.

"You'll find out soon enough," Olíriá muttered, with a direct look at Jak. "It's certainly one of your father's creations, that's for sure. However, I have never seen its like."

Crŷs looked bleak. Even Ínrío gave his sister an alarmed glance.

"And he made it and just gave it to a mortal?" Crŷs muttered.

"He did," Olíriá confirmed. "He made her a sword from one of her own bones. I'm the only reason she's alive to tell you about it, and Jim and the boys are the only reason she's able to move today."

"Wait, back up," Crŷs demanded. "He helped heal her? That's what he's doing here?!"

"Don't make it sound so scandalous, babe." The all-too-familiar, leering voice sounded behind them. They all turned as one. Jim was leaning on the back of the wagon with a steaming mug wrapped in both hands. He had that early-morning, slightly-tousled, just-woken look about him. It suited the dimpled smirk. None of them had even heard the caravan open, but the doors were pulled back. Jim watched the congregation with his cheekiest expression.

Jak couldn't even look at him. Her face was burning, and half of her wanted to cry. All of her hoped no one noticed.

Dora redirected everyone's attention as soon as the Ha'Cās descended the back steps. The two beautiful faeries looked as soft as ever in the morning light, if slightly dazed and sleepy. As soon as the little girl saw them, she squealed in delight.

"Kode!" Dora yelled. She was on her feet and racing straight for him before anyone could stop her.

"Hey, baby girl!" Kode beamed. He caught her and swung her up into his arms. Dora laughed as he snatched her up and threw her arms around his neck. He poked her fondly in the cheek with his nose. "You look like you're doing a lot better than you were."

"I am!" Dora declared. "Allie told me Jim made me sick, but you guys didn't know he made me sick, and then once you found out, he healed me, but then you all left again, and then Jak left to go and get a sword she can use to kill Jim… but I don't know why we're killing Jim. Everyone keeps saying he's a bad man."

Kode looked around the collection of people, including his own, as though seeing them for the first time. His soft lavender eyes took in the sword, and the D'Ihne clustered around Jak, and Krill and Jim standing by the wagon. He observed the tension in the air. His big eyes looked at Jim in confusion as he held the little girl close.

"Jim…?"

"Yes, babe?"

"Are you a bad man?"

"Of course not," Jim smiled reassuringly at him. His expression was so honest it was almost enough to make Jak believe him. Almost, but not quite. Jim motioned to his lover. Kode returned Dora to Allie and scampered back to his husband. He was naïve, but he wasn't stupid. He knew something was going on.

"So, Jak," Jim grinned. "You going to get that thing out and wave it around for us now? It looks like it might be bigger than Ínrío's, and it's definitely bigger than Crŷs'."

"I use two," Crŷs countered, his fingers itching like he was about to try. Ínrío kept a tight hand on his brother's shoulder.

"So does he," Jim jerked his head at Krill. "And he's better at it. Go on, gentlemen. Who wants to go toe-to-toe with the D'Hiris? Or are you going to leave the little girl to fight your battles for you?"

No one moved. Crŷs' chest rose and fell like he was breathing to calm himself. His fingers twitched. Krill saw. He stepped forward. It wasn't much. It wasn't even a challenge. He just placed himself very casually in front of Jim and Kode. Jak felt the D'Ihne draw back beside her. She only saw it out of the corner of her eye. They were afraid of him. They were gods, but they were afraid of fighting Krill. The faerie himself was watching them with eyes like topaz. Golden, and hard as they were bright.

Jak unfolded from the ground in front of her sisters and the D'Ihne siblings. She took up her sword. One hand clutched the scabbard, and the other tightened around the hilt. It was smooth and warm in her grip. Perfect. Like it was made for her. She ground her teeth against the pain as she took a step forward.

"Fuck it," she snarled. "He's mine."

Someone caught her wrist instantly and stopped her from drawing the blade. Olíriá was beside her, staying her hand. The goddess' eyes were warning, and her expression was dark.

"Rule number one," she warned. "Never play his game."

"Oh, come now, Olí," Jim chuckled. "She's his apprentice. If she wants to get schooled, who are we to stand in the way? A little education never hurt anyone."

"I wouldn't hurt her, Olíriá," Krill promised.

"I know you wouldn't, Elkrillendé," Olíriá sighed. But she didn't loosen her grip.

"Oh, come on," Jim teased. "Don't we at least get to see him? What's his name?"

"It doesn't matter." The voice came from all around them. Powerful and commanding. It was like a clap of thunder. Jak flinched back towards Olíriá. It felt like the ground shook. Like the sky was clouding over and the sun was going out. None of those things occurred, but Jak felt a shiver in her bones. They were not alone. In the second it took her to blink, they were there. She saw the black armour of the D'rö-Hadās as the assassins stepped out of the shadows of the treeline. They surrounded them. Dark steel glinted in a ring around the group, and the crowd behind Jak had grown.

Jak felt her eyes widen, and she shrunk back in fear and awe. They were here. They were all here. The gods of Roïgola'a'lanaū. The three D'Ihne with her had been joined by their siblings and parents. Clōudiá stood at the front, and she was the one who had spoken. The Queen of the gods was an imposing woman. Her skin was the colour of storm clouds and it shone like the sun lit it from behind. She had hard eyes the shade of the evening sky, and they were fixed on her nephew. Giant feathered wings spread from her back.

"You stole from us, Fæmör. This is treason. I will collect what is mine, and you will stand trial for your crimes against the crown." When she spoke it seemed as though the heavens rumbled. Jak looked to the sky. She could see it. The cloudbank was parked above

Fäsaírm. Roïgola'a'lanaū was here. Every fibre of her wanted to cower in fear. Then Jim smirked.

The mug vanished from his hands. In its place, a glittering golden crown hung from his fingertips. It was sharp and spiky like an amalgamation of stars. Jim tossed it casually around his fingers like a hoop. He grinned at them.

"Come get it," he taunted.

No one moved. Jim's grin widened.

"You will return it," Clōudiá commanded. There was no room for dispute. Even Jak felt a strong urge to return the crown, despite not having it.

"No, auntie dearest, I don't think I will," Jim replied with mock tragedy. He clapped his hands together and the crown vanished in a small puff of smoke. All the D'Ihne drew back slightly at the sight. "You see," he continued smugly, "the days of the Faerie Queen are over. You don't own it. You didn't earn it. So I'm taking it back. No one should have that kind of power. I know that in my hands no one is using it, and I'm the only person I trust. Even if you agreed to my terms of banishing slavery from your kingdom, which you wouldn't, I can't imagine you keeping your end of the bargain. So, my loves, this is what we call an impasse."

Both sides watched each other. The breeze stirred the trees, but otherwise the world held its breath. And all the while Jim kept smirking. It was like nothing could wipe the smirk off his face. Jak could feel it under her skin. That look he'd always given her. When they met. When she'd been bathing at the spring. When he'd found her at the ball. Last night on the back step of the caravan. Right now. Jak gritted her teeth and ripped herself free of Olíriá's grasp. She staggered forward. Her hand tightened again on the hilt.

"Oh, Jellybean," Jim looked delighted. "Come get some!"

"I'm going to rip that nasty smirk off your smug face!" she growled.

"You want some flesh, Jellybean, I'll give you more than a pound," he grinned, stepping forward to meet her. "You support my cause — this is just personal."

"If you actually had a cause you'd be rallying people to support it, not driving everyone away and hiding behind it like an excuse!" Jak snapped. She was struggling to walk, but she pushed forward. Jim watched her pityingly. He eyeballed her.

"Jellybean, you can't even swing that thing in your condition."

"I can do enough," she growled. Jak unsheathed the blade. The dark steel whispered as it rushed from the scabbard. It glinted sharply in the morning light. The runes down the centre shimmered with force.

Everyone recoiled. Even Jim paled and drew back at the sight of it. Krill looked like someone had slapped him. Jak gripped the hilt in both hands and raised the blade in front of her. The boys could all get a good look. She glared them down.

"This is Shrïgkyvsh," she introduced him. Everyone flinched at the name. "He was made for me — from my own blood and bone."

Jim wasn't smirking anymore. If anything, there was a slight sneer of disgust and outrage crinkling his nose.

Olíriá's reaction to the sword had only been the baseline. The D'Ihne were horrified. Jak was holding something blasphemous.

Only one god had failed to move away. They stepped forward now, slowly and hesitantly. Jak could feel the fae presence behind her, the same way she had sensed Krill and the D'rö-Hadās in battle.

"Jak...?" The voice of a goddess came urgent, questioning, and desperate.

Jak turned. She knew who the woman was. She had seen her likeness in images before. The majestic goddess had skin darker and richer than the soil, and she was clothed in a simple dress bound with flowers and leaves. Thænäri. Goddess of the earth. Her green eyes were tragically imploring. Jak didn't want to falter, but faced with the sad eyes of Jim's mother, her hands trembled. Except the goddess never looked to her son. Her expression was distraught as she looked the girl up and down.

"Jak... what are you doing here? What happened? How did you get like this?"

Jak lowered the point of her sword in confusion.

"Do I... know you...?" Jak asked. She could hear hissing off to the side. Allie was trying to hold Dora back as the little girl dragged her sister towards the ensuing chaos. Dora broke free and rushed up beside Jak. She clutched Jak's sleeve urgently, and stared at the goddess with hopeful wonder.

"Mum?!" Dora called to her.

"What?" Jak exclaimed.

"Hello sweetheart," Thænäri smiled at Dora.

Behind them all, Jim groaned loudly and pinched the bridge of his nose in exasperation.

"For fuck's sake, Mom," he grumbled. "What did you do?"

Thænäri finally glanced his way. She didn't acknowledge him, but she let her D'Ihne form melt into the body of a human woman. A very familiar human woman.

"Mum!" Dora cried delightedly. Jak threw Shrïgkyvsh down and snatched her sister back. The sword fell harmlessly into the grass. Jak grabbed Dora so tightly her sister yelped. The struggle pulled Jak's wound so hard she couldn't hold back a cry of pain, and she felt the bandages at her side begin to grow hot and wet. Dora was fighting her, but Jak tightened her grip so hard she knew it must be hurting.

"Let go!" Dora screamed. "It's Mum, Jak! Let go!"

"It's not Mum!" Jak yelled back. "It's just a trick! It's not actually Mum, Dora! It can't be! That's impossible!"

"It's Mum!" Dora shrieked.

"It can't be." Allie was at their side. She stood composed beside her fighting sisters, although her face was flushed. "If Mum was a goddess then..." she glanced back at Krill and Kode. "Then we'd be Ha'Cās..."

"Exactly!" Jak snapped. "It's not possible. You can't be our mother! What did you do with her?! Where is she?!"

"In your father's grave..." Olíriá sighed. Everyone turned to look at the young goddess. She was standing back, with her hand linked in Crŷs', but her eyes were settled on Thænäri without judgement. The goddess of the earth nodded back and shifted again. Jak felt a hot tear splash down one cheek as she looked at the man standing in Thænäri's place. Her throat was too tight to speak. Her chest felt like it was about to forcefully explode. Allie spoke for her.

"Dad…"

"Hey girls…" his smile was more like a grimace. He was waiting for the fallout. Jak felt like the sight was going to kill her. It was more painful than facing Ĝoŕgomghōul. Her hands dropped from Dora. She couldn't hold her sister back anymore. The strength wasn't there. But Dora wasn't struggling anymore either. She was confused. They all were.

"Wait…" Dora muttered, pulling a face. "What? Dad? But… but Mum…"

"I'm… both, Sweetheart," he told her. "To you, anyway. I was always Mum to you, but, well, technically… I suppose…"

"WHAT THE FUCK?" Jak roared angrily. Everyone shut up. Her sisters cowered. Dora clung to Allie's skirts. Blood was spotting through Jak's shirt beneath her vest. Shrïgkyvsh was on the ground, but people were still afraid of her now. More than anything, they were afraid of her fury. It radiated from her like light from the sun. Hot and bright. She stared her father down. "What the actual fuck?! Where is she?!"

"Dead," he replied sadly. "For years now. She died in childbirth."

Silence reigned. Jak didn't have anything to say to that. No more tears had fallen. The single one at the sight of him was all that had managed to escape her burning rage. She was too angry to speak. Thænäri continued.

"Things went wrong," he tried to explain. "Even with all my power, I couldn't save her. She made me promise to save the baby, but I couldn't save them both. I loved her, Jak. I truly did. Suddenly, I had three baby girls and my wife was gone. Belladora… she was my everything back then. I wasn't ready to let her go. It was easier to be her and bury my own identity, than lose her once she was gone."

"You have got to be shitting me…" Jak muttered.

"That…" Allie murmured. "That makes us…"

"Half fae," Thænäri nodded. "I was going to tell you, once you were old enough. Your mother… Bella… she… she didn't know. I hid your fae blood. I figured it was something you could come into once you were grown. It was safer that way. Girls… what are you doing here?"

Jak didn't answer him. She turned to Olíriá. Those blue eyes had been watching her for what felt like a long time, and they were apologetic.

"You knew," Jak accused. Olíriá barely nodded, but Jak didn't need her to. She wasn't even mad at the goddess. Olí hadn't been the only one. Jak rounded on Krill. Her Master wasn't sorry, but he was resigned. He stood with his arms folded and his gaze steeled. "And so did you!" she bellowed. "You fucking knew!"

"You knew?" Jim looked at him.

"I suspected," Krill shrugged. "She carries Thænäri's pottery, and the D'Ihne of the earth is the only one who could have hidden demigod blood in her children. Given the talents of the girls, it was more than likely. Two of them can sense magic, the other one is abnormally mature and intelligent for her age. It was so far from normal, but… still, nothing was certain."

"That means…" Jak finally looked at Jim. She turned away instantly, covering her mouth and making loud noises of horrified disgust. He sighed and rolled his eyes.

"Yes, Jak," he muttered. "I'm kinda wishing I hadn't been your first kiss too."

"Wait, you kissed him?!" Allie exclaimed.

"Well, not like I am now…" Jim elaborated.

"I made out with my sister…" Jak choked into her hands, like she was trying not to puke.

"Half-sister," Jim defended. "It's not that bad, Jellybean. Come on, my mom is your dad — we're barely related."

"Jim, you selfish cunt, shut up," Crŷs growled.

"Wow," Jim rolled his eyes. "How many times do I have to explain to you idiots that I'm not the bad guy here?"

"This doesn't really look like the crowd to try and make that argument to, Jim…" Krill warned softly. His sharp eyes were cautiously watching the calamity unfold. He alone seemed undistracted by the drama. Krill had not forgotten that they were surrounded by his old army, and the gods of the Golden City. He didn't give anyone an opening, yet his face was marked by sympathy for the girl before them. "Jak…" he began gently. "Are you alright?"

Jak was on her knees in the grass hugging her body. She looked sick and tortured, and she was bleeding again. She shook her head in response, and he could see her holding back tears. They all could. Thænäri sighed and came forward.

"Jak," he addressed his daughter soothingly. He reached out to comfort her.

"GET AWAY FROM ME!" Jak roared. Thænäri flinched back. Allie clutched Dora out of the way as they watched her with pained expressions. Jak sat shivering in the grass like she was struggling to contain herself. She looked up with tears on her face, and glared at her father. The glint in her dark eyes was uncharacteristically murderous.

"Don't you dare touch me," she threatened. "I am done. I am done with your shit. I am done with your magic. I am done with your kind. My entire life is a lie. I don't even know who or what I am anymore. You lied to us and abandoned us. We are in this mess because your entire race is a fucking disaster!"

No one moved. All the D'Ihne were staring at Shrïgkyvsh lying in the grass beside Jak. The air was thick with the tension of immortality finally contemplating their own demise. The girl's words were not lost on them. She sounded like she was prepared to fix the problems of the world, and for the first time in all of creation, someone had the power to kill a god.

"Jak... please..." Thænäri tried to reason with her gently. He didn't move closer, and respected her boundaries, but his dark eyes were heartbroken. "Sweetheart, I never meant for any of this. I was going to come home. I was going to put things right, but this business with the crown—"

"Is your fault!" Jak accused. "And I cannot believe you don't see that! All you D'Ihne ever do is fuck things up and then deny responsibility and run away. You're all fucking cowards!"

"Enough!" A giant man with golden skin and horns stepped forward. His red hair flickered up from his scalp like flames. Frézíān, god of fire, didn't seem to appreciate being called a coward. Thænäri raised a hand to her brother to try and signal him to stop.

"Frézíān, please, she's my daughter—"

"Obviously," he sneered. "And now she's as problematic as your first born."

"Back up, Frézíān!" Jim commanded. He stepped forward and the air seemed to crackle. The D'Ihne flinched back from him as one. Jim still bore the crown, even if none of them could see it. "No one's as problematic as me. Don't insult my family like that."

"No, because you're the only one allowed to hurt your family," Frézíān retorted. He stepped forward and the grass smouldered as it was scorched under his feet. "What are you going to do about it, Fæmör?"

Jim might have been prepared to answer, but Jak didn't give him the chance. She snatched up Shrïgkyvsh and hauled herself to her feet. The D'Ihne looked ready to bolt, but no one was prepared to be the first to flee. Jak raised the sword in a tight but trembling hand. Her face was twisted in a sneer. She levelled the blade at Frézíān.

"It's Jim," she told them. "If you can keep track of all

your homewrecking identities and lost children and slaves and whatever, then you can remember what his preferred name is."

"Jak," Crŷs protested. "You cannot seriously be defending him!"

"She can make her own decisions, Crŷs," Thænäri sighed. "She's an adult."

"But I don't want to be…" Jak breathed. She looked back at her father. Her eyes were exhausted and full of heartbreak. "I don't want to be an adult. I didn't want to be one when Dad died and you told me I had to start being responsible. I didn't want to be one when Mum left because you abandoned us. I don't want to be one now. I just want to stay a kid. But I can't. I don't get to choose that. My childhood is over, and you all took it from me." Jak stared between them all, and then slowly lowered her sword with a sigh. She looked to Thænäri.

"He had that thing for a year…" Jak reminded them. "And none of you realised, even though you were supposedly scouring the world for it. Did you even think to ask? When was the last time you checked up on him? Was it even this decade? In my lifetime? The whole year you were gone you never came to check up on us once. Not even a minute to tell us what was going on. Would you really have come back? If this hunt had kept going, if it had gone on for years, would you have ever come back to us? Or would we have just finally and quietly accepted that Mum must be dead too, and we'd never really know where or why or how? You're all so mad at Jim for what he's done. He lies and cheats and steals and covets attention, claims he's fighting for freedom for the lonely and enslaved. If he's even half as lonely as you left us…" Jak scoffed quietly. "No. Fucking. Wonder."

"Jak…" Jim breathed quietly behind her. She'd never heard him speak her name so softly before. He actually sounded genuine. She turned to face him. It shocked her a little to see him look so sincere, although she didn't show her surprise. For the briefest of moments, there was no trace of his pride or lust or snark. He looked gentle. Jak sighed again, and she levelled Shrïgkyvsh at her half-brother.

"This doesn't excuse any of the terrible shit you have done, Jim," she warned him. "I can start to put this right if I have to, but you have to make the first move. Give the crown back. You stole it, and I can't barter for goodwill on those terms."

"The crown is our only bargaining chip, Jellybean," Jim replied, instantly recovering from his moment of weakness. "I'm not handing it back."

"You say you're doing this for the Ha'Cās?"

"I am."

Jak turned to look at the D'rö-Hadās all around them. She twisted slightly and winced, touching her side, but she kept her eyes on the circle of assassins.

"Well?" she invited. "He's doing this because of you lot. You're Ha'Cās. He wants to buy your freedom. Do you want it?"

The shuffle in the circle was barely discernible. Most of the Head Hunters didn't move at all. They were like statues of darkness at the edge of the trees. A few seemed to breathe at Jak's invitation, but nothing more.

No one defected.

"Enough!" Clōudiá ordered, and her voice shook the heavens once more. Her sunset eyes were cold and hard. Her soft white hair drifted around her face like clouds, but her gaze burned through fiercely. "I have tolerated your displays long enough, human. You do not get to influence my army. Move aside, or face my wrath."

"I'm trying to help you, Your Majesty," Jak replied. "Everyone deserves the right to choose what they do with their lives, and you're up against someone holding all the cards."

"You are insolent," Clōudiá sneered. The Queen raised her hand and struck.

Jak heard cries and screams around her, but they were drowned out by the bolt of lightning. A golden streak of light smashed down at her from the sky. She didn't even flinch. Jak stood with Shrïgkyvsh raised and let her instinct take over. Shrïgkyvsh recognised an attack, and he wasn't worried that it didn't come from a blade. Jak raised her sword into the light as the strike engulfed them. It was pleasantly warm. In seconds, there was nothing. The ground around her smoked and charred. Shrïgkyvsh crackled and sparked, but the runes burned hungrily in his centre and quickly devoured the magic. She could feel a little static, but not much else. She felt stronger with the new blade in use in her grasp. Even her side hurt less. Jak kept the sword up with both her hands tight around the hilt. She stared the Queen down.

"You want to go again?" Jak asked. She was actually

hoping Clōudiá would, but she knew she had sounded far too threatening. As much as she enjoyed the benefits of the magic, she was pissed the Queen had just tried to smite her. A little intimidation might be good for her Royal Stuck-up-ness. Clōudiá looked stunned. Slowly, Jak eased back and relaxed her stance. She addressed her brother without turning around.

"Jim," she called. "Wipe that grin off your face."

"I can't," Jim protested in delight. "I actually physically can't, and I don't know if I ever could again. That was gorgeous."

Jak sighed and turned to face him again. He was beaming. His joy had gone full-dimple and he looked like he was going to be happy for the rest of his life. It was so hard to negotiate anything when both sides were so difficult, and saw each of Jak's moves against the other as a win for themselves. Just because Jak had faced down Clōudiá didn't mean she was on his side.

"Jim, give the crown back," Jak repeated slowly and patiently.

"That's your stance on this?"

"It is," she insisted.

"Well then..." Jim spread his hands helplessly. "You're just going to have to catch us first." He clapped his palms together with a bang. In an instant, he and the boys and their wagon were gone. Jak groaned and lowered her sword. That dickhead. Without Jim around to posture for, she let the tip of Shrïgkyvsh sink into the ground and leant on him, pressing a hand to her burning wound.

"How did he do that?" Crŷs demanded. The D'Ihne

of trickery looked furious. He strode fiercely to the spot Jim had just been standing in and began to inspect it.

Jak sighed and shook her head. "It's just what he does. He teleports everywhere all the time. Fuck knows where he is now."

"Yes, but, how…?" Thænäri asked in confusion. Jak looked at her father. Thænäri bore a quizzical look in his dark eyes. He wasn't the only one. Jak looked around them all.

"It's magic," she stated like they were stupid. "You can all do it."

"Not like that," Clōudiá admitted. "That isn't magic like the rest of us can do, and it wasn't the magic of the crown."

"Nothing!" Crŷs exclaimed from where he was examining the area. "Not a blade of grass. Not a bird or bunny. Nothing. How the fuck did he do that?!"

"It has to be the same way he took the crown…" Olíriá mused. The other D'Ihne looked to her and nodded. They all looked deep in thought. "He's found some way of using magic without casting and without burning."

"What does that mean?" Jak asked.

"Magic, Jak," Crŷs said in a tone that implied it was explanatory. "Remember? I told you how it works. You can cast it with runes or you have to burn something to create the energy. Except he didn't mark or touch anything."

"Neither did your Mum when she tried to blow me up," Jak gestured accusingly at Clōudiá.

"I summoned the power of Roïgola'a'lanaū," the

Queen intoned. "The power of the Golden City is my power as its ruler."

"We all have certain areas we excel at," Crŷs agreed. "People call us the gods of all kinds of things. Yes, my mother can summon lightning without much trouble — just like I can make it snow. Jim can win any game he likes — we've never been able to beat him. That is where his skills lie. This is different. He was able to magic away the crown while it was on our Queen's head, and then vanish into nothing before our eyes."

"What about what we did?" Jak turned to Olíriá. "You magicked me here."

"Different again," Olíriá sighed. "I used the magic of nature. Fae come from the energy of the earth, and there are realms that still belong more to us than to humankind. I can move through a fae forest or a body of water as easily as stepping into another room — that is simply what it is to be fae."

"This sounds like the rules are a bit bullshit," Jak rubbed her forehead wearily. "You all think it's simple because you know them, but to the rest of us it sounds like you're making it up as you go along."

"There are rules, Jak," Crŷs insisted.

"And Jim is breaking them and you don't know how," Jak sighed.

"It's some kind of sleight of hand trickery she's bested you at," Ínrío mused to Crŷs, pointing at him knowingly. Crŷs spread his hands and shook his head.

"It's not," Crŷs assured. "Believe me; I'd know. I put plenty of safeguards in place against his trickery. He is not pulling one over on me ever again. I would know the instant he tried. This is… this is genuine, whatever it is."

"Ĝoŕgomghōul…" Allie said quietly. Only half of them heard her. Jak turned to her little sister while the others continued to bicker. Allie still stood off to the side with Dora, trying to keep out of the way of the chaos. She looked between Jak and Thænäri, who was also watching her curiously.

"What do you mean, baby?" Thænäri asked gently. "You think Jim's father is helping him?"

"No," Allie shook her head. "Jim learnt Ĝoŕgomghōul's magic. He told us that when we were camping with him."

"He did say that…" Jak recalled as Dora nodded eagerly at Allie.

"Well, shit," Thænäri muttered.

"Dad," Jak rebuked, knowing full well her own language had been far from reproach recently.

Thænäri ignored her and sighed deeply. He rubbed his weary human face with both dark hands, like a tired, rundown father feeling his years.

"What ails you, Thænäri?" Frézíān asked.

"The girls just said Jim bragged to them once about learning his father's gift with magic," he sighed. "Ĝoŕgomghōul is the oldest and wisest of us all. He has many talents we do not. If Jim learnt even half of them… we will never catch him."

"We'll never catch him anyway," Olíriá shrugged. "He has the crown; even without it he's as wily and powerful as any of us. If he has Ĝoŕgomghōul's ability with magic too, that's just the final nail in the coffin.

Most importantly, he has Elkrillendé. I just watched you all balk from him and he never made a move. You're all as afraid of him as I am — and I know he likes me. Clōudiá, you've had your army pursuing them the entire time — not only has every single soldier failed to best him, but they couldn't even recognise him behind Jim's magic."

"Now we know what we're dealing with," Clōudiá countered. "We know it's him. We can adapt accordingly."

"How?" Olíriá argued. Crŷs touched her arm warningly, but she ignored him. "How do we beat them? Jim's never met a game he couldn't win, and at this point he knows he's playing with us. Even if we discount the crown, if Thænäri's daughters are right, he is more dangerous now than he has ever been."

"We attack their weakness," Clōudiá answered simply. The D'Ihne shared contemplative glances at this. Olíriá looked murderous. Her blue eyes clouded like a storm over the ocean and she stared down the Queen.

"That is suicide," Olíriá accused.

"That is how to beat Elkrillendé. Once he is out of the way, Fæmör will be easier to subdue."

"If that's what you think, then Jim is right and you are not fit to wear the crown," Olíriá declared.

"Olí!" Crŷs hissed at her, grabbing her arm. Clōudiá drew herself up and the two goddesses stared each other down.

"What will you do, Clōudiá?" Olíriá demanded. "Strike me down? Without the power of the crown to back you, I think not. You are on the same level as the rest of us for once, and I think you know that, although you haven't been down here long enough to remember what it's like. What you are talking about is a last stand that will cost you your life, so I don't care if I'm being rude to force you to hear reason. If I am wrong, Elrïlani, then tell us." Olíriá turned to look at the D'Hiris at the edge of the trees.

Golden eyes glinted out of the dark mask of the leader of the D'rö-Hadās. For a moment, it seemed as though she wouldn't speak. Her gaze shifted between the two goddesses. Then her stance shifted as well. She seemed to sigh, although no sound was heard.

"Lady Olíriá is right, Your Majesty," Elrïlani admitted. "The instant you give us the order to move on Kodell, all our lives are forfeit. Elkrillendé will kill you and anything that stands in his way to you. He has the ability. We all know this."

"In the year you have been hunting them he has not killed a single one of you, D'Hiris," Clōudiá replied. "He is rusty."

"Nay, Your Majesty," Elrïlani pleaded. "Elkrillendé is a great many things, but he is not rusty. He had no desire to kill us. He had no desire to kill us when he left the Golden City, and he has had no desire to kill us since. If Fæmör's claims are true, then his only desire for us is that we are offered the freedom he took for himself. He wants us to be happy, not dead. That is the only reason we are alive. If you provoke him to lethal action, we will be slaughtered."

"There are hundreds of you and only one of him."

"Yes, Your Majesty," Elrïlani bowed her head. "Exactly. There is only one of him. There has never been another like him in our ranks. He would have been D'Hiris forever, if he had wanted it. You know it grieves me to say this, but none of us have ever matched him in even combat. Even against us all, I cannot guarantee our victory. The D'rö-Hadās are trained so that we would be able to slay a D'Ihne should they become rogue and dangerous. Elkrillendé was the best of us all."

"And now he serves the rogue D'Ihne and you're telling me I have an entire army of trained assassins for this purpose and you can't beat them?" The Queen sounded dangerous.

"He trained us," Elrïlani finished bluntly. "You may send us if you wish, but I tell you now that if you threaten Kodell, only a fifth of your army would return, and they would do so empty handed. I would not be among them."

The breeze rustled the trees as everyone took in what the D'Hiris was saying. There was a gentle sigh from the edge of the forest. A familiar blonde faerie stood in the shadows with his arms folded. Elrïlani's predecessor met her eye.

"If you threatened Kode, without so much as moving a single hair on his head, I might let you keep a quarter of your army," Krill warned.

The entire ring of Head Hunters were instantly armed. D'rök blades reflected the sun from every angle like a circle of mirrors. Krill didn't move.

"Seize him!" Clōudiá ordered.

"Halt!" Olíriá commanded. "Once again you have

failed to see all the threats you are facing before you attempt to act, Your Majesty." Her voice was a warning growl, and she pointed.

The gods had all but forgotten the children amidst their squabbles. Jak still stood with her hand on the hilt of Shrïgkyvsh. She gripped the handle so tightly her knuckles paled. Beneath her, the grass was dying. The circle of death was spreading slowly like a viscous ooze from where Shrïgkyvsh pierced the ground. Green stalks browned and crumpled in an ever-growing ring. Jak was glaring at Clōudiá with pure contempt.

"Jak... sweetheart..." Thænäri edged back nervously. Jak ignored him and addressed the Queen.

"Clōudiá, if you so much as think of going after Krill and Kode to get to Jim, I will stop you," she threatened. The grass had been dying ever since the Queen had first suggested going after Kode. It stopped as Jak drew the blade back out of the ground. The air of death still hung about it.

"You are weak and injured," Clōudiá scorned. "You—"

"Shut up!" Jak ordered. She turned to her old master. "What are you doing here, Krill?"

"I came to barter," Krill admitted, unfolding his arms and showing his empty hands in a gesture of peace. "Your Majesty, we both have something the other wants. I also knew this conversation would be happening and I wanted to head it off. I shadow walked to get back here. Jim doesn't know I'm gone and I don't have much time. I don't want to kill anyone, Your Majesty. I don't want it to come to that." He straightened and raised his chin. "But if I think for a second that you would give the order against Kode, I would make sure it never came to pass. I would take your head to your one-time lover. The blade he would make from it would serve as a banner to all your kind that none of you are safe from me, and you don't have the power to stop it. I would give Jim his war."

"But you don't want to," Olíriá pressed.

"I do not," Krill agreed softly. "I do not want this to end in death. You cannot catch him or trick him, but I can. I would give you James and return your crown. If, and only if, you promise to let Kode and I go free. We get to live our lives in freedom, without fae interference or retribution for the events that have led to all this."

"An interesting proposition," Clōudiá agreed. "Why should I believe it is not another of Fæmör's tricks?"

"He already holds all the cards," Krill shrugged. "Why would he bother? What would he gain?"

"Those are the questions," Clōudiá nodded. "Why, too, would you turn on him? By your own admission, he holds the cards. Why change sides when you're winning?"

Krill was silent. He laced his fingers together and bowed his head with a sigh. Jak stared at him with the wound in her side burning, and the pain dull in comparison to what she felt for her lost master.

"Because you're still a slave," she answered for him. The tragedy of it made her voice thick. "You're bartering for freedom, because you still don't have it. You're just his slave now instead of hers."

"I have felt him in my head over the last decade,"

Krill admitted miserably. "So many times I have felt him in there — poking and prodding and changing. I am not myself. He alters my thoughts, and bends me to his whims. I wish to be free. Truly free. That is why I am here. If I can get you the crown, you can arrest him. Without his magic, Kode and I can be ourselves. We can live our lives."

"Krill, are you sure about this?" Olíriá asked urgently.

"I am," he nodded. "Those are my terms."

"And intriguing terms they are," Clōudiá mused before Olíriá could say anything else. "I am prepared to make this trade, Elkrillendé. Bring me the crown and Fæmör, and you and Kodell can go free. We will seek no retribution — provided you adhere to the terms of your current banishment."

"Then we have an accord," Krill agreed. He looked away. "To the east is a lake. You will find us camped upon the shore. Be at the camp in half an hour — no sooner, and we can trade." He paused. "Maybe make that an hour." As soon as he was done speaking, he stepped back into the shadows of the trees and vanished. No one had time to respond. Clōudiá looked pleased. Olíriá didn't.

The gods began to move again in the wake of the standoff. The Queen turned away with a smug and satisfied smile. Thænäri shifted into her natural form and rushed to speak with Clōudiá. Olíriá had shrugged Crŷs away. She motioned to one of the other gods and approached Jak.

"You're bleeding again. Let us help," she requested.

Jak had nothing more to say. She sheathed Shrïgkyvsh and sank down to the grass. It was crispy and coarse beneath her now. She felt bad about killing it, although she wasn't wholly sure how she had done that. Obviously her sword had a great many powers she would have to learn to wield responsibly. Notably, one that could suck the life out of its surroundings.

Olíriá joined her on the grass and carefully placed her gentle hands to help hold Jak up. They were joined by someone Jak only recognised from the window art. Créātā, Olíriá's sister and the goddess of rain and medicine. She had Clōudiá's soft white hair, although on her it drifted up in a mohawk, and Äluāknā's faint scale pattern across her smooth grey skin. She knelt on the grass with them and, at Olíriá's bidding, Jak let Créātā lift her shirt and inspect the wound. The goddess pulled away the wet bandages. She pursed her lips and clicked her tongue.

"That is quite nasty, isn't it? Who's been working on it?"

"I did some of it," Olíriá admitted. "I used blood magic to stop the injury from killing her — her own blood, so it wasn't as potent, given that she was losing it anyway. Krill spent quite a while stitching it with rune magic, and Jim used something as well. I don't know what."

"I can see. Whatever he did, it's weird, but not bad… I can do better." Créātā didn't wait for a response, but moved her hands through the air as though reaching into another plane of existence. The goddesses continued to whisper around Jak as Créātā worked.

"Cré," Olíriá hissed nervously. "What are we going to do? Your father's about to get her crown back and arrest Jim!"

"What would you like me to do, Olí?" Créātā replied. She reached into seemingly nowhere, and plucked a contented fat pigeon out of the air.

"Clōudiá is going to want to make an example of him. She won't tolerate what he has done and she will want retribution. Thænäri will fight for her first born. Ínrío will turn on his mother in Jim's defence. I want to know where you stand. Would you advocate for him?"

Créātā let her eyes flick over her family clustered in various debates. Her graceful fingers reached over the pigeon and snapped its neck. She began to squeeze the plump body and it shrivelled in her hands. Jak resisted the urge to scream as Créātā started to feed the light she drew out of the bird's body into Jak's side.

"I would stand with my brother," Créātā whispered softly, glancing at Ínrío and conversing as though she wasn't in the midst of an intense spell. "You know well that Ínrío and I have always been deeply and sincerely fond of Jim. There was a time when the three of us were all there was of our generation. I take it you would stand with us?"

"Absolutely," Olíriá sighed. "It terrifies me that wounded pride might be about to permanently cripple and fracture our society."

"I mean…" Créātā pulled a face as the last light from the pigeon fused Jak's flesh, and the bird's desiccated corpse crumbled to dust. "As much as I love her, Jim made her own bed. Stealing the crown and trying to get the Ha'Cās to fight us is… well… treasonous. Besides, what are her brothers going to do?"

"Talámh will be on our side," Olíriá insisted. "They've had their differences, but he doesn't bear that much ill will against Jim. As for Crŷs…" Olíriá trailed off with a sigh.

"Crŷstïar won't help," Créātā shook her head. "If father orders Jim's execution, her little brother would probably volunteer to swing the sword."

"Not if he wants to stay married he won't," Olíriá threatened darkly. "I don't know, Cré. I'm really hoping that Crŷs will surprise us all. He does have a knack for surprises."

"You want him to turn the tables? Prank everyone and fix everything?"

"Does it sound delusional?"

"Yes," Créātā grinned. "But then, you two always were, and it's seemed to work for you in the past." The goddess reached down and pressed her fingertips firmly to Jak's side, prodding along the wound. Jak flinched. "Still tender," Créātā diagnosed, "but you shouldn't have any problems with it tearing again. It's much better than it was. I would tell you to rest it, daughter of Thænäri, but we have yet to hear where you stand."

"What?" Jak asked numbly.

"Krill is about to betray Jim to Clōudiá," Olíriá whispered to her directly. "If the Queen calls for his execution, would you stand by? He's your brother too."

Jak did not like the question. She felt slightly woozy, although she was grateful the pain had lessened. She didn't want to have to answer. She didn't want to have to think about it. But two pretty goddesses were staring at her like it was a matter of life and death, and she was the keeper of the Godslayer blade. Half of her wanted to throw Jim to the wolves for everything he had done, but as deep as her anger and hurt ran, half of her was prepared to admit she loathed Clōudiá a lot more than him. Also, as much as she hated it, Jim was her brother. The thought somehow managed to be both traumatising and comforting. She wasn't prepared for such a conflict. It made her wonder if there was something deeply and profoundly wrong with her.

"I don't know." She replied with the only response she could think. "So I guess I'm just going to have to come along and see how I react when it goes down."

***

The shore of the lake was warm golden sand on the edge of the wild and tangled forest of Vætor-ō-Ĝōul. The sand was shallow and densely packed on the hard rocks, but it was pretty. Reed grass and wild flowers grew together in patches like splashes of coloured paint across the golden ground. The Banging Wagon was conspicuous on the otherwise picturesque landscape.

It had been an hour, and the gods were arriving. Jak had explained to her sisters that she was going too, and Allie had retorted that they were also tagging along. Thænäri didn't want any of them coming, but given that Olíriá was prepared to bring them the point had become moot. Olíriá had managed to convince Crŷs to help, when she got his attention.

He spent most of the hour with his face set in a deep frown of intense contemplation. Every now and again, he would pull a face and mutter 'how did he do it?!' Jak and Olíriá had watched his frustration and decided it was best to leave him to it.

Créātā's healing had done wonders, and Jak appreciated the help. Her side was stiff and achy, but it wasn't a burning pain any longer, and she didn't think she could tear the wound again. Travel through the trees had left her feeling queasy once more, but at least she had been prepared for it. It seemed to have a similar effect on Allie, and both sisters shared a dark look at the chirpy Dora who didn't appear to have any issue traveling by magic.

Their group, including the D'rö-Hadās, stayed quietly at the edge of the trees. The thought that this might still be a trap was not lost on the D'Ihne, but Jak knew it wasn't. She could feel in her soul that Krill wasn't lying. She had seen his pain. He didn't want to do this, but he didn't know what else to do either, and he seemed to think this was the best way to protect his husband and stave off the killing. Jak could feel a great weight of sympathy in her chest for her Master's plight. She agreed that he was probably doing the right thing, even if Olíriá's expression spoke volumes about her disagreement.

The back door of the wagon banged open. Jak flinched. She wasn't the only one. Krill walked out alone. He had a wide cloth belt tied around his hips, but he was otherwise naked, and he carried the crown. Jak felt a hot blush flare up at his lack of attire. Even though, technically, she knew she'd seen him in less, it didn't feel like it. Clōudiá strode out to meet him. The gods began to drift onto the shore as they realised Krill was making good on his deal. Everyone wanted to see what would happen. Jak drifted with them. She kept Shrïgkyvsh strapped to her side, and she couldn't take her hand from the hilt. Her instincts were screaming at her to draw the blade, but there was no reason to. Not yet. The instant it looked like Clōudiá might renege, Jak would protect her Master. It did not occur to her that Krill might break his word. He was a great many things, but Jak felt he had always been honest. Even if he was only honest about keeping Jim's lies.

Clōudiá walked with unwavering purpose, although the soles of her white boots left no imprint on the ground. The streams of her long skirt and the feathers of her wings flared around her. Krill approached her with more caution, and there was a fear in the way his fingers loosely clutched the crown — as though any second he was prepared to lock his grip. They neared each other, and the crowd on the shore simply watched.

"Krill!" Olíriá called warningly. Everyone froze. He looked to her, and whatever her concern was, she tried to convey it in her expression. Clōudiá glared at her, but the Queen was already in reaching distance of her goal. Krill was already holding the crown out. Someone else called his name.

"Krill!" They all heard Jim calling from inside the wagon, and he didn't sound happy. He burst out the doors in his human skin, fully clothed. Kode was behind him, half dressed and confused. Jim's eyes went dark with shock and anger as soon as he took in the beach. "Krill! Don't!"

Doubt and fear chased each other across Krill's face, but he'd already done it. He'd already brought the crown back into the Queen's reach. Clōudiá snatched it from him before he could change his mind. It was like lightning hitting the shore. Jak tore her eyes away. The light was blinding. In a flash it was over. The boom still echoed. The fae were moving so fast Jak struggled to follow it, but that was how they worked. She focused.

Krill was collapsed at the water's edge. He looked like he'd been blown back by the force of Clōudiá's power. Kode was with him, clutching him in concern, as his bruised husband tried to prop himself up. Clōudiá was floating. Her crown sat atop her head, and she radiated power. Her wings were flared and from her hands trailed a glowing golden chain. The chain led to Jim. It shackled him around the neck, wrists, and ankles. It burnt away his magic.

He stood in his exposed fae body, and his pale skin glowed brighter than Jak had ever seen. His dark curls were a tumbled mess around his shoulders, and his violet eyes burned. Not even the illusion of the robe was kept. He had nothing. He struggled and pulled against the chains around his wrists. If anything, they tightened. Jak felt like a mist was lifting from her mind and eyes — as though she could think clearly for the first time. Jim's magic was being undone. All of it. Behind him, the Banging Wagon began to crack and fall apart like the broken junk it was. He struggled, but Clõudiá didn't even have to tighten her grip.

She watched him in amusement. Then she yanked the chain. Jim crashed with a yell as she pulled him over and dragged him across the rough ground. He struggled and cried as his bare skin scraped across the rocks and sand. The glow burned brighter from his arm and leg on the side he was dragged, as though he was bleeding light. Several of the D'Ihne winced as they watched. Clõudiá dragged him to her feet, where he curled struggling and grimacing against his chains.

"Fæmör," the Queen declared in her thunderous voice. "The crimes that you have committed against us know no bounds. Always you have been a trouble-maker, but never before has our kind known suffering like you have caused. I hereby charge you with the highest order of treason. The punishment for such an offence is death. However, I am nothing if not reasonable and considerate. You will stand trial in the golden halls, and I will hear justice served." She stared down on him. He stared back with a burning hatred, before baring his teeth and spitting at her. Clõudiá smiled. "It begins," she declared. In an instant, the Queen and her prisoner vanished completely.

"Clõudiá!" Thænäri called in a panic. The forest goddess vanished after them, and the D'Ihne all began to disappear as they followed after the action. Jak stood with her hand shaking on the hilt of Shrïgkyvsh. The blade was half drawn, but she hadn't committed. It didn't matter. It was over.

552

CHAPTER TWENTY

Jak let out a soft sigh. She let Shrïgkyvsh slip safely back all the way into the scabbard. Things were different now. She felt lighter, yet wearier. It was as though everything that had happened since she'd first met Jim was catching up with her, and she was exhausted. She felt like she could just float away and sleep on a cloud. Behind her, Allie and Dora were still staring wide-eyed from the treeline where they clung to each other. In front of her, where the waves were rolling in, Kode was carefully helping Krill to his feet. Not all the gods had left. Olíriá and Crŷs were still standing on the beach. She was watching the Ha'Cās. He was watching her.

"Ah," Crŷs murmured in revelation. His sudden understanding appeared deep, but he did nothing to elaborate. Olíriá sighed and turned away. Crŷs held out an arm to her. For a moment it seemed as though she might turn from him, but she walked to his embrace and curled in against him.

Jak averted her eyes from the fae and looked back at her sisters. The shock of what had just happened was written on their faces. Jak didn't know how much they had been able to see or follow. Aside from that, they seemed fine. They were watching her like they expected her to do something. She nodded at them. Their expressions didn't change, so she turned and walked further onto the shore. The fae were so light footed she was surprised how much her soles sunk into the sand. She headed for the Ha'Cās, but Olíriá and Crŷs were between her and her friends.

"Jak?" Olíriá called to her as she passed.

Jak turned to her. Olíriá had mostly detached herself from Crŷs, but the two still stood close. The D'Ihne were looking at her in concern.

"Are you alright?" Olíriá asked.

"I guess," Jak shrugged. She glanced to Krill and Kode. They two of them were standing at the edge of the water. The waves lapped around their feet as they conversed in whispers. Krill was shaking as Kode held him close. Jak turned back to the gods. "I mean… it's over now, right? We're done. Jim will stand trial, and then… then Dad— Mum— whatever— Thænäri! Thænäri will come back and we can work out what to do. We can… I dunno… maybe… maybe go back to Kosvo and… and try and fix things. We can explain to everyone that it was just Jim, and he's been dealt with."

"You would be content to let Clōudiá decide your brother's fate?" Olíriá asked.

"He's not much of a brother," Jak pointed out. "D'Ihne committing D'Ihne crimes get D'Ihne justice, right?"

"That's one way to look at it," Crŷs agreed.

"I thought you'd be on your Mum's side," Jak looked to him.

"So did I," he sighed, rubbing his face wearily. "I'm not sure what side I'm on, Jak. Clōudiá will kill him.

She's a lot of things. However, despite what she says, reasonable and merciful are not two of them. She's putting him on trial to humiliate him and make an example of him. My mother is vengeful. When all is said and done, she will execute him — unless I stop her."

"Would you do that?" Jak asked.

Crŷs pulled a face as both the ladies looked to him.

"Crŷs!" Olíriá insisted. "This isn't some trick you get to pull! This is final! You really want to see what happens to our people when we start killing each other?"

"No," he shook his head. "I don't. I don't want Jim to die either, I just…" he trailed off with a grimace. Crŷs tightened his hand into a fist and raised it like he was looking for a wall to punch in frustration. "I just… I just want him to be sorry! I don't want her to kill him. If she does, he will always believe he was right — until his dying breath, he will think he was right, and that she was a tyrant, and I was just her son. He will die righteously spouting that bullshit if we can't teach him he was wrong! I just want him to be fucking sorry!"

"Then start by apologising."

The three of them turned. The Ha'Cās had approached. Kode was staring at them with his lavender eyes sad and serious. He still had his arms around Krill, as though helping to keep him up and walking. Krill looked like death. Jak had never seen him look so awful — not even when he was hungover. Kode looked to them, afraid and pleading. It was a tragic sight on his usually optimistic face.

"You tricked him into murdering a whole town,"

Kode reminded. "How can you expect him to be sorry for his trick, if you were never sorry for yours?"

"They were just—!" Crŷs cut off his indignant defence quickly. He shot an embarrassed look at Jak and finished lamely, "mortals…"

"And you knew he cared for mortals more than you did," Kode rebutted. "That's why you did it. You used that excuse so often he realised it was easier to think like you. He started two wars — after all, they're just mortals. But he's always been caring, and that had to go somewhere. It went to us. You lot were so toxic to him he detached himself from his feelings. He didn't care about killing humans or D'Ihne. He just wanted us to be free, and everything else could be damned."

"Don't put this on me," Crŷs growled.

"I'm not putting anything on you," Kode clarified. "I'm just trying to teach you. I've spent my whole life catering to the whims of the D'Ihne. They have taught me everything they like and don't like. All I have learnt is that a little bit of kindness can go a long way. Jim was my patron. I have always loved him. He was always kind to me. Everything that has gone wrong with all of you has always been because you couldn't just be kind to each other. I know that he is as much at fault there as anyone else, but if he won't learn first, perhaps you can."

Crŷs was silent in the wake of Kode's speech. Jak stared at the two blonde faeries feeling strangely proud and humbled. Sometimes it was easy to forget how wise Kode was, but this was not the first time he had been the one to put things in perspective for her. Her awe unfurled fresh and alive, like a flower opening in her chest. She felt as though her feelings had been unlocked. Everything was so new and bright and intense. The more she thought about it, the surer she was that Kode was right, and the more the concept of Jim's execution began to scare her. Beside her, Crŷs sighed and shook his head.

"It would just make things worse," he argued. "As long as she holds the crown, she will want to execute him, and she will have the power to do it. If we take the crown, this whole debacle starts all over again."

"Then we have to find another way!" Kode insisted. "Please, Crŷs! Olí! You have to help us!"

"We will do everything we can," Olíriá promised. "But Crŷs is right about Clōudiá. Kode, sweetheart, even if we can sway her to a different sentence, Jim will be imprisoned by her power for a long time."

"And what good will that do?" Jak asked. "Olíriá, you tried to teach me that there was no point killing him, because it wouldn't do any good, and it wouldn't fix what he had done. I get that now, but how is Clōudiá keeping him in chains any better?"

"He has to answer for his crimes, Jak," Crŷs pointed out. "It's the punishment we're debating, not his innocence. He's definitely guilty."

"For crimes against the D'Ihne?" Jak turned on him. "For what? You're calling it treason, but really, he just stole his aunt's crown and led you all on a wild goose-chase for a year. That's not exactly a capital punishment offence. For crimes against humanity? For that, you're all pretty fucking guilty, but we can't exactly take our justice out on gods."

"Jak," Krill spoke her name softly. She looked to him. He met her eyes with pain and determination. "Please," he implored. "Save him."

She gave a brief nod. There wasn't anything else she could do. Even though he had followed Jim in abandoning her, he was still her Master, and he had never asked her for anything so desperately.

"Are you dying?" she asked thickly, afraid of the answer. Her gaze traced the scar on his side for any sign of injury. Krill shook his head. The action dislodged tears he had been keeping back, and the drops plunged suddenly and silently down his cheeks.

"Worse," Olíriá sighed. "His wound was healed a long time ago. He doesn't need magic to keep him alive." She turned to him. "I'm sorry. I tried to warn you. Your natural apathy will come back. It just feels intense right now because it was so powerfully increased."

"Your apathy?" Jak echoed in confusion. Then she realised. It all fell into place. What Kode had just said to Crŷs. Her own feelings bursting out again. Krill's fear of what Jim was doing to his mind, coupled with his reaction to freedom. Jim's powers had been shut off, so now... "You're in love with him," Jak sighed. "Like, really truly, properly. He wasn't messing with you to make you like him — it was the total opposite. He put the doubt there." She paused as she thought about it. Her mind was whirling so fast her mouth was struggling to keep up. "He does it on purpose. He did it to me, just a little bit. That's why he's such a jerk. He doesn't want us to like him… he doesn't want to get to close. He's… afraid of his own feelings." Jak pulled a face. "What a fucking child!"

"Aptly put," Olíriá smiled gently. "Jim has always foolishly believed that feelings get in the way of fun. Stupidity isn't a crime, but it has made him commit a few. He keeps people at what he considers a safe distance. Not that it helped him much. He wouldn't have messed with your minds if he didn't care about you so deeply."

"That doesn't make any sense…" Crŷs muttered.

"It's because he's an idiot, my love." Olíriá placed a gentle hand on his chest.

"Now it makes perfect sense," Crŷs nodded.

"I don't care that he's an idiot," Krill asserted. He wiped his eyes. "He's my idiot, and I betrayed him. We have to get him back."

"Oh, we will," Jak assured vehemently. "Although, I can't help but feel he sort of brought that betrayal on himself. Even so," Jak drew her sword and the faeries all flinched back as one. "We're going to go sort out my loser of a brother, and I'm going to deal some mortal justice!"

"That sounds more dangerous than D'Ihne justice," Crŷs wavered.

"Not if you know her," Kode smiled.

"Take me to Roïgola'a'lanaū!" Jak demanded, pointing with her sword. The fae scooted back to give Shrïgkyvsh a wide berth.

"We can't," Crŷs admitted.

"We have to get there," Jak insisted. "You have to

take us."

"No, Jak, he's right," Olíriá sighed. "We can't. Mortals cannot set foot in the Golden City — even demigods. That is the most sacred law. It has never been broken, and even if we wanted to, we physically can't. Crŷs and I don't have the magic it would take to get you there."

"We really don't," Crŷs lamented. His expression shifted halfway between nervous and sly. "However… we know someone who might…"

Jak didn't have to ask. She had felt included in that 'we' and she knew who he meant. Footsteps shuffled in the sand behind her. Dora was leading Allie by the hand towards them. The youngest sister had a determined look on her face. Jak was all set to run into danger again, but she couldn't leave the girls behind. She couldn't do what Thænäri had done. Besides, they had the permanent look of limpets. They had come to witness this, and they wouldn't stay behind for the next adventure either.

"We're going to go rescue Jim now, aren't we?" Dora questioned. Both girls looked unsettled seeing Krill and Kode so upset. They wanted to help put everything right. Jak felt her brow crease into a frown. They didn't know what this was about to turn into, but even if they did, she knew she would struggle to convince them to stay out of it. At the end of the day, even if she didn't want to think about it, Jim was their brother too. She turned to her sisters and squatted slightly to face them.

"How brave are you feeling?" she asked.

***

The darkness was still cold. Jak couldn't imagine feeling like it wasn't. Dora had been acting particularly brave, until the magic transportation had worn off and they had been standing before Fäsaírm. Staring into the eternal darkness between realms, Dora's bravery had faltered, and Jak had taken the lead. Dora was right behind her, clutching the back of her vest, and Allie had an arm around Dora's shoulders. Allie was more afraid than they were, but her biggest fear was being left behind. Krill and Kode brought up the rear. Neither of the fae had been afraid to enter Ĝoŕgomghōul's lair, and it helped Jak settle her little sisters to have them there. If she was completely honest, it helped to settle her too.

Jak knew how Fäsaírm worked because she had been here to trade before. She knew that having Crŷs and Olíriá there would have hindered more than it helped. Which was why she had been happy to agree to meet them in Roïgola'a'lanaū. Jak had only met Ĝoŕgomghōul once, but she already felt like she knew him. She knew that he had no respect for people unwilling to fight their own battles or barter their own trades. If she wanted to go to Roïgola'a'lanaū, she had to ask him herself.

The dry cold settled around them. Jak could feel her little sisters shivering behind her. It no longer scared her. She couldn't explain it, but the space between worlds was comforting now. Maybe because she knew that she too was something from halfway between worlds. Their collective footsteps on the hard ground echoed back in respective clangs and whispers from the realms beyond. Jak kept a steady calm pace, and hoped her confidence would resonate with the girls. She looked back at them.

In the darkness everyone was invisible. But not for her. Not forever. She could see her sisters' eyes, wide and afraid, as they peered up at her. She could see Krill and Kode, almost luminescent in the darkness. Kode clutched Krill's arm tentatively, although his eyes were filled with absolute trust. Krill looked to Jak. He had been here before too. Many times. Both of them had made sacrifices here. He could see her conviction. Her faith. He smiled. Jak knew that the only reason she could see the people behind her was because light, however faint, was emanating from a source. She turned back.

"Jak of the Mortal Realm," Ĝoŕgomghōul addressed her with a smile. The old fae was as skeletal as she remembered, with his dark, wraith-like cloak, and his pale gaunt face hidden behind thick black beard.

"Ĝoŕgomghōul," she replied, bowing her head.

"You return once more, so soon after departing. I am pleased to see you. Although, you may forgive that I am not the least bit surprised."

"Of course," Jak nodded. "You knew I'd come back, and you know why I'm here."

"Indeed," his deep voice intoned. "You wish to travel to Roïgola'a'lanaū." He looked over her party and his three red eyes blinked at them. "It is the oldest faerie law that no mortals shall set foot in the Golden City. Crŷstïar didn't have the power to bring you there or face the consequences. Yet, you all believe I do. You think I can bring three mortals, and two who were forever banished, into Roïgola'a'lanaū? That I can summon that much power?"

"I know you can," Jak told him, meeting his gaze. A broad grin cracked the old god's thin lips. Crow's feet deepened around his eyes.

"And what would you trade, Jak of the Mortal Realm, for such a feat?"

"I would trade a feat of my own," Jak replied, resting a hand on the hilt of Shrïgkyvsh. "I would save the life of your son, if you would take us to the Golden City."

"My son?"

"Jim. Your first-born."

"Ah," Ĝoŕgomghōul nodded. "My first-born indeed. Even at this moment, Clōudiá threatens Jim's life. One could argue, however, that James made their own bed, and is simply facing the consequences."

"Oh, that's absolutely what's happening," Jak agreed. "And one of those consequences is us busting in to the rescue. He may be a complete dick half the time, and there are times when I think I'd quite like to be the one to stab him, but he's saved my life enough times that I have to save his. We might fight, but he's family, and we've got his back."

Dora gave a small woop of support behind her. Even Allie smiled.

"Then your feat is simply for yourself," Ĝoŕgomghōul shrugged. "How is this a trade?"

"Jak," Krill whispered softly. He stepped from Kode's grip and touched Jak's shoulder briefly as he strode to meet his old Master. Jak could feel his intent in the tips of his fingers. He was telling her to stand down. Ĝoŕgomghōul straightened taller as Krill stepped silently forward on bare feet.

"Elkrillendé," the dark god nodded.

"Ĝoŕgomghōul," Krill bowed his head. "You need a sacrifice to bring forth magic. Something to burn of equal value to the spell you cast." He raised his chin defiantly. "If it will save Jim to have them there, then use me. We don't have anything else to offer, and we beg with empty hands, but my life would burn powerfully. Burn my heart. It will take them to Roïgola'a'lanaū."

Jak felt like she was going to scream. That was not a trade she was prepared to make, but the cold and the shock had frozen her body and her lips were sealed. It was an unnatural paralysis, and she could only imagine that Kode was also caught by it. In horror, she watched Ĝoŕgomghōul step closer and lay a thin white hand on Krill's bare chest. The god's long skeletal fingers rested over Krill's heart. Ĝoŕgomghōul smiled, and made no move to break his old apprentice's skin.

"You forget, Elkrillendé," he murmured. "Your heart is no longer yours to trade. You cannot offer it to me." Ĝoŕgomghōul looked over Krill to where Kode stood in the darkness. "It belongs to your husband," he smiled. "And, if I am not mistaken, my first-born."

"Then what?" Krill begged. "There must be something! We are running out of time!"

"Time is relative," Ĝoŕgomghōul dismissed. He was still looking at Kode. "Before we negotiate, I would meet Kodell."

"Kode?" Krill echoed, turning to look. Kode blinked innocently at them. Ĝoŕgomghōul motioned him forward and Kode walked obediently past the girls to join them. Ĝoŕgomghōul watched him approach with an unreadable expression.

"Long have I been curious about him. James has spoken in awe of Clōudiá's young half-breed for many years now, during visits. Jim called Kodell their most gifted student. They said they had never met a soul like him. He was a creature powerful enough to turn even my most formidable disciple." Ĝoŕgomghōul glanced at Krill. "You gave up your armour, your title, and your life for him. I had barely believed something that could sway you so even existed. So, you can see where my curiosity is born." The D'Ihne reached out a hand to Kode. "I will not hurt you, child."

Kode went to him with absolute trust. Ĝoŕgomghōul cupped his cheek and stared into his lavender eyes. Kode stared back. The god's expression softened as he looked. Jak watched the interaction fearfully. Ĝoŕgomghōul gazed at Kode like the faerie was the most beautiful thing he had ever seen. Yet, Jak wasn't sure the god had given Kode's physical body enough of a glance to know what he looked like. He was seeing something else. Ĝoŕgomghōul let his hand fall and the connection broke.

"I have seen you," the god intoned. "And you are everything I could ever have hoped for."

"It is nice to be seen," Kode smiled sweetly back.

Ĝoŕgomghōul smiled in return, as though looking

down at a child. He turned his smile to Krill. "I can see why you made your choice. It would take a heartless creature to make any other."

"And now what?" Krill asked.

"Now what indeed…" Ĝoŕgomghōul turned back to Kode. The sweet faerie was still smiling at him.

"You don't like going to Roïgola'a'lanaū," Kode stated. "You don't like getting involved in the politics of the D'Ihne. You think they are foolish."

"That is very true."

"Do you want Jim to die?" Kode asked, his big eyes wide.

"I do not," Ĝoŕgomghōul answered.

"Then, isn't Jak right?" Kode asked. "When she offered to trade her feat for yours? She would save his life, and spare your involvement, if you simply get her there. Does that not seem fair?"

"Taking you there is involving myself," Ĝoŕgomghōul countered. "That is an action I would have to own. The consequences would be mine to deal with. The ramifications of what would occur would keep me from my work here in Fäsaírm for lengths of time as yet unknown. It is not in me to return to Roïgola'a'lanaū and involve myself in managing my brethren. I told them long ago that they are their own people, and must do as they see fit."

"Then a new deal," Jak countered. Everyone looked to her. She had been listening intently and inspiration had sparked. Ĝoŕgomghōul had rules, but chaos and eloquence were his children. The phrasing was important. "You take us to Roïgola'a'lanaū, and in return, I will do all that is within my power to fix what has been wronged — however long it takes."

"Do you know what it is you offer?" Ĝoŕgomghōul checked.

"Pretty sure I do, yes," Jak nodded.

"And you offer it willingly?"

"Eagerly."

Ĝoŕgomghōul grinned. Trickery was his child too, Jak was well aware, and he looked like he had been waiting for her to pass his test. It also looked like she finally had.

"Then we have an accord," the god declared. His bony hand caught the edge of his tattered cloak hanging over his robes, and he pulled the cloak open.

***

In the mortal world the floating city of Roïgola'a'lanaū appeared as a massive cloud bank drifting through the sky. But in the mortal world all fae and their magic presented as illusions. The realm of mortals could never hold such splendour. In their own world, the illusions were no longer necessary. The clouds were invisible from the inside, and the island drifting in the air was wrought of soft warm light. From the soothing glow rose a city of gold, which shimmered and gleamed with the magnificence of a gentle sun. White marble and pearl served to reflect and compliment the gold, and all graced the halls of the gods in quantities the mortal realm couldn't comprehend.

Ĝoŕgomghōul was a stark contrast in these halls.

While most of the gods revelled in their paradise, with glowing skin and richly coloured adornments, the god they called Wisdom stalked the golden corridors like a shadow of death. The path to Clōudiá's hall was wide and dramatic. The sounds of arguing voices carried down it like echoing bells. The sounds Darkness associated with the realm. There were no doors. No grand entrances. He didn't need one. Ĝoŕgomghōul strode from the corridor into the gigantic hall.

The walls stood fifty feet high and rose into a vaulted ceiling. Pillars shimmered in two rows on either side of the massive room, effortlessly holding up the intricate ceiling. Everything glittered in gold. It was ostentatious to the god who had once been primarily responsible for its construction. Between the furthest two pillars, Jim was bound in magical golden chain. He had been strung up before the throne, and Clōudiá sat upon it with the same delicacy her crown sat upon her brow.

The rest of the D'Ihne were gathered between the Queen and her prisoner, and they argued. Some were pleading for the traitor's life. Others insisting that he be eliminated. Jim and Clōudiá stayed silent. Their eyes were on each other. Her expression was unforgiving. His was challenging. He was daring her to do it. Then silence fell.

The gods had noticed their company. Everyone looked to the shadow in the doorway. Ĝoŕgomghōul walked softly into the room, wreathed in his tattered black. The hood hung deep, and cast thick shadows over his hairy skull of a face. Nothing had ever looked so out of place in the Golden City.

"Brethren," he intoned in his deep voice. It carried.

"Ĝoŕgomghōul," Clōudiá nodded respectfully. "I see we have drawn you from your cave."

"Wisdom," Thænäri addressed him irritably. She raised an arm and indicated the woman on the throne. "Talk some sense into her. She can't do this."

"Your child is a traitor, Thænäri," Clōudiá insisted. "There can be no other way. Having Ĝoŕgomghōul come and argue your case is not enough, although, he is always welcome in these halls."

"You silly bitch," Thænäri shook her head. "He is smarter than you will ever be. He gave you that crown to make you a peacemaker. If you renege on your duties, he will take it back."

"And would you try?" Clōudiá challenged the god. "How am I failing at the justice we all agreed I would manage? Ĝoŕgomghōul, you gave me a crown and an army that could take down a D'Ihne, should one of our kind ever go rogue. Have you really come here to challenge me just because the traitor turned out to be your son?"

Ĝoŕgomghōul reached up a hand. He pushed back his hood and he sighed. He sighed the sigh of someone who was born too tired to deal with people, and who has only become more exhausted with the passage of eternity. He looked to the pillars.

"Hello Jim."

"Hey Dad," Jim smirked. "How's it going? Are you here to sit on the side-lines and watch noncommittally while everything happens around you?"

"I certainly hope so," Ĝoŕgomghōul sighed. "I am

already far more involved than I would like."

"Alright then," Jim retorted snarkily. "Let's help you keep out of this. Either auntie dearest is going to lift her laws on the Ha'Cās, or she's going to kill me. We'll see what happens then."

"No," Ĝoŕgomghōul replied. "We'll see what happens then. You won't. The thing about suicide, James, is that it is very final. You think that your death will be the final word on the matter, and that the others will rise up and fight on your behalf once you're gone. That you will be martyred. Your death would only be the final word on your narrative. Everyone else will keep going. They will change the story, without you there to contribute. They will fight about it all for so long that, by the end, they may not even remember you were there at the start."

"I'm not going to surrender," Jim argued. "And I won't apologise."

"I expect nothing less," Ĝoŕgomghōul agreed drily. "As long as there is a crown, you will fight it."

"So, if there was no crown..." Crŷs mused off to the side. Everyone looked to Ĝoŕgomghōul's other son. He adopted a startled expression and waved his hands. "No, I was just hypothesising out loud."

"You never think out loud," Clōudiá growled. "What are you up to?"

"Such suspicion, mother!" Crŷs protested. "Why question me? Jim's chained up and humiliated — what part of that would I not love?"

"Really?" Jim smirked. "You want to out your bondage fetish here?"

Crŷs turned his icy blue eyes to his wife with an expression of reluctant patience.

"Do I really have to be party to this?"

"You have to do what's right for you," Olíriá replied simply.

"Party to what?" Clōudiá demanded. "You would turn on me? For him? Crŷstïar, surely even at your worst, you would not bring your father here to betray me."

"It's not betrayal, Clōudiá," Ĝoŕgomghōul insisted. "It is choice. Make yours, and we shall make ours."

"I will not be strong-armed in this manner," she declared, rising to her feet. "He is a traitor and he shall be punished in a manner fitting his crime. Challenge me, if you dare."

"Not me," Ĝoŕgomghōul shook his head. "Them."

He opened his cloak. Layers of black robes kept him eternally shrouded, but the entirety of the universe swirled in the lining of his cloak. Stars and galaxies, worlds and moons, all danced endlessly in a sparkling serenade. Five people burst out from it.

It was like being sprung from the faerie trap. Jak knew the feeling. This time, she was ready for it. She launched herself from the void. In one fluid motion, she hit the ground, rolled, and came up drawing Shrïgkyvsh. The sword rushed from its scabbard with a metallic hiss. The D'Ihne yelled and scattered back. She wasn't aiming for them. With effortless grace, she rose up and struck. The dark blade cut clean through the chain binding Jim to one of the pillars. It met no resistance. The chain splintered like glitter and vanished.

Jim crashed to the floor, one side still bound, but no longer suspended. He looked up, unable to hide his bewilderment.

"Jellybean...?"

Jak didn't reply. She didn't even glance his way. A fight was coming. It moved faster than she could follow — despite already turning to meet it. A blade stopped inches from her throat. She hadn't even seen it coming. It stopped with a resounding clang. Elrïlani sought her head. Krill stood back-to-back with his apprentice, his blade between Elrïlani's weapon and Jak's neck. He stared his sister down. Everyone froze.

Behind them, Ĝoŕgomghōul loitered to watch. Near him, Kode held the girls out of harm's way. He kept Dora scooped in one arm as she held on around his neck, and the other arm around Allie. The god of darkness loomed like a mountain of shadow behind them, and even his own followers could see the threat he posed.

"TREASON!" Clōudiá thundered. "Seize them! The first to bring me their heads—!" her crown vanished. She knew instantly that it was gone. Her eyes flashed with a homicidal rage as she stopped short. Everyone looked at Jim. He was still flopped on the floor with one arm chained to a pillar.

"Don't look at me," he shrugged, tossing his free hand to conjure the purple silk robe. It draped modestly across his body, which was a suspicious action for him, until you accounted for the fact that he found the rescue attempt mildly arousing, and was concerned that if Jak noticed, she might decide not to save him after all. What he clearly didn't have was enough magic to free himself or take the crown.

Everyone turned slowly to Crŷs. Given that he'd all but admitted he was going to do it, he had a slightly miffed look on his face regarding how long it had taken everyone to consider him. He was supposed to be the annoying one, and he was sick of being shown up by his older sibling. It showed in his pout as he tossed the crown loosely in his fingers.

"Frosty," Jim beamed at him. "You worked out how to do it. Good for you. Took you long enough."

"What can I say, Fuckface," Crŷs retorted. "Watching you bleed was inspiring. It gave me a whole new perspective on the situation."

"My, you are getting sadistic in your old age," Jim teased. "We can work with that."

Crŷs looked at Olíriá painfully. "Do I really have to do this?" he begged.

"I'm not making you do anything, my love," she sighed. "All these actions were your choices, and now you hold the crown. The next move is yours."

"That is most terrifying thing you have ever said," he smiled. "No one wants this kind of power in my hands. Imagine what I would do with it…"

Silence reigned in the moment while everyone contemplated it. Several of the D'Ihne grimaced. Notably Ínrío. Clōudiá stepped forward gently. She wasn't moving to startle anyone, but she had her eyes on the crown.

"Crŷstïar," she bade her youngest softly. "Darling,

this is all fun and games, and everyone is amused, but give it back. Now is not the time for jokes."

"Then consider, Clōudiá, that we are not joking," Olíriá replied. "We won't let you kill one of our own. Jim isn't the only who has found a way around the magic of the crown anymore. There is room for negotiation, but we cannot resort to lethal action. The ramifications of the death of our own kind are terrifying when you can look beyond the immediate gratification of vengeance." She looked to her husband at her side.

"Mm," Crŷs offered in agreement, although he didn't really sound like he agreed.

"Jak," Jim hissed quietly behind them all. "Cut me free. Cut me free and we can end this. Now! While she's distracted!"

Jak looked back at him. He was a determined force in a sprawl of purple. She didn't move. Krill still stood with his back pressed against hers and his blade holding back Elrïlani's. The former D'Hiris kept his eyes on his opponent, but was every inch aware of exactly where the other D'rö-Hadās were. No one was getting past him. He wouldn't look at Jim though.

"What happens next is up to you, my love," Olíriá smiled at her husband. "You might not trust yourself with that kind of power, but there must be someone you trust with it. Someone you think will do the right thing."

"There is one..." he nodded. Olíriá placed an understanding hand on his arm. Crŷs looked over at the warriors stalemated before Jim. "Stand down, you two," he instructed.

Both Ha'Cās lowered their blades slowly. Both were hesitant and ready to strike as soon as the other flinched. Neither did. Crŷs turned from Olíriá and walked away from her. He headed straight for them. For a moment she looked surprised. Then she clutched a hand to her face in a desperate attempt to silence her own laughter. Everyone else watched in surprise, waiting for the joke. Crŷs stopped in front of Jak. He held the crown out. Jak looked around. Crŷs moved to place it on her brow.

"STOP!" Clōudiá ordered. No one listened to her.

"Wait, what?!" Jak ducked away. "What are you doing?"

"I'm giving you the crown," Crŷs answered solemnly. "You're the only person I trust to use it."

"Is this another trick?" Jak glared.

"No," Crŷs shook his head. "I've been talking with Olí about you. You're the only person right now that I trust is going to try and do the right thing — instead of what best serves them." And with those words, he sat the crown of the fae on her head. No magic had been woven to change or disguise it. It was big and heavy and pushed her curls down around her face. Jak was just confused and bewildered.

"Why me?"

"I just explained why you," Crŷs smiled.

Olíriá was still doing her best not to laugh, but there were tears of mirth in the corners of her eyes. Jak looked between them, and suddenly she got it. Her expression settled and she leant in closer to whisper to him.

"I thought we were 'just mortals'," she reminded

him. Crŷs shrugged. Jak smirked and continued. "Jim caught love off your wife… you didn't happen to catch caring about mortals from him now, did you…?"

Crŷs glanced at his brother, still chained to the floor. It was a flicker of a look, and then his eyes were back on the girl he had just crowned.

"He cares about you very deeply," Crŷs whispered. "In his own warped way."

"Yeah," Jak nodded, straightening back up and stepping away. "It's messed up, but then, so's the entire family."

The rest of the D'Ihne had watched wide-eyed as Crŷs had crowned Jak. Some in awe and some in horror. It had taken a moment for the effect to sink in, but now the moment was over. Clōudiá let out a revolted cry.

"What have you done?!" she shrieked. "We didn't just let mortals into the Golden City, you gave them the crown of the D'Ihne as well?! As though we have not done enough to condemn all our people have held sacred since time began! And not just any mortal — one who would dare wield Godslayer in these very halls! You are more a traitor than your brother could ever be! My own flesh and blood!"

"Oh, shut up," Jak scoffed. She was new to the crown, and didn't know how to work it when it was unfiltered. So she was surprised when Clōudiá's voice seemed to vanish, and the goddess was left yelling without sound. Everyone else looked somewhat surprised too. "Oh," Jak muttered awkwardly. "I can fix that…" She just wasn't sure how yet.

"Don't," Jim encouraged. "This is a vast

improvement, I assure you." Jak turned to face him. He was grinning up at her, and overall looked far too happy with himself. "This confidence is a great colour on you, Jellybean. You should finish cutting me free and I can check how long you can make it last. Durability and endurance are things I'm good at."

Jak lowered the point of the sword to his chin. She moved it closer. His grin started to falter. His smile fell nervously as the steel brushed his skin. He was still bound, and so much as a shaving cut from a D'rök blade was liable to have serious consequences.

"You are going to start behaving," she ordered coolly. "I'm not saying you can't be yourself. I'm not saying you have to stop being a desperate and tragic flirt. But I wouldn't be here if he hadn't begged me to." She glanced at Krill. Jim glanced too. Krill only met his eyes for a second, but it was enough. Jim looked suitably humbled. Jak continued. "You don't get to use people anymore. No more being creepy and rapey. You're going to behave yourself," she repeated, lifting his chin with the point of her blade. "Or I'm going to cut your balls off with a sword that won't let you grow them back. Do you understand?"

"Crystal clear," Jim croaked.

"Good," Jak lowered her sword. "Then there's the matter of me freeing you. Clōudiá wasn't entirely wrong — you've done some really terrible shit, and you need to answer for it."

"So what?" Jim grimaced. "You going to imprison me here? Banish me from the city?"

"What good would either of those do?" Jak grinned

at him. "I'm not banishing you from anywhere. And imprisoning you? Aside from the fact that it probably ties into one of your numerous weird fetishes I don't want to know about, imprisoning you is no better than killing you. Neither of those options do anything to fix the problems you've caused. It will take hard work to fix the messes you've made, and, Jim, I know how much you hate hard work..."

"Wait..." his eyes narrowed as he caught on. Jak poked the golden chain with the tip of her sword, toying with it.

"Jim, I'm going to cut you free, and then... then, big brother, you're going to come with me back to the mortal world, and we're going to stop all those wars you started, and fix all those lives you ruined."

"That could take years!" Jim protested.

"Yup," Jak stared him down. "So you better get used to me and my big sword."

His face cracked into an enormous grin. "Well, that's not an offer I've ever been able to refuse from anyone."

"I figured," Jak nodded. "We're agreed?"

"It seems fair," he nodded.

Jak looked over at Ĝoŕgomghōul. He still stood protectively behind Kode and her sisters, watching over the whole ordeal. This had been their agreement. She hoped she was doing it right, even if she was only a third of the way there. She took a deep breath and turned back to Jim.

"Then we have an accord," she announced, hoping that she sounded authoritative enough for the D'Ihne, without letting Jim think she was just copying his dad.

She cut through the last chain. It shattered into glitter and vanished. His arm dropped. He rubbed his wrists as he climbed to his feet. The glow that he hadn't been able to hide while his magic was bound dimmed, and the illusion of his fae form became more corporeal. Instantly, his smirk returned.

"Ah, it's good to be free," he grinned at his silent aunt. The moment of glory was short lived. A fist to the face sent him sprawling back on the ground. Krill stood over him. He had turned his back on Elrïlani, but she appeared to still be obeying Crŷs' order to stand down. Krill grabbed Jim by the front of the robe and hauled him up with one hand as he punched him in the face repeatedly with the other.

"You stupid, selfish, manipulative, toxic, piece of garbage!" Krill growled, landing a punch with almost every word. "This is your fault!" He dropped him heavily back on the ground. "You were messing with my mind! You had no right! No right! I only betrayed you because you tricked me!"

Jim groaned from the ground. He touched his face tenderly where he bled from the nose and the corner of his mouth.

"I'm very into this," he replied. "But can we save some of it for later?"

Krill hit him again. Repeatedly. Jak just stood and watched. Crŷs watched beside her, and he seemed to be enjoying it more than Jim was. Someone else moved at Jak's other side.

"Aren't you going to stop that?" Thænäri asked gently. She watched her daughter with familiar and caring eyes.

"No," Jak decided. "That's between them, and it's probably part of the restorative justice."

Thænäri raised an eyebrow. Jak shrugged at her, and raised a hand to steady the crown as it slipped.

"What can I say, Mum? I'm fifteen. If you don't like the way I do things, you can blame the people that raised me. I shouldn't have to deal with all this pressure anyway. I'm not cut out to be a queen." She gave up trying to steady the crown and pulled it off. Then she tried to push her hair out of her face with her wrist and nearly poked herself in the face with one of the spikes. She sighed. "Okay Krill, you can stop hitting him now."

Krill climbed off his boyfriend and shook his bloodied knuckles. His expression was still dark, and his golden eyes flinty. Jim followed him up with a groan as he pushed himself to his feet. He ran his hands wearily over his bloodied face, and the injuries vanished. With a shudder, he shook himself out.

"Invigorating," Jim commented. Krill looked like he wanted to punch him again. Jim noticed. His violet eyes were soft as he looked at his lover. "For what it's worth," he spoke genuinely. "You were right. I should never have done that to you, and I am sorry."

Krill didn't reply, but he looked less violent. Jim glanced at Jak, and then back to Krill.

"Is it true?" Jim asked. "What she said? She wouldn't be here if you hadn't asked?"

Krill shrugged. "She's not the type to lie, and I did ask." He met Jim's eyes. "I begged her, actually. Once your magic was shut off, the idea of losing you went from appealing to painful. You psychopath." He glared. "You never did this to Kode?"

"No, never," Jim shook his head. "I never had to. Kode loves everyone, and everyone loves him. It's not weird. He's basically kindness personified."

"But it was weird for you to care about me," Krill criticised. "It was weird for me to care about you, so you had to put a stop to that."

"I sound like an asshole when you phrase it like that," Jim protested.

Krill stared him down. "I believe the word your sister used was 'coward'."

Jim rubbed his cheek awkwardly. He turned his eyes to the floor and his dark curls tangled around his face. For a brief, and frighteningly vulnerable, moment Jim hugged himself against reality. "Look, I did wrong. I know unwaveringly I did wrong, and I am so sorry. You don't have to forgive me. I love you, and I am… fucking terrified of that. It's very new to me. I'm sorry I did it so badly."

Krill reached out and pulled him in. Jim didn't even seem to realise it was happening until Krill kissed him.

"You're an idiot," Krill whispered. "And I hate you. And I'm going to hit you again later."

"That is everything I wanted you to say," Jim breathed, kissing him back.

The room was entranced.

"I can't tell if that's cute or unhealthy…" Jak mused.

"It can be both," Thænäri shrugged.

From the side of the room, Dora supplied a third opinion with a loud 'Ew' sound. There were several chuckles, not least of all from her mother.

"Come here, baby girl," Thænäri invited. Kode led the girls over and Thænäri embraced them as he joined his lovers. Jim and Krill smiled as he approached, but Jim's expression flickered to panic. Jak saw it happen with a second to move. She dodged towards him. Behind her, Clōudiá snatched for the crown. The queen was still moving silently, and she looked ready to kill. She raised her hand and brought down her magic. Jak had a second to raise Shrïgkyvsh, but it was all she needed.

In this world the magic was pure. Unfiltered. It crashed down around her so hard it was like an electric shock. Pain stabbed through her fingers and toes, but the sword took the blow. Jak staggered away. One hand gripped Shrïgkyvsh, and the other still clutched the crown. Everyone else had leapt away. Thænäri had pulled the girls back. Jak turned, still smoking at the edges. Her vision felt hazy. She felt like she could see thousands gathered. Then she realised that she could. That had been her other job. The other part of her feat to fix what was wrong. At the edges of the halls they were gathered. They were watching. The Ha'Cās. Jak twisted back and glared the Queen down. She held up the crown and shook it.

"You want this?" she taunted. "You know the only reason I got it was because I didn't, right? The power made you cruel. You're no longer fit to be queen, Clōudiá. But I don't want to be. So, you know what?" Jak held the crown up in front of her. "Maybe no one should have this power." Before anyone could stop her, she swung Shrïgkyvsh straight through the crown. Clōudiá leapt for it.

The sword cut through the crown the same way it had cut through the chains. All its magic broke. The crown dissolved into glitter and vanished. Clōudiá hit the floor. Her wings flared as she prostrated herself despairingly where the glitter trickled to nothing.

"NO!" she cried desperately. Jak looked down on her pityingly.

"Is it wrong..." she asked softly, "that I expected more from gods?" She brushed her hand on her vest, but there was nothing there. Not even a shining speck of dust. She looked up. Jim was staring at her in awe. "You were right," she told him. "You just went about it in the worst way possible." She sheathed Shrïgkyvsh and turned from the D'Ihne to the people in the shadows. The ones that served and were never seen.

"The crown is gone," Jak announced. "No one is ruling, and no one is controlling. No one will make you do anything. If you like your life, you are more than welcome to stay, and I imagine that will be appreciated. However, if you want to build yourself a new life, there are no laws or powers keeping you from it. The age of the Queen is over."

"Stop her!" Clōudiá yelled, scrambling to her feet. "You dare talk to my subjects like that?! You... you... mortal! Kill her!" Clōudiá pointed a damning finger of execution at Jak. No one moved. The D'rö-Hadās didn't budge. Elrïlani stayed standing. With a slow hand, she reached up and removed her mask. Clōudiá's eyes widened as she realised what was happening, and she fell silent again in horror. Elrïlani dropped her mask to the floor. It clanged like a gong as it crashed down. The D'Hiris was grinning from ear-to-ear as she looked around the room.

"I'm going to be a pig farmer!" she announced happily, and then turned and strode from the hall. Everyone else shared bewildered looks.

"Did she just..." Jim started.

"Yes," Krill answered beside him. "Probably more of a sanctuary than a farm. She really likes pigs. Always has." He kept his eyes on his sister as she vanished out the doorway with a joy of purpose she had never before shown. Jim looked between the doorway and his lover with aloof interest. Krill was smiling.

"No accounting for some people's taste..." Jim shrugged. Krill gave him a cautionary look. "No?" Jim checked. "I can't get away with saying stuff like that?"

Krill shook his head. "No. You really can't."

"Fair enough." He turned to Clōudiá with a big satisfied smirk. "How's the worst day of your life going, auntie dearest?"

"You will pay, Fæmör..." she warned softly. Her eyes were wide with a fresh madness as she watched her empire collapse around her, and her soft white hair drifted loose and unkempt around her face. "I don't know how long it will take me to wreak vengeance, but I will have it."

"I'll get scared when you get as powerful as I am," Jim shrugged. "In the meantime, I suggest hard liquor and prostitutes to get you through the next few years."

"Jim," Thænäri scolded.

"What?" he shrugged. "They're a solid coping mechanism. Tried and true. I only recommend things I've tested myself. Besides, Crŷs and I can both do more powerful magic than she can. What do I have to be afraid of? A woman scorned?"

"Start by being afraid of me," Jak supplied. She looked to Clōudiá. "I'm sorry it had to be this way, but I really think it did. The behaviour of your D'Hiris just proved me right. You couldn't keep them as slaves. I hope that in time you will realise that this wasn't the end of everything and that things will be okay."

"In a mere hundred years your bones will be dust, child," Clōudiá scorned. "Your sword will fall into new hands, and we will see who's sorry then..."

"There are plans for that..." Ĝoŕgomghōul announced from across the hall. Everyone looked to him. He still stood on the fringes. Now he stood alone, shrouded in his galaxies and darkness. He watched the room with three patient red eyes. He watched like he'd been waiting for something. No one tried to coax more information out of him. If he'd wanted them to know, he would have told them. He had made the sword, given it to Jak, and brought her here. He had made the crown centuries before for Clōudiá. Then he had made something that could destroy it. They were all aware that he had known exactly what he was doing.

"The age of the crown is over," he announced. "The age of the sword is beginning." He looked to the windows of the hall, where everything outside was a soft and comforting light. "Welcome to the dawn of a new age." Then he turned back to the room. He looked to Jak and raised a hand to motion her forward.

For a second, she felt like she was back in Fäsaírm, but it only lasted a second. She strode forward to meet him. They weren't finished. Not yet. Both had kept their part of the deal, but he was going to hold her to the rest of it, and he was going to do something to make sure she couldn't escape. He was going to unleash the rune on her soul. He was going to affirm her destiny. They stood alone at the edge of the hall and he held out his hand.

"Shrïgkyvsh," he requested.

Jak drew her sword and presented it to him on one knee. It felt appropriate. Ĝoŕgomghōul was the theatrical type. Something about him commanded things be done a certain way. A ceremonial way. After all, he lived in a cave between worlds with a magic cauldron, brewing the heart of all faerie power. He took the sword from her and bade her stay kneeling with a gesture. Gently, he lowered the point of Shrïgkyvsh over her shoulder.

"Jak of the Mortal Realm, first of your kind to set foot in these halls, the actions you have taken today will change the course of all worlds. You are true of spirit, true of heart, and true of courage. By these actions and these qualities, I mark you a knight of Roïgola'a'lanaū. The Golden Knight of the Golden City." He touched her shoulders with Shrïgkyvsh and then lowered the sword. "Rise, Champion of the Gods, and take our blessings into the world with you as you go."

Jak stood slowly. Ĝoŕgomghōul smiled and handed her back the sword. She took it with nervous and sweaty hands.

"That's an awful lot of pressure…" she commented.

"You promised you would fix everything, no matter how long it took. Now, I hold you to that. You are the one who will balance the ramifications."

"Okay," Jak agreed. "But I'm using his magic," she pointed at Jim. "And maybe his too." She pointed at Crŷs.

"Yeah," Jim smirked. "We learnt the good stuff. Aren't you proud?"

Crŷs didn't want to be seen agreeing with Jim, but he couldn't help but look to his father for approval. Both of them waited. Ĝoŕgomghōul out-stared them. He sighed.

"Yes," he replied. "Well done. You both finally got there. Only centuries after I expected you to."

Jim and Crŷs shared a look of frustration.

"Can you just go back to being an absent father now?" Crŷs grumbled.

Ĝoŕgomghōul nodded with a smile. He pulled his hood up and stepped back into nothing, vanishing completely. His part in all this was over. He could walk away without any trouble, and anyone who wanted to argue his involvement would have to face his champion. The champion in question was still standing at the edge of the hall, leaning on her sword. With a sigh, she sheathed it again and headed back to her family.

Dora jumped from Thænäri's arms to run to Jak's. Jak scooped her up as Dora threw her arms around her sister's neck.

"You did it!" Dora exclaimed. "You fixed it, Jak! You're a hero!"

"And a knight," Allie gave her a cheeky grin. "A proper demigod knight. Jak... this is the stuff of legend."

"It is indeed," Jim agreed. "And it will be. You freed the Ha'Cās and changed the world. There's no way the faeries won't gossip this story from here to the end of the time." He grinned. "You did good, Jellybean. You're your own story now, just like those heroes of old."

"I can't think of myself as a legend," she shook her head at him.

"Well, you've got time to get used to it," he grinned. "Besides, once you've stopped some wars you might find it easier to believe."

"Once *we've* stopped some wars," she corrected. "You need to fix up that shitty wagon. We've got a long way to go." She looked at Krill and Kode. "I presume you're coming too?"

"Wouldn't miss it for anything," Krill smiled. "Besides, you'll need help managing him."

"Will I ever..." Jak sighed. She looked at the Ha'Cās still smiling at her. Her master and his gentle husband. The one who had seen. "Did you know?" she asked him.

"Know what?" Kode asked, tipping his head to the side curiously.

"That I'd end up here? That things would get this out of control? You were the one who said you saw Domhanda on my soul. You said I had a destiny — well, I don't think even I can argue against that now." She shook her head. "I feel like I've been given a pretty big destiny."

"No one would argue that..." Krill agreed. "But Kody never said anything to us."

"I didn't know anything," Kode shrugged. "I could see Domhanda, but that was all." He smiled cheekily. "It burned pretty bright though."

"Maybe it was better not to know in advance," Jak muttered. "I might have panicked and run away instead, if I'd had any idea where this was all going." She bounced Dora on her hip to stop her from slipping down, and turned to Allie and Thænäri. "I'm sorry we can't just go home now. I wanted to after this was over — I really did, but it's not over yet, and I don't know when it will be."

"Pfft," Allie pulled a face. "You think we could just go home? After all this? You're not a peasant anymore, Sis, and those handsome princes won't rescue themselves. We're coming too."

"We're going into a war zone, Allie," Jak reminded. Allie rolled her eyes.

"As opposed to a divine rebellion? Don't be such a wet blanket."

Jak looked to their mother. She tried to convey with her eyes the need for someone to step in and help. Thænäri just smiled at her. The goddess wasn't going to make that decision for them. Rather, she looked like she thought Jak should be used to Allie fighting her by now. She stepped forward and kissed Jak gently on the forehead.

"I'm so proud of you, baby girl," she smiled.

"Thanks… Mum?" Jak still didn't know what to call her. Thænäri laughed at her obvious confusion.

"Ready to go save the world again?"

"Ready as I'll ever be," Jak shrugged. "Once Jim's got our transport sorted, we can hit the road."

"It's the Banging Wagon, babe," he smirked. "It's always ready to roll."

For a brief and enraged second, Jak regretted absolutely everything. Then she steeled herself with a deep breath, placed her hand on the hilt of Shrïgkyvsh, and got ready to roll.

Did you enjoy this book?

Please consider leaving a review for it on Amazon or Goodreads — even a simple sentence or two about your favourite bit helps. Every positive review allows me to spend more time writing books for you to enjoy!

591

LIKE THE HEROES OF OLD

THE D'IHNE PANTHEON

FREZIAN
FIRE
DESTRUCTION

CLOUDIA
SKY
QUEEN OF THE FAE

GORGOMGHOUL
DARKNESS
WISDOM

ALUAKNA
WATER
DIRECTION

THAENARI
EARTH
GROWTH

CRYSTIAR
SNOW, ELOQUENCE,
TRICKERY, POETRY
CLOUDIA + GORGOMGHOUL

OLIRIA
LOVE, BEAUTY,
MUSIC, BATHHOUSES
FREZIAN + ALUAKNA

FAEMOR
SEX, GAMES,
PARTIES, ECSTASY
THAENARI + GORGOMGHOUL

CREATA
RAIN, MEDICINE,
TRUTH, MATHEMATICS
CLOUDIA + ALUAKNA

TALAMH
TRAVEL, COMMERCE,
FOOD, HEARTH
FREZIAN + THAENARI

INRIO
SUN, ANIMALS,
FORGE, FAMILY
FREZIAN + CLOUDIA

Rune:	Name:	Literal Equivilent:	Meaning:
	Arsaid	Messenger	Communication, Source
	Nari	Earth	Fertility, Growth
	Ellaigh	Cattle	Money, Wealth
	La	Day	Breakthrough, Dawn
	Capall	Horse	Speed, Progression
	Ezian	Fire	Burning, Destruction
	Bronntanas	Gift	Gift, Surprise, Luck
	Ollmahor	Darkness	Monster, Chaos, Wisdom
	Stiar	Ice	Quick, Cold, Sharp
	Bliain	Year	The Harvest, A Cycle
	Creachta	Wound, Torch	Transition, Healing, Light
	Uisce	Water	Sea, Flow, Direction
	Daonna	Man	The Self, Humanity
	Niochta	Magic	Power, Danger, Knowledge
	Talamh	Home	Birthright, Possessions
	Draimor	Risk	Gamble, Chance, Pleasure
	Ondia	Sky	Life, Peace, Unity
	Marcha	Riding, Carriage	Journey, Travel, Transport
	Sorio	Sun	Warmth, Wholeness, Energy
	Trodai	Warrior	Courage, Justice
	Neart	Beast	Strength, Virility
	Marleid	Moon	Balance, Equality
	Othas	Love	Joy, Happiness, Romance
	Domhanda	World	Destiny, Beginning, End
	Fasairm	Yew and Birch	Offering, Sacrifice, Bound
	Fora	Forest	Protection, Shelter

OTHER BOOKS BY KATE HALEY

Welcome to the Inbetween

The Light After Earth

The Vincent Temple Trilogy

Gateway to Dark Stars

Tomb of Endless Night

Fortress of the Shadow Reich

The War of the North Saga

Footsteps into the Unfamiliar (short story collection)

1. Steel & Stone

2. Magic in the Marshes

3. Forest of Ghosts

4. Women of the Woods

5. Spirit & Sand

6. The Prince and the Witch

7. Gods & Dragons

ABOUT THE AUTHOR

Kate Haley is a speculative fiction author who works predominantly in fantasy and horror.

While currently content to fill their days with writing and table-top RPGs, their grander plans involve world domination. Something akin to the tyranny of the greatest city atop the Disc would be an acceptable standard. They believe a super-villainous overlord would be an upgrade, given that our current villains lack style and imagination.

After all, super-villainy requires Presentation.

If you like their references, consider visiting their website www.katehaleyauthor.com for short fictions and merchandise, and join the mailing list for early access and exclusive cool stuff.

You can also get in touch through the website regarding their work, your position in future slave armies, or a general interest in all things nerdy and wonderful.

LIKE THE HEROES OF OLD